THE Empress' GIFT

THE VOLGA FRONTIER

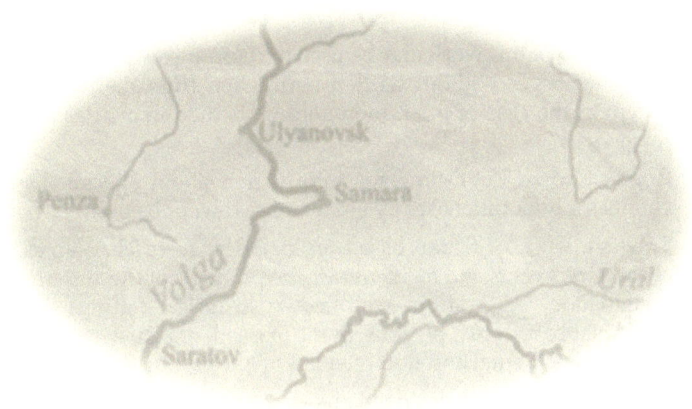

ELLEN LAUBHAN

Rowe Publishing

ISBN 978-1-64446-015-3

Contact Rowe Publishing for information about special dis-
counts for bulk purchases by email: info@rowepub.com.

This is a work of fiction based on historical research. Names,
characters, events and incidents are the products of the author's
imagination. Apart from well-known historical figures, any
resemblance to actual persons, living or dead, or actual events is
purely coincidental and not intended by the author.

Map illustration was designed and created by James E. Stafford
(© 2022).

3 5 7 9 8 6 4 2

Printed in the United States of America
Published by

Rowe Publishing

www.rowepub.com

DEDICATION

For my Mother, Mary Eleanor Trenfield Laubhan,
who taught me the joy of reading

"The German is like a willow,
No matter which way you bend him,
he will always take root again."

–Aleksandr Solzhenitsyn

PROLOGUE

SARATOV PROVINCE, RUSSIA

February 1765

*A*s the sleigh glided across the frozen river, the horses sensed the wolves' approach. Ears pricked forward and muzzles snorting, the two sturdy native ponies sped up to outrun the starving pack. The wolves attacked the horse on the left, the lead wolf jumping again and again to bite its neck while others snapped at its back legs. The horse's frenzied kicks found their target, forcing the yelping wolves back.

Recoiling toward Rein on the sleigh's narrow wooden seat, Amila shivered, less from the cold than from the savagery. Minutes before, Rein had calmly prepared her for the likelihood of an attack, the ferocity of which she had heard about but never seen. Now the ice was black with snarling wolves closing in, mouths open, teeth bared, and coats bristling while paws fought for traction on the snow-covered ice. If the wolves brought down one horse, the second would fall, the sleigh capsize. She gulped the frigid air burning her lungs, trying to swallow her fear. Amila glanced at Rein. He had repeatedly experienced these attacks alone, transporting provisions for the colony. It was reckless, putting himself in peril this way. She winced, knowing it was her actions propelling them into danger today.

Rein's steady voice asking for a musket calmed her slightly. She handed him one of the heavy, single-shot rifles. Resting it across his lap, he quickly wrapped the leather harness straps around Amila's trembling hands, shouting above the din to steer the sleigh forward through the lightly falling snow. With the wolves too near the horses to shoot, Rein clenched a whip with his free hand and lashed out, landing stinging blows on the wolves' backs and heads. They fell back, giving the horses time to gain a slight distance from the pack. At last, Rein could fire. Immediately, a red patch spread across the snow.

The sinewy wolf stumbled and fell, struggling in vain to regain its footing. The other wolves halted the chase, turned on their wounded brother, and ravenously tore him to pieces. Knowing the wolves would not be sated for long, Rein picked up the second musket, fired, and another wolf dropped on the ice.

Amila and Rein watched the gruesome scene for a tenuous moment, feeling kinship with the wolves' powerful instinct to survive the brutal Russian winter. Then Rein reloaded both rifles. Amila turned the sleigh across the Volga River and urged the horses forward. It was still more than a mile across the massive river to the safety of the west shoreline.

One danger averted, heavy snow began to fall in place of the feathery flakes. High winds swirled the stinging crystals, limiting vision beyond the sleigh. Soon, Amila and Rein wore the white of the storm, the wet, spring snow clinging to their coats and faces, to the horses and sleigh. Rein had driven the sleigh in heavy snowfall, but never in a blizzard with such hypnotic power. He tenderly wiped the snow from Amila's face and pulled her closer, lifting a fur hide over her head. Gritting his teeth against the bitter air, he wrapped the scarf of his *dokha* tighter around his head and face. His Russian friend's words hounded him: *beware Mother Volga, source of life and death, hope and sacrifice.* Rein gave the Kalmyk ponies their heads, trusting in their instinct to survive. The horses heaved the sleigh through drifts in a direction Rein hoped was Dobrinka.

Amila shouted above the wind's deafening howl, pleading with Rein to take cover. He relented and she pulled the hide over their heads, sheltering them from the storm's wrath. Whatever happened now, they would face it together. Surely they hadn't come this far, only now truly finding one another, to die like this.

PART ONE

CHAPTER 1

June 1763

*A*mila settled into the saddle, cantering Gabe over the stone bridge guarding the entrance to Nassenwald Manor. Halfway across, a richly adorned carriage came into view. She scowled, realizing she had lingered too long at the stable. Now there would be no escaping an encounter—the narrow bridge was the only way in and out of the castle. Well aware her stepfather, Count Tundorf, had sent a messenger saying he would arrive today and expected to see her immediately, she slid off the gelding's back and faced him, blinking away an involuntary twinge of her eyelid.

"Stop here and let me out. Get the carriage inside." The count bellowed at the driver and stable boy who had come running. "Take Lady Amila's horse. She won't be riding today."

The boy hurried to carry out the harsh order. "I'll take Gabe back to the stable myself," Amila intervened, unwilling to relinquish her ride that easily. Noting they were off to their usual start, Amila extended her chin defiantly.

He stepped quickly from the carriage, forcefully prodding the uneven stone of the bridge with the tip of his ornate cane. Even his daytime attire was formal, with a long waistcoat and knee-length breeches of fine fabric and powdered hair tied with a black ribbon at the nape of his neck. The lanky count pursed his lips, drawing attention to his broad forehead, longish nose, and chin that came to a bit of a point.

"Don't pretend you didn't get my orders," he admonished, harshly inspecting Amila's worn riding habit and unruly hair.

Amila attempted to pull back her wavy auburn hair and straighten her frayed jacket, aware she looked more like a serf than a young noblewoman. She had rarely seen his temper flare so quickly. "I was hoping for a short ride and planned to hurry back to greet you." She had seen her mother try pleasantry, sometimes with success.

With the carriage and servants out of sight, the count moved in close. "You look like a common stable hand. You're grubby, of little use like this. Stop this behavior immediately or suffer the consequences."

Amila straightened, shoulders back. Her height put her almost eye-to-eye with her stepfather. She leaned against Gabe slightly for support. "I ride every day. It's just to take some exercise and…"

The count interrupted, raising his voice to a level of contempt usually reserved for servants. "Return to the manor immediately. We have guests arriving soon, one you may well remember. Duke Herman of Zwuibrücken." He paused and cleared his throat, suddenly in high spirits. "His Lordship has asked for your hand in marriage. I have consented."

Amila cringed and shrank back. She grasped her throat, thoughts spinning. Duke Herman was arrogant, fat, and at least thirty years her senior. She winced, recalling the time he had cornered her and tried to grope her body.

"No. You can't ask this of me. Surely you know what he's like. You must allow me to meet young noblemen and consider other suitors. My...my mother never would have made such a cruel match!"

Count Tundorf's clenched teeth and piercing glare forced Amila to step back. He lunged and grabbed a handful of her hair, pulling her so close she felt his stinging words penetrate her skin. "I'm not asking; I'm telling you. Your mother is dead and your preference of no concern." He held her rigid, met her stare and dared a response. When he finally released her, he pushed her roughly to the ground and turned away. Wiping his gloved hands on his breeches, he turned his attention to the horse.

"In the war, our soldiers learned to hobble the enemy's horses by cutting the tendons of their front legs." Tundorf touched the point of his cane behind Gabe's hoof. "The horse falls, trying, again and again, to stand before finally succumbing to the pain. Alas, they have to be shot or struggle and die slowly. It would be a shame for this horse to suffer such a fate."

The count hovered as Amila huddled against the bridge, holding Gabe's reins. "Now, you'll do what I say. Look your best at dinner and be attentive to the duke. Your engagement will be announced soon after the contract is worked out." He turned and crossed the bridge, striding toward the castle gate.

Amila hugged her knees, staring into the distance while Gabe nuzzled her. He'll carry out that threat, she thought. Opening her mouth to cry out, no sound escaped. Since her mother's death two years ago, she was terrified the count might use her as a token in his self-serving ambition. Young women of high birth were expected to marry titled noblemen. She knew it would be her fate. But not this match, never a match like this.

Rising slowly to her feet, Amila put her arms around Gabe's neck and watched the water in the Wörnitz River flow gently by. The melodic churn of water rising and falling through the nearby mill wheel was a constant she had come to depend on. She had crossed this river hundreds of times in youthful exuberance, its calming current an anchor that assured her world was secure both inside and outside the castle. Now the river looked different...uncaring, unfeeling, no longer offering comfort.

Amila watched the stable boy's shy approach, ready to carry out the count's orders to stable the horse. She raised her hand feebly to stop him and mounted, determined to cast off the prospect of the dismal evening ahead. She yearned for the solace of these daily rides. Though increasingly, the depleted woods and parched fields left her deeply troubled. The landscape wore the battle scars of seven years of war and a crippling drought.

Once across the bridge, Amila saw young Eva Lundgren, her house maid and friend, rushing toward her. Eva's face showed strain. "Amila, you've got to come right away. Mother is gravely ill, and she's asking for you. We've called Rein, too. He's coming from the fields now. Hurry!" Eva turned and ran ahead to her family's cottage near the village.

*R*einhardt Lundgren swung the sharp metal blade of the reaping hook near the ground, firmly pressing down shocks of wheat with his free hand. Cutting the straw at the plant's base assured the entire strand could be harvested with no waste. He yawned and stretched his arms above his head. The repetitive motion honed Rein's tall, muscular frame, and at age 22, he was able to work all day. Although his body ached from long hours swinging the sickle, he should be able to stay ahead of the other farmers and villagers, who were gathering the wheat into bundles and tying them into sheaves.

It was tradition for all the manor's serfs, both those who lived in the village and those who farmed the estate's land, to help with the intense harvest labor. It was also a necessity—all either shared in the bounty or went hungry. With war taking a massive death toll among the manor's men and drought damaging crops the past three years, every hand was needed. Even the village weaver, shoemaker, baker, and blacksmith had joined farmers in the field to bring in this crop. Rein's family plot had ripened first—once it was cut and stored, he would help the others harvest their crops.

"Why is your wheat always the best yield among all the parcels?" chided Johann Heft, who paused to survey the field ahead. Johann was head stableman and had left his post to assist.

Rein paused, leaning on the scythe, and grinned at his lifelong friend. "It's a mystery to me, Johann. Perhaps it's because I'm stingy about saving the best seeds to plant next season. And for some reason, the deer don't graze in my fields at night."

"And where do the deer go, I wonder?" Johann knew quite well Rein's skill with a bow.

Rein winked and resumed swinging the scythe, feeling his muscles burn but keeping his focus on the repetitive rasp of the blade. Inside, he fought bitterness. The serfs' plight was unfair. Deer on manor property were allowed to graze wherever they wandered, even destroying the farmers' crops. But it was against the law for serfs to hunt.

Though appearing weary, workers nearby smiled warmly at the banter between the two young men. Rein thought highly of the manor's serfs, the peasant class he had grown up with. They accepted their status most of the time but weren't always such humble servants. To Rein, hunting the forbidden deer was a way to vent frustration. Like others, he practiced small, crafty acts of retribution on his master's property. An occasional stag found its way to a villager's table, supplementing meager diets. Though if caught, the manor's lord could exact any punishment he felt suitable. Rein believed that, when roused, the peasants could unleash their rage. For the most part, he and the others were *tuckischen* by nature— doggedly stubborn in dealings with their master.

The children were busy with the next task, stacking sheaves upright in small triangular shocks. Once dried, the shocks would be loaded onto wagons and moved near the barns for threshing. Rein didn't plan to put down the sickle until the field was cut or darkness fell. The work was demanding, but the mood lighthearted, a celebration of the first decent yield in years. Every grain of wheat would be bagged and sold to nobles able to pay high prices. Rein knew the income would pay some of the heavy taxes and rent owed Count Tundorf, but not all. His and the other serfs' bread would come from left-over barley, oats, or rye, whatever portion of grain they were able to keep for themselves.

At ease in the field, Rein had learned every detail of farming from his father, Daniel. He loved the feeling of his hands on the wooden handles of the plow and watching seeds sprout and thrive. The summer sun bronzed his skin, complementing the dark brown hair and deep brown eyes inherited from his mother, Maria.

Daniel and Maria had named him Reinhart for its meaning, "brave counsel," but he thought the common meaning "thinks like a fox" more appropriate. With Johann, he enjoyed a childhood trying to outwit authority, occasionally landing both in trouble. Now he found himself thrust into the role of head of household, assuming responsibility for his sister Eva and heavy debt on the leased land.

He was no longer called Reinhart, but Rein. It meant "kind and strong." He frowned, contemplating that. With so few coins left after taxes, and energy drained by four days of *socage* he and the other serfs were required to work free for the count each week; he felt neither, only exhausted and frustrated.

Rein glanced over his shoulder, half expecting to see his father working by his side. First harvest without him. Daniel had been among villagers who had perished in the war with France and Austria. Seven years of battles, much of it on German soil, had laid waste to the countryside, followed by a cruel drought and failed crops. His father died—not as a soldier—but while delivering wagonloads of supplies to the army's frontier fortress. All Rein had learned about his father's death was that Daniel and other villagers were ambushed by the enemy, and food and ammunition stolen by the French army.

More debilitating news followed the ambush—the count proclaimed serfs would receive no payment for the wagonloads of food and supplies because the Prussian War Office refused to pay for goods never delivered. Families had counted on the income to pay the taxes, land rents, and to feed themselves the coming winter.

Rein welcomed the demanding physical work to numb the frustration at the needless loss of his father and others in a war none of them understood or cared about. He fought heavy guilt, having been spared conscription to farm. Even though the war had ended, serfs were still being conscripted—sold by their lords to rebuild the Prussian army. Rein sighed, knowing it was a matter of time before he was taken.

While work continued, a boy came running from the village and stopped short of breath when he reached Rein. "You've got to come right away. Eva sent me. It's your mother."

𝓔va led Amila into her family's cottage near the village of Nassenwald. As tenants with high standing, the Lundgren family lived in a solidly built stone house with a straw roof surrounded by a fenced farmyard with a simple barn. Even though the manor owned the cottage, Eva and her brother had spent their lives here. Amila looked around the clean, humble dwelling and saw Maria propped up with pillows in a bed moved near the window, where fresh air flowed into the room. Amila covered her mouth with the back of her hand at the sight of Maria's weakened state. Used to witnessing the woman's unflagging energy managing domestic operations of the castle, Amila fought back tears. She moved closer, taking Maria's age-spotted hands in her own. She had known Maria's health had deteriorated since her husband Daniel's death. Still, it was shocking to see the woman who had always been like a second mother in this condition. Her pale skin and cloudy eyes, weary of life, reminded Amila of her own mother the days before she died.

"Amila, my beautiful child, you look more like your mother every day." Maria summoned a smile and patted Amila's cheek. "I told your mother I would try to protect you from hardship, but I won't be here for you or my children."

"No, Maria, you mustn't speak like this. You'll be fine. Please rest. We'll take care of you." Amila's eyes darted toward Eva, who was quietly weeping.

"My dear Amila. You always believe the best will happen, just like your mother. She was so precious to me, as you are." Maria coughed deeply and struggled to clear her throat. She then turned to her daughter. "Eva, would you bring fresh water and watch for Rein outside?"

Maria raised herself from the pillows, clutching the blanket. Her gaze followed her daughter until the cottage door closed, then her voice became urgent. "Amila, listen carefully. I don't know how much time I have. You must believe what I have seen and heard."

Amila never doubted Maria, who knew better than anyone what took place inside the castle walls. Maria had observed joyful events and family matters best left untold. Rarely out of earshot of nobles living within, servants harbored many deep secrets and confided in Maria. Most were harmless. But with the arrival of Tundorf several years earlier, the tenor of life in the castle had changed.

Gasping, Maria leaned forward and continued. "I know what the count has in store for you and my children. He will see you married to better himself. Your life may even be in danger if you don't obey. And soon, he will send more of the manor's men to the army. Rein will be among them."

She drew Amila closer and spoke quietly, voice cracking. "Amila, he hurt Eva. He caught her alone near the storehouse and…violated her. She told only me, she feels such shame. He continues to pursue her."

Amila shuddered and let out a soft whimper. Through the window, she could see young Eva waiting beside the gate. "No, not Eva! How could he be capable of such a vile act?"

"Amila, it has happened before with servants, both before and after the countess' death. You must not tell Rein. He will kill the count and be hung for murder." Maria squeezed both Amila's hands firmly. "You must take Eva and Rein and get away from him, forever. *Their lives are in your hands.*"

Amila stiffened, staring back open-mouthed and shook her head. *She must not mean me.* "Maria, I believe you're telling the truth. But what you're asking of me, it's impossible. What can I do?"

Maria released Amila's hands to reach under the bedcovers. "I took this from the count's study." She handed Amila a leather-bound packet. "It must be proof of what he is planning or has done. I don't know what it means, but I saw how carefully he hid it and know it holds a secret. No one knows I took it. I dared not risk telling Rein and Eva, should I be caught. I have read the documents written in German, but some are in French, which I can't understand. I believe somehow these documents will protect you from him."

Amila took the packet and tucked it beneath her riding jacket. She turned as she heard Eva enter the room with Rein, hurrying to their mother's side. Rein scowled, jaw clenched at Amila's presence. She stepped back, giving them space to embrace their mother.

"Reinhardt, you are here." Maria fought for strength. "I love you so much, my son. You have grown to be so strong and good. Your father would be proud of you, as I am, every day."

Maria motioned to Amila to come close again. Tension surrounded the crowded bedside. "Now, you must listen to what I have to say. It is time for all of you to leave this place, forever." She paused to gaze from one face to another. "You must know what the count is planning to do. I overheard him say he will soon conscript more men to serve as soldiers. Rein, your skill as a farmer has kept you from this fate. But you are next to be taken. You will die a senseless death, like so many before you. You must be here for Eva when I am gone. And I believe the count will soon betroth Amila to a noble, not of her liking nor deserving of her."

Amila knew the truth of Maria's foresight. "He informed me it is so. I am to be betrothed to the Duke of Zwuibrücken, who arrives here today."

Maria nodded, unsurprised. "Amila, when your mother came to know what the count was capable of doing, she asked me to watch over you. Now I'm asking the same of you—for my daughter and son. *You must all escape.* If you stay, this is the end of your lives. If you go, it is a beginning."

The three gathered by the bedside gaped at one another, bewildered.

"There is a way," Maria pointed to a circular lying on the kitchen table. "They talk of this in the village. Amila, read it to us."

Maria and her children were literate, having learned to read the Bible. Unfortunately, they couldn't afford books or even the circular news sheets distributed in the village occasionally. But Maria had obtained a copy of this news circular. It was from a larger village a few hours away, dated July 22, 1763. Amila scanned the document, an advertisement formally stating Empress Catherine of Russia's manifesto, a colonizing decree inviting people of Germany and Europe to emigrate to Russia.

"This is remarkable. Can it be believed?" Amila exclaimed, looking up from the lengthy document. "It says German people, no matter their station, are invited to come and settle on free land. Money for travel will be provided. Colonists are to have many privileges: the right to govern themselves, freedom from military service and taxes, freedom of religion, and land ownership. It lists the lands open to settlement."

Absorbing what Amila had read, they waited for Maria to speak, her voice deepening and more insistent. "Think what this means—land to farm, freedom. You speak Russian, Amila. You have traveled, and you are stronger than you know. *You can lead my children to this new home.* Life has more in store than that demon has planned for all of you. This is my wish. You must all go!"

Maria's forceful words drained the remaining strength from her body. She lay peacefully, eyelids slightly open, holding her children's hands as she rested. No more words were spoken. After a few minutes, Maria's breathing became more labored, her eyes closed. Rein and Eva huddled near as their mother lost conscious-ness and took her final breaths. Amila began to tremble. Eva's sobbing increased, and Rein's burning gaze fixed on a distant wall. Soon, Rein enfolded his tiny sister in his arms. Amila stepped forward, extending her hand toward Eva's shoulder. A chilling glare from Rein drove her back.

Stunned, Amila closed her eyes tight attempting to fight back tears. Her disturbing encounter with the count an hour earlier had been enough to bear. Now she had lost the wise guardian whom she depended on and loved so dearly. She opened her eyes downward to the cold, uneven stones covering the floor. Glancing up at Eva and her protective brother, she wanted to share in the pain but was clearly unwelcome. Clutching the advertisement in one hand and securing the leather pouch beneath her jacket, she quietly left the cottage.

CHAPTER 2

June 1763

$\mathcal{H}$urrying to her bedchamber, Amila secured the heavy metal latch inside the door. Her hands shook as she filled a mug with water from a pitcher resting on the dressing table, gulping down the liquid to soothe the burning sensation in her stomach. She sat heavily on the window seat and slid open the wooden shutters, allowing light from outside the upper floor window to flood the musty room. Amila's heart beat wildly, disputing the tranquil view. Her patchwork world extended as far as she could see, illuminating in sharp contrast the slow-moving river, farm plots, grass-covered pastures, sparse woods, and tiny village nestled in the valley. She leaned forward to scan the castle complex directly below, where winding cobblestone paths connected gray stone buildings inside the protective wall. The familiar surroundings lent no relief from events that had just upended her life.

Somehow, she must regain strength for the evening. Remembering the count's harsh words about her appearance, she glanced around the room in search of her brush, not seeing it. Look your best, he'd commanded. Amila picked up the looking glass, a gift from her mother, and studied her reflection—deep green eyes with long, dark lashes framed by unruly waves of auburn hair. She raised an eyebrow, almost able to hear her mother's oft-cited reprimand. "Don't do that. It makes your pretty face unattractive. You look as though you're annoyed, even suspicious." Setting the mirror down, she opened the wardrobe. She hadn't had a new dress since her mother died two years ago, and they all fit snugly. Amila was becoming used to the shapely curves and long, graceful neck that had replaced gangly limbs of youth. Now, at age 19, she didn't dwell on her appearance. When comparing herself to other young women, she thought herself too tall and plain to be attractive.

The warm summer sun streamed in, usually energizing her. Not today. With both parents gone, no siblings, and the isolation of the estate from the few cities in the fiefdom of Württemberg, she had come to accept loneliness. Every day she missed her mother, Countess Margaretha, while her father, Count Philipp of Wallerstein, was a distant memory. As an officer in Prussian King Frederick's army, he had rarely been home and died in battle when Amila was a child. Her father's death had drawn Amila and her mother close, like confidantes.

In the early years of the Kingdom of Prussia and German Nation's war with France and Austria, Count Karl Gottfried of Tundorf married Lady Margaretha, becoming Amila's stepfather. The count's position with the Secretary of War for King Frederick frequently kept him away, as did his small property in a nearby fiefdom, which provided him the title of count. However, almost overnight, the changes he forged sent tremors through the Nassenwald estate. Amila had asked her mother why she felt compelled to remarry. Her mother said only that Count Tundorf had been persistent and offered protection, especially important given the threat of war encroaching.

Protection. From that black-hearted, evil man? Amila flinched. How wrong Mother had been. Once married, all pretense of kindness disappeared. Tundorf immediately took control of the manor's property and serfs, ruling with an iron fist. The count relied on brothers Ebald and Axel Stein to oversee the estate. The lazy pair and several other paid ruffians were the only men allowed to carry— and use—guns. She detested the shiftless brutes, who browbeat and threatened serfs, doling out punishment to massage their egos. They were little more than bullies and spies, reporting anything of note that had happened when the count returned following an absence.

Her mother was held in high regard by the serfs, who belonged to the land and thus the manor. She respected and treated them fairly. But once married, Tundorf no longer allowed her to manage the estate or determine treatment of serfs, whose taxes, rents, and work burdens were increased to unattainable levels. Amila and her mother realized the horror the count was capable of committing when Ebald and Axel caught a serf poaching venison in the manor's woods. The count ordered the poacher executed for theft and his corpse suspended in an iron cage.

It was heartbreaking to watch how Tundorf treated her mother, who spent hours crying in her bedchamber. Amila heard him berate her and believed he assaulted her physically. She wasn't surprised to hear that the count had forced himself on servants but was horrified Eva was among the victims.

Even though Tundorf controlled the estate, Countess Margaretha had insisted she retain the right to oversee her daughter's education. Amila wasn't sure why, but the count acquiesced. So Amila's lifeline to outside knowledge was allowed to continue. The countess assured an appropriate string of tutors instruct her daughter in not only music and the arts but also history, literature, and the French and Russian languages. Amila had accompanied her mother to Frankfort and London, where the countess introduced her daughter to society. To Amila, the young people she met seemed gay and interesting but anchored in the trivialities of the moment. Amila felt little in common with them.

Since childhood, Lady Margaretha had repeatedly explained Amila's fate: marry, provide an heir, and carry out the duties of a countess. But covertly, Amila believed her mother wanted more for her, especially since Tundorf's arrival. In the absence of a son, the countess was preparing her daughter to manage the estate while maintaining the responsibilities of a high-born woman. Her mother said every part of her own life had been controlled by men. First, by her father and male relatives, then by her husband, Count Philipp, and finally Count Tundorf. She remembered the priorities her mother made clear: "You belong to the household and are subject to the paternal rule of your father and eventually your husband. You must be a chaste daughter and faithful wife. Your reputation for chastity is a *rechtsgut*, a legal entity for which you will be highly regarded."

Despite her mother's lectures, Amila resisted the subservient role she was being groomed to assume. After all, her experience was not the same as her mother's. Her father had died when she was young, and she had no uncles or brothers, thus no dominant males influencing her life. That, in addition to growing up with the privilege of her class, had likely given Amila a bold and independent streak. Even though the countess was preparing her for the same life she had lived, Amila felt she might be hoping for a better life for her daughter—more freedom, the ability to determine her own destiny. At least that's what Amila told herself. But it was another of her mother's messages that bolstered Amila to resist the influence of her detested stepfather. According to laws in their fiefdom, Amila would inherit the manor, property, and serfs since she had no brother. The count had temporary power over the estate, but only until Amila married. At that time, she would acquire the title of countess and the estate with her husband, and their heir would be named the next Count or Countess of Wallerstein.

Her mother's sudden illness and death two years ago had left Amila adrift. Now Maria, her remaining source of comfort and strength, was gone. Opposing forces of despair and hope consumed Amila. How could they recover from the loss of Maria? What of the grand offer from the empress? She desperately wanted to believe the far-fetched promises in the empress' manifesto. But was escape possible? If she didn't try, she'd be trapped in marriage to a man she abhorred. Dinner was approaching, and Amila dreaded what might transpire. Look your best and be receptive to the duke. With some work on her appearance, she could become presentable. But how could she feign interest in the duke when his attention was the last thing she desired? And a lifetime of that, however many years he lived?

Delaying preparations for the evening, she turned her attention to the packet Maria had taken from the count's study to see if she could understand its significance. It contained several pages of correspondence, all bearing the count's official seal and signatures. Some pages were written in German, listing inventory, food items, feed for horses, swords, sabers, muskets, and munitions. These records seemed to relate to the count's work as Undersecretary to the War Office, procuring supplies for King Frederick's army. Other documents were written in French and would take more time to scrutinize. So, why would he take such care to hide them separately from other official documents? She leaned out the window to examine a scrolled page in direct sunlight when she heard a knock on the door. Startled, the page slipped from her hand. She lurched forward to grab it, nearly falling out the window. "Who's there?" Amila scurried about the room, searching for a place to hide the packet.

"It's Eva. I've come to help you dress for dinner."

Amila sighed and pushed the documents under the window seat, then hurried to open the door. "Eva, are you all right?" Her words were enough to stir raw emotions in both young women. Amila told Eva she knew about Tundorf's attack. They embraced and let a cascade of tears flow. Finally, Eva was able to talk.

"Ladies from the village came to prepare Mother's body for burial. I can't bear to watch. Rein went back to the field. He's a great comfort to me but is suffering. Amila, how can we bear it? Father's death, and now Mother."

Amila listened, not knowing how to comfort her friend. Few families were untouched by war, famine, or both. After seven years, many of the men and older boys in the village had disappeared, having died in battle or newly conscripted to fill the ranks of those who had perished. Amila didn't understand the complex rationale for the war. She only knew that the German states, as a part of Prussia and King Frederick's kingdom, were fighting with England against France, Austria and its allies. She was aware the conflict extended to the colonies in America, where the French and Indians were fighting the English. But battles near home had caused widespread devastation. Three years ago, troops from France stormed and occupied Nassenwald, burning houses, barns and crops, while pillaging farm animals, grain, and anything of value. Knowing fighting was near, Amila and her mother had found refuge with distant relatives in Munich. Once Prussian forces had retaken the region, they returned, shocked by the destruction. Most villagers were left alive but lacking stores for winter. Amila and her mother shared what food they could, temporarily keeping hunger at bay. The ill-timed drought resulted in failed crops and even greater famine. Finally, after seven bloody years, the war ended. Announced after a treaty signed in Paris, Prussia and its allies, including Germany, were the victors. Unfortunately, nothing had improved.

Amila hugged Eva close. Only 16 years old, she seemed so delicate. Her blond hair, blue eyes, and pale skin lent a softness that matched her timid demeanor. Amila's dark hair and green eyes were a marked contrast, as was her bold, headstrong nature. Today, the two young women had in common a fragility brought about by grief. After a time, Eva began the motions of helping Amila prepare for dinner, giving both young women a mindless ritual to temporarily escape the day's reality.

"Today, the count called me dirty and unkempt." Amila frowned as Eva vigorously brushed her tangles. It was true Amila's hair did more closely resemble a matted horse's mane at times. But as Eva brushed it smooth, attractive highlights began to shine through.

Amila felt determined to protect her young friend from the count, knowing Eva was more vulnerable now that her mother was gone. A ferocious contempt seized her. It wouldn't be easy to contain this hateful distaste in his presence—tonight or ever again.

Her hair now brushed and arranged off her neck with an abundance of pins, Amila stepped into the purposefully plain dress she had chosen, a dark blue gown of summer fabric with a modest oval neckline. "I don't care what he thinks of me." Amila hoped her words would help summon confidence for the evening. "Eva, I want you to know how much I despise the count. Even so, I will face him with resolve tonight."

*A*mila took a deep breath as she entered the drawing-room where the count and his guests had gathered. On special occasions such as tonight, wall sconces and iron chandeliers overflowed with candles, giving the gloomy, high-ceilinged room an amber glow. It was apparent Tundorf was trying to impress these guests.

"Good evening Amila. How lovely you look." The count delivered a severe sidelong warning glance. "You will remember, of course, his Lordship Duke Herman of Zwuibrücken?"

The portly duke came forward and bowed slightly, feigning a kiss over Amila's hand. Then he paused to look her over from head to toe, seeming bored and unimpressed. Amila tried unsuccessfully to disguise her lack of enthusiasm.

"I'm honored to introduce the duke's cousin, Stefan August of Sulzbach, and his wife Marianne," said the count.

"I'm pleased to meet you." Amila curtsied, relieved she wouldn't be alone with the count and duke this evening.

Marianne's beauty and vibrancy enlivened the room. Immediately apparent was the manner in which the couple related to one another. Her husband was attentive and doted on her every word. Amila had never witnessed such deep devotion and found it touching. Was this what love was like? And, Marianne's smile upon meeting her was genuine, giving Amila the impression of an ally for the evening.

Introductions complete, they moved to the dining room, a corner of the massive table set for the small group. The meal already placed on the table was meager compared to larger estates, she was sure. However, Amila could see the count had ordered the best available. Dishes included fish with onion sauce, calf's head and trimmings, the interior of a pig in various dishes, a goose, and two hares. Wine from the manor's cellar was decanting.

Amila knew it was her role to remain silent, to simply adorn the room. She had learned ladies might speak when spoken to and interact with persons seated nearby. Still, ladies were not welcome to engage in serious conversation. Amila was satisfied to avoid the limelight and relieved her intolerable engagement would not be announced tonight, at least.

Amila reflected on the duke's appearance. She supposed he was dressed in the height of fashion, wearing a deep red waistcoat of embroidered silk, a ruffled shirt with full sleeves gathered at the wrist, and matching breeches. However, she didn't know what to make of the oddest part of his visage: two small black splotches of fabric protruded from his face, one on his cheek and the other on his forehead. Evidently intended to embellish his stylish look, instead they presented a disturbing contrast with his heavily powdered face and wig. Amila had seen this a few times when attending formal events in London. Like his showy clothing, she guessed the affixed moles were a statement of the duke's status and wealth. By his appearance and behavior, the duke seemed to believe himself far above her station. She exhaled quietly, suddenly filled with hope His Lordship would lose interest in a mere country bumpkin.

Seated across from Marianne, Amila took the opportunity to learn more about the friendly young woman. "I'm delighted to have you here, Marianne. It's clear you are comfortable in society. Please tell me about life in the city."

"We spend most of our time in Stefan's home at Sulzbach, which is not a large city." Marianne sounded pleased by the interest. "I'm from a much bigger city, Stuttgart, where I grew up and learned ballet."

Amila smiled. "That is why you move so gracefully. It's as though you dance with every step you take! I've never seen ballet, but I've heard it's quite beautiful."

"Stuttgart has become the center for ballet in Germany," explained Marianne eagerly. "The ballet is becoming very popular with the aristocracy and spreading quickly around Europe. I danced in opera productions for the Court, and that's where I met Stefan. But of course, now that Stefan and I are married, I no longer dance."

"Don't you miss it?"

"No, not really." Marianne glanced warmly at Stefan. "And we are fortunate to attend ballet performances when in Stuttgart visiting Duke Herman, which is fairly often."

Amila overheard the men's conversation transitioning from horses and hunting to more serious topics.

"My serfs and the children of my serfs are lazy beggars," complained Tundorf when asked about the status of the manor's holdings. "They have unhealthy bodies and are often subject to loathsome diseases, of which many die at a young age. As a result, they don't live long enough to serve me well."

His Lordship pursed his lips in distaste. "Then they have much in common with my servants in the city. They have few virtues and are simply subordinate to us in every way. Hence, many are to blame for their own misfortunes."

One of Amila's tutors had explained to her the absolutist position held by most of the ruling class: the belief in nobility's supreme authority over lower classes of people based on bloodlines and heredity. These were undoubtedly the leanings she heard repeated now and were quite contrary to her first-hand knowledge of the manor's hard-working serfs.

"I find my serfs rude and overbearing to those whom they do not fear." The count disregarded the fact that the objects of his verbal attack were entering and leaving the dining room, serving and pouring wine. "It's necessary to keep them in their place. Upon finding one of my serfs had poached venison on my property, I had him executed to remind them who owns the forests. I've had to deal with rebellious upstarts in other situations as well."

Upon hearing Tundorf brag about the atrocity, Amila raised an eyebrow and lifted her chin. She opened her mouth to speak, held her tongue, then words poured out.

"In studies with my tutor, I read authors who describe peasants otherwise. If I remember correctly, one writer called them an indispensable foundation of the other classes of human society and as making great contributions to agriculture and the trades."

She continued in a strong, clear voice in spite of the count's scathing glance. "I studied the writings of the great German philosopher, Immanuel Kant. He believes there's a way to reconcile individual freedom of peasants with authority of the upper classes. I believe he wrote, 'Always recognize that human individuals are ends, and do not use them as means to your end.'"

A smothering silence filled the room, all eyes on Amila. Tundorf stormed back, his voice filled with rage. "Amila, as a woman, you are ignorant of such matters. Your opinion is not welcome at this or any table. Apologize to our guests immediately for your foolhardy outburst. See that this never happens again!"

Amila flushed and stared down at her plate. Finally, she mumbled. "Please forgive me, Your Lordship and guests. I was wrong to speak out."

"So, I see this young woman has spirit in her." The duke looked from the count to Stefan as if Amila were absent from the room. "We'll see what can be done about such impudence."

The men picked up the conversation, seemingly more enflamed, confirming Amila's words were indeed of no consequence. "King Frederick mistakenly thinks himself an enlightened monarch, trusting in the teachings of the upstart French philosopher Voltaire," offered the duke. "Frederick misguidedly believes his principal occupation is to combat ignorance and prejudice, to enlighten minds, cultivate morality, and even make all people happy. It is likely one of the reasons his Prussian Empire is losing strength and our local princes gain power."

Stefan snickered, head nodding with every phrase the duke uttered. "Frederick has gone so far as to say that his royal power emanates not from divine right but from a social contract to improve the lives of his subjects. I've heard the King is now allowing commoners to become judges and senior bureaucrats, even military officers. Can you imagine?"

His Lordship held a handkerchief to his nose. "Likewise, I see the city's rising class of artisans swagger about in fine dress, riding in their ornate carriages. I think to myself: be as ostentatious as you will, you will never be equal to us. We alone possess the superior qualities that come from having noble blood run through one's veins."

"Well said, My Lord!" Stefan clapped his hands, eliciting a positive lift of the chin from the egocentric duke.

Amila could understand why the duke enjoyed Stefan's company. Her mind wandered from the distasteful conversation and the count's reprimand. What a heartless match this would be. Whether ignorant of reality or simply narrow-minded, the duke's words shocked her. So unlike Mother and Father, who cared for every individual of the manor, be they noble or serf. They taught me to treat all with respect. If Duke Herman were kind and reasonable, perhaps she could bear it. While he didn't seem to be like Tundorf—a cruel, vicious tyrant— his 'superior breeding' sickened her.

References to emigration and soldier conscription brought her focus back to the conversation. They were discussing the war's end and the fact that King Frederick's troops were dwindling. The king had recently circulated an edict to replenish the army. Amila knew the impact on the manor's serfs and had heard alarming stories. Nobles like the count forced their serfs into conscription and received payment for each person. When conscription was not successful, the king employed recruiters who used every tactic available, including kidnapping young boys.

"I say, let the peasants and new middle class emigrate to the British colonies of the Americas, or even to Russia at the recent bidding of Empress Catherine. Good riddance to bad rubbish!" concluded the duke, as if to wash his hands of the ignoble problem of the lowborn.

Coughing nervously, the count responded boldly. "I forbid my serfs to emigrate. As my property, they're obligated to stay and work the land, care for my estate, and pay taxes. A better solution is to send some of the men to fill the ranks of the king's army. Above all, with Frederick's payment for soldiers filling my coffers, it's a solution that benefits both my purse and future war efforts."

Amila froze, determined not to glance in the count's direction. There it was, all as Maria had foreseen, an open admission of his plan, as well as forbidding the option that could save them.

*D*inner concluded, the count dismissed Amila, Stefan, and Marianne to a small sitting room cooled by a summer breeze while he met with the duke privately in his study.

At last, thought Tundorf, as a servant placed snifters and a bottle of the manor's finest brandy on a side table. It had taken years to find a husband for Amila who met all his requirements. While appearing to delay a betrothal for Amila to allow a proper mourning period, in reality he'd been seeking the right candidate. And, keeping Amila cloistered at the castle for two years with no access to other suiters had allowed him the time.

As they sipped brandy and made small talk, the count reviewed what he knew about Duke Zwuibrücken. Tundorf had learned a great deal through private inquiry—he was a non-ruling duke, ranking just below grand dukes and royalty, a rank far superior to himself and even Amila's family. Rent from farmland and ownership in coal mines provided more than enough annual income to support his lavish lifestyle, including a baroque residence in Zwuibrücken, a grand palace built over the last 30 years. Most importantly, his first wife had died without providing an heir. The duke seemed urgent for an heir, presumably due to his advancing age. It had taken more in-depth inquiry to confirm the real reason. Tundorf had suspected it, having seen physical evidence in other members of the noble elite. The heavy powder and fake moles masked scars and signs of the 'French evil' disease, syphilis, contracted through brothels and various partners. It was even rumored the duke's wife had succumbed to the disease. All the more wisdom in taking his own pleasure with healthy, young servant girls such as Eva. Perhaps the old man didn't have long to live. Even better. Produce the coveted heir, and he himself would be able to control the Wallerstein holdings along with the duke's estate through Amila's heir following the duke's death.

Tundorf offered the initial foray. "Your Grace, I'm honored by your interest in dear Amila as the future Duchess of Zwuibrücken. As the daughter of the Count and Countess of Wallerstein, she is of noble blood, as well as healthy and quite beautiful, as you can see. With no male heir or other siblings, the title and estate pass to her and her heir. I've waited to consider a betrothal to allow her a grace period to mourn the death of Countess Margaretha, my dear departed wife. It's been two long years."

"I, too, have been lonely these past few years, mourning the loss of my own wife." The duke sighed. "Now it's time to remarry. As you may know, I do not have an heir."

"Yet I wonder about your cousin Stefan, now that he is married. Would not he or perhaps his child be in line as your successor? He seems very devoted to you."

Duke Herman laughed, belching loudly from the large meal and brandy. "Oh yes. Stefan panders to my every word to assure my favor. I do enjoy the constant flattery and companionship. However, against my wishes, Stefan married a commoner well below his station. Quite distasteful. I assure you--his dowdy dancer will never become the duchess. Neither will his offspring be entitled to my title or estates. Unequal marriages among classes are frowned upon by royalty, you know, and put claims of inheritance at risk."

The final barrier removed, he breathed comfortably, ready to advance negotiations. "What then do you propose, Your Lordship?"

"That we enter into a marriage contract immediately. A modest dowry is important only for appearances, as all her property will pass to me through her heir. You assure she is healthy and able to bear children? I will require a certificate of virginity, of course."

"I assure you she is quite chaste. Indeed, a physician's examination will confirm she is intact and able to provide an heir. You will have the certificate before signing the contract." Secretly, Tundorf was concerned. Amila had been largely unsupervised since her mother's death. No matter. If she didn't pass the exam, he'd pay the physician to procure the necessary document. Now was the time to broach his greatest concern, a point of negotiation he'd been pondering. "However, Your Grace, I must confess the loss of this estate will weigh heavily on my own situation."

"Ah, you are hesitant to give up her estate's income. Provide the sum in the contract and we'll negotiate annual compensation. Clearly, I will require you to continue to manage this manor, as I have no interest in it. And, of course, you will receive a large sum at the birth of an heir."

Tundorf smirked. "Then let us toast the union of the two families. I will obtain the appropriate document from our minister to show that the banns have been announced. A posting of the banns for three weeks? That would be near the date of my annual birthday hunt here and the dinner that follows. Can we announce the engagement at that time?"

"Agreed. As long as the wedding follows quickly. A small, private ceremony. We will move immediately to my palace. Let's meet with my solicitor in Stuttgart the day after tomorrow. I leave in the morning. Shall we rejoin the others?"

In the sitting room, Amila listened enthusiastically to Stefan and Marianne's stories about life in the city. Rarely able to converse with guests near her age, she found herself smiling and laughing aloud. However, as the count and duke entered, she immediately became silent. It was hard to miss the smug looks on both faces. Knowing what it might mean, a profound exhaustion suddenly overtook her following the tumultuous events of the day. She said good night and left, hoping her lack of interest in the duke's company, coupled with her outburst during dinner, would be enough to discourage further interest. She could only hope he would leave and never return.

Walking up the stairs to her bedchamber, she found Eva peeking around the corner. "Amila, the count left word for me to bring him a cordial tonight in his chambers. What should I do?"

"Come with me." She put an arm around the frightened girl's shoulder and urged her forward. "Spend the night with me, safe behind my locked door. Then we'll see what tomorrow brings."

CHAPTER 3

June - July 1763

$\mathcal{A}$s Amila had hoped, the two men wielding control over her future left the next morning, but not before Tundorf took her aside and delivered more devastating news.

"The details of the marriage are settled, and the engagement will be announced in a month. He paced jauntily behind her father's desk. Amila couldn't remember ever having seen him giddy. His eyes darted around the room, then fixed on some lofty prize floating in the air. "My annual birthday hunt and banquet will be the perfect occasion. We'll invite the highest-ranking nobles in Württemberg. A splendid opportunity to spread the marvelous news that you'll be the next Duchess of Zwuibrücken!"

With a dismissive flip of his wrist, he ordered her to procure a wardrobe, whatever might be needed, including an appropriate gown for the engagement dinner. He didn't care how much she spent because her fiancé would pay all expenses. But the news most difficult to bear—the engagement would be short. After a private wedding ceremony, Amila would leave the castle immediately for the duke's residence. Then the count rode away in his carriage with no word regarding when he might return.

Amila encountered the duke and his small party briefly at breakfast. She remained quiet throughout, still digesting the grim news. At last, obviously unimpressed with the gloomy castle, he yawned and informed her he was anxious to return to the comforts of his palace. Duke Herman ordered his personal servant to load their baggage, and he and his companions left immediately.

The moment the carriage was out of sight, Amila traded her plain morning dress for the previous day's riding attire and hurried to the stable.

"What's so urgent this morning, Lady Amila? You look as though you're being chased by the devil." Johann got no answer as she darted toward Gabe's stall. He set down the harness he was repairing and followed. Just a few years older than Amila, he'd taught her to ride and, over time, had proclaimed himself Amila's guardian.

"Oh, Johann. That's too close to the truth. I want to ride a bit further than usual today. I may not return until late afternoon." She had hoped to avoid his attentive eye, knowing he would disapprove of her riding as far as Donauwörth alone. Tucked inside her jacket was the leaflet with Empress Catherine's colonizing decree, which listed the nearby town as a place to meet with a Russian emigration agent. Donauwörth was about an hour's hard ride from the castle. Eva, who sometimes rode with her, was nowhere in sight.

"Don't worry, I'll be fine." She finished saddling Gabe and lead him out of the stall. "You know few horses can catch Gabe. I don't plan to slow down for anyone."

After crossing the stone bridge, Amila spurred Gabe to a gallop, both rider and horse exhilarated to traverse the open road.

Returning hours later, she stopped by the kitchen storeroom to gather root vegetables, bread, then meat from the larder, tying the items in a bundle. She found Eva tending herbs in the manor garden, called to her, and extended her hand to climb up behind on Gabe. They rode to Eva's cottage, then released the weary horse to graze in the meadow.

Darkness had fallen by the time Rein returned from the field. The aroma of freshly roasted pork invaded his nostrils when he stepped through the cottage door. He blinked and breathed deeply, certain he must be imagining it. Intense hunger pangs reminded him he hadn't eaten since a meager breakfast before daylight.

His eyes widened upon seeing plates heaped with roasted pork, new potatoes, carrots, and heavy brown bread filling the table in front of him. A feast. Most meals were bread only. He smiled at Eva, about to ask her where it had come from. When he saw Amila rise from a stool near the hearth, his smile disappeared. He turned away, mumbling, then spun back to face her, pointing at the table. "Is this an act of goodwill? It's too late for that. This is our home, and you have no right to be here."

His mother's body lay in the bedroom upstairs, awaiting burial the next day.

Amila stepped back timidly. "I want you to know how sorry I am for the loss of your mother. I grieve with you. You, you must know I loved her too."

Ignoring her, Rein approached Eva, folding her in his arms. After a time, he broke the silence and spoke tenderly to his sister. "When I got home late last night from the field, you were gone. I didn't know where to look for you. Eva, I have only you now."

"Eva spent the night with me, in my chamber," Amila started to say more but didn't. She had promised Maria.

"You must never do that again." He responded sternly to Amila, too tired to care that she was the lady of the manor and far his superior.

Amila stood in silence and felt her eyelid twitch. Careful not to glare at him, she felt uneasy, as if an unprecedented shift was underway. She was uncertain how to react. Grief undoubtedly emboldened him to deliver such a reprimand, almost an order. This was their home and the first day of their lives without either parent. If it made him feel better to scold her, so be it. She needed his help.

Eva broke the uneasy silence. "Sit down, please, Rein, and eat. I've been cooking this afternoon, and I know you must be hungry. I asked Amila to stay. She, well, she is hoping to talk with us about Mother's wishes. She went to Donauwörth today."

"What were you doing there and why should we care?" Rein responded dryly. His mother's death, a sleepless night, and the day's work blinded him to everything but the food before him. He sat down and began eating.

"The decree Maria gave us, it directed me to see a man in Donauwörth." Amila had noted his scornful response and proceeded cautiously. "I'm a stranger in the town, so I decided it was safe to go and ask. At first, no one seemed to know anything. But then a woman directed me to a man named Gunter Rohlwagen, a recruiter for emigration to Russia. He's German but works for the Russian government. I met with him for several hours in the dining room at an inn. He told me everything in the empress' manifesto is true!"

Amila could no longer contain her enthusiasm—details of what she'd learned began to flow unbridled. She told them Russian Empress Catherine, like them a German, was seeking settlers from all walks of life, especially farmers and craftsmen. "They want settlers of sterling character, orderly, thrifty. Rich or poor is of no consequence. The agent simply creates a contract that emigrants sign. Then colonists receive money for the journey and provisions for several years until they are established."

After a pause, Amila looked back and forth between Rein and his sister. She took a breath and continued. "Settlement is just beginning. Emigrants must first travel to Lübeck, a German port city in the far north, where temporary living quarters are arranged, and colonists receive a daily allowance for food. Then, they travel by ship across the Baltic Sea to a gulf near St. Petersburg, Russia, and on to settlement locations. *Farmers receive their own land. They own the land outright.*"

Finally, Rein had his fill of food and Amila's outrageous rant. "Lady Amila, no one knows better than you that serfdom binds us to this land, this manor. We are forbidden to leave. It's a law enforced by your kind! I know villagers who've wanted to leave here and go to America but have been told by Tundorf they can't."

His voice was gaining force with every word. Glancing up at the thatched roof ceiling, he shook his head slowly from side to side. "If we leave without permission and are caught, do you know what Tundorf will do? We'll be arrested and put in prison. He can take away everything—our right to farm, all our possessions, our home. Remember what his guards did to Jacob, who was caught poaching deer? What do you think he'd do to us if we were caught? And helping *you* escape, Amila? What would the punishment be for that?"

Amila sat deflated, staring at her hands folded in her lap. She glanced at Eva and held her gaze, unwilling to accept the reality of Rein's words, which continued to flow.

"All our lives we've been told by the lord we're bound to this plot of land. We are to raise crops, pay taxes and try to feed ourselves. We can't leave this manor unless the lord sells or transfers us to another manor or the army. We must ask permission if we want to change trades or even marry. We have no power against the actions of the lord. *Do you not see that you are tempting us with a life that can never be?"*

Eva began to sniffle, wiping her eyes. "Rein, I can't stay here any longer. I just can't! Don't you remember Mother's dying wish for us?" She began to sob and ran from the cottage.

Rein watched Eva's departure, baffled. Why would she declare she could no longer live here? Perhaps it was the loss of Mother. He was still deep in thought when Amila responded.

"I spoke too boldly. Perhaps it's too soon to talk about this. But an idea worth your consideration has occurred to me. Am I not the lady of the manor, with rights over the serfs who reside here? If I grant permission for you to emigrate, then it would be legal."

She gave him a chance to consider the suggestion. "Eva isn't the only one who feels she must leave. I will not marry the duke. I have only a month before the engagement will be announced. The wedding will take place soon after."

Rein pounded the table with his fists, the force making the empty plates bounce. "What has your privileged life to do with our future?"

Amila met his hateful stare and took deep, slow breaths. She waited until his anger subsided. "It's all as Maria told us, Rein. Last night at dinner, the count informed guests he's preparing to conscript another group of the manor's serfs to the army very soon. If this happens, *you will be lost to Eva.* They'll take Johann too, I'm sure. Even your skill as a farmer and Johann's as a saddler won't protect you. I can grant permission for you to emigrate to accompany me to the new colonies. I know you find me and 'my kind' repulsive. Like it or not, we need each other."

Amila's final argument was perhaps the most compelling. "Your mother and mine wanted a better life for us. We must try."

Elbows on the table, hands covering his face, Rein closed his eyes and willed her away. His mother was always so wise, had such good instincts. She knew a bold step must be taken and had given them a path. But who was this crazy young woman before him? The same child who climbed too high in trees, rode horses too fast, and swam in the river where it wasn't safe was now a bigger version of that little girl, scheming to drag him and Eva deep into trouble.

"I don't believe what you've been told by this man. No one wants farmers, and giving away land—that is preposterous. Who would pay to bring poor peasants to their country? I'm willing to meet with this recruiter just to hear his crazy story for myself." Rein sighed, giving in to the mental assault as well as the physical exhaustion. "But it must be in secret. Not a word of this to anyone, do you hear?"

$\mathcal{A}$ few days later, Amila, Eva and Rein rode to Donau-wörth to meet discreetly with the enroller. Though the thought was distasteful, Amila justified the trip to visit a dressmaker for her wedding trousseau. She had made one hasty trip to Donauwörth several days earlier to seek a seamstress and make sure the recruiter could meet with them today.

On that trip, Johann had accompanied her for appearance's sake, insisting she needed protection. Certainly, Johann's stocky, muscular frame from years of black-smith, leather, and stable work made him formidable. But Amila knew well the gentle giant beneath. She smiled, recalling the way he could always lighten her mood. Since childhood, he'd known how to temper her desire for bold adventures as well as cheer her up when she was discouraged. It was a natural friendship, with Amila soaking up every bit of his extensive knowledge of horses, at the same time taking advantage of the sta-bles as a convenient hiding place from Tundorf. Amila had shared with Johann the real reason for the visits to Donauwörth and sworn him to secrecy.

Today, Amila and Eva rode double on Gabe, and Rein rode a horse Johann had chosen from the stable. Since this trip wasn't at breakneck speed, they had time to talk, and Amila took full advantage to convey to Eva and her skeptical brother all she had learned from Gunter Rohl-wagen.

Amila said Herr Rohlwagen had traveled the world and currently works for a Russian ambassador from Lübeck, where emigrants embark by ship. The ambassador had engaged Gunter and other professional enrollers to meet with potential colonists all over Europe and dispatch them immediately to the Russian Capitol.

"He's an official emissary of Empress Catherine herself. He seems like a kind, knowledgeable man. Just please listen to what he has to say." Amila had noticed Rein fidgeting in the saddle. Of course, she realized—he's not used to riding. Farmers used plow horses, but the giant beasts were rarely ridden. Amila hoped discomfort wouldn't keep him from listening, at least. She held him captive on the two-hour ride and planned to present a full recitation of what she had learned.

Amila explained the enroller had told her most of the emigrants would be coming from German-speaking lands. However, the empress' manifesto was being distributed far and wide across Europe. He said there's intense competition from other countries seeking settlers, especially from Austria and Hungary.

"If we were to go to either of those countries, I'm afraid Tundorf would find us and make us return…or worse." Amila proclaimed her opinion of the best option. However, she didn't tell them everything—that she planned to return one day to reclaim the estate. But on her own terms, without the threat of a loathsome forced marriage. She had been sure to ask Gunter the question foremost on her mind. In response, he assured her colonists could return to their land of origin at any time.

At last, Rein responded. "Why not America? We know families from nearby villages whose relatives have gone there."

"Herr Rohlwagen has been there. He told me America is indeed beautiful, with fertile land, rich forests, and abundant water. But travel is dangerous, and no expenses are paid, not even for ship's passage. The journey lasts several months. Many sicken and die. Once they arrive in port cities, colonists are auctioned off to farm or business owners, where they work as indentured servants for five or more years, just to cover the cost of their passage. Only then are they free to pursue a life of their own choosing. He says the most generous terms by far are from Russia."

As they left the meandering Wörnitz River and followed the road the seven miles to Donauwörth, Amila noticed Eva and Rein craning their necks in all directions and commenting to one another with great interest. Then she understood—the two had never been beyond the boundaries of Nassenwald village and lands. As they entered the narrow, cobblestone streets in the town center, the siblings paused and gazed at the ornate parish church and massive monastery crowning the hill. With bridges across the converging Wörnitz and Danube rivers, the town attracted a bustling trade. They looked on curiously as they rode through the crowded market where noisy vendors were hawking their wares.

They found the well-dressed, talkative Herr Rohlwagen leaning against a two-story building under the sign of the Black Bear Inn, where they had arranged to meet. "Greetings! Let us enter and sup together." The recruiter looked over each shoulder as he hustled the travelers inside. He nodded to the innkeeper, and no sooner had they sat down than a tavern maid arrived with a welcome midday meal of traditional German food. Amila saw Rein and Eva glance wide-eyed at platters heaped with gefulte noodles filled with meat, bowls of farina soup, pumpernickel bread, and tankards of beer. Amila knew it was likely more food than they saw in a week.

He insisted they call him Gunter, not Herr Rohlwagen, then encouraged them to eat and drink as he launched into his pitch.

"So, you are a farmer?" asked Gunter. Rein nodded. "Russia wants skilled farmers more than any other tradesmen. You can settle anywhere you want, even on the great Volga River. The river is the biggest you'll see in your lifetime. Hundreds of streams flow into it to provide abundant water. And wait until you see the land. Although the ground has not yet been broken, it's so fertile you can grow everything necessary to live. Eyewitnesses have told me the land resembles the warm provinces of France."

He let them digest his words along with the food. "And so much land for each family—50 hectares to farm. When you colonize vacant lands, you pay no taxes for ten years. We have maps that show tracts available. Some are meadow, forest, and streams, where of course you are allowed to hunt and fish. Once you arrive, you will receive horses, cows, sheep, pigs, and money to purchase tools and supplies until the first harvest. Some of the funds help start the farm and are never to be repaid. This is very generous of the empress, is it not?"

"Have these lands been settled? Does anyone live there?" asked Amila.

"Ah. Because of the current peaceful situation with Persia, there is extensive trade with the neighboring Kirghiz, tribes of nomads who live in the area. And the Russians are the most peace-loving and kind people."

"How do colonists pay for ship's passage?" Rein had finished eating and crossed his arms.

"Your passage is paid. As soon as you enroll, you receive expense money for the journey north." Gunter pulled out a circular listing currency they would receive in silver coins. He handed it to Rein, who gasped.

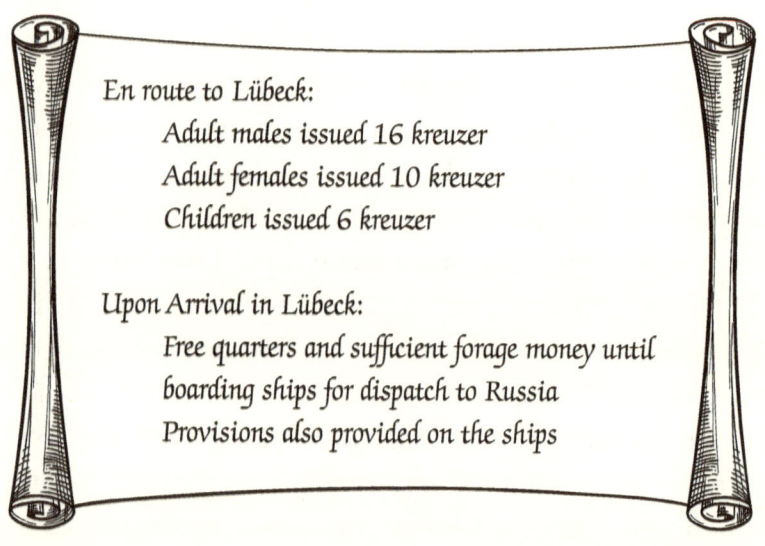

En route to Lübeck:
Adult males issued 16 kreuzer
Adult females issued 10 kreuzer
Children issued 6 kreuzer

Upon Arrival in Lübeck:
Free quarters and sufficient forage money until boarding ships for dispatch to Russia
Provisions also provided on the ships

Rein stared at the sheet of paper, brow furrowed. He traded for most of the food and other goods they needed to survive but was still aware what these sums would buy. The 16 kreuzer to travel to the port city was more money than he and his family had to live on in a year after a successful crop, paying rents and taxes. With less than one kreuzer, he could buy a great deal of food, many loaves of bread, flour, cheese, and butter. And 16 kreuzer was about the price of a cow and calf or a young plow horse. Two persons' expense money would buy a pair of pistols. It was hard to believe they would receive additional funds once they reached Lübeck.

Gunter suppressed a smile, sure he was beginning to convince the most reluctant recruit. "I've traveled across the Baltic Sea. It's a restful trip on the sailing ship and takes less than two weeks to reach Oranienbaum, near St. Petersburg. Once there, Empress Catherine herself may welcome you, as her summer palace is nearby."

Amila sat dumbfounded by the promises she heard. She and Eva exchanged encouraging looks. Amila glanced in Rein's direction. The stoic gaze that had dominated his face through most of the discussion had softened. They sat quietly, looking at one another, not sure what else to ask.

Gunter summoned a more serious voice. "How many families might come from your manor? A large number would be better. A sufficient number of colonists are gathering now in Lübeck to fill the first ship. Farmers go to the top of the list. You need only show an affidavit signed by the lord of your manor saying you may emigrate and are a farmer in good standing. Then there will be no delay. You could leave on a ship right away, soon after you arrive in Lübeck."

Amila recognized this had crossed over to dangerous discussion. She had explained previously to the recruiter that as the lady of the manor, she would be granting permission for her serfs to emigrate. Amila and he both knew that was a privilege usually granted only by the lord of the manor.

Rein frowned and lowered his voice. "What if we are forbidden to leave?"

Gunter leaned closer so no one beyond the table could hear. "If it's forbidden by your lord, we work secretly and with caution. The ambassador I work for said we simply do not issue passports. Lady Amila's signature as the lady of the manor once you arrive in Lübeck will be enough. *They can do nothing to stop you.* Go directly to Lübeck and enlist as colonists. But you must hurry. After September and for the remainder of the year, no reception of new colonists will be possible."

Reading Rein's uncertainty, Gunter rushed on. "I don't know why you hesitate. I know a bit about what your life must be like. A serf is obligated to work for his lord four or even more days every week without pay. Think what you could accomplish on 50 hectares of land farming all the days—for yourself?"

Gunter stared unblinkingly and continued. "Aren't you tired of being treated like property? Your petty rulers are so puffed up with ideas of grandeur and self-importance, they don't care to see you are starving. Are you aware the nobles have put the burden of debt upon you to finance their war? And that when they cannot afford their lives of splendor through taxes, they can sell you as soldiers into forced military service for Prussia? It's a system that benefits the upper class quite well—the nobility leads the army, the middle-class supplies the army, and the peasants die in the army. I know. I have been an army recruiter, a job I'm not proud of."

Rein was stunned by the recruiter's bold words. "Then why are you doing this?"

"Ah, yes, why would I spend my time on this endeavor? The war is over, and soldiers are no longer dying so quickly. Vast numbers of new soldiers are not needed, although Prussia must now replenish its ranks somewhat. So I'm working with Russia now. I'm to be paid three guldens for each emigrant I deliver to ships in Lübeck. That's significantly more than if I were recruiting soldiers. I'm afraid I'm guilty of dealing in human merchandise. I have even been called a 'soul seller.' The ambassador has instructed me to use every sort of seduction needed, whatever it takes to get colonists to Lübeck. You see, the empress desires settlers this much, and what is wrong in that?"

The recruiter left the table and paid the innkeeper for the meal, announcing he must meet with other prospects. He bid them goodbye with a tip of his hat, reminding them they could find him here for the next few weeks, should they wish to procure documents. The visitors quietly left the inn, and Amila led them to the dressmaker's shop. The selection of clothing for her trousseau included the formal gown, and two sturdy travel dresses for herself, two for Eva, and heavy cloaks.

On the return trip, Amila kept quiet but glanced occasionally at Rein, who stared straight ahead. Finally, Rein turned and spoke to Eva. "We would be taking a huge risk trusting this man with our lives. But I'm beginning to wonder, what is the alternative? If even some of what he promises is true, then the new life would be better than we have here. Eva, are you prepared to take this risk?"

Eva lifted her shoulders confidently and nodded. "I feel safe with you, Rein, no matter where we go. But I'll no longer stay here."

Neither needed to ask Amila what she wanted to do.

Several days later, Rein was in the field helping neighbors harvest wheat when Tundorf rode past toward the village. Alongside were his guards, Ebald and Axel, and a Prussian soldier in formal uniform. They stopped only long enough to post a decree in the village. Having seen this before, Rein and the other farmers stopped their work, walking downcast to the square. They gathered with tradesmen from the village to read it. From past experience, they knew it was senseless to resist.

"By order of King Frederick II of Prussia, we hereby requisition all able-bodied men to defend the nation in order to drive enemies from the land. All unmarried males from ages eighteen to twenty-five years are required to report, and no one may obtain exemption for service to which he is summoned. They shall meet, beginning tomorrow morning, at the town square of Nassenwald, where they shall practice manual exercise daily while awaiting the hour of departure. Count Karl Gottfried of Tundorf is responsible for taking all measures necessary for the prompt execution of the present decree."

The following morning, Rein hesitantly reported with other young men of the ages conscripted to begin military training. He thought how ironic the charade—they were forbidden to marry until age 25, and then only with permission. This assured all men under age 25 could be taken. They grudgingly lined up and signed in. A brief examination determined all were fit to serve. The Prussian soldier addressed the recruits, about 50 in all, with a well-rehearsed message.

"I am Sergeant Braun. I will prepare you to be a soldier in the Prussian Army." He shouted, walking up and down the lines. "You will drill in infantry formation, use of swords, firing of flintlock muskets, and bayonet charges against advancing cavalry.

"As a soldier in the Prussian army, you will never be without bread, very rarely without vegetables, and even more rarely without a half-pound of meat issued each week. If you distinguish yourself in battle, you have the prospect of a commissioned rank, perhaps even elevation to the nobility.

"Military discipline will be enforced, and punishments will include whipping and running the gauntlet for minor offenses, and hanging, for deserters."

So began each day for the coming weeks, time spent training for military service while ripened crops wilted in the fields.

Tonight, by moonlight, Rein walked wearily to his parents' graves in the churchyard. He reviewed in his mind the decision he'd quickly come to, hoping it was the right one for him and Eva.

Each evening after the day's military training, followed by work in the field to bring in much-needed crops, Rein felt crushing exhaustion. When the time finally came for sleep, he dreamed of being separated from Eva, caught in spiraling water, struggling against a current that threatened to pull him under. He would awaken covered in sweat. What he wanted more than anything was to protect Eva. How could he do that as a soldier in a remote place? Family... his mother's dying wish... that was what mattered. As skeptical as he was about the empress' promises, he had decided emigration to Russia was the quickest and best opportunity.

Rein stood looking down at his parents' graves marked with simple wooden crosses. He had taken so little time to grieve, and this might be the last time he would come here. He had learned so much from his parents, had loved and respected them deeply.

Daniel's death had left a void not only in the family but in village leadership. He had played a key role in helping the farm community develop a finely tuned process to produce enough to pay taxes, rent, and feed themselves. By assisting in the settlement of land disputes, supervising grazing rights, maintaining public order and Christian morals, Daniel had been well respected among the most prominent tenants and a village leader.

Rein knew Daniel's greatest contribution was the innovative operation of the estate's watermill on the Wörnitz River that ground wheat, rye, and barley into flour and meal. Rein wondered how his father had found time to manage the mill as well as the farm. Daniel's improvements made to the water-powered wheel meant more food for the villagers and revenue for the manor's lord. Knowing the mill's value to his estate, Count Philip had wisely agreed to a contract Daniel proposed: he would continue to serve as the mill overseer and operator. If, over the next 15 years, the mill became more profitable, Daniel and the entire Lundgren family would become free men. Along with their freedom, they would be granted hereditary rights to the land they farmed and would no longer be forced labor. *Free men.* His father had kept his part of the bargain—the mill flourished under his leadership. But Daniel had died a year before the 15 years stipulated in the contract. Tundorf nullified the contract upon Daniel's death.

Rein pulled the weeds growing by the crosses and tried to make peace with the senseless loss of his father and then his mother, who seemed to have lost the will to live. He pondered leaving the only home he'd known, either as a colonist or if their escape failed, as a soldier. Either way, it was unlikely he would return.

The desire to protect Eva drove him to be confident about their future. Without a doubt, pursuing this plan to emigrate was risky, demanding that he ally himself with the class of people he detested. He was disgusted by everything the nobility stood for. Rein replayed the shocking message from the recruiter about nobles' inhumane treatment of serfs. Was this devastating reality concealed from him, his family and friends, all their lives? No. They knew but had grown to accept it, having lost all hope through generations of oppression.

The recruiter's words pounded in Rein's temples as the count demanded more of the servants' energy to prepare for his annual hunt and Amila's engagement dinner. Eva and other servants' work had tripled to prepare for overnight guests and serve vast amounts of food. Guests would begin arriving tomorrow, with the hunt and extravagant dinner the following day.

Over the last few weeks, Rein had fine-tuned escape plans. He took the lead plotting a way to leave undetected. At the same time, he had encouraged as many families as possible to meet with the recruiter and emigrate, go somewhere, anywhere, at the same time. Rein, Eva, and Amila would travel to Lübeck on horseback, hopefully concealing their destination. His gut ached at the thought of involving Amila. He didn't trust her, but they needed her help to board the ship at Lübeck.

Fighting fatigue while sorting through details of the plan, Rein was startled by footsteps approaching. He turned to see Amila. "Eva told me I might find you here."

"I wish she had not told you. This is where my parents lay at rest. You have no right to be here." Rein thought his response seemed unusually harsh, but it felt satisfying.

"I knew and loved Maria too." Amila spoke gently.

"You knew her only because she was a servant in the castle." Moonlight masked Rein's features. He moved away to adjust the wooden cross on his mother's grave.

"No, she was much more to me than that, Rein," countered Amila. "I loved her for her kindness but also for her guidance. Tundorf was brutal...to my mother. I know he sometimes beat her, although she hid it from me. Maria comforted me. But more than that, she told me repeatedly to never allow a man to treat me that way, that I deserve respect and must stand up for myself. That lesson will never be lost on me."

Rein nodded his head slightly. "I'm glad she was able to help you. But she suffered too. Did you know she lost a child? My younger brother. He died when he was a baby. After that, she was ordered to work in the castle with little time left for us, although she did her best. Later she managed the household for your mother, then cared for her during her illness. In my lifetime, you had more of my mother's attention than I."

"It's clear you resent that." Amila turned to walk away.

"Wait. What is it? You must have come here for a reason."

"I wanted to ask how much I can carry with me." She smiled when she saw the roll of his eyes, likely thinking she meant a wardrobe befitting her station in life. "No, not a trunk. I know better than that. But just a small satchel? I want to bring important papers and a few small items that belonged to my mother."

Rein puzzled as to how she had read his thoughts. "That is reasonable, as long as it can be tied behind a saddle. Eva is bringing a supply of herbs. As you know, our mother was very learned about medicinal herbs, and

Eva carries much of that knowledge. But she doesn't know what we'll find there, what grows in the wild. I'm bringing seeds as well. If the land is as fertile as we've been told, we need only throw seeds over one shoulder, and crops will magically appear."

Amila laughed softly at the light-hearted break-through. "I'll pack carefully. I'll see you the day after tomorrow."

CHAPTER 4

July 1763

"*L*et the hunt begin!" From horseback, Tundorf swept his arm toward the villagers, commanding them forward through the field and into the woods. Determined to impress his guests, the region's princes—counts, barons, and landgraves who ruled estates in nearby fiefdoms— he had seen to every detail. As the early morning sun crept above the horizon, the manor's serfs were ready, lined up where the cultivated ground bordered the dense forest. The chase began as the villagers walked steadily forward, swinging nets and noisemaking rattles to flush out wild game.

The count sat elated aloft his mount. His smaller Tundorf estate in a neighboring territory had no remaining woods, making Nassenwald's vast forests even more appealing. He recalled how a few years earlier the farmers had skulked when he demanded they remove all the fences and hedges separating farmland from woods to assure no impediments to wildlife and the chase.

He smiled inwardly at how favorably this year's event was progressing thus far. No matter that serfs complained about damages to their fields. They were too ignorant to understand the importance of this day. He planned to take full advantage of the German princes' fondness for carnage—trapping or shooting whatever they could. Hosting a hunt was a grand way to demonstrate his growing status with the upper class and, of course, his power over the peasants and the beasts. After all, 'the nobler one is, the more one knows about venery,' the princes were fond of reciting.

In preparation, servants had filled their masters' muzzle-loading rifles with shot and accompanied them to reload the black powder guns. The princes charged through the fields with horses and hunting dogs, uprooting and trampling crops, seeds falling from ripened stalks. As the villagers walked through fields and into sparse areas of the woods, the hunting party began shooting game birds flushed out of hiding—partridges, pheasants, and woodcocks. With little cover in woods scarred by drought and overhunting, the animals were easy prey. Deeper in the woods, the hunters shot larger game, wild boar and red deer, as well as rabbits and foxes.

On his way back to the castle, the count ordered the serfs to apportion the meat so the visiting nobles could take it home to their estates. Fresh meat was scarce and highly prized. It was another opportunity to elevate his relationship with the princes. As an independent lot, they ruled their fiefdoms like small kingdoms, even lacking common laws across boundaries. Certain he was gaining their esteem, he felt assured of future invitations to their estates to hunt and socialize. After all, the upper class practiced the noble value of reciprocity.

Tundorf reached the castle before the other hunters, hurrying inside to check on preparations for the evening banquet. He ordered servants to halt preparations long enough to wait on the approaching princes. Then he sought out his guest of honor, Duke Zweibrücken, to make sure his every need had been seen to and discuss tonight's announcement. It was a shame the duke had declined to ride in the hunt, thought the count. But his portly physique and ill health might have led to an injury. He wanted the duke healthy, for now.

"I am comfortable enough but wish to return to my residence very soon." Even the new décor in place for tonight's banquet failed to impress the duke. "Were you able to secure the Lutheran minister? A small ceremony attended by just the three of us tomorrow morning, then we'll be on our way."

"Yes. the minister will be here in the morning to preside over the vows, Your Grace," assured Tundorf with a slight bow. "The announcement at tonight's dinner will be a pleasant surprise for our guests. We'll drink a toast to Duke Zweibrücken and his soon-to-be Duchess! I trust you received the copy of the signed wedding contract and certificate requested?"

"Yes, it is in order. It is peculiar that I haven't seen Amila since I arrived." The duke frowned.

"She's busy preparing for the evening and assures me her gown is worthy of the occasion. I promise she is charmed by Your Grace and will happily fulfill her duties as your wife. At tonight's grand celebration, be assured the best wines will flow like a river."

Satisfied by the attention, the duke joined the princes and their wives gathering in the drawing-room to share tales of their hunting prowess.

Tundorf allowed a close-lipped snicker to escape as he exhaled. Over the past month, he had scrutinized

Amila's behavior and detected no resistance. Her trips back and forth to the dressmaker were frequent, and she seemed, if not ebullient, at least accepting of her fate. He hadn't told her the wedding would be tomorrow morning but was sure he could coerce her to cooperate. She had asked if she could take Gabe to her new home, and he had agreed. Tomorrow, after the ceremony, he would tell her he had changed his mind. The duke had plenty of horses in his stable. Amila's gelding was worth a great deal, perhaps even as a warhorse. Expenses for the hunt and dinner had drained his purse, and taxes from serfs were becoming more difficult to collect. However, soon his income from the duke would commence. Combined with upcoming payment for serfs conscripted to the Prussian army, his financial problems would be altogether alleviated. While Amila would no longer be underfoot, he would nevertheless continue to benefit from her property and control her from a distance. He was surprised she hadn't asked if her servant Eva could accompany her, but he wouldn't have agreed to that either. He had plans for Eva. Although he hadn't been able to catch her alone since the first encounter in the woods, he knew opportunities would abound once Amila was gone.

*A*mila shifted nervously about the room as Eva trussed her into multiple layers of the evening gown. "I keep assuring myself, be calm. It will be over soon," Amila repeated to Eva for at least the tenth time. "I don't have to speak at dinner. Unlike the last time, I'll hold my tongue."

Amila had forced herself to model acquiescence all month. In the company of Tundorf, she smiled and went about her duties, even pretending to show interest in plans for the hunt and banquet. She had made it through the puzzling physician's examination, which felt degrading and quite odd. The physician had arrived one day insisting on seeing her in private. Evidently the count had enlisted him to make sure she met the chastity requirement for marriage, whatever that meant. Amila balked but finally agreed, once assured Eva could remain with her throughout the ordeal. The physician had asked her to urinate in a bowl, the output of which he scrutinized for some time before announcing it was clear and lucid, even sparkling. He then required her to strip to the waist and looked at her breasts from a distance. Following an agonizing pause, the physician uttered some words she didn't understand and told her she could cover herself. Amila knew she must have passed whatever requirement this might have been because he never returned, and thankfully, no more was said.

As she ran her hands down the silky soft bodice, Amila was keenly aware the dress fit like a skin, a lovely skin. It was more beautiful than any gown she could have conceived wearing. And following numerous fittings at the dressmaker, she was even getting used to the discomfort of the tightly laced stays. After tonight, she wondered if she would ever see the dress or wear it again.

The seamstress told Amila she would be dazzling in this style. She assured her many noblewomen chose this style but few had the figure to showcase it as well as Amila. The dress was of coral silk brocade etched in tiny flowers, with a revealing neckline trimmed by a lace ruffle. Where the fitted bodice met the wide hoop skirt below the waistline, the fabric slit in front to reveal a cream-colored petticoat, also of silk. Close-fitting sleeves extending elegantly past the elbow were trimmed in fine lace to match the petticoat. The long skirt showed only the tips of her slippers of pale cream-colored fabric with curved heels and shiny silver buckles.

Most of the women and men attending the dinner tonight would be wearing white facial powder, a fashion trend she had observed when visiting London. But Amila didn't like how dry it made her face feel, and the arsenic in it had an odd smell. Consequently, she chose only to wear pale coral rouge on her cheeks and lips. Eva had arranged her hair in rolls of curls piled high on her head, with a few cascading down her back. Peering at her image in the full-length mirror, she tilted her head sideways, not entirely comfortable with the stranger gazing back.

"You look breathtaking." Eva stepped back and stared in awe of the young woman before her. "Everyone will be quite taken with your beauty, Amila. Are you... sure? Sure you don't belong here? Do you really want to leave all this?"

"Oh, Eva! After all this time, do you not know me?" Amila responded without hesitation. "This isn't who I want to be, especially not with Tundorf in control of my every breath. He's an evil, horrid man. No one knows that better than you. And the duke? I don't care how rich he is—I won't spend even a day as his wife."

Amila adjusted a stray curl, then took a slow, deep breath. "I think fondly of my mother and father and of your dear mother, Maria. I'm glad for the stubborn child they allowed me to be. Because now I have the strength to resist the count and take charge of my life, beginning tonight."

$\mathcal{A}$mila felt her jaws tighten as she took the count's outstretched arm and entered the great hall, already filled with guests. For the occasion, the hall was richly decorated with costly carpets, huge Venetian mirrors, impressive silk hangings, and tapestries.

Awaiting her entrance was Duke Herman of Zwuibrücken, dressed even more grandly than the last time she'd seen him. She noted an air of approval on his pale, well-powdered face as she took his arm. It felt like a bad dream from which she desperately wanted to awaken. Be calm, she reminded herself. We have a plan.

Duke Herman had invited several princes and their wives from estates near his Württemberg landholding. Amila smiled when she recognized the duke's cousin, Stefan August, and his wife, Marianne. The couple exchanged looks of apprehension upon seeing her take the duke's outstretched hand. Tundorf's guests included his hunting acquaintances, lesser princes and their wives from nearby manors.

Amila took her seat between the duke and count, who sat at the head and side of the long, formal table set lavishly with dinnerware, silver, and flickering candelabra. Amila presumed by positioning her beside him, Tundorf was confident he could control her behavior, including silencing her if need be. She was aware the dinner would last at least two hours, and the count's surprise announcement would take place after the first course, as dishes were removed and fresh dinnerware placed on the table.

As soon as guests were seated, the first course commenced. Servants placed more than fifteen dishes of soups, fish, pastries, and great pies filled with pheasant and partridges from today's hunt on the table. As guests chose two or three of the dishes nearest them of which to partake, servants poured liberal amounts of locally produced Riesling, Elbing, and Spätburgunder wines.

Amila overheard conversations about today's hunt, the latest gossip from the King's Court, and banter about music and art. It was as if the war had never happened. She thought how absurd this lavish dinner was amid poverty and hunger merely for one unconscionable man to celebrate his birthday and maintain the pretense of nobility. None of these people had any idea what peasants were going through, nor did they appear to care. At least the servants and their families would eat well tonight, enjoying the food left over from the table. She heard a voice thick with phlegm and forced herself to be attentive.

"You do look beautiful, my dear Amila." The duke inspected her from head to toe. "I hope you were able to assemble a trousseau to your liking? Given the bill presented to me today by your stepfather, I would assume so."

His gaze made her skin crawl. Summoning calm, she thought about the new travel attire for Eva and herself and smiled at the thought. "Yes, Your Grace, and thank you."

"Once the ceremony is over tomorrow, we'll leave right away for my residence."

"As soon as tomorrow, Your Grace? My stepfather failed to inform me." Amila raised an eyebrow toward her stepfather.

"See that you are packed tonight, so there will be no delay in the morrow." The duke turned his attention to his plate overflowing with food.

She nodded her head in agreement. "I most certainly will, Your Grace."

Relieved no further conversation was called for, Amila diverted her attention across the table where Marianne and Stefan were seated. Stefan was conversing with a well-dressed baron seated on his right. She heard a strain of the conversation.

"What a horrid little village Nassenwald is. Clearly in turmoil. I sent my driver to the village today, requiring only the service of a wheelwright to repair a carriage wheel," complained the baron. "My driver returned saying he was unable to find anyone to help. The frenzy of activity among the villagers and wagons being loaded made the streets nearly impassable."

Stefan responded. "That's odd. I've been through the village with the duke several times and have found it an orderly place, though not prosperous by any means. I'll notify the count. He won't approve if his guests are being treated poorly in the village. Perhaps he can send his guards to see what's afoot."

Stefan turned toward the count, opening his mouth to speak.

"Count Tundorf, I've heard exciting tales of the hunt today." Amila leaned toward her stepfather, smiling warmly. "But I've not heard yours. Please tell me, what was your most impressive kill?"

His nostrils flared. "Well, it was a grand hunt indeed. I shot a huge stag, as big as I've seen in these woods, from a hundred paces. It is, however, the vast numbers that are most impressive—a fine slaughter! Hundreds of stags and wild boar and too many game birds to count. The fox and hare pelts alone fill an entire wagon, I'm told."

He paused and peered down his nose at Amila, who was listening intently to his every word. "I'm glad to see your behavior is improving, Amila. You see, Your Grace, what an agreeable companion she will make?"

A moment later, Tundorf stood to capture the attention of the guests. "I would like to thank all of you for coming to take part in the raucously successful hunt, and of course, to celebrate my birthday."

Puffed up by the polite applause that followed, he continued. "And now, I have a profoundly exciting announcement to share with all of you. His Lordship, the Duke of Zweibrücken, has graciously asked for the hand of my stepdaughter, Amila, the future Countess of Wallerstein, in marriage. We are pleased to announce their engagement and the joining of the two families. Accordingly, I ask you to raise your glasses to toast the Duke and soon-to-be Duchess of Zweibrücken!"

Amila tensed and blushed as all eyes turned her way. Glasses clinked as guests offered congratulations. Amila noted many heads tilting to whisper to one another. Did they know or object to something she didn't understand? Looking back and forth from the count to the duke, she saw no overt concern on their faces. Undoubtedly, it was the dramatic difference in the bride and groom's ages that made guests react in such a subdued manner. No matter, she thought.

The general banter in the room resumed as the second course of lighter main dishes and fruit tarts, jellies and creams arrived. Amila continued to engage the count and duke in lively conversation, squelching Stefan's line of questioning. She found it especially easy to keep Duke Herman talking about his property, palace, and lifestyle. When a lull occurred, she asked Tundorf another question about the hunt. Finally, dessert consisting of dried fruit, nuts, small cakes, confections, and cheese was served. After more wine was poured and disappeared with the final course, Amila took her cue as hostess and rose so that the women at the table would follow her, leaving the gentlemen to smoke and converse.

In the drawing-room, women whose names were unfamiliar surrounded Amila to congratulate her for raising her status to a duchess and becoming mistress of the opulent palace owned by the duke.

Marianne, wife of the duke's cousin, approached Amila and spoke with more candor. "I offer my congratulations to you, Amila. I'll be honored to have you as a cousin. But there is something I wonder if you know about Duke Zweibrücken."

Seeing Amila's puzzled look, Marianne pulled her aside to speak privately. "No one must know I have told you this. His Grace has an incurable disease, one that is easily passed to those he is, um, intimate with. It is sometimes called the lover's disease or 'French evil.'" She looked down and hid her eyes demurely, then went on. "His dear wife died of it after a long and painful illness. For Duke Herman, it seems the disease comes and goes. Although he takes mercury treatments, nothing seems to completely cure it."

Amila gasped, then covered her mouth to control her outrage. "Is this common knowledge in the duke's circle?"

"Yes, quite so. He has been seeking a wife of noble blood for some time, but fathers have thus far declined his offers to their daughters, even though he is quite highly positioned."

Face tingling and rising in heat, Amila struggled to contain her anger. Her only reassurance was that she'd made the right decision. "I want to thank you for your honesty when many others know the truth but offered only their congratulations." And, of course, the count knew.

She looked toward the doors of the drawing-room, knowing they would soon open and the gentlemen would join them. "Marianne, I'm afraid I'm not feeling well. It's been a fatiguing day. I would like to retire. But would you please assure Stefan that everything is tranquil once again in the village? Earlier in the day, the villagers were hurrying about to bring supplies for tonight's banquet. It was a bit chaotic. Perhaps Stefan can tell the baron to take his carriage to our stable. Our stablemaster is a skilled wheelwright and can help with any repair needed. Now, I hope you will excuse me." A handkerchief to her nose, Amila ambled slowly toward a side door used by servants and fled the room.

*W*ell after midnight, Rein urged the nervous horses pulling a wagon of rotting carcasses toward the castle gate, the only way out of the castle. Due to heavy carriage traffic, Tundorf had posted guards Ebald and Axel at the gate leading to the bridge. Rein had learned about this development only two days ago, allowing little time to alter the plan.

Rein eased the wagon toward the gate, glancing up at the ominous overhead iron grate and the single lever that could drop its metal spikes, keeping unwanted visitors out or imprisoning those within. The passageway was fifteen feet wide, enough for a wagon to pass through, and fortified by ten-foot high stone walls on both sides. At the end of the passageway was the stone bridge and river that led to the countryside and freedom.

"Halt. Who goes there?" Ebald never hesitated to exert superiority over the peasants.

"Greetings Ebald." Rein pulled the team gently to a stop and respectfully kept his head tilted down. "By order of the count, we are to take these pelts to the furrier in the village before they spoil. The hot weather is giving the courtyard an unpleasant aroma and drawing flies. Guests are beginning to complain."

The guard sneered. "Oh, it's you, Lundgren. I've no orders to let you pass. Only guests may leave in a wagon or a carriage. We must search servants to make sure you haven't stolen anything." He walked toward Rein.

"Come on, Ebald, we're dead tired. And be careful—the horses are flighty around all these dead animals. Do you really want to get your hands in this stinking pile? The count's orders are to deliver the pelts to the furrier as soon as possible. It might be a mistake to disturb him now. He and his guests hunted all day and dined in high spirits. We were told to get these pelts ready and deliver them."

"Aye, I've been on duty for days now, and my brother lays here and snores." Ebald motioned toward Axel. "But why do you have a horse tethered behind? Isn't that Lady Amila's gelding?"

Rein smiled and nodded. "You're worth your salt today, Ebald. Nothing gets past you. He has a loose shoe. Johann hasn't time to repair it, with guests' horses to care for. So we're taking him to the blacksmith in the village."

Ebald started toward the back of the wagon, where an easily visible coffin-sized wooden box was attached to the undercarriage. Near the wagon, he stopped. "Get out of here with that foul-smelling mess. It's my turn for a nap."

Rein slowly urged the mismatched team forward, not looking back. At a distance, darkness should help obscure the box beneath the wagon. He expected the guard to recognize Amila's horse. Thankfully, the guard had not asked why the horses pulling the wagon weren't a matched team. The methodical clip, clop of the horses' hooves on the cobblestones steadied Rein's nerves. Once across the bridge and onto the dirt road, he hastened the horses to speed up, and it took only minutes to reach the cottage, where Eva was hopefully waiting. Rein tethered the saddle horses that had performed so calmly and jumped down from the wagon to pry off the wooden box fastened beneath. The box dropped suddenly, and Amila hit the ground with a thud.

"Oof! That hurt!" Amila cried out, breath knocked out of her. Her body felt stiff from lying motionless in the tiny box. But the discomfort was well worth it. After learning about the count's duplicity, Amila was willing to do much more than ride beneath a wagon full of rotting carcasses to escape.

Rein clumsily dragged Amila out from under the wagon by her boots. "There, you're out. I never said it was going to be comfortable."

"At least it worked. I had my doubts. But thank you." She sat up and felt her tender head, then rose to her feet, holding her small bundle of belongings. "Eva, are you here?"

"Yes, over here!" Eva materialized out of the darkness, wearing her new travel dress and cloak, hugging a large fabric bag bound with leather cords that contained her belongings. Amila rushed to hug her, squeezing her so hard both could barely breathe.

"It's over. I made it through without any blunders. But one of the guests heard about the disorder in the village today and nearly told Tundorf. I must tell you, I've learned something disgusting about the duke. I hate them even more now, more than I thought possible."

They hurried to help Rein, who had unharnessed the horses from the wagon and was saddling all three with gear Johann had smuggled out of the stable several days before. Eva reminded Rein to change into his new clothing, complete with a well-fitted shirt, leather breeches, a cloak, boots, and a hat. He balked but went into the cottage and emerged minutes later pulling at the unfamiliar clothing, but looking the part of a middle-class traveler. Amila had insisted Rein, too, have new clothes, eventually convincing him they mustn't look like peasants or war refugees, or they would attract undue attention—as emigrants stealing away in the night. Satchels were tied behind the saddles, food from the cottage stored in saddlebags, and water bags were thrown over saddle horns. They had studied the route and knew a long journey lay ahead to reach Lübeck.

As they mounted, Amila exhaled, taking a moment to scrutinize her two travel companions. Rein peered over his shoulder at the cottage, squinting through the darkness at the only home he'd ever known. Eva held tight to the reins like a frightened child determined to be brave. Amila thought about how little they had in common. But they did share a common desire—the willingness to take risks necessary to choose their futures freely. She hoped it would be enough to see them through.

After behaving so well through it all, Gabe snorted and pawed at the ground, primed for the hard ride ahead. Moonlight beckoned them forward.

CHAPTER 5

July 1763

$\mathcal{T}$undorf rose well before sunrise and locked the study door behind him, seeking privacy before guests stirred. Hardly able to sleep, all night he lay basking in the success of the day's events. The festivities couldn't have gone better, he thought, a malicious smile fixed on his face. How easy this is going to be to elevate one's station within the German nobility. Amila, a duchess, and Nassenwald Manor his own. The ultimate birthday gifts. He brought out the copy of the marriage contract and examined it. Soon, he would be rid of Amila but continue to control her estate and expand his power once the old man was dead. No longer would the burden of debt threaten his lifestyle here and at his small, depleted estate. And perhaps it was time to take a personal residence in Stuttgart.

Today was important for another reason. It was the day he had decided to destroy the documents he'd been hiding since last winter. He was quite pleased with the cleverness of his plan. With the war now over and a treaty in place, he no longer needed the double-edged protection the documents provided.

Checking again that the study door was locked, the count went to the bookcase that covered one entire wall in the study. Standing on a chair, he reached up and removed the books from a section on the highest shelf. He used a pry tool to lift the false wooden piece that covered the back shelf and extended his arm into the dark void. Nothing. Thinking it must have shifted a bit, he reached further and moved his hand from side to side. Empty? Frantically, he pulled more books off the shelf, letting them drop to the floor, and tore away the remainder of the back shelf with his bare hands. His fingers went numb, digging in the dark space, and his hands began to shake uncontrollably. The entire cavity was completely empty! He looked around the room, thinking he had moved the packet. No, he hadn't. Someone had taken it. He began to feel the room spin, panic quickly turning to outrage at this theft. *Who would dare?*

Rushing from the study, Tundorf raced up the stairs two at a time until he'd reached Amila's chamber. He banged on the door. Hearing nothing, he turned the handle on the unlocked door and burst through. The room was quiet and empty, her gown from the previous night crumpled on the bed, which was undisturbed by sleep. Rage building with every movement, he furiously searched every possible hiding place in the room.

At last, he stopped, forcing himself to think. Had she run away with the documents? A heavy sweat began to coat his body. He ran from the room to the kitchen below, where sleepy-eyed servants were noisily banging pots and pans to prepare breakfast. Realizing he must not alert the duke or his guests that something might be amiss, the count struggled for composure. The servants jumped to attention when they saw him enter.

"Have you seen Lady Amila this morning? Any of you?"

"No, milord." The cook glanced at the other servants to see if they had a different answer. One by one, they shook their heads and hung back, fearful.

"What about Eva?"

The cook was unsure if they had done something wrong. "Why no milord, we didn't see her after she helped in the kitchen last night."

Barely waiting for her to finish the sentence, Tundorf turned and left the room, taking the swiftest route to the stable. There he found a weary Johann and several boys carrying water to the guests' many horses quartered in the stable.

He looked past the stableman into Gabe's stall and saw it was empty. Fearful and furious what it might mean, the count shouted. "Where did Lady Amila go? When did she leave?"

"I didn't see her this morning, milord." Johann's eyes were downcast. "When I got here, her horse was gone. She must have left very early."

"You idiot! You should have been on duty here through the night."

Johann replied respectfully. "I worked all night in the dining hall and kitchen, helping other servants clean and prepare for today, Lord Tundorf."

"I'll have you whipped for leaving the stable unguarded!" bellowed the count, spittle flying. "Saddle my horse immediately!"

The sun was rising when Tundorf reached the castle gate where he'd stationed Ebald and Axel. Rounding the corner, he found both guards asleep. Fuming, he kicked one then the other violently. They jumped to their feet, moaning. "By God, you'd better tell me no one has passed through here this morning!"

"Don't worry, milord." Ebald rubbed his painful ribs. "No one has entered or left. Although we were resting a bit, we never left our post."

"Did Lady Amila leave here this morning?"

"No, she hasn't passed through this gate." Ebald was ever confident they had done their job. "We did see her horse tied behind the wagon of hides that you ordered be taken to the furrier last night."

"I gave no such orders, you fools! I told you to let no wagons pass with servants. Who was driving the wagon?"

"It was Reinhardt Lundgren, the farmer. He said you told him to take the carcasses away because of the stink," offered Axel, fear mounting. "It was late last night after the dinner."

The count clenched his teeth. I've had to deal with that family before, he thought. He turned to his guards. "Come with me. You'll all suffer for this if we don't find her, and quickly!"

Tundorf and the two guards raced over the bridge to the Lundgren cottage. Near the entrance sat the wagon of ripening carcasses. Harnesses were attached to the wagon, but the horses were gone. Pistols drawn, Tundorf motioned for them to enter the cottage with him. Moving from room to room, they found it deserted. Rooms looked lived in, tidy and undisturbed. The only items out of place were a single pile of ragged clothing on the kitchen floor. Near the table, the count picked up a sheet of linen paper, recognizing it as a well-known circular, *The London Gazette*. It was dated April 11, 1763. He scanned it quickly. The news sheet had traveled a long way, he thought. It listed an account of the signing of the treaties of Hubertusburg and Paris. Old news—the Treaty was signed in February, ending the war... with no spoils for Prussia.

"Seven years of war and nothing to show for it here. What an idiot King Frederick is," mumbled Tundorf, eliciting quizzical glances from the guards.

Another news piece caught his eye. It was an advertisement from a shipping company recruiting emigrants to the British Colonies of America. A map of Virginia showed boundaries for each colony being settled. He scanned the words next to the map.

"In America, immigrants can forget the subordination that servility has taught you. Flee the contentious domains ruled by exploitative aristocrats and kings and flock to this great American asylum, where you will feel liberated by the abundant and fertile land of a vast continent. Here, thousands of poor men own their own farms instead of working for a landlord. You, too, can become resourceful and enterprising, energized by the ability to keep the fruits of your own labor. It is here, then, that the poor become rich!"

Tundorf clutched the circular and hurried from the cottage, cursing for Ebald and Axel to come along. Riding as fast as they could back to the stable, the count found Johann feeding the horses. "Guards, bring him here and hold him!"

Tundorf came close as soon as the guards held Johann firmly. All the venom he'd been holding inside spewed forth as he punched Johann in the face and stomach.

The stableman sustained the blows, shaking his head to remain conscious. "Now, tell me where they went, or I'll kill you."

"I don't know…"

The count grabbed a board lying nearby and hit him across the face. A steady flow of blood now dripped from Johann's temple and nose.

"All right, all right, stop. I'll tell you what I know. They've run away…to America. Amila and Eva met a sailor at an inn in Donauwörth when Amila went there to see the dressmaker. I rode with them once or twice. The sailor was home visiting his family and carried news sheets from his ship's captain. He said the skipper told him to hand them out to all who came to the inn."

Tundorf seethed. "There must be more you're not telling me. Go on. Or I'll give them the order to finish you."

"They asked me to go along with them, but I said no." Johann yanked a hand loose from the guard's grip to wipe away blood with his ragged sleeve. "I didn't know when they were going to leave. They didn't tell me. Three horses were gone when I got here early this morning."

"Quick, what route were they going to take?"

"Turn me loose, and I'll tell you." Johann used his freed hands to realign his jaw. "The sailor's ship was out of Belgium, a port called Antwerp. The sailor told them the ship would be there another two weeks until it was filled with passengers and goods bound for America. That's all I know, milord."

"Saddle the two fastest horses. And tell no one what has happened, do you hear?" the count ordered as he left the stable, motioning for his guards to follow. "Come back with me to my study. I'll give you money for provisions and a map. If you ride hard along the road to the west, you can catch them before they reach the city of Mainz. I want you to kill the Lundgren man but bring Amila and Eva back alive."

Johann watched them leave, then rose and limped toward a water bucket to cleanse his wounds. He exposed a half-smile toward the loft where his uncle crouched behind a pile of hay, a bow and quiver of arrows ready but thankfully not needed.

By mid-afternoon, Rein had guided Eva and Amila north for ten-straight hours, pushing the horses at a brisk pace. He pulled out the map he'd studied in preparation for the journey. Gunter had given them the map and assured them it showed the latest roads, complete with distances between towns and the occasional larger city. On heavily trafficked routes, milestones precisely listed distances to the next town, although small villages were rarely included.

Rein looked warily over his shoulder each time they reached a vista with a clear view behind them. With so much time to think, he revisited information the recruiter had imparted, believing that at least the travel instructions and existence of the ambassador's office in Lübeck were probably the truth. After all, Gunter wouldn't receive his 'human merchandise' payment unless they arrived in Lübeck and furnished his name as the recruiter sending them.

Having recently arrived from the north, Gunter prepared them for this first leg of the long journey. With Rein and Eva lacking travel experience and Amila having traveled only in a carriage with handlers, they were hungry for every crumb of information he could offer. Gunter said it would take them about a week to reach Lübeck, depending on the number of hours they were able to ride each day. He emphasized lodgings and provisioning horses would be a constant concern, so they must stop at inns in towns well before dark and stable the horses. Gunter explained they would be required to pay customs fees at borders as they traversed through each small German territory. And as an afterthought, either to minimize the danger or perhaps the opposite, he warned them to watch out for highwaymen.

"Can we rest soon?" Eva was used to hard physical labor but unaccustomed to riding a horse for long periods. Rein realized early that Johann had wisely selected a mild-mannered horse for Eva. And all three mounts had stamina, critical for this pace.

"I'd like to rest as well." Amila looked for a shady area off the road. Luckily, their travel attire included hats to shield their faces from the hot July sun.

In some places, the road was paved with old stones, remnants of what Gunter said were Roman roads more than a thousand years old. But in most areas, the road was more like a wide bridle path. Still, the riders saw a surprising number of carriages. Weary passengers peering out the windows seemed to be suffering on the deeply rutted roads.

Determined not to bring attention to themselves, they gave other travelers only a glance and continued on. Gunter had assured them they could pass for working-class travelers since they were well-dressed and rode good-quality horses.

It was only the second time Rein had agreed to stop since leaving Nassenwald, each mile lessening fear of being followed. They had watered the horses, and eaten dried fruit and bread from packs before quickly continuing on horseback. Riding single file, they had hardly spoken.

Rein relented. "I hear a stream nearby. I'll find a path, and we can water the horses again." He was gone only a few minutes, motioning for them to follow, nervously watching the path behind for any sign of danger. In his satchel of belongings, he had brought his bow, arrows, and hunting knives for protection. The first chance he got, he planned to buy a sword and pistol with the travel funds Gunter had supplied.

As the horses drank from the stream, the weary travelers splashed water on their faces and drank. They filled leather water pouches, also furnished by Gunter, who seemed to have a limitless supply of items to outfit their trip. He had also given them expense money to travel to Lübeck: 16 kreuzer for Rein, and 10 each for Amila and Eva. It was more money than Rein had ever possessed at one time in his life, and it made him uneasy. It seemed like a fortune, mostly because he didn't owe any of it in rents or taxes. But what had he done to earn it? He harbored a deep skepticism of the empress' offer. Many nights he continued to awaken in a cold sweat, thinking it crazy to be putting their lives in the hands of a man they'd met twice in a tavern.

"I hope Johann is all right." Eva was the first of the three to speak aloud a common concern. Johann had volunteered for his role in the escape plan, putting himself in harm's way for their benefit. "By now, he and his uncle's family should be on their way north to join us. They'll be much slower, traveling in a wagon. Maybe they can reach Lübeck in time to travel on the same ship."

Rein wondered how badly Tundorf's goons would rough Johann up to make him admit where they'd gone. Johann had laughed at the prospect, recalling that he and his friends, including Rein, often went at fisticuffs for fun. The pain would soon be forgotten, and wounds heal, Johann had assured him. "If the count has taken the bait, then his guards are well on the wrong trail. If not, then I don't know which way he'll go, if he cares to chase us at all."

"Oh, he'll try to find us," assured Amila. "The humiliation of not seeing me wed to a duke will make him livid. I'm nothing but a possession to him, albeit a valuable one, to further his ambitions. The faster and further away I can get, the better."

"No one else really knows which way we've gone, do they?" It was more a hope than a question from Eva, who sat tucked into a shady spot, wiping her face with a wet cloth.

"So many families were planning to leave during the night and going many directions. Even we don't know where they're all going. It's better that way." In case he catches us, Rein thought.

At least Amila had encouraged the manor's serfs to leave the manor at the same time and emigrate somewhere. Over the previous few weeks, Eva secretly brought travel and emigration documents to Amila, who signed all placed before her. However, she dreaded the thought that those who remained would be subject to the count's wrath.

Now that the war was finally over, Austria, Hungary, the Prussian states, Russia, and America were actively seeking colonists from Germany, the country hardest hit by the carnage. Those who chose America knew they were taking on a great burden. Known as 'redemptioners,' they would be granted passage to American colonies by selling themselves into years of indentured servitude to pay the shipping company for the transatlantic voyage. In the end, the empress' offer seemed best to Rein and Eva, as it had to Amila all along.

Rein and Johann covertly coordinated with those planning to leave. Still, turmoil overtook the village as wagons were packed the day of the hunt and banquet. Serfs began to leave by the cover of night after the banquet, as Rein, Eva, and Amila had, or as soon as the guards were on the false trail.

Rein pondered what they had encountered on the journey thus far and wondered how the others would fare. Having never traveled beyond Donauwörth, he was shocked at the widespread devastation along the route north. The landscape of farms and villages they passed through was disturbing—houses poorly patched, churches and buildings charred to piles of rubble, vineyards and fields deserted. The land lay fallow with immense cracks. The residents moving lethargically around dilapidated dwellings seemed barely alive, surviving but shrouded in hopelessness. He recalled with contempt the wasteful hunt and lavish dinner Tundorf had held for his—and Amila's—high-born friends the previous night. Somehow, they were able to continue their extravagant lifestyles as if nothing had changed. Rein glanced over and saw Amila adjust Gabe's bridle and fan flies from his face. His eyes narrowed. She represented a way of life contrary to everything he believed in.

"I know some friends guessed our destination." Rein kept his attention and comments directed to Eva while pulling out the map again. "Hopefully, if the count finds out, we'll be so far ahead he won't come looking. We must try to make it to Lübeck before the first ship sails. Are you ready to go on? The map shows we'll reach a city called Nuremberg in the next few hours. We'll stop there for the night."

Near the outskirts of Nuremberg, carriage, horse, and walking traffic increased significantly. Their horses, used to the serenity of the country, began to fidget nervously. It was clear they were approaching a large city, and Rein felt intimidated by the unfamiliarity of everything before him. Swallowing hard and looking over at Eva, he saw a dazed look on her face as well.

Unsure whether Amila had noticed his discomfort, Rein was nevertheless relieved when she rode Gabe to the front of their little procession, forging a path through the noisy, congested city streets.

A flood of sights, sounds, and scents engulfed the travelers. Residents seemed unfazed by the racket of horses' hooves pounding the overcrowded cobbled streets and rumbling from carriages and carts. Loud, shrill voices competed to be heard above the clatter, angry and insulting, laughing loudly, often conversing across streets and out of windows. No one stopped to listen to the bell from a nearby church, nor to pay attention to small handbells hawkers rang to sell their merchandise. The stench from raw sewage, rotting waste, and unknown filth invaded their nostrils.

"Amila, do you have any idea where you're taking us? We've got to get away from this bedlam and rest the horses," shouted Rein in an effort to be heard above the clamor.

"I'm looking for an inn with a stable for horses," Amila bellowed back over her shoulder, irritated at his tone. She veered toward a large, two-story building with a sign that said Wayfarer Inn. Amila dismounted and motioned for Rein to hold her horse while she went inside. What seemed like an eternity later, she returned, retrieved Gabe, and told them to follow with their horses. Behind the inn, they found a modest stable and corral. Amila sought out the stable boy and doled out several pence, giving him specific instructions for the horses' feed and care as she patted Gabe's neck. Once confident the horses would be well cared for, the three gathered their belongings and wove their way through the crowd to the front door of the inn.

As they entered the busy inn, Rein and Eva halted, their backs to the door, staring open-mouthed at guests sitting at long wood tables and milling around the noisy tavern. They saw a boisterous mix of old and young, men and women, peasants and what must be middle-class diners. Some were finely dressed, others clothed more like peddlers. A clergyman and his family graced a nearby table. The perfect place to hide, Rein thought. No one would give them a second glance.

They watched Amila stride to a table and sit down, motioning for them to join her. Rein stifled a grin. He didn't remember ever seeing her look quite so pale and spent.

She delivered news in a weary voice. "They have one room left upstairs. It's all they have. The innkeeper says we're lucky to find anything this late in the day. It cost us one kreuzer and includes supper."

As if on cue, a tavern maid pushed her way through the crowd with a tray of plates heaped with wurst sausages, cabbage with onions, potato pancakes, bread, and beer. Without uttering a word, they ate and drank their fill.

Again following Amila's lead, they rose to find their room. Rein noticed Eva wobble a bit, likely a result of the strong beer. A tired smile creased his lips as he steered her up the stairs, where they found the small, sparsely furnished room with one small bed. The heavy wooden door gave the room an illusion of privacy but didn't block the noise rising from below. The summer sun was still high enough to let light in through the small window, allowing Amila to pour water from a pitcher into the basin. Oblivious of Rein's presence, she and Eva began washing their faces and necks, sharing the single cloth furnished.

Rein felt his face redden and looked down and away. Discomfort overcame exhaustion. "I'm going to check on the horses and wash in the stable. Lock the door once I leave."

Half an hour later, Rein returned and knocked lightly on the door. When no one answered, he flooded with fear. He tried the latch and found it unlocked. Entering uneasily, he was relieved to see why they had failed to respond. Amila and Eva were lying fully clothed, side-by-side, asleep on the bed. Breathing a sigh of relief, he locked the door and slumped to the floor, falling into an uneasy slumber.

*T*emples throbbing, Tundorf paced back and forth in front of the chair where Duke Zweibrücken sat waiting. The count kept up the pretense that everything was as expected while other guests were fed and graciously sent on their way. Now he faced an agitated bridegroom, far his superior, who'd been deserted at the altar.

"I'm sorry to inform you that Amila has been kidnapped, stolen away from the castle in the night. I was astonished when I learned the details this morning. My dear stepdaughter has vanished!" The count rambled on, glancing over to see if the duke was buying his hastily fabricated story. "I had to beat the stable hand into submission to find out who has taken her and where they have gone. I sent my guards to rescue her. We'll soon have her back safely. I only hope they aren't asking a ransom for her return."

The duke opened his mouth to speak, then paused, a grimace possessing his face. "Do you take me for a fool? Evidently, you do, you imbecile! You have no control over that uncultured little harlot. She has run off with a servant, and you're trying to convince me you now need money to pay a ransom."

No longer holding back, the duke struck thunderous blows. "To think I would ever have considered her as Duchess of Zweibrücken! You've broken the terms of the marriage contract, which I will take great joy ripping to shreds. Have my carriage prepared immediately. I'm finished with this godforsaken place and with your scheming and lies, forever."

The duke rose and strutted proudly from the room, leaving Tundorf staring at his wake. Soon, the reality of the turn of events shocked him back to the present. The plan was in ruins. His finances were in shambles with huge debts overdue. He ran his hands through his thin hair, feeling the rapid pounding at his temples. He needed to think calmly. All was not lost. Funds would be coming in from serfs he had conscripted to the Prussian army. And his guards would return with Amila and her treacherous companions by the end of today. Oh, how he would take pleasure in beating her and having Reinhardt shot, if he was not already dead. Then, he would find another nobleman to marry Amila.

The count spent most of the day counting what little money he had left, reviewing his strained finances, and watching nervously out the window. He was unsure how much, but several guldens were missing from his desk. Amila had likely taken the valuable coins to pay ship's passage to America.

Finally, impatience overcame him. He decided to ride in the direction his guards would be expected to return. At the stable, he found no sign of Johann. He deserved the beating, thought the count. A stable boy saddled his horse, and he rode toward the village. He noticed a lack of activity in the fields, the same in the village. It wasn't Sunday, the only day of rest. He rode back to the castle and crossed paths with Sergeant Braun, who should be drilling new recruits.

"Have you turned them loose for the day? Are drills over?" Tundorf noted the soldier's irritation.

The soldier grumbled back. "Only a few were here. Out of fifty, perhaps eight showed for mandatory drills. I asked them where the others were, threatening they would be disciplined. They just said the others were gone."

"Gone? Whatever did they mean, gone?" The count felt bile rise in his throat.

"Gone from here, entire families. They've left their homes and the manor." The sergeant shrugged, riding away.

Tundorf dismounted and bent over to retch. At last, he wiped his mouth and stood up straight, seeing Ebald and Axel approaching from a distance. The count was afraid to hear what he read in their downtrodden demeanor.

"Sorry, milord. We rode all the way to Mainz," reported Ebald. "We couldn't find 'em. Nary a trace."

CHAPTER 6

July 1763

$\mathcal{A}$mila opened her eyes to the morning sun streaming in the small window. Glancing around and sitting up quickly, Eva began to stir. Slowly recalling their whereabouts, she wondered if they'd slept only an hour or two. The new angle of light from the window confirmed they had slept the night through. Peering around Eva at the floor, she saw no sign of Rein nor evidence he'd been there.

"How do you feel, Eva?" Amila asked gently as Eva stood and stretched, gathering her belongings.

"My bones ache like an old woman, but I'm not as tired as last night." Eva smiled valiantly. "A mixture of herbs in tea would help, but I'll not part with my precious leaves. Will the soreness from riding ever go away, do you think?"

Amila assured her it would. They left the room and found Rein in the stable, horses saddled and ready. He was seemingly in good humor, despite blood-shot eyes. "I was hoping the horses would still be here. I'm afraid I didn't sleep well, wondering if they would be. When I returned to the room last night, neither of you moved. Even the noise from the tavern and street didn't cause you to stir."

Amila noticed his eyes darting around sheepishly. "Why are you blubbering on about sleep? We have to go." Oh, she realized it must be the sleeping arrangements. While she and Eva were used to sharing a bed occasionally, Rein must be uneasy about sleeping in a room with two young women, one of whom was not his sister. Was he watching them sleep? Did that keep him awake? Well, it was his problem. He could sleep in the stable from now on for all she cared.

"I've been ready to leave for hours." He matched her ill-temper. "Next time, I'll wake you both before I leave the room."

With the horses fresh from a night's rest and feed, the riders mounted with filled canteens and food stored in satchels. Still on the city's southern outskirts, the ride north through Nuremberg took them along narrow, winding streets that led to the market square, where they paused to marvel at water flowing through a fountain with tiers of carved figures. Just when Amila wondered if they would ever pass through the seemingly endless tract of buildings with red-tiled roofs, wooded hills emerged. Amila pulled Gabe to a stop and stared at a familiar view—a massive castle perched on the hilltop. It should elicit homesickness, regret. She waited for an emotion to engage her but felt nothing. No sadness or sense of loss, just emptiness. After a few moments, she urged Gabe forward, finding comfort in his lively gait on the uneven trails that passed for roads.

Soon they began to encounter entire families of refugees, left homeless by the war or fleeing other desperate circumstances, some traveling toward Nuremberg and others north alongside them. Lacking saddle horses or carriages, they shuffled by, women and children riding in carts sometimes pulled by a tired-looking horse, but more often by male family members. Rein carefully steered around the lethargic groups of refugees.

Eva leaned toward Rein and asked in a hushed voice. "Where do you think they're going?"

"Wherever they believe they can make a new life for themselves. Maybe we'll see some of them in Lübeck," reflected Rein.

As they paused to talk, a woman jumped from one of the carts and scooped up a tiny handful of grain that had fallen into a rut on the roadway. She brushed away the soil and carefully placed the grain in a small cloth bag. Once settled back in the cart, she continued her vigil for other bits of food.

Amila watched in sorrow as refugees passed by, wondering how serfs from Nassenwald would fare. Families from across Germany had been forced to abandon their homes, bodies stricken with hunger and beaten down by exhaustion, staring at the empty expanse ahead. Yet, they appeared to possess a determination she deeply admired. Like her, they were running from the past without knowing what their future could possibly bring. But they were determined to try.

The long hours and days on horseback blurred, the weather often began with early morning mist that penetrated their clothing, converting to high clouds and sweltering afternoon temperatures. Amila was amazed by the variety of landscapes they traversed. Steep hillsides overlooked valleys through the patchwork of German principalities. Some rivers were swollen by rain, while small streams trickled with just enough water for the horses. The scenery alternated between dark forests and flattened plains with occasional bogs, marshlands, and moors. Each mile, hour, and day they advanced without detection lessened the tension for the three riders.

They had settled into a routine toward the end of each day—stop at a village, seek an inn to eat, sleep, and stable the horses. Rein would wait until the two women had washed and were in bed before returning to the room to sleep on the floor. He rose early and left the room before dawn to prepare for the next day's journey, returning to rouse them with a gentle knock on the door. The desire for rest at the end of each long day in the saddle diffused the unspoken strain of sharing a room.

On the fifth day, drawing closer to Lübeck, they continued riding well after dark, taking advantage of the cool evening temperatures. They approached wooded hills as the moon shone high above a jagged, rocky terrain. Just enough muted light filtered through the dense growth of pine and spruce trees, allowing the travelers to continue along the path.

On a somewhat steep section of the road, Eva's horse stumbled slightly.

"Are you all right?" Rein had pushed them farther today than any so far.

"Yes, but how can the horses see the road?" Eva's horse balked, moving forward even more slowly than before.

"It isn't safe to keep riding, and the horses are tired. Is there somewhere we can stop?" Amila peered into the darkness surrounding them.

"Stay here with the horses, and I'll try to find a place to shelter for the night." Rein disappeared into the dense woods. When he returned, they followed him off-trail, up a steep hill to what looked like ruins of a building nestled among the rocks. They found a grassy area nearby and unsaddled the horses, attaching rope hobbles before releasing them to graze.

By moonlight, they sat down wearily inside the building's one standing wall and ate the last of the day's provisions—cheese, fruit, and bread Rein had bought that morning.

"When do you think we'll reach Lübeck?" Amila asked Rein. She had to admit Rein's proficiency with the intricate maps had improved each day, making the distances between points easier to predict.

"Tomorrow or the day after at the latest." The last town was several hours behind them. He had hoped to reach a village marked on the map and spend the night there, but the rocky landscape had slowed the horses' progress.

Rein turned to Eva with a sense of wonder in his voice. "Eva, today I was thinking of all we've seen. Do you realize we've traveled farther in these few days and seen more than our parents did in their lifetimes? And we have much farther to go and more to see."

Amila listened silently as Rein and Eva talked excitedly about the marvels they had seen along the way. Rein was amazed by the oil lanterns that lit up the city streets at night, and Eva spoke in awe about the churches' windows of stained glass. She wondered if the bright sun would make the colorful scenes dance when viewing the windows from the inside.

Amila stared down at her grimy hands, darkness hiding the sullen look she gave her two traveling companions. Her mouth turned down in a pout at once again being excluded. She stood and stretched, then walked away from camp toward the sound of the stream where they had watered the horses. Alone again. Most of her life, she'd been alone, with no cousins or companions near her age. Her closest friends had been her mother and tutors, and now Eva. She knelt to splash water on her face and wash her hands. It was clear that Rein and Eva were very close to one another, and she was an interloper. She felt at a crossroads—did she belong to their world, hers, or neither? The sound of someone or something approaching through the woods wrestled her from thought.

"Who's there?" Amila cried out. "Make yourself known!"

"You fool." Rein suddenly unsheathed days of restraint. "What do you think you're doing, walking into the forest alone? If the bears don't get you, the wolves probably will. You have likely never been in the woods at night in your life, and you start tonight, here? Do you even know the way back to camp?"

Amila gathered her skirt and glared at him. "How dare you talk to me that way! I can take care of myself. Of course I know the way back."

"I don't believe you. If you do, then point to the North Star." He paused when she looked blankly at the sky and then at the ground. "I thought so. We seldom become lost in the woods because we set our reckonings by the sun during the day and by the North Star at night," lectured Rein. "My father taught us how to read the moon, the morning and evening stars, and the constellations so that we could tell the hour within fifteen minutes of clock time. Can you do that? Or anything useful?"

"That wasn't part of my tutoring, I'm afraid. So, I'm useless, am I?" She bit back defiantly. "What about helping people escape the manor and helping you and Eva? Is that useless? What difference does it make if a bear eats me anyway. It's just one less person to tag along as far as you're concerned."

Rein grabbed her arm and shook her thoroughly, then released her. "Once we get to Lübeck, you can behave like the selfish, spoiled child I know you to be. But out here, you must listen to me and do as I say. We need you to sign the papers. You have to be alive to do that." He turned to walk away. "Now, come on."

Amila looked around for a rock or branch, anything she could grab to hit him with. But he was disappearing into the night. Glancing around, she realized how dark it had become. Grudgingly, she followed at a distance, bristling with every step.

As they approached the camp, Rein heard voices. "Karl, watch while I search the packs. I've got her tied up and gagged. What a fine young thing she is! Wait. I heard noise from that direction." The second man came to the edge of the woods, holding a pistol and peering in the direction Rein and Amila were approaching. Rein stopped and reached back, motioning for Amila to crouch down behind him. Then, after putting a finger to his lips, he pressed her shoulders to the ground, long and hard enough to convey what he wanted her to do.

Rein pulled his newly purchased pistol, ball, and powder from pouches in the waist of his breeches and carefully loaded the single-shot. Having drawn the long knife from his boot in his other hand, he began to slowly, soundlessly circle to the camp and approach from the opposite direction. Rein drew close enough to see two men: the armed man had stowed his gun beneath his belt and was hurriedly saddling the horses, while the other thief rummaged through packs. Both looked over their shoulders from time to time.

Just then, Amila paraded boldly into the camp from her hiding place, hurrying to Eva's side. "Leave this place immediately and don't touch our horses!" she shouted. The two men stopped and looked at one another, grinned, and confidently started toward her, one with gun in hand. As she crouched down by Eva, a shower of sparks and burst of gunfire shattered the silence, and the armed man fell to the ground, groaning. The second man turned to see the source of the shot and faced a knife inches from his throat, held tightly in Rein's hand. The thief looked for his knife and saw it lying out of reach beside the packs he had been searching. He scrambled back, turned, and ran into the woods, not pausing to look back.

Amila quickly untied Eva. "Are you all right?" The young woman had been crying softly. Amila hugged her tightly.

Rein looked at the man on the ground, who was bleeding profusely. He reloaded the flintlock pistol and checked the area for more thieves. When he returned to the camp, he found Amila attempting to comfort Eva, the girl's head resting on Amila's lap. Rein kept watch until Eva fell into an uneasy sleep.

Amila walked to the edge of the camp where Rein was leaning against the crumbling wall, standing guard.

"What possessed you to do that?" Rein demanded, keeping his voice low enough that his sister didn't awaken. "Didn't you understand what I told you to do, to stay where you were? Eva could've been hurt."

"I had to do something," she blurted, still shaking. "It was my fault she was in trouble, and I couldn't just lie there. I knew what you meant, you brute! I thought they might chase me and give you a chance to surprise them. As it turns out, it worked."

"It was your fault. At least you admit it," Rein blasted back. "Amila, you know nothing about surviving in our world, and I won't let you put Eva in danger ever again."

"The last person I want to hurt is Eva. It wouldn't have happened if we had stopped in a village for the night," Amila countered through clenched teeth. "It's your job to read the maps. We shouldn't be out here."

Rein fought to contain his anger. But he wasn't going to let her have the last word. "Do you never flinch, Amila? Don't pretend you care about Eva. She doesn't need you. And we don't want you with us."

She covered her ears with her hands to repel the stinging words. Yet, they seeped into her mind like fresh blood through a thin bandage. The message was clear— she wasn't welcome in their lives. After a moment, she looked up and wiped her nose with her sleeve, then nodded her head. "All right. Once we get to Lübeck, you go your way. I'll go mine."

"Agreed. Once the documents are signed, we part ways." Rein turned away.

After dragging the now dead man away from camp, Rein stayed awake the entire night, thinking about having killed a man and how dangerous this journey had suddenly become. The threat hadn't been from Tundorf's pursuit but from another peril he should've seen coming. He admitted to himself both he and Amila shared the blame for what had just happened. He'd been stupid not to realize thieves would watch for travelers at night on long stretches of road like this—he'd left them vulnerable. But it was Amila's fault the thieves were able to tie up Eva and very nearly take everything they owned. He looked skyward in a moment of honest reflection. What would've happened if they had all three been asleep when the thieves attacked? Perhaps Amila's thoughtless actions had played a part in saving them. Still, it was best they went their separate ways in Lübeck.

They left at sunrise without a word spoken.

$\mathcal{B}$y mid-afternoon, Lübeck appeared in the distance as they descended the higher elevation to the seaport below. Amila fidgeted in the saddle and patted Gabe's neck, knowing what she must do. She'd been looking for a prosperous farm along the way. The one they were approaching seemed perfect.

"I want to stop here to see the owner. It won't take long," Amila urged Gabe forward, disregarding her travel companions' puzzled looks. They followed her through the pasture toward a farmhouse.

Amila dismounted and knocked on the door. She waited until a well-dressed man and woman were summoned to the door and began talking with them, out of earshot from Rein and Eva. Soon she led the couple, introducing them as the farm's owners, to where Gabe was standing and her companions waited.

"You won't find a better riding horse, strong and dependable, and a desirable disposition, spirited yet responsive," sighed Amila. "Will you take him, please, and care for him? I assure you, he isn't stolen. I raised him from a colt. I must give him up now and wish for owners who will take good care of him. We're going by ship to a faraway place, so you see, I can no longer keep him."

The farmers seemed a bit confused but pleased with the offer of such a fine horse for their stable and agreed immediately.

Amila removed her possessions from Gabe's saddle, lingering to give the horse's neck a long hug and whisper a message in his ear before handing the reins to the farmer. Tears stung her eyes as she climbed up behind Eva onto her horse. She looked back until the farm was out of sight, vowing to remember the exact location when she returned.

On the outskirts of the city, the riders crossed a bridge spanning the Trave River that surrounded the island city of Lübeck. An intimidating stone gate guarded the entrance, and church spires shaped the distant skyline.

"We're here; we made it! Where is the sea? And when can we see our ship?" exclaimed Eva in a series of unrestrained bursts.

Amila and Rein smiled at her childlike enthusiasm, finding it contagious. Amila had not forgotten nor forgiven last night's angry discourse. Given Rein's aloof demeanor, he hadn't either. But she believed a sensible bargain had been struck. They had at least made it this far together. Long days in the saddle were over, and they'd soon be trading horses for a ship and another challenge, although separately.

"I don't see any ships from here or even the sea. But don't worry, Eva. We'll keep looking," laughed Rein. "We are to seek out the Russian ambassador, and hopefully, he'll tell us what to do next." Rein continued to harbor misgivings that the emigration offer was a hoax, but they had to try.

After the long day and restless night on the road, they stopped to board the horses and find lodging and a decent meal since they hadn't eaten all day. They stopped at the first inn that looked promising. As they voraciously ate the food placed before them, they learned about Lübeck from the talkative innkeeper.

Used to seeing newcomers, the innkeeper proudly conveyed information about the city and its commerce. Lübeck was called a 'free city' because of its long and successful shipping and trade relations with Russia and other northern countries bordering the Baltic Sea. "Ships arrive with full cargos every day—especially salt. The goods are stored in enormous stone warehouses along the harbor. The city is on excellent terms with Empress Catherine of Russia, and many representatives of her government have offices here."

Amila asked where they might find the Russian ambassador for emigration, and she noticed Rein breathe a sigh of relief when the innkeeper responded there was, indeed, such an office and told them where to go.

After a short walk, Amila, Eva, and Rein turned a corner and encountered a crowd filling the street facing the two-story building they'd been directed to find. Ignorant of what to expect, the first surprise was a large number of what must be prospective colonists milling about in boisterous conversation, shuffling forward in lines outside the office. Gunter had warned them to be discreet en route to and once they reached Lübeck, for fear of being arrested and returned. But cautious talk was absent from this street.

"For the first time, I believe the promises we were told may hold some truth. I've never been so glad to be wrong," admitted Rein. "And now we know others are willing to take the same risks."

Market day in the village. That's what it felt like, thought Amila. She always enjoyed market day, where all were welcome to attend regardless of the clothes on one's back or coins jingling in one's purse. The street swelled with faces and voices participating in that rare event that is blind to human differences. Amila felt the air tingle with excitement as she moved between the clusters of people, trying to discern the languages being spoken and glean bits of conversation. She heard German dialects and tried to recognize other languages, to no avail. She felt sure she heard no Russian. Amila had a rudimentary understanding of Russian from study with her governess, who insisted all German nobility must learn the complex language because their fellow countrywoman, Catherine, was now the Empress of all Russia.

Amila wandered back to her companions, and the three moved to the back of the long, snaking line progressing toward the building entrance. In front of them stood a couple dressed in what must be their Sunday best, waiting patiently as the line eked forward. The plump wife held the arm of her husband and slowly fanned herself. Joining the line behind them was a family of four. Their threadbare clothing must have been all they owned. The haggard mother rocked the child she held back and forth, trying to comfort the coughing toddler, whose face was pressed into her mother's shoulder. A young boy held his father's hand and looked up occasionally for reassurance as they eased forward in line. Despite their differences, Amila concluded everyone on the street held common ground—the human plight where desperation seeks out hope.

It took several hours to reach the building entrance and an audience with Ambassador Jacob Rehbinder.

"It's obvious you aren't refugees like many on our rosters. We have all sorts of riff-raff, a jumble of settlers. Who are you?" asked the ambassador, scrutinizing the three with a practiced glance. He spoke German with a slight accent Amila thought was Russian. Given their wait and the line outside, it was apparent he had limited time and patience for any single group.

Amila and Rein glanced at one another, both a bit uneasy.

"I'm Lady Amila Wallerstein, and these are my traveling companions, Rein and Eva Lundgren. We are from the south of Germany, near Donauwörth." Amila took the initiative to begin, causing Rein to lower his eyes and look away.

"Ah, a noblewoman. We haven't any of you yet, but there are sure to be more." Rehbinder eyed Amila with great interest, then pushed documents toward them along with a quill freshly dipped in ink. "I assume you two are married, or will be soon, and wish to enroll as a family?"

The speed at which both Amila and Rein blushed and vigorously shook their heads got the ambassador's full attention.

"No! We traveled here together, but we plan to go our separate ways now," Rein rushed to say. "My sister and I will be enrolling together."

"Rein, what are you saying?" Eva broke in. "Amila is going with us. We're staying together, aren't we? You don't mean what you're saying." Hands on hips, Eva looked from one to the other, determined to clear up the misunderstanding.

"Hmm. I believe there is more afoot here," assessed Rehbinder. "Now, why don't you tell me what's going on." He put the quill back in the inkpot and motioned for them to sit down.

Amila started slowly, explaining that Rein and Eva were, in fact, servants at her manor— and wished to emigrate along with her. She told him they had met several times with a recruiter named Gunter Rohlwagen. While preparing them for the journey, he had advised them to travel together discreetly because the lord of her manor, Amila's stepfather, did not wish to give his consent.

"I'll be signing the permission form as the lady of the manor, as well as the farmer affidavit. I can assure you that Rein is a skilled farmer, as has been his family for many generations. We must leave right away."

Rehbinder paused to reflect before continuing. "Oh yes, Gunter, such a resourceful man. He's been busy indeed, having already sent us many families. Be assured, you're not the only ones stealing away. It seems every colonist here is running from something or someone. I won't press you for more details. I'll accept you without official passports and send you on to Russia as unaccredited colonists. Many colonists don't have official documents, and the ship's passenger logs, well, they're never very…complete. No one will be able to find you."

Amila sent a sidelong look of relief to Eva and Rein, and they reciprocated.

The ambassador continued. "Our dear empress wants to give all her fellow countrymen and women a chance for a new life in Russia, regardless of their, shall we say, personal situations. She knows the war has been devastating for her German people, especially the poor, and welcomes all with open arms. Farmers are especially desirable. It's simply my job to send as large a contingent of settlers as possible."

Rehbinder's assurances ended there. "There is one problem. No woman can be accepted if she is 'unaccompanied.' You will either have to find someone suitable to marry right away or be accepted into another family. Many of the colonists in this situation are marrying before they sail. You'll receive more land once you arrive there if you do."

Amila opened her mouth to respond but was unsure what to say. Quickly the ambassador launched into the remaining details he was used to reciting before obtaining new colonist signatures from Rein and Eva and the farmer affidavit from Amila.

With final words, he waved them on their way. "You'll be quartered here in Lübeck. Your arrival now and farmer affidavit assure you'll be on the first ship. And you'll receive 16 shillings per person each day as 'butter money' for food and other expenses while here. Lady Amila, I suggest you stay with townspeople who host colonists at a fair price, as you'll be more comfortable there. While you're there, you can consider your options. But you best hurry if you wish to enroll."

Then, motioning to Rein and Eva, "You two will stay at the warehouse with all the others. It's important for you to meet fellow emigrants and join a colony—immediately. No individuals are accepted. You must join a colony. You'll be settling the first colonies as a community."

"When will the first ship sail?" asked Rein when he could finally get a word in.

"We have no idea," Ambassador Rehbinder admitted. "As I said, not until it's assured we have enough passengers to fill a 'pink.' That's a type of ship. But likely within the next few weeks."

"And how long will it take to reach our new home?" asked Eva.

"Ah, Gunter didn't tell you that." The ambassador was unsurprised. "First, you will go by ship to St. Petersburg, where the Kontora, the Office of Oversight of Foreigners, will process you as colonists. They'll decide your colony's location. Farmers are in great demand on the Volga prairie, or steppe, as they call it. If that's your final destination, you have some traveling to do to reach your land. You'll travel by wagon and probably float on a barge down the river. Most assuredly, you'll arrive by next spring or summer, once the Volga River thaws."

The ambassador motioned to his assistant, who hustled the three out of his office as the next group entered. Rein and Eva left the office armed with directions to the warehouse and 16 shillings each as newly enrolled settlers bound for Russia. Amila received directions to a local resident's home for lodging but received no 'butter money' because of her undetermined status as a colonist.

As they left the ambassador's office, the transformation from excitement to perplexity was immediate. Different concerns plagued each of the three.

"If the Volga River is as large as they say, how can it freeze in the winter? And I've never heard of a shilling, only kreuzer. I wonder what a shilling is worth," Rein thought aloud while inspecting the coins in his hand.

Eva presented a solution to the problem she was most concerned about. "Amila, you should be a part of our family, then you can stay with us." She looked toward Rein, who didn't respond.

Amila walked behind them silently, lost in thought, wondering why someone was always demanding that she marry.

Overwhelmed by all he'd just heard, Rein led the trio into the street. He swallowed hard, struggling with a harsh reality—he and Eva had just signed documents casting their lot with strangers thrust together for a common cause but with little in common. Rehbinder's disturbing words found a deep well inside him: *It's simply my job to send as large a contingent of settlers as possible.* The ambassador was paying little attention to the type of people he accepted, regardless of fitness for farming, knowledge of trades, or strength of character. He had said they must join a colony. This seemed like a momentous decision, one that would have a far-reaching effect on their lives. How exactly would he and Eva do this? And what of Amila, whom he continued to believe didn't belong here at all?

Having committed to a room at the inn, the three returned there as the eventful day ended. Overcome with exhaustion, they once again fell into the lodging routine: Amila and Eva shared the bed, Rein slept on the floor, and he was gone before they awakened.

*E*arly the next morning, Rein returned to the room overflowing with news and energy. "I've found someone willing to buy the two horses for a good price. Just as with your gelding, we can't keep them anymore. The stableman gave me a name. Once sold, all the money will, of course, be yours, Amila. Since you don't have 'butter money,' it will tide you over." He was surprised to feel somewhat sorry for her, being rejected as a colonist and having to give up Gabe. She was truly alone. But it was relief, not regret, he felt about ending their troublesome partnership.

"I walked to the harbor to see the ships and found the warehouse where we'll stay, Eva," he continued. "It's fascinating to see all the activity. I don't know what a 'pink' is, the type of ship we'll travel on, but I saw many ships loading and unloading cargo. Come downstairs when you're ready. The innkeeper has breakfast for us."

Rein departed to the dining room below. The farther away from Nassenwald they traveled, the more energy he had. He wondered if a primary reason was simply food, recalling only a bottomless hunger for many years, perhaps since childhood, certainly since before the war. But more than that, he burst with hope and excitement for this new life. *The offer to emigrate was real!* However, restlessness was setting in. Used to dawn-to-dark physical labor, he was unsure where to direct his energy. This morning he'd walked for hours and absorbed every shred of information he could. He'd learned that a shilling was the type of currency used in northern Germany and worth about the same as a kreuzer. He felt nervous but anxious to meet other colonists. Would they want him and Eva as part of their colony? And how would they know who to trust?

During the hearty breakfast, Amila kept a civil tongue as Rein eagerly shared exploration details from the morning. Her mind dwelled on the uncertainty of her future and what seemed like few options. She told Rein to go ahead and sell the horses since he had more of a grasp on what money was worth here. Amila had plans for the rest of her and Eva's morning.

"I can't remember ever feeling so dusty, clear to the bone." Amila led them to a dressmaker's shop that looked promising. "It's time to purchase more garments since we can now have travel bags. Well, each of us a separate bag, I suppose."

At the shop, they found some articles of clothing ready-made and were each fitted for two dresses, again sturdy enough for travel, and were told to return for the custom-made clothing in a few days. They returned to the inn to wash, bolting the door before stripping off the trail-weary dresses. Amila remembered the most unique part of their dresses, the inner pockets. Not having removed the dress for a week, she was relieved the valuables hidden inside were intact.

"It feels heavenly to finally wash," Amila indulged in the scent of the sweet-smelling soap purchased from the dressmaker. They took turns washing their hair and lathering their faces and bodies, rinsing with large basins of water, much of which ended up on the floor. As they finished drying off and putting on newly purchased undergarments, Amila asked why her friend was so quiet. "Eva, please tell me what's on your mind."

"I don't understand why you keep talking about leaving us, Amila," she explained. "You're like a sister to me. We belong together, don't we? Why do you want to leave us?"

"Eva, your brother and I don't get along. I know you can see that. He's angry at me all the time. Not only that, he's bossy, and he blames me for everything. Fortunately, we made it this far, and that's remarkable. But we must take separate paths now."

"Amila, this is not the way he usually acts," Eva pleaded. "Since Father died, he's been so angry. He tried to take care of us and do everything, and still, we lost Mother. Won't you please give him another chance?"

"Oh, it's evident he wants to send me on my way. But Eva, I'll miss you so much! I'm in a predicament. I can't go back, and I can't go forward. Let's hope Johann and his uncle's family arrive in time for me to join them." Amila pressed her lips together and shrugged. "I'm certain about one thing. I'm not going to seek out and marry a total stranger."

Clean hair gleaming and donning their spare travel dresses, Amila hugged Eva and told her to bolt the door and wait for Rein while she went in search of the lodgings the ambassador had recommended. Eva flashed a pathetic look and slumped onto the bed.

Within the hour, Amila had found the home of an elderly couple, Luise and Charles Ulrich, retired merchants who had rooms to rent in their large, modestly furnished townhouse. Amila told the proprietors a portion of her story, and as a noblewoman, they were pleased to board her. However, the hostess looked shocked when Amila explained both her parents were gone and she might be traveling to Russia alone.

Amila stored her few possessions in her room and was about to leave when Mrs. Ulrich stopped her. "Lady Amila, before you go, I'd like to introduce you to one of our other guests. This is Mr. Christian Bengler. He, too, is planning to travel to Russia."

Amila extended her hand to the young man standing before her. He was about Amila's height with shocks of curly blond hair and bright blue eyes. He wore clothing befitting a middle-class tradesman and smiled warmly.

"I'm pleased to meet you, milady." He bowed and tipped his hat. "And please call me Christof, as my friends and family do. I'm patiently awaiting a ship to Russia to explore that vast land. And you?"

"I, too, hope to be on a ship very soon," Amila smiled, realizing how few times in her life she'd had the opportunity to talk with a young man near her age and of a similar social status. "How long have you been here, and where was your home, if you don't mind my asking?"

The talkative young man seemed more than willing to share his background. Christof explained he was the son of a manufacturer from Hanover and was intent on world travel. "I received a good education for a middle-class merchant's son. Schooling in geography has created in me a craving to see the world. My parents kept me home until I was of age, then gave their consent. I had planned to go to America. I learned that if I agreed to be a soldier, I would receive free passage in exchange for serving in the army and be paid as well. However, it would be many years before I'd be free to go where I wanted."

Christof explained that a Russian recruiter urged him to give up his plan, calling it highly undesirable, even dangerous. "He assured me it would hardly be different from the way the slaves are stolen from Africa."

"Was the recruiter's name by chance Gunter Rohlwagen?" laughed Amila. "We received much the same warning about America."

"Why, no, it wasn't. But perhaps there's some truth to it if you heard it too," Christof continued. "The recruiter pointed out a different option. He showed me the royal manifesto from the Empress of Russia. Everything he claimed was written there, just as he had promised. He lured me here for the adventure of settling in a new land and meeting Russians and Kirghiz and a host of other unknown people. And, of course, the offer of free passage and financial support to settle anywhere, at my own discretion, was not without merit. Anyway, I changed my mind, and here I am. That's my story. Not very exciting, I'm afraid. Where is your home?"

Not sure how much to reveal, Amila shared similar information she had with the ambassador: that both her parents were gone and that her estate near Nuremberg was in the care of her stepfather. She explained she had been traveling with two of her servants, a sister and brother who would be emigrating, and she planned to do so as well.

"The most frightening thing that happened on our journey was an attack by highwaymen late one night between villages." Amila hoped to divert the conversation away from her true reasons for leaving and her plans from here forward. "Luckily, we escaped without injury or losing our possessions."

"Oh, how awful! I'm so glad you were unharmed. And tell me, have you already joined a colony, as the ambassador says we must?"

Amila bit her lip and considered a response. "No, well yes. I mean, I'm hoping more servants will arrive in time to travel with me. The ambassador informed me it's not possible for an unaccompanied woman to become a settler without a family, as well as a colony. So now I'm wondering what to do."

"If you will pardon my boldness, I may have an idea." Christof was suddenly wide-eyed and even more enthusiastic. "I've joined a group I believe to be of high principles and reputation. I could introduce you to some families, and perhaps you could accompany one of them?"

Amila smiled warmly and agreed to meet with them. Finally, a solution that didn't involve marriage. She took Christof's outstretched arm and accompanied him out to the street.

CHAPTER 7

July 1763

*R*ein found Eva hunched over at the foot of the bed when he returned to take her to the new lodgings.

"Eva, what's wrong? Are you unwell?" Eva sobbed. Realizing he wasn't calming her but making it worse, he sat down beside her and tried another approach, silently taking her hand.

Eva jerked her hand away and wiped her tears, then jumped up to confront him. "You've driven her away! Now Amila has no one and nowhere to go. We've lost Mother and Father, our home, and you won't let her come with us. Don't you realize she's like a sister to me?"

Rein's eyes widened at his sister's uncharacteristic outburst. Eva had been quiet since they left the ambassador's office. Now he understood why. "No. I suppose I didn't want to admit how close you two have become. But Eva, we both know she's different from us and always will be. She's from the class of people who have controlled us all our lives. She and her stepfather sent our friends to their deaths as soldiers and raised our taxes and rents, knowing we couldn't pay and still feed ourselves. They want to own us, not live among us and treat us as equals. *She's exactly the kind of person we are running from.* Amila belongs with her kind of people."

Eva moved across the room as far from her brother as she could and folded her arms defiantly. "I don't believe she's the person you say she is. She helped us escape, and now you want to desert her. How can you be so cruel?"

He went to stand beside her and put his arm around his sister's shoulder. "All right. Let's find her and make sure she has somewhere to go. We'll make sure she's not alone. But we still have problems of our own to solve. We need to find a colony of settlers to join."

Eva sniffled and nodded once, skeptical and yet temporarily pacified. They left the inn in search of their new lodgings in the warehouse.

Rein and Eva found the giant *salzspeicher,* or salt storehouse, among a long row of brick buildings along the Trave River. People were milling about outside the warehouse recently converted to temporary lodging. A clerk stopped them at the entrance, asked to see their emigration papers, noted their names on a ledger, and asked the name of their colony.

"We, um, don't belong to a colony yet," Rein responded. "Can you tell us how to go about finding one?"

The clerk shrugged and waved them on. "Go inside and talk with others. And when you have a colony name, come back, and I'll log it beside your name. The papers authorize you to stay here, but you won't be able to board a ship until you join a colony." He quickly dispensed cursory instructions for lodging: watch your possessions carefully, as thieves are about, and don't leave any food uneaten because it will attract rats.

Rein and Eva paused just inside the building and gaped. It wasn't the first time the siblings had been awed by sights and sounds on the journey. But it was perhaps the most dramatic scene they had witnessed. High windows welcomed unfiltered light into the cavernous yet overflowing warehouse that reverberated with voices and squirmed with the movement of newly arrived residents. Children of all ages were sleeping on cots amid the noise or crying and running freely, and groups of adults filled the space with lively discourse. Like the refugees they'd passed on the road, many looked sickly and weak. However, the 'butter money' and makeshift sleeping quarters already showed signs of improving the refugees' prospects. Still, Rein thought the most feeble needed more time to grow stronger before taking on a sea voyage.

He and Eva began to wander through the maze of people sorting through their meager belongings and engaging in daily routines. When he heard a familiar German dialect being spoken, Rein stopped near the group to listen, understanding enough to be encouraged by what he was hearing. This wasn't like gatherings in his village where eyes were downcast and shoulders hunched in despair. While he heard voices in dissent, an aura of hope still emanated from most conversations.

Rein noticed a man, shoulders held high, walking briskly from one area to another. Upon seeing Rein, he stopped abruptly, speaking in a German dialect similar to theirs. "Who are you looking for? Maybe I can help you find them."

"I thank you for your kindness, sir. My sister and I just arrived from the south and don't know anyone here," responded Rein nervously.

"Well then, you are fair game for us." He extended his hand and grasped Rein's confidently, then bowed slightly to Eva. He introduced himself as Georg Müller, the group leader from the small German city of Bremen and the rural area surrounding it. "Do you have additional family members with you? What is your trade?"

"My name is Rein, Reinhardt Lundgren, and this is my sister Eva. Our parents are gone, and we have no other family. I'm simply a farmer. My sister has greater skills than I do." Rein winked at his sister fondly.

Georg nodded his head enthusiastically and told them the Bremen colonists waiting for transport had elected him to be *vorsteher*, or leader of their group of emigrants, as the ambassador required of each colony. Unused to his duties but willing to try, Georg said it was his responsibility to pay regular allowances to his settlers, look after their welfare on the long trip to Russia, and oversee the formation of the colony.

"I'm also supposed to make sure no one deserts after they've enrolled, although I don't know how I'm supposed to enforce that." Georg shrugged.

He said their colony had about fifty families registered thus far. While most were from Germany, several families came from Hungary, Denmark, and Poland. The ambassador required each colony to have at least 200 people, so they were actively seeking additional members. Georg explained what he'd been told about the importance of belonging to a colony: The empress believed the success of each new village would depend on the cohesiveness and combined skills of its members.

"I'm a merchant's son, the youngest of five," continued Georg, who used a variety of hand gestures while talking, a mannerism Rein had never seen but found quite engaging. "My wife, Elisabeth, and our young son are with me. We have some farmers and many trades represented—a blacksmith, cobbler, tailor, baker, builders, and a minister who will also serve as our schoolmaster. We are to be a colony of the Lutheran faith."

Rein immediately felt at ease with the man. He was certainly confident and optimistic. Georg continued. "All of us have farmed or at least gardened plots to feed our families. With so many tradesmen in our colony, we plan to start a settlement near one of the Russian cities, perhaps even St. Petersburg.. But we need more skilled farmers. The ambassador has made it clear that farmers are highly desirable for each colony. The quicker we meet the minimum number of colonists—and recruit additional farmers—the higher on the list we will be placed to ship out. Would you like to meet some members of our group?"

Rein nodded, and he and Eva followed eagerly. Georg led them to an area where his group had gathered their possessions and commandeered cots. He introduced them to his wife Elisabeth and other colonists. They met families with young children and several girls Eva's age. Most interested in talking with the group's farmers, Rein heard about new techniques and crop varieties, and they listened intently to the innovative methods he had tried, and about his mill experience. At the same time, all expressed common concerns about growing food in the new climate and soil. Overall, Rein sensed optimism among the people he met, a determination that filled him with hope.

Rein asked a farmer about Georg. "Will he be a wise and fair leader? Do you trust him?"

"He didn't want to be our leader at first but finally agreed. We chose him because we've known him all our lives and we trust him. And we know he won't rule with an iron fist. We've had enough of that. He's already organized a leaders council to be decision-makers for the colony. It's a bold idea. But Georg says that way we're more likely to hear the best ideas and share responsibility."

Rein had heard enough. He asked Eva to come with him to a less chaotic area of the building to speak privately. "What do you think? Are they the kind of people you could see yourself living with in our new community?"

Eva giggled. "Did you see how some of the young ladies looked at you? I think they would welcome you right into their open arms. I like the people I talked with. I met a woman who shares an interest in herbs and healing. And Elisabeth is very kind. They seem to be good people, like our friends from home. And when Johann and his family arrive, we must try to make room for them as well."

Rein hadn't noticed the women in the group. He was too busy assessing the farmers and offered his impressions. "The farmers are smart and dedicated to our craft. I can imagine working with them, side-by-side, in the field. I didn't know each group was required to elect a vorsteher. But everyone speaks highly of Georg Müller. All agreed they were fortunate to find a man like him to be the colony's leader." Eva seemed giddy with excitement, and Rein felt a deep-seated relief when they returned to tell Georg they would like to join the Bremen colony.

Georg, too, was ecstatic. "That's wonderful news! It's been a lucky day for us. Earlier today, a well-spoken and quite beautiful young lady joined our colony. She's going to become a part of my family and travel with us."

"What's her name, do you recall?" Rein asked hesitantly, a crack in his voice.

"Her name is Lady Amila Wallerstein. You just missed her. She was here earlier with the young gentleman who introduced her to us. They've gone to see the ambassador and complete her enrollment."

Eva squealed and hugged Rein, who stared blankly into the distance.

$\mathcal{T}$en days later, Amila and Eva dragged their shared trunk up the ramp of the Russian ship, the *Elephant*—a cargo ship refitted to carry colonists bound for St. Petersburg. As they boarded the ship, Eva looked back and waved vigorously to Johann, who waited in line with Rein and other members of the Bremen colony, signing the ship's log. Once the nearly 300 passengers finished the tedious boarding process, the *Elephant* sluggishly pulled away from the dock and labored up the Trave River toward the Baltic Sea. Solemn faces turned toward the lighthouse onshore as land disappeared, passengers whispering regret that this might be their last glimpse of Germany. Amila uttered a determined vow—it was not so for her.

Johann had arrived safely in Lübeck several days earlier with his cousin, his cousin's wife, and their three children. He told them the trip from Nassenwald was uneventful, and the Bremen colony quickly adopted the Heft family. One of the things that had always endeared Amila to Johann was his ability to put an amusing twist on life's challenging situations. Johann told Amila sheepishly he had taken the liberty of borrowing horses and a wagon from the manor's stable for travel to Lübeck and was now returning them directly to her. She laughed and said she was glad, as he had cared for the manor's horses from the time he was old enough to carry a water bucket. As a result, she insisted the money from their sale be his to keep for his work and inadequate pay over the years.

Johann confirmed what they had come to suspect, that Tundorf had taken the bait and sent his henchmen on the wrong trail after Amila and the others. Johann joked about the beating he took to convince them, saying he yelped loudly and begged for mercy before finally divulging the false route. Johann reported many serfs had escaped Nassenwald the same day for different locations, leaving the manor looking deserted. When Amila pressed for information about where others might be going, Johann thought some planned to go to America, other parts of Prussia, and Austria. She was disappointed to hear no others would be coming to Russia.

Christof edged in close to Amila and Eva on the deck. He clutched a satchel full of precious maps close to his chest, anxious to consult them on his first ocean voyage. Over the past week, Amila had enjoyed his company at their common lodgings. In the evenings, he amused her with tales of his travels thus far and knowledge of various subjects. She decided his greatest gift might be a love of storytelling and an ability to converse with total strangers in a relaxed manner, regardless of their stations in life.

Before leaving Lübeck, Christof had sought out and quizzed sailors about the upcoming voyage. He learned the ship was called a 'pink' from the Dutch word *pincke*, the name given to a class of fast sailing ships with narrow sterns able to navigate in shallow water such as rivers, streams, and canals with locks. Like other pinks, this ship had a large cargo capacity. The sailors had assured Christof the Russian naval captain, Lieutenant Sergey Petrov, was experienced sailing this route, although with cargo, not necessarily passengers. The voyage was to take nine to eleven days, depending on favorable winds.

On cue, the first mate's whistle and announcement directed passengers below deck. They began to follow Georg Müller, who found an area for members to congregate. As they descended the wide staircase into the hold, Amila realized why passengers had been allowed to stay on the upper deck until well out to sea—had they known they would be forced to travel in the dark, dank cargo hold, many would have left the ship.

Sailors drove passengers down the stairway into the nine-foot-high hold as waves from the open sea began rocking the ship, the swaying motion making it difficult to stand. Passengers tumbled against one another as more and more entered the ship's cavity, filling it beyond capacity. Food stockpiled in barrels and crates had been lowered through the cargo hatch, which was now covered with a metal grate.

Amila held tight to Eva, afraid they might be separated. She gazed up at the confining grate overhead, which afforded some light and airflow to the hold. A few lanterns lit the cargo area, barely enough to see. Portholes were closed for protection against the waves, shutting out further ventilation.

"This must have been what Noah's Ark was like," Eva shouted above the wails of passengers squeezing in behind them. The prayers and curses of adults combined with the cries of children to create strange, woeful echoes off the walls and low ceiling. Soon, passengers of all ages began to groan and heave with seasickness.

"Eva, Amila, over here," Rein waved his hands above the crowd. Taller than most, they could see Rein's head as he maneuvered closer. Once together, he led them through the crowd to the area staked out by the Bremen colony. As their leader, Georg had been charged with bringing food purchased with funds from the ambassador. The group's biscuits, dried fruit, and smoked meat were packed in barrels and crates nearby. They were told food would also be available from the ship's captain in case of shortages. However, no one was prepared for the horrid conditions in the ship's hold.

A ship's officer came and went quickly, delivering more distressing news. "The captain has ordered that no passengers will be allowed on deck during the voyage because their presence will interfere with the sailors' work."

A momentary hush preceded a reverberating outcry from passengers as they began to comprehend. Day after day, with no release from the hold in overcrowded and unsanitary conditions with little ventilation meant people would become sick, and very soon.

"Let us out! We'll die!" a woman screamed, having given up trying to comfort her children. Widespread cries and threats to the captain and crew filled the hold.

Georg climbed on top of a barrel and shouted over the panic-stricken voices. "Please, you must try and remain calm! Tend to your children. Group leaders, listen! Come and meet here. We must work together to see what can be done and take our demands to the captain. Bring anyone from your group who has dealt with conditions such as these before."

Leaders from the four groups soon pushed through the crowd to reach Georg, bringing others along. Amila lingered at the edge of the gathering. Georg spoke first. "We must determine what we can do ourselves and what we need from Captain Petrov. We'll take our demands to him. He must hear us out."

A woman who accompanied one leader had learned to care for the sick in a type of hospital for the poor established by King Frederick of Prussia. She suggested ways to keep areas clean so illness didn't spread. Her ideas and others formed concerns recorded for presentation to the captain: plentiful clean water to drink, seawater in buckets to wash, strong soap, and as many slop buckets as could be found. They would also demand that small groups of passengers be allowed on deck for short periods each day, assuring the captain they would not disturb the sailors. This way, each passenger would have some exposure to fresh air.

As to their own actions, they would open portholes when possible, create a walking path for passengers to pass through, and clean often with the seawater and soap. Blankets would be hung around privy buckets for privacy, and all passengers would be required to use them and dump buckets regularly.

"Assure your colonists it will only be for ten days, maybe less," encouraged Georg. It was now obvious the space was woefully inadequate for day and night— passengers would have to stand or sit on the floor during the day, as there were no bunks or furniture and no blankets. At night, passengers would have to sleep lying on the floor or lean against a trunk, barrel, or one another.

As the leaders made their way back to groups and shared directives, some of the panic subsided, although widespread seasickness continued. Georg and two other leaders soon headed toward and banged on the bolted cargo door, determined to meet with Captain Petrov.

Thinking the movement of the ship felt like the gait of a wobbly horse one minute and a bucking stallion the next, Amila felt queasy, but so far, not seasick. However, she was used to being alone and fought off the uneasiness she felt in such close quarters. At least these people were not all strangers. Amila rejoiced at being back with Eva, and now Johann had joined them. She knew Christof and, of course, Rein, whom she had successfully avoided since learning they had unintentionally joined the same colony. The adoption by Georg and Elisabeth had been fortuitous. She looked fondly at Elisabeth holding her young son, who was sleeping fitfully in his mother's arms.

The captain listened to and grudgingly met most demands. The days began to pass calmly, although slowly. He agreed to let small groups go above deck for short periods, under orders that passengers not talk or make noise. The constant rotation to the deck freed up some space in the hold during the day. Another of Captain Petrov's conditions required passengers to buy food from him at shore prices, which leaders agreed to do. In response, Georg and the other negotiators agreed to provide a favorable report to the ambassador once they arrived safely in St. Petersburg, thus increasing the likelihood that the *Elephant* would be engaged to carry passengers on upcoming voyages.

With excessive time to fill, Amila dug through the trunk and pulled out the tightly-bound leather packet of documents smuggled out of the castle. During the month leading up to the escape, she had studied them but never thoroughly. The past two weeks, she'd all but forgotten them. Just holding them in her hands now made her nervous. She glanced around to make sure no one was watching and leaned close to the porthole for light. The documents were complicated, but she was determined to decipher their meaning. She noticed first how very official they were, all bearing Tundorf's seal and signature.

Among the papers was a mortgage document stating that a great deal of money was due on loans against the manor's land. Her land! Correspondence from the bank showed default on the debts would result in forests being felled and sold and livestock on the manor procured by the bank, including livestock belonging to the manor's serfs. *How could he!*

Two documents—one written in German and the other in French—showed detailed inventories of supplies ordered from Nassenwald Manor to be delivered to the Prussian army. The recipient for payment was, of course, Tundorf. Amila had heard him profess the importance of his role many times—as an Undersecretary of War for Prussia, he ensured regular supplies of food, ammunition, and animal forage were delivered to the army's field locations. The document stated clearly that the count was selling Nassenwald Manor supplies to the Prussian army. She squinted in the poor lighting to translate the French inventory list, for the first time comparing each item to the German version. Line by line, the two documents were—identical. Why had two documents, in two different languages, been created for the same purpose? Closer inspection showed one was an invoice to the Prussian war office, and the other an invoice to the French army—the enemy! Tundorf had been paid twice for the same supplies. The date for delivery was the final months of the war, for twenty-five wagonloads of supplies from Nassenwald Manor.

Amila grasped the pages tightly, recalling that Maria's husband Daniel had been among those chosen by the count to deliver those wagonloads of supplies to the Prussian army's frontier location. But the unarmed serfs were ambushed by the French, all killed, and supplies…taken. The gravity of her discovery slowly dawned. Tundorf had arranged the ambush and death of his own serfs so he would be paid twice. *Murder and treason!* Amila cringed, eyes glaring at the pages. Involuntarily, one trembling hand reached up to cover her throat. She didn't know why Tundorf had kept these documents, but he had. And now she had them—proof of his guilt. He would realize they were missing and that she had likely taken them. Tundorf would come after her to retrieve them—and silence her now that she knew his horrible secret. The evidence dear Maria thought would keep them safe had instead plunged them into grave danger.

She clenched her fists to calm her trembling hands and tried to think. Not only did these documents put them in danger, but Maria had also provided the evidence she needed to ruin Tundorf. Now her vow to return was stronger than ever, to make sure the count paid for his sins. Amila remembered his boasts of violence. Her hand moved from her throat to the coat pistol hidden in a dress pocket and to the knife in her boot. She must protect herself if he found her first.

Amila looked across the room and saw Rein squinting in her direction. She quickly turned away. After a moment, she carefully folded the documents and stored them deep in the travel trunk.

Rein followed Eva, both stepping over people packed wall to wall, carrying items needed to tend the sick. It gave him something useful to do while trapped in the hold. "You're a natural at this, you know." Only sixteen years old, she had long ago taken on the responsibilities of an adult. "Mother and Father would be very proud, as am I."

Eva smiled at the mention of her mother. "Some of my earliest memories are accompanying her into the woods in search of herbs. Over and over, I saw how she used her knowledge to heal. I hope to do the same."

Passengers were sore and bruised from the motion of the ship. Some had scrapes on their faces and hands from falls. She helped clean minor wounds and apply cloth bandages. But most in demand were herbs for fever, coughs, and stomach complaints.

"They're getting worse," Eva whispered to Rein. "Those already sick or weak before we left are at great risk if conditions don't improve soon. I'm afraid for them, especially the children. Soon I'll run out of peppermint and fennel."

By the eighth day, Rein thought passengers' spirits might be lifting, knowing the end of the voyage was near. At least they were becoming used to the fetid conditions. Occasional sounds of laughter, singing, and reading aloud could be heard, still accompanied by constant wails of seasickness and impatient cries of the children.

For a land-loving farmer, Rein felt he was doing passably well, keeping food in his stomach most of the time.

He had never anticipated traveling on a seafaring ship. From talking with Christof and seeing the geographer's maps, Rein had learned the Baltic Sea was not nearly as large as the vast oceans ships crossed to reach faraway places like America. He shook his head in disbelief when Christof told him those seas had much more powerful winds and waves.

On a visit above deck, he was fascinated by the sailors' work. Rein watched the confident seamen climb the rigging in high winds, perhaps as high as eighty feet, to pull down ripped sails that were flapping violently. The ship's sailmaker sat on deck mending the tears with oversized needles and twine. Upon repair, the sailors climbed up the tall rigging and set the sails in place once again. On rare days, the water was calm and the breezes gentle, allowing passengers to bask in the sun and fresh air, a welcome break from the ship's heaving. But the ship didn't cover much distance on these rare days.

Rein worried. They needed to reach their destination immediately, for everyone's sake. During another turn on deck, he noticed sailors leering at the women. It was Amila who attracted the most attention, although she seemed oblivious. Rein stayed near Eva and urged the men never to let women go above unaccompanied. Hah, he thought. It wasn't the passengers whom Captain Petrov feared would misbehave.

Even with efforts to keep the hold clean, the spilling and overflow of privy buckets and lack of ventilation had made the air putrid. By the tenth day, Eva's fears came to pass. Fever and dysentery claimed six lives, four of which were children. Parents sobbed and clung to their children's bodies as they were stitched into canvas bags and cast overboard. Eva feared many more would die if they didn't reach their destination soon.

Seasickness continued for the most vulnerable passengers, and heat in the cargo hold had become oppressive. Even though many passengers had eaten smaller amounts due to seasickness, food stores were beginning to run low. He saw Georg and the other leaders return from a meeting with the captain. Stern and pale, Georg addressed the group.

"Petrov has informed us we are far from our destination. He said the winds have not been favorable, and the weight of the passengers, which he calls cargo, have slowed the ship considerably." The news was met with surly mumbling.

"How much longer will it take?" Johann was faring well but looked across at his cousin's family with grave concern.

"The captain says at least a week, perhaps more." As Georg shared the news, outcries swelled to a roar across the passenger hold as other leaders delivered the same grim report. "I know, this seems impossible to me, too. Please listen. Our food is running out. We have no choice but to buy food from the ship's supplies. And he has informed us it will be triple the price we paid in Lübeck. What this means is, I'll need to collect money from each of you to ensure no one goes hungry. I'll share in the cost for my family and myself. We must all share this burden."

Already disgruntled, voices now turned to outrage. Rein saw Christof step forward and ask to speak with Georg privately. Along with several others, he followed to listen.

"I have long had an interest in geography," Christof told the small group. "I have a set of maps with me and at least some knowledge of ocean navigation. I charted our course for the voyage, and for several days I've been confused by our lack of progress. I thought I must have made the wrong calculations. But now I understand. We're off course. It's a lie that we've had unfavorable winds. I believe Petrov is purposely taking us on a longer route. Now we know why—to force us to buy his food at outrageous prices."

"What should we do? We can't continue like this, or more people will die," said Johann, echoed by others.

Georg spoke first. "We must somehow confront the captain; tell him we know what he's up to. Demand that he right the ship on the route to St. Petersburg. If we don't, we could be at sea for weeks more."

The first mate's whistle sounded, ominous and ill-timed. "All passengers will remain below deck for the remainder of the voyage by captain's orders." The sailor quickly retreated, slamming and locking the door behind him.

Georg's usually strong voice faltered. "Petrov also told us today he will no longer meet with us." Now they understood why.

*L*ater that day, crew members removed the overhead grate covering the cargo hatch just long enough to lower provisions. A seemingly generous act, providing food and water so critical to survival, Rein thought with disgust. This method assured the passengers had no way to leave the hold and confront the captain. Determined to break out, Rein and Johann stacked barrels and climbed atop to study the crew's movements through the metal grate. By the next morning, they had a plan, agreed to by Georg. But they needed Amila's help.

Rein and Johann found her sitting by their shared trunk, Eva napping by her side. "Amila, can we speak with you?" Johann asked Amila softly, motioning for her to come alone. Raising an eyebrow, she followed them to an area that afforded some privacy.

"Amila, you know the situation we're in, that we're at the captain's mercy and trapped down here?" Rein asked. She nodded. "Johann and I have a plan to break out, and Georg thinks it could work. We need your help."

Now they had her full attention. "Of course, I'll help! They can't hold us prisoner like this. What can I do?"

"Tonight, we'd like for you to climb to the top of the barrels, near the iron grate where the guard will be able to see and talk with you. We want you to talk to the sailor on duty. See if you can talk him into opening the door to the deck," Johann explained in his gentlest voice. He and Rein had discussed it, and both thought this request would be more acceptable coming from Johann.

Amila looked from one to the other. "What do you mean? And why are you asking this of me?"

"You know, talk with him, and flash that lovely smile I see from time to time." Johann seemed somewhat at a loss for words, unlike him. "What a woman does to get attention from a man, tease him, charm him. Pretend to be interested. Ask if he will open the door and allow you to come to the deck for some night air and to... pass the time with him."

Amila shrugged. "But why would he open the door for me?"

"Well, I've seen the way sailors look at you when we're above deck," Rein offered. "You have captured the attention of more than one crewman."

She backed away wide-eyed. "Oh, no! You don't mean for me to seduce him! How could you ask that?" She knew enough Russian to understand what crewmen were saying as they leered and bantered when she and other women were on deck.

"No, no, of course not! We just need for him to open the door so you can pretend to pass through. We'll be there, right beside you," promised Johann.

"You see, we watched last night, and we know they have only one sailor watching the hatch during the night and no one guarding the hold," explained Rein. "If we can get on deck, we can make our way to the captain while most of the crew is asleep. We've talked to Georg, and he agrees to the plan. You see, Amila, we're desperate, or we wouldn't ask this of you. More passengers are weakening and will die if we're trapped here much longer."

Rein found the intensity of Amila's resulting stare unnerving and lowered his eyes. Finally, she responded. "All right. I'll try. But I have my pistol and a knife in my boot. I'll use them if necessary. And I don't have any idea how to pretend this way, so I better find out."

Amila stalked off to find Elisabeth and announced she had a delicate subject to discuss. Georg guessed what it might be, so he took the child and motioned for her to go. When Amila explained what she was being asked to do, Elisabeth placed her hands on Amila's shoulders in a motherly way. "Are you sure you can do this?"

"Yes, we must get out of here. I'll do it, but I don't know how. That's the problem. Johann told me to act this way, and I need guidance."

"Oh my, of course, my dear. Have you ever read a book or seen a play where a woman plays the coquet? It's more than smiling. I can give you some tips. Don't worry—you'll be very convincing."

Around midnight, Amila climbed atop the stack of barrels and sat where Rein and Johann had scouted the night before. The night was clear, and the moon shone through the metal grate of the hatch, allowing muted light to filter in. She caught the attention of the lone crewman guarding the hold.

"Good evening." Amila had opened the top few buttons on her bodice and held a fan to her face and neck. Her hair fell loosely around her shoulders. "It's so late. Everyone is asleep. It's still very hot, isn't it?" She leaned forward so the sailor could see the outline of her face and neckline as she balanced on top of the barrels.

"Oh, you're the one I've seen above deck, aren't you? The tall, pretty one with the long wavy hair? I've noticed you, I have." The sailor moved closer. "What is it you want?"

"I've noticed you as well. The most handsome of all the crew. I just want to feel the night air. I can't sleep, like everyone else. If only there were a breeze." Amila fanned her face and neck furiously with one hand while lifting the hair off her neck with the other. "It's so lonely down here. Would it be possible for me to come to the deck for some night air, to pass some time with you?" This time she licked her lips and smiled at him while loosening another button on her dress, more tips from Elisabeth.

The sailor's response came more rapidly than she expected. "Crawl down from there and meet me at the door to the hold. But be quiet. Don't wake anyone."

Amila climbed down, falling several feet off the last two barrels and cursing under her breath that she'd made too much noise. Limping slightly, she appeared at the door as quickly as she could, where the sailor could see her through metal bars of the tiny window. He unlocked and pushed the heavy door open. Appearing rapidly from the side of the doorway, Rein grabbed the sailor by the shoulders and pulled him inside, while Johann quickly passed through and up the staircase to make sure they hadn't been detected. The surprised crewman was bound and gagged.

Rein glanced back at Amila and swallowed hard before averting his eyes. He joined Johann and the small band of armed volunteers now gathered at the top of the stairs. Knowing a full watch of sailors would be aloft and a helmsman at the ship's wheel, Georg led the delegation roundabout to the captain's cabin, recalling the location from previous meetings. They passed crewmen asleep in hammocks, some snoring loudly. As far as they could see, no sentries were posted near Petrov quarters. When they reached the door, it was locked, as expected. Johann and Rein put their shoulders to it, and it gave on the second try.

They found Petrov slumped over his table, an empty glass and bottle of vodka nearby. While guards watched the door, Rein grabbed him by the collar and shook him, awakening Petrov to the sobering presence of unwelcome guests and a loaded pistol aimed at his head.

CHAPTER 8

August 1763

$\mathcal{F}$or the next two days, Rein and Johann guarded Petrov day and night, wielding guns to assure the crew didn't attempt a rescue. Crewmen scowled when their captain first appeared on deck held at gunpoint. But the crew knew what their superior had been up to. They had grumbled among themselves that sailing in circles in the Baltic Sea put no extra jingle in their pockets. After that, the first mate efficiently navigated the ship toward St. Petersburg, and the crew's behavior was genial for the rest of the trip.

Rein was amused by the colonists' treatment of the sailor whom Amila enticed to open the door to the hold—he was being hailed as a hero and basked in the notoriety. The sickest passengers improved rapidly when immediately brought on deck to breathe fresh air. Food was handed out free of charge.

Once Petrov gave orders to turn the ship back on course, it had taken only two days to reach the island harbor at Kronstadt, the Russian naval base near St. Petersburg. From his post at the captain's side, Rein watched the crew maneuver the *Elephant* close to the dock under sail, then throw heaving lines to soldiers waiting to help secure the ship to the dock.

Colonists crowded on deck as the ship approached land, falling silent at the sight of the imposing stone fortress that guarded the Russian sea lanes to St. Petersburg. The fortress overpowered the tiny island, but it was land nonetheless, and cheers rang out when docking was complete.

Georg and the other leaders were uncertain what the consequences might be for taking the vessel's skipper captive. But charges against Petrov were clearly more severe—imprisoning passengers in the hold, resulting in loss of lives, and deviating from the route in the interest of personal financial gain from inflated food prices. Not knowing who they would report the charges to once onshore, Georg demanded and received a full refund for the food they had been forced to buy from the captain, and drafted letters stating the grievances, which Petrov eventually signed. The letter was addressed to both the Russian ambassador in Lübeck and his counterpart in St. Petersburg, whom they had not yet met but believed would be sympathetic to their cause.

With docking complete and a ramp in place, a group of surly, bearded soldiers wearing dark green uniforms boarded the ship, rifles in shoulder straps and sabers sheathed at their belted waists. Rein and Johann stepped clear of Petrov, weapons out of sight.

"Greetings, Captain Petrov. I assume you had a pleasant voyage? I'm here to make sure your ship carries no contraband. As is the routine, we will oversee the unloading of cargo. What is your cargo this trip?" Hearing a foreign tongue made Rein uneasy. He and

Johann exchanged nervous glances from their position behind Petrov.

Fluent in both German and Russian from frequent naval trade between the two countries, the captain responded to the officer in the local language.

Amila stood on deck near Christof, Georg, and his family. She moved closer and listened carefully to the exchange. Then, turning toward Rein and Johann, she began to translate words she could understand. "The conversation isn't about you. It's about the ship's cargo. They want to inspect it. Petrov is agreeing. I can't understand it all. It's the first time I've heard Russian spoken so rapidly."

Rein and Johann gaped open-mouthed. Christof smiled and tipped his hat. Georg shouted, "Bravo, Amila!"

"It's not cargo at all, but passengers." Petrov swept his arm across the deck full of people. "They're the first colonists invited by Empress Catherine to settle here. Given the waiting list in Lübeck, many shiploads will follow."

The captain and officer continued their conversation privately as they walked toward the ramp. Seeing no sign of betrayal, Rein breathed a sigh of relief. He and Johann made their way toward the hold and gathered their belongings. Once back on deck, Rein and Eva entered the long line to disembark, just behind Amila and the Müller family.

Several passengers leaned over the ship's side where a woman in a dinghy had approached and was trying to steady her wooden boat while holding food for them to see. It was clear she was trying to sell them something. Amila tried a few words of the difficult language aloud and smiled when she finally understood. The woman was offering fresh *kalachi*—small, sweet breads. Hungry for fresh food, colonists bought all she had. Eva handed one to a nearby soldier, who hungrily snatched up the delicacy.

"Lord God have mercy on me!" he exclaimed and crossed himself three times before eating it. Amila cast a confused look toward the soldier and at the woman in the dinghy. The woman laughed. "Oh, it's nothing to worry about. All Russians say that before they eat." Amila translated for passengers, and their laughter lightened the mood during the long wait to disembark.

Bolstered by the cool ocean breezes, Amila waited patiently to exit the ship's ramp. Once ashore at the naval station, they suffered through another painstakingly slow process, registering as colonists.

"Spell the name, and very slowly, please," Amila heard the clerk say in German with a heavy Russian accent as she and the Müllers progressed through the line. The clerks told her they worked for the Russian Chancery of Oversight of Foreigners. Their job was to create detailed lists with each colonist's city, state, and country from which they came, as well as occupation, age, and members in each family.

Amila backed away, realization buffeting her like a freezing gust of wind. "I can't. I can't do this."

"What do you mean?" Georg was puzzled. "Have you changed your mind about coming here?"

Her mind raced. "No, no, it's just that I don't have official travel documents. I'm afraid it may be a problem."

"Well, what do you have?" whispered Georg, looking over at Elisabeth, who shrugged her shoulders at Amila's hesitation.

"I'm what the ambassador called an unaccredited colonist. We arrived in Lübeck and left within a fortnight. There was no time to procure a proper passport."

"You need not worry, Amila," Georg assured. "When we boarded in Lübeck, I registered you with us on the ship's log, listing your name alongside ours. There was no problem then, and I don't know why it should be a problem now."

Elisabeth took Amila's arm in the crook of her own. "I'm sure you have nothing to worry about."

Amila's knees felt weak. Two easy trails for Tundorf to follow, the ship's log in Lübeck and registration lists here. Amila tried to remain calm. But she wondered if the Müllers could see through her attempted self-restraint. Amila glanced back at Rein, who stood close enough in line to hear. She pulled her cloak tight around her shoulders and smiled at Christof, hoping to disguise the depth of her fear.

*W*aves tossed the wooden rowboat in which Rein and Eva sat shoulder to shoulder with eight other passengers, the first to travel the short distance from the island port to the Russian mainland. Recalling seasickness on the voyage, passengers waiting their turn on the dock began to mill about nervously.

Six Russian sailors waited silently in each of the three sturdy rowboats. As soon as colonists filled the boats, the rowers began pulling toward shore. Rein admired the way the sailors worked in unison to propel the boat through the swirling waves, sometimes using long, powerful strokes, then shortening strokes to accommodate the changing contours of the waves. At times the experienced rowers' blades barely dipped into the water as they angled the boat sideways into the wind, assuring it wouldn't capsize. It reminded Rein of ways he had honed his body to accomplish difficult farming tasks using hand tools and muscle power, not always afforded the luxury of a team of horses or oxen. Plowing, planting, harvesting, and threshing crops all required a finely-honed rhythm. His muscles too long at rest, Rein wished he could row back and forth with them and learn their techniques. The skills might come in handy if they settled near the sea, with its dangerous waves and currents. Before Rein was ready for the ride to end, but to the relief of fellow passengers being tossed about, they arrived at the shore, still somewhat dry. As soon as they stepped out of the boat, sailors pushed back into the waves for the next load.

"Where do we go now?" asked Eva, edging close to her brother.

He was unsure how to answer. They looked back toward the sea, where more colonists were approaching in boats, and peered forward toward the land that beckoned. A fierce reality greeted them, announced with certainty by the cool zephyr blowing toward shore. Rein filled his lungs and faced the land. He saw a foreign country where they neither spoke the language, knew the customs, nor knew what challenges lay ahead. Nearly a foot taller than his petite sister, he put a reassuring arm around her. "I don't know, Eva. But there's no turning back."

Once the final load of new arrivals reached shore, they were reunited with their meager belongings from trunks and crates brought ashore. Soldiers barked orders in the unrecognizable language. When no one moved, they motioned for passengers to climb into wagons, each pulled by two heavily muscled horses Rein found very curious, almost comical looking. With short legs, thick necks, and strong hindquarters, their capacity to pull heavy loads was immediately evident as the overflowing wagons lunged forward.

Rein studied the horses excitedly. "Eva, do you suppose we can get a team of horses like that? Think what they could do hitched to a plow."

"You are always the farmer," she laughed. "It should be high on our list if we wish to eat. But I'm most anxious to see what herbs grow wild and gather them before winter. How far do you think we have to travel in these wagons?"

Amila was riding in the same wagon, conversing with Christof, and overheard Eva's question. She leaned forward to ask the driver where they were going and engaged with him in her clumsy Russian for several minutes. "He says it will take an hour or two to reach a town called Oranienbaum, a small city near St. Petersburg. They've been told to take us to soldiers' barracks. We'll be quartered there." The passengers in the wagon immediately nodded at the word Oranienbaum, recognizing the German word for orange tree. Amila explained. "He says the city got its name for Empress Catherine's summer palace, for the greenhouses full of orange trees and other exotic plants. The soldier says the empress may even be there now."

"Would you ask if we may walk alongside the wagon instead of riding?" asked Rein, fidgeting uncomfortably. "After so long on the ship, I welcome the ground under my feet."

Following another exchange, the driver nodded while curiously eyeing the tall, broad-shouldered passenger who jumped off the wagon to walk instead of ride.

Amila had noticed Rein keeping clear of her since their arrival and wasn't surprised he'd rather walk than be near. Every time she and Eva were together, he strode away. She, too, preferred it that way, pleased to be near Eva, with whom she was becoming closer every day. The more distance from Rein the better, since they consistently seemed to irritate one another.

She resumed a comfortable banter with Christof, reflecting on the new landscape. They compared the hilly German countryside of home with the flat contours before them, agreeing this land had few admirable physical features, except for an abundance of tall pine trees. Eventually, they arrived at a line of long, poorly constructed wooden buildings that would be considered barns or huts at home. The wagons stopped, and passengers were told these were the military barracks where they would be housed. Dreary looking buildings with no windows, the doors were propped open to let in the summer breeze. Inside, they found bunks and little else. Weary from the eventful day and relieved to be free of the bowels of the ship, they moved possessions inside and awaited instructions.

Amila was surprised at the level of organization of the colonization effort thus far. Theirs was the first shipload of emigrants to arrive in Russia, yet the attempts to transport and house them seemed well thought out, though far from comfortable. It wasn't long until a German-speaking representative of the Russian government appeared and called colonists outdoors for the next step in their welcome, a message repeated in German at the door of each of the long, narrow buildings.

Once assembled, a tall, formally dressed man addressed them—again in German—in a bold, confident voice. "It is my honor to welcome you to Russia. I am Count Yuri Demidov. Empress Catherine has appointed me Commissar of the Guardianship Council for Foreigners. Tomorrow, the empress herself wishes to greet you at her summer palace." He paused, lifting his chin proudly as he moved stiffly from side to side.

"You will now be invited to the church of your choice to take the Russian oath of allegiance as our new citizens. At the entrance, my clerks will be issuing forage money and clothing. You will be provided with an allowance of 12 to 18 rubles, depending on the size of your family, and four rubles for single men."

The welcome ended as abruptly as it had begun. Amila did as she was told, huddling close to her adopted family as they moved forward in line. Georg signed and received the allowance money, peering at the foreign coins. Once again, they would all need to learn the value of a new currency, this time Russian rubles.

"May I ask, what is the purpose of our signatures?" Georg asked. The clerk looked at him with a blank stare— and then ignored the question. Amila restated the question in her broken Russian.

"Ah, you speak some Russian." The clerk's attitude shifted slightly, from disapproval to indifference. "We have been ordered to record each loan into account books. If you need clothing, an amount will be entered for the value of each item." The clerks were issuing shoes, stockings, hats, and a heavy, dark blue cloth they said was for kaftans.

"What loans?" Amila asked the clerk as accurately as she could in Russian.

"Each allowance is an interest-free loan, to be repaid to the Russian government in ten years." The clerk motioned them on.

"Were you aware of the loans?" Amila whispered to Georg, who shook his head. Since arriving, they had noted a consistent brusqueness in the clerks' treatment and responses, and some officials spoke a German dialect, some spoke only Russian. The colonists began passing information about the loans on to those next in line, who looked equally surprised. Many of the colonists were in dire need of clothing and shoes, especially for their children. Compared with their German lords' annual taxes and payments, ten years seemed like a lifetime to pay back a loan. After a quick discussion, Amila and the Müllers decided to accept all the items, especially the kaftan cloth, as it seemed of high quality for winter cloaks and a blanket for their child. They didn't know when the next opportunity to obtain clothing might come.

Once through the line, Georg led the Bremen group towards the Russian Orthodox Church, where colonists seeking a protestant church were directed. Some settlers they had met on the ship were Catholic. These delegations moved toward another building. Amila joined her fellow travelers gawking at the church's unique architecture. The sides of the multiple-storied wooden building were of log cabin-like layers painted white. Affixed on the high, slanting roof were three onion-shaped domes of shingled wood, tapering to points and topped by crosses.

Inside, they crowded into an empty chamber able to accommodate large groups. A German-speaking pastor, again with a Russian accent, addressed the colonists, packed shoulder to shoulder. "I ask you to declare your oath of allegiance to Russia. You will repeat after me. Please state your name. He divided the oath into sentences the colonists could easily repeat.

'I swear that, by taking the citizenship of Russia, I will observe the laws of the Russian Empire and the rights and freedoms of its citizens;

That I will fulfill my duties as a citizen of the Russian Empire for the welfare of the state and society;

That I will protect the freedom and independence of the Russian Empire; and that I will be loyal to Russia.'"

Amila glanced nervously at her fellow colonists. It appeared she wasn't the only person hesitating to take a vow of loyalty to a country she knew nothing about and felt no kinship with. She followed the lead of many near her, who simply moved their lips. She wondered if, like her, some felt the time would come to return to Germany. That was one of the promises in the manifesto—the assurance colonists could return to countries of origin at any time.

Filing out of the church to make way for the next group, a heavy silence hung in the air. Flashing back through the day's momentous events, Amila felt alternating waves of physical exhaustion, excitement, and bewilderment. What had she and her companions gotten themselves into?

*E*arly the next morning, Eva plopped down on the bunk where Amila slept near the Müllers. "Could it really be true? Do you think the queen of all Russia will greet us today?" Waking colonists were abuzz with news they would be taken to the nearby summer palace where Empress Catherine would welcome them.

Last evening, she and Eva had found a private area with other women and children to wash and change. Then they ate delicious fresh food sold by venders who had gathered nearby, knowing the new visitors had rubles to spend. They feasted on boiled fish, bread and butter, and sliced carrots. Amila learned that four rubles, her share of the allowance the Müllers received, would buy a great deal of food. She still had German kreuzer and shillings, and Georg was already inquiring about exchanging it for Russian currency.

Amila had told no one she kept her most prized possessions, her mother's jewelry, concealed in pockets sewn into her dresses. She knew the jewels were worth a great deal, but they meant more to her as keepsakes, and she hoped never to part with them. Her other source of income was several guldens, gold coins worth much more than kreuzer, taken from the Tundorf's desk the night she left the castle. She felt no qualms—the money was hers from the estate, and she hadn't taken it all, just what she could conceal in her clothing.

Eva floated out the door as colonists were called to gather. As boldly as he had the previous day, Commissar Demidov appeared to address the colonists. However, this time he was accompanied by a troop of soldiers, who stood at attention near the wagons. "I bring wonderful news. The empress wishes to address you. Soldiers are here to take you to the summer palace."

Food and rest had replenished the travelers. The prospect of seeing the German-born empress was almost too much to comprehend. After all, it was she who had brought them to this new country, was willing to feed and clothe them, and give them land, when no one else would. Amila glanced about at the colonists' beaming faces. Most were half-starved peasants who had barely survived seven years of war. They'd been treated as lowborn servants all their lives. Like Rein and Eva, most had never traveled beyond the boundaries of the manor where they were born and to which they were shackled. Swathed in hope and bound together by the belief that a better life awaited, they rushed to fill the wagons as if in a dream from which they didn't wish to awaken.

As the wagons approached the summer palace, undercurrents of nervous excitement stirred the air. Amila asked the driver to tell them what he knew about Empress Catherine.

"Ah yes, the princess became empress only a year ago, when her husband died somewhat suddenly. There was some turmoil, but now the country is united behind her," he chose the words carefully. When he continued, it was with sincere respect and admiration. "Czarina Catherine has captured our hearts! Even though she came to us from Germany, she is empress of all the people, even a lowly soldier like me. How do we know this? It is with pride that we recite the words greeting visitors at her palace entrance: the sign says, 'Your pretense of birth, pride, or other sentiments must be left at the door.' We feel she is mother to all of us, and yet a mother who rules with a firm hand."

Amila translated as best she could, eliciting a respectful silence from the riders. As the wagons entered the grounds surrounding the palace, whispers ensued as if approaching a reverent place.

"This is what heaven must look like," uttered Eva. "There must be hundreds of windows and rooms, just on this side." Elisabeth, seated beside Amila, whispered, "In all my life, I never thought I'd see anything so grand!"

Amila had seen drawings of the French palace of Versailles and other luxurious residences for Europe's royalty, and this must be as grand. No drawing could prepare her for the scale of the summer residence. The massive stone palace was painted pale yellow and trimmed in white. The center building stood several stories high with wings of rooms that stretched in each direction beyond their view. At the center, a wide marble staircase divided two levels of terraces to a balcony large enough to hold hundreds of people.

Their wagons passed over a bridge covering a canal, then halted along an avenue near manicured gardens decorated with fountains and sculptures. Once colonists were out of wagons, Commissar Demidov hastily moved from group to group, arranging the guests in rows by colony. At the head of each group, he positioned the colony's elected vorsteher. Children fidgeted impatiently, hushed by their parents as the wait continued.

After what seemed like an endless length of time, Empress Catherine sauntered into view, strolling along the avenue, followed protectively by a royal procession of attendants.

Never having seen a queen, the colonists gawked in awe at the young empress. Amila stood behind Georg, near enough to study every detail of the czarina's appearance. The diminutive empress wore a dress of pale gold, embroidered with beads and pearls and adorned by a royal blue sash that accentuated her tiny waist. Her jewels—gold and pearl earrings and necklace—matched jewels on her dress and those woven in her hair, which was piled high and made her appear taller. Amila knew all too well about wide petticoats, but the pannier side hoops underneath this gown made it almost as wide as it was high. The gathered ruched sleeves created a sort of ruffle from the shoulder to the top of the wrist. Amila had seen the same type of sleeves on blouses worn by Russian peasant women. They conveyed a quaintness, perhaps for the empress to identify with her subjects, including the poor colonists before her. But it wasn't the attire that most impressed Amila; it was the sense of authority the young woman radiated, every attribute fortifying her rightful position as queen of an empire.

Head held high and shoulders back — the empress emanated confidence. She exchanged bows with the colonists, stopping before Georg, who was positioned as their group leader. In her native German, she asked him about their shared homeland and his occupation, for which he stammered replies, nearly overcome by the occasion. She presented her hand for him to kiss before moving forward to the next group.

Standing near Georg, Amila was close enough to hear the young queen lean over and converse in Russian with a well-dressed man beside her.

"I find myself in possession of large tracts of virgin land along the lower course of the Volga River," she told him, likely believing no colonists could understand. "It is my plan to turn this region into productive agricultural land, as well as to populate the area as a protective barrier against the nomadic tribes who inhabit the region. You know as well as I do that it has been attempted before. I wish these people well and will help provide for them insofar as I can."

Able to understand the substance of her words, Amila kept her eyes lowered out of respect and feeling a bit guilty for eavesdropping on the private conversation of a monarch. Surprised she was so much taller than the empress, Amila wondered how one so tiny could convey such an intimidating presence. Empress Catherine's demeanor seemed thoughtful and friendly. Yet Amila felt a strong desire to back away.

More boldly and with a sweep of her arms to both her royal entourage and the colonists, the empress concluded, "From these people, I hope for both economic progress and above all cultural progress for the backward people whom I rule."

Once she had greeted the leader of each colony, Catherine addressed the first colonists in a regal voice befitting a queen.

"Dear children! You are the first to come from my native land to another country, to our State. The places where you lived were doubtlessly holy to you. Nature, the love of your princes, and state oversight made them so for you. And this country to which you, kind children, have come will be made for you just as dear and holy.

Having invited you to Our Empire, under our protection, I greet you: Welcome! My love for the German people has caused me to invite Germans to our country from abroad, to warmly accept them and care for them. You responded to my invita-

tion and, in the hope of God and My protection, came here. Be assured that all that is promised will be delivered for you and all of our descendants' lives.

You, in your turn, dear children, must respond to this with love, truth, and devotion, as instructed by our state laws. Be industrious and diligent in all your undertakings and thoughtful and sympathetic to all who serve you. We have decisively resolved to protect you. May the Almighty protect you and your descendants!"

Amila studied the beaming faces of her fellow colonists, gazing transfixed as the address ended. A moment later, with a raise of the empress' hand, servants opened baskets and cast out handfuls of rubles over the heads of the emigrants. As the paper currency rained down, the astonished colonists hurried to collect their share. Roars of gratitude shattered the silence. Standing apart, Amila reeled as the disturbance sent birds careening from the nearby trees.

*R*eturning to the barracks, Rein heard hymns of praise mingled with laughter and excited chatter as colonists relived moments spent in the presence of royalty. He felt hopeful, but ingrained mistrust of nobility left him wary. Showering peasants with money? He had never heard of such a thing. But still, he had picked up his share.

Commissar Demidov's carriage followed the caravan of wagons returning to their lodgings, and he wasted no time calling the colonists together outside the barracks to listen once more. This time he was accompanied by a formally dressed man Rein had seen standing in the crowd during the ceremony. He was a thin, somber man who seemed to be scanning the crowd nervously.

"My dear citizens, now that you have received the blessing of our empress, your journey can continue." The commissar's voice boomed above the noisy crowd. "I want to share with you plans for the next step in your journey. You'll soon leave by wagon, then travel on the river to settle in the beautiful farming region of the lower Volga River. It may not be possible to arrive there before winter, and if that is the case, you'll stay with villagers until spring. With more settlers arriving here by ship every week, and winter approaching, you are to leave immediately."

High spirits melted to murmurs of surprise and then protest. Shouts of disagreement echoed throughout the crowd. Several men came forward to express their objections. "You can't mean all of us. Perhaps only those who wish to become farmers? We were told we could settle anywhere we wanted. Many of us are bound for St. Petersburg, where German tradesmen live. We are not farmers. We are tradesmen!"

Demidov stood firm. "Empress Catherine has decided what Russia needs now more than anything are farmers to settle in the Volga River region near Saratov. Those of you who wish to go there will leave without delay. I suggest that if you are a tradesman, you practice your trade there, in addition to farming. Otherwise, you'll stay here, housed in the conditions you see before you."

"Then we'll return to Germany!" yelled the spokesman, supported by a chorus of cheers.

"I'm afraid we don't have ships to send you back to Germany or other countries." The commissar said calmly as if prepared for the unruly response. "If you refuse to go to the Volga colonies, you'll simply have to remain here in the barracks all winter, perhaps even longer, in very crowded conditions."

"Are we to be your prisoners then?" shouted Georg. The crowd fell silent.

"My soldiers are here to protect you and to make sure you follow the laws you have embraced as new Russian citizens."

The stunned colonists gaped at one another as though waking from a familiar nightmare. "This is betrayal!" a man in the back row yelled.

The commissar ignored the accusation. With a nod of his head, he summoned a column of armed soldiers to join him at the front of the crowd as if nothing untoward had occurred. "On your way to the Volga, you'll be provided with money for board until you reach your destination. Those who go will receive all funds necessary for fares and expenses for an entire year, at least until your first harvest."

He rushed on amidst the mumbling, angry stares and clenched fists. "I wish to introduce you to the government official who will oversee the colonization program on the Volga. His name is Chancellor Ivan Grekov. He'll lead the Chancery of Oversight of Foreigners, or Kontora office, in the frontier city of Saratov. Chancellor Grekov will travel ahead of you to Saratov, where he'll make preparations for your arrival." Grekov bowed slightly then quickly stepped back.

Demidov spoke loudly to pacify the wary crowd. "Each family will be given horses, livestock, wagons, harness, a variety of farming tools, and seeds. Tracts of land will be assigned to each family, which you will own and pass on to heirs." The commissar instructed soldiers to hand out printed sheets listing inventory to be issued to farmers once they traveled to Saratov then on to land set aside for colonies. Among muttering voices, hands reached for the flyers.

Rein studied the list with great interest, relieved it was printed in German. Titled "Provisions for the Volga Frontier Colonies," it listed:

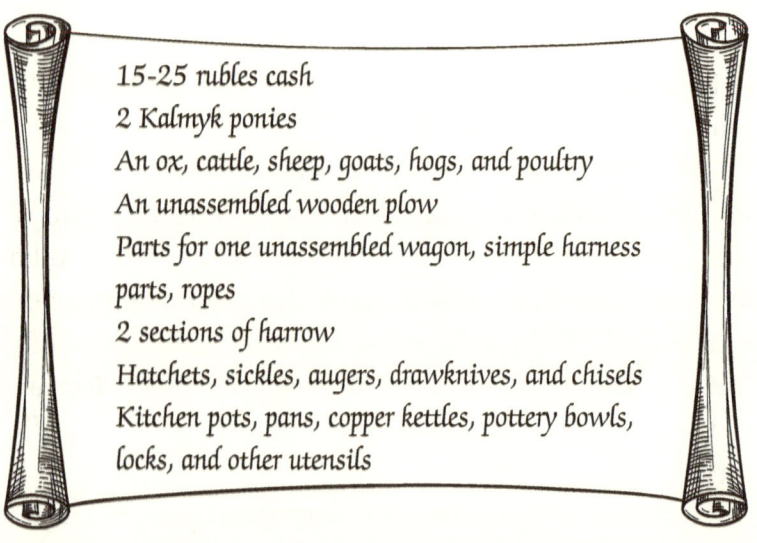

15-25 rubles cash
2 Kalmyk ponies
An ox, cattle, sheep, goats, hogs, and poultry
An unassembled wooden plow
Parts for one unassembled wagon, simple harness parts, ropes
2 sections of harrow
Hatchets, sickles, augers, drawknives, and chisels
Kitchen pots, pans, copper kettles, pottery bowls, locks, and other utensils

Rein scanned the crowd, observing widespread misery coupled with irate whispers. For the first time, he realized why farmers were in such demand by recruiters. This was the empress' plan all along. Betrayal softened by bribery in the form of gifts—rubles thrown to the crowd and free farming implements. Compared with the farm equipment and livestock back home, this list seemed a good start, though sorely incomplete. The experienced farmers could make do. But what of the tradesmen who had no knowledge of farming and, worse, no wish to learn?

"Tomorrow, you'll receive details pertaining to the rest of your journey. You must now return to your barracks," finalized the commissar. With another nod, the soldiers disbursed, but not until they had safely escorted him and Grekov to the carriage from which they had emerged.

Rein joined the Bremen colonists already gathered, berating their leader for this shocking development. Georg explained he was surprised as well, asserting he had no prior knowledge of such deception. Like Rein, some who intended to farm were more accepting, but most were dumbfounded. Tradesmen forced to farm? And all colonists to be forcibly sent to the Volga frontier when they had been promised freedom to settle wherever they chose? Rein took a step back and listened, trying to absorb what this meant to him as well as to the people with whom he had committed to start a new life.

The small village of Nassenwald where Rein grew up had few true tradesmen. The isolation of the village and widespread poverty required the villagers to be self-reliant. Almost everything they needed, they made, grew, or raised. They built their own cottages, made their own furniture, clothing, and tools, plowed and planted the land, raised their livestock for food, and hunted and fished if they could do so without getting caught. His village had a few tradesmen with specific skills, such as a blacksmith, a wheelwright, a leatherier, and a schoolmaster. But at harvest, these tradesmen stopped their work to help farmers in the field, earning a share of the crop to feed their families.

Expert craftsmen from Bremen and other cities honed very specialized skills, where middle- and upper-class residents were able to pay for their services. On the journey here, Rein had talked with some of these men—a pewterer, bricklayer, and a weaver—and Rein was impressed with their knowledge and dedication. But they admittedly had no knowledge of farming and no desire to learn, as Rein heard now. He knew how physically demanding farming could be and wondered how a new colony would fare with few experienced farmers and the rest forced into the profession under protest.

Deep down, Rein should have known they had been lured to Russia by promises that would be impossible to fulfill. He shook his head in disgust and made a vow to pay more mind to the inner voice he'd trusted many times in his life but had ignored with the urgent decision to emigrate to Russia. Now, they would be rapidly diverted to the Volga frontier, a mysterious place they knew little about. A weight suddenly descended as he listened to woes expressed by the craftsman—he and the few experienced farmers would be responsible for feeding this throng of settlers in the wilderness.

Volga River Region
Russian Empire 1763

Area Shown

German States

St. Petersburg

Veliky Novgorod

Tver

Moscow

Ryazan

Kazan

Penza

Petrovsk

Samara

Saratov

Dobrinka

Kamyshin

Astrakhan

Caspian Sea

CHAPTER 9

August-November 1763

*T*undorf smirked as Ebald and Axel dragged the man from Donauwörth into the stable. Still furious he'd been fooled into believing Amila had stolen away to the British Colonies in America, he had waited weeks to find an outlet for his anger. Once he realized they'd laid a false trail, he took out his frustration on the few serfs who remained, as well as a servant girl he'd found to be quite vulnerable. Of course, the stableman, Johann Heft, had been a part of the deception, sending his guards in the wrong direction that very morning when his guards could so easily have intercepted them if they'd gone north. Then the lying wretch had made off with his horses and another family, undoubtedly following Amila's escape route. He'd sent his guards to Donauwörth to covertly inquire about who Amila had really met with there, ultimately finding the man before him, the Russian recruiter. Now he'd find out where they had gone. And this time, he'd make sure to extract the truth.

"Who are you? And where did you send my stepdaughter Lady Amila Wallerstein and my serfs?" asked the count, the point of his knife at the man's throat.

"My name is Gunter Rohlwagen. And please, put down the knife. I'll tell you whatever it is you want to know," he volunteered, expressing his unwillingness to take a beating, or worse, for what he'd done. "I'm under no orders to keep the transactions a secret."

The two guards had approached him at the same tavern in Donauwörth under the guise of becoming Russian colonists. Once they learned Gunter was who they were seeking, they bound and gagged him and threw him in the back of a wagon, heading for the castle.

"How do I know you'll tell the truth?" the count demanded.

"I keep a list of the colonists recruited for Russia. I'm paid for each man, woman, and child who boards a ship in Lübeck. I go there occasionally to meet with the Russian ambassador and collect my money. If he registers them as settlers, then I receive payment for them. If you'll untie me, I'll show you," he pleaded, meekly looking up at the hovering men.

"Untie him." The count sheathed his knife but pulled out his pistol, standing back but aiming it at Gunter's head.

The recruiter carefully pulled several sheets of linen rag paper out of a pocket and began looking for specific names on the sheets. "I remember them well. They were nervous, especially the man. Here it is: Reinhardt was his name. And two young women. Lady Amila, what a beauty! I met with them several times."

The count grabbed the list and read the names carefully logged alongside the date. Reinhardt Lundgren. Eva Lundgren. Amila Wallerstein. He looked through the list for more of his serfs and found the name Johann Heft and another Heft family, likely related to his stableman.

He mumbled, realizing he didn't remember the names of most of the manor's serfs and threw the pages back at Gunter.

He slapped the recruiter with the back of his hand and signaled for his lackeys to grab him again. "Take this deplorable crook to the estates of the other nobles in the region and show them his wretched lists. Then beat him within a breath of his life, and dump what's left in the river."

Gunter spoke up for himself, declaring his innocence. "You must know I have the protection of the Russian empress and her ambassador in Germany. That being the case, what I'm doing is legal. It's much like when princes sell serfs to the army. So go ahead, send me to the princes. I've handled many transactions for them. I know them well."

The count punched the restrained man in the face, kneed him in the groin, then turned away in disgust.

Striding back to the castle, the count shook off the encounter and considered options. He now had the information he needed. There must be a solution—he'd faced more difficult challenges. He mentally reviewed the predicament. With the war over, his job with the Prussian War Office had ended. Even the substantial double payments from France and Prussia for delivering his serfs' supplies last fall weren't enough to free him from looming debts. All his sources of income had halted, and most of the remaining serfs were too old or sick and hard-pressed to make the drought-stricken land yield and pay the rents necessary to maintain his lifestyle.

Red-faced, he sat down heavily behind his desk, recalling Amila's escape and the resulting humiliation from the Duke of Zweibrücken. His stomach churned at the longer-term concern Amila's absence created. Without her, he no longer had an official claim to her lands. He knew of distant relatives who could legitimately petition for the property and its income. If Amila were to alert them, he could be cast out altogether. He put his head in his hands and massaged his pounding temples, determined to stop punishing himself with such negative possibilities. Amila was just a stupid girl who lacked the wherewithal to know she had any power over him.

The other lords in the region must be as desperate as he. Given the number of names on the recruiter's list, their serfs were also deserting. Although the lords wouldn't readily admit it, he guessed they were in similar financial circumstances. The princes ruled their own fiefdoms across Germany with no central oversight. It infuriated Tundorf, but he knew what the recruiter said about his activities was true. It wasn't illegal because no universal laws were in place across the German provinces barring serfs from emigrating. But for generations, each manor's serfs knew they were bound to the land and their lords. How dare they desert him!

$\mathcal{T}$he count quickly scanned the letter he'd been awaiting for weeks. He threw his glass of port across the room and watched it shatter against the stone wall. Imbeciles! Weeks wasted, and another failed strategy. Knowing time was of the essence to intercept the serfs, Tundorf had taken action to demand their return. Under his leadership, the princes had sent a joint letter beseeching Prussian King Frederick to issue an edict forbidding Russia from further recruitment in the Prussian states and insisting that Russia return German serfs to their lords.

One of the most powerful princes had delivered the request, and Tundorf held in his hand the prince's deflating response. King Frederick was sympathetic, dealing with a similar exodus among citizens from all parts of his far-flung kingdom. However, the king referenced the sensitive political situation he was in, precisely because Russia had played a critical role in helping Prussia win the war. King Frederick said he had already communicated strong displeasure about the colonization program to the young empress and asked her to halt it, to no avail. Empress Catherine had responded that she intended to continue and even expand the manifesto's reach until Russia's vacant lands were adequately filled with German and other European settlers.

Enraged by the news, Tundorf called for his carriage and ordered one of the few house servants remaining to pack a bag. Over the next few weeks, the count would meet secretly with the region's princes, one by one, to solicit their support for a bold plan. If the king would do nothing to help, then they'd take matters into their own hands. He would enlist the princes' support to take whatever covert action was necessary to ensure the Russian colonies failed. Then the serfs would come crawling back, and no more would dare desert their lords.

$\mathcal{A}$ caravan of forty fully outfitted wagons, each pulled by a team of two stocky Kalmyk horses, lumbered along the streets of St. Petersburg, embarking on the long journey southeast to Saratov. Residents of the Russian capitol stopped to stare at the seemingly endless procession. Along with most members of the newly combined groups of colonists, Amila fought anxiety created by the forced orders. Every jolt of the wagon took her farther from Nassenwald, reducing her chances of confronting Tundorf and regaining her estate. She still felt the biting sting of Commissar Demidov's command to leave immediately for the Volga region and forget returning to Germany. She laughed inwardly at the idea that she, too, was expected to become a farmer.

It was early August, but Amila noted a chill in the air, unlike this time of year in Germany. Before departing, soldiers issued heavy winter clothing, boots, blankets, and cooking pots and utensils to each family, preparing them for the long journey.

The commissar had returned several times to make more pronouncements, reinforcing the empress' plan to expeditiously send all settlers to the Volga River region. Two more ships full of Europeans had arrived the past week, were registered, and given the oath of citizenship as rapidly as the Bremen group. These newly arrived colonists were combined with Müller's group to comprise one large contingent of settlers but were separated to travel to Saratov by two different routes—the Bremen colonists were among the half traveling the 7,000 *verst*, or about 1,000 miles, by the overland route to Saratov. The wagons would pass through Russian towns and cities with curious names—Novgorod, Tver, Moscow, Ryazan, Penza, and Petrovsk—before finally arriving in Saratov for the winter. The other group of colonists would travel a slower route by water on barges, the last segment of which would include a portage 200 miles to the headwaters of the Volga, where they would float the remaining distance to Saratov.

Amila recalled the meeting of the newly formed leadership group for the combined colony. Georg Müller had resisted but been elected leader, nevertheless. He led the vorstehers in a discussion to confront the new reality being forced upon them—not really a choice—to remain here for the winter in crowded conditions with little or no hope of returning to their home countries, or travel to the Russian frontier. Not invited to participate, Amila lingered close enough to overhear the discussion.

"Isn't this just a new kind of oppression, exactly what we hoped to escape by leaving Germany?" lamented one of the new leaders.

Amila wondered if the oppression being forced on her by Count Tundorf was that different from the unjust tyranny these good people must now bear. Neither they nor she were free to pursue the life they sought. Her face began to redden in anger for all of them.

"How can we abide by these orders to become farmers when we were promised the freedom to settle wherever we wished and pursue our trades?" asked Lars Heckmann, a shoemaker who had been part of the new middle class in Bremen. "We were poor in Germany, but we were free to practice our crafts. What other lies have they told us?"

"I'm the son of a manufacturer. I learned factory work, but I know nothing of farming," added Christof. "I was educated as a geographer, and I want to travel, see the world and create maps. Not farm."

Amila's eyes turned toward Rein, as did many, eager to hear what a dedicated farmer had to say. "I must be honest with you—farming is a difficult life. Back home, we worked the fields every day—many days of the week for our master—but still, our families went hungry. Our crops were sold to pay huge taxes to our lord, debts we could never fully repay, no matter how hard we worked."

Johann nodded sadly. "The day before we escaped, our manor's lord held a hunt for all the region's princes. Our friends and the families in the village were forced to trample our own crops, walking through the fields to flush game for them to slaughter. Then the demon made us dress all the meat, more meat than we had seen on our tables in a year! And he gave it to the princes. They enjoyed a feast that night, which we prepared. We were left wondering how we would feed our families in the coming months."

Rein stepped confidently to the front of the group. "I live to work the land; it's in my blood. It must be how you feel about your trades. I agree this is a betrayal, and I can understand why you feel that way."

Chin raised and shoulders held high, Rein took a deep breath and continued. "On this journey, I've had much time to think, too much perhaps. I've made a decision for myself, though I do not ask this of you. But I'm at peace with it. Even with the lies and uncertainty of what we will face on this frontier, the life they offer is still better than my existence in Germany, no matter what my trade. I believe we can create a good life there."

"Aye," shouted Johann. "I'm here with my cousin and his family to escape the tyranny of the lords. If we're farmers here, with what they are offering, we'll be free and can at least feed our families from our own land."

From her vantage point, Amila observed subtle changes in the group, heads nodding slightly, a softening of facial expressions as the two young men's enthusiasm caught hold. She wondered—was it freedom that appealed to them or something broader, perhaps a yearning for adventure. Perhaps both.

Rein spoke up again. "Did you see the list of provisions we'll receive once we arrive? In my entire life in Germany, I might never have been able to own so much! And we have ten years with no taxes to repay our loans. We can be successful farmers with this start. I know we can. But by far, the most appealing part of the offer is this—I had lost hope of someday owning my own land. Now I believe I will." He shut his eyes and dipped his chin slightly before continuing. "And I don't wish to boast, but I know how to farm. For as many generations as I can remember, my family has tilled the soil. My father taught me, and he was very good at our trade. We farmers can teach you as well if you wish to learn."

Johann smiled. "Rein is as good a farmer as was Daniel, his father. I've seen the magic he works on the land to make it yield. He and the other farmers here will see that our families don't go hungry."

"The wisdom of your words is not lost on us," Georg said to both men, scanning the faces of the group. "Can we agree, then, that we are to become a colony of settlers headed for the Russian frontier—to farm?" He scanned faces and saw heads nod grudgingly. "Then what we must do is this: commit as leaders to believe in this, and show others a better life awaits. We will make every effort to succeed together."

Amila knew Rein and Johann's portrayal of their former life was true and that her stepfather, and others like him, were at fault. She believed it likely that serfs on the other princes' manors were treated equally egregiously. Given the likelihood that little was ever going to change under Tundorf's authority, Rein had good reason to feel optimistic about opportunities here. She shuddered to think what Rein would say and do if he learned the depth of the count's treachery. Would Rein's antagonism toward all nobles convict her as a co-conspirator? She turned toward the leaders, leaning forward slightly to hear what they would say next. She knew that women weren't supposed to participate in serious discussions, much like at the count's table. Recalling that harsh lesson brought discomfort, but surely no harm could come from listening now. When she caught Rein's eye, a scalding look informed her otherwise. His message was clear. *You're one of them, Amila. You have no right to be part of this.* She turned away and left.

Eva's excited voice summoned her back to the present and the bone-jarring movement of the wagon on stone-covered roads. At least Eva didn't hate her, too. That Amila couldn't bear. Eva pointed and gasped as they passed through the Russian capital of St. Petersburg and home of the queen and her government.

So unlike the German cities she had visited, Amila joined Eva in awe of this remarkable foreign city. Wagons traversed the endless streets, bridges, and canals of St. Petersburg bathed in summer. Amila told Eva what she remembered about the city from her studies: it was named for Czar Peter Alexeyevich, a ruler of Russia known for his modern reforms and efforts to bring European advances to his country. He had ordered the city to be built almost entirely of stone instead of wood construction commonly used in the country. They passed impressive palaces, a museum, a college for study and education, and cathedrals, all of which dwarfed the empress' summer palace in Oranienbaum.

Thinking back on Empress Catherine's speech, Amila wondered how it was possible for anyone, especially a woman, to wield so much power, and to use that power to initiate a massive colonization program and mobilize the resources to support it. It was as though the queen had spread a protective cloak around the shoulders of her colonists. But at the same time, the cloak seemed lined with doubt stemming from the manifesto's half-truths and newly discovered demands to do her bidding. As the distance between the colonists and the empress increased, would the lies be compounded to suit her goals? More importantly, could she extend the reach of her protective shield as they traveled a thousand miles from St. Petersburg? Amila shivered when the long line of wagons left the city at last and lumbered off into the countryside.

Once again, Amila found herself in the company of a Russian soldier driving the wagon in which she rode. She watched as the officer assigned to her group of wagons rode his mount back and forth to check on progress and keep the caravan moving.

Before leaving, Commissar Demidov introduced the colonists to the regiment's leader, Captain Misha Kachinov, who was in charge of the Russian military escort. Suspicious about anything Demidov now had to say, the colonists closely scrutinized the man. The tall, lean officer greeted the colonists with no words but instead used a formal tip of his *ushanka*, the sheepskin hat trimmed in fur and worn by every Russian soldier. Amila noticed the captain was older than his troops, perhaps the age her father would be had he survived. Captain

Kachinov had a neatly trimmed beard and mustache and wore a long tunic adorned with an insignia across his shoulders denoting his rank. The soldiers and officers in the regiment snapped to attention and saluted when their superior was introduced, clearly communicating who was in charge. Amila raised an eyebrow at the soldiers' brisk responses, wondering whether the show of discipline resulted from earned admiration or harsh leadership.

Prior to leaving, the commissar explained in German that food and water were to be supplied by the army, from whom colonists could buy items with their daily allowance, as much or as little as desired. Upon learning the captain and his soldiers spoke only Russian, colonists looked at one another in dismay. Unaware of anyone other than herself who had begun to learn their complex tongue, Amila realized that she needed to rapidly improve her language skills.

Having seen soldiers only at a distance in Germany, she wondered how colonists would get on with the troops. In her limited experience, military officers were arrogant young noblemen who strutted around in uniforms expecting privileges due to birthright. It was clear these soldiers and officers had been given strict orders regarding the treatment of settlers: they kept to themselves, making little eye contact, as if the colonists were merely cargo to be delivered to a far-flung location.

She sensed an urgency from the officers hustling wagons forward. The colonists had been informed it would take at least two months to reach the frontier outpost town of Saratov. Many of the army freight wagons were overloaded, filled with both provisions for the journey and farm supplies. To spare the teams of horses and increase the pace, Amila and her fellow colonists took turns walking beside the wagons. Oh, for a horse, thought Amila. To have Gabe on this journey would be heaven.

After traveling as far as possible each day, Captain Kachinov and his officers would confer and locate a large, grassy area to stop. The soldiers pulled the wagons into a circle for shelter and safety, with the center area providing a corral where the horses could graze. Amila eagerly wandered the nearby forest to gather wood for campfires while Eva searched for herbs, wild roots, and berries. Once started, the evening's campfires lit up the circle of wagons like a giant beacon. Soon, stews made from cured meat or wild game bubbled in pots, aromas beckoning families to gather around. Dried fruit and biscuits or porridge made from oats and wheat rounded out meals. Amila admittedly knew little about cooking, instead she watched over Elisabeth's young son to assure he didn't stray too close to campfires or horses. Children stretched their legs with games, and light-hearted banter filled the evenings. The weather was mild but cooling each day and most noticeably at night. Families slept huddled near the fires, the wagons too heavily loaded to provide shelter. The occasional nighttime rain shower sent families scrambling for cover under wagons.

Long travel days passed slowly and uneventfully, one day blending into the next. Although riding in the wagon was uncomfortable, Amila was curious about the new country, its people, and customs. So, each day during her turn in the wagon, she climbed into the seat beside the driver, who introduced himself as Pavel Mirnov. At first skeptical of her frequent appearances, in time, he seemed to realize the days passed more quickly with conversation. Pavel often snickered at Amila's clumsy use of Russian words and phrases. She bristled and asked him to instruct her, not make fun of her.

Amila was fascinated by the scenery. On her long rides in the home country, she had become familiar with the hilly woods of Nassenwald. She had since seen new regions of Germany on the journey to Lübeck. This landscape intrigued her, especially the trees that were unlike any Amila had seen before. Vast forests of tall, straight trees with green needles and giant wooden cones covered the landscape. At home, they would have been called pines, but Pavel called the forests *taiga* and said they covered much of the land they would be traveling through. He said they would encounter hills but no mountain ranges and many lakes, bogs, and rivers. The roads were worse than those of Germany, though Pavel told her they had been used for hundreds of years as trade routes.

One day, after talking for some time, Pavel shared information about his family and home. "My parents and four older brothers and I served a baron and worked the land. We worked very hard for our master many days every week—digging, planting, and harvesting crops. Then we worked for ourselves the rest of the time." Pavel fiddled with the reins and avoided her eyes. "We were very hungry, such a big family, never enough to eat. Winter is the worst. I got caught trapping animals for food, which is forbidden at any time. Under the empress' new laws, our masters have the right to punish us with exile to labor camps in Siberia. That is like a death sentence; it is so cold there. But I was lucky. Instead, my master sent me to the army. It's a good life. I have food to eat and a warm place to sleep in winter, although, I don't know where we will be this winter. Maybe Saratov, maybe somewhere else?"

Amila shivered, not from the thought of cold but thinking of the similarities between this Russian's life and that of German serfs so far away. But she was most shaken by the empress' harsh new law to punish Russian serfs. This was the same sworn protector of German and European emigrants whom she was giving land, provisions, and the right to govern themselves.

"It seems the empress can be as cruel to her own subjects as are the lords in our country," commented Amila. "Why is she offering so much to us? Payment to come here, supplies and livestock, land for our colony? Why wouldn't the empress do this for her subjects instead?"

Pavel shrugged. "We never question our rulers. We are born *muzhik*, peasants, and remain so all our lives. Of course, some runaways defy the nobles. It's the army's job to hunt them down. If we can find them, they are dealt with harshly."

Sore from hours of jarring impact on the wagon seat, Amila sought out Christof, who was attempting to etch details of the countryside despite the bumpy wagon ride. She asked if he'd like to walk with her a bit, and he willingly put down his materials and jumped off the wagon to join her. Remembering he had openly expressed his opposition to becoming a farmer, she wondered how he was coping.

"I haven't given up on becoming a mapmaker. In fact, I'm recording the terrain on the entire route to Saratov to see if it will be useful to the army. What about you, are you resigned to becoming a farmer? Or perhaps some lucky man's wife?"

Amila frowned. "Oh, not you too! I'm weary of being asked that. I successfully avoided that sort of trap before leaving home, but just barely."

"I see. I was wondering if you might be running from someone. But then, aren't we all? We're on quite an adventure, but something drove us all here to begin with—some unpleasant memory perhaps?" Christof looked off into the distance, deep in thought.

"I'm trying to leave a distasteful, um, situation behind. But in truth, I'm not sure what I'm doing *here*, in this place." Unwilling to share more, she asked Christof if he hoped to return home someday.

"Sadly, my father asked that I leave. And I'll be unable to return any time soon." He sighed. Walking next to her, he was able to avoid eye contact, which made confession a bit easier. "You see, I formed a liaison with a woman in Hanover. A dear lady whom I love and perhaps always will. But the match is impossible. Not only is she of a higher social status, but she is also married, although unhappily. When my father learned about the relationship, he demanded it cease. I told him my heart belonged to her, and I refused. According to my father, I disgraced my family, and he has disowned me. So you see, I must become a wealthy and famous cartographer. Then I can return."

"Oh, Christof, I'm so sorry. For me, it was just the opposite—I escaped a ghastly match being forced upon me." Amila stared ahead pensively. "I can't imagine being so much in love. What is it like?"

Christof coughed and cleared his throat. "Now that is a question for all time, milady! All I know for certain is love is a powerful force of nature—you can't do a thing to stop it, no matter how hard you may try. But only you can answer that question for yourself."

After many long, dusty days on the road, Amila succeeded in convincing Captain Kachinov to let the women find streams or lakes for bathing and washing clothes in the evenings. He agreed only if they took along several armed soldiers. Amila thought it a small price to pay for the luxury of being somewhat clean. The soldiers respectfully turned their backs when the women bathed in their underclothes in the cool, clear water.

Tonight, after bathing, the ladies were fortunate to find what they had begun to call *schwartzbeeren*, smooth black berries growing in brambles near streams and rivers. The small berries were tart. But simmered in a pot of boiling water with a bit of sugar and doughy dumplings, the dish had become a highly sought-after campfire meal. Fascinated by what she found growing in the woods, Eva stopped on the remote trails every few feet to gather wild herbs. Amila crouched low to the ground where the *schwartzbeeren* berries grew in clusters, pleased her plucking technique had improved. Elisabeth teased her at first—ever impatient, Amila would squeeze too hard and the fragile berries would burst, leaving her with a palm full of gooey seeds. They bent low, picking until darkness made it difficult to see even their hands. The soldiers had been urging them to finish and return to camp, using brusque Russian commands the women had come to understand but weren't always quick to obey.

As they finally started back toward camp, Amila heard a loud rustling in the thicket, accompanied by a deep growl. Soldiers nearby hurried toward the sound. Amila looked frantically in every direction for Eva and began to call her name, with no response. Louder and louder, she screamed Eva's name until it became a roar in her own ears. She heard a soldier's gun fire, followed by more shots exploding nearby. "No, please, not Eva!"

Hearing Eva's name called out in panic, then gunfire, Rein sprinted into the forest, followed closely by others. He found Eva unharmed, kneeling beside Amila, who was sprawled on the ground. Praising themselves for their sharpshooting, the soldiers nearby gathered around the body of a large brown bear, excited about the fresh meat and many rubles the pelt would bring.

"I was gathering herbs in the woods and got sepa-rated from everyone. I came as soon as I heard her call. I think she's all right," Eva told Rein as she examined her friend.

Rein hesitantly knelt to help. Eva leaned in close and could hear Amila's even breathing. "I don't see any signs of blood. Maybe she fainted from the shock."

"The way she screamed your name, she sounded terrified. She must have thought the bear was after you." Rein scooped up Amila's limp body and carried her the remaining distance to camp. He laid her down beside the campfire, where Elisabeth quickly appeared. Waiting a short distance away, he heard Eva and Elisabeth confirm Amila had fainted but was now awake and recovering.

Rein sighed and rolled his eyes. The other women didn't faint when they heard the bear and gunfire. He hurriedly left the campsite to join the soldiers busily skinning the bear. He had never seen a bear, although his father had told him the beasts used to roam forests near home. He couldn't help but wonder if these massive creatures might be found in the woods near their new home. If so, he better get a bigger rifle.

*I*n early September, Captain Kachinov announced they were more than halfway to Saratov. As they passed through the village of Tver, the wagons lumbered across a bridge covering a small, rapidly flowing river. The captain waited beside the bridge as each wagon passed, pointing repeatedly at the river, wanting to share something important with the colonists.

Amila did her best to translate his message. "He says these are the headwaters of the Volga, the great river that is our destination."

Rein and Johann looked at one another and shrugged, unimpressed, recalling rivers in Germany. "It looks more like a stream than a river," commented Johann.

Amila translated, and the captain shook his head briskly. "The Volga gathers strength from snowfall in the mountains and underground springs. Eventually, hundreds of tributaries feed Mother Volga. No one even knows how many. This is why the Volga is called the river of rivers. Wait until you see it when we reach Saratov. You will understand."

Days passed uneventfully as they continued to travel through the sparsely populated countryside. Then, as the wagon train crossed a stone bridge over the Moskva

River, the skyline of a large city loomed ahead. The line of wagons halted along an intimidating stone wall that stretched forward beyond view. A wide moat protected the wall. On the other side was a sprawling marketplace. Hearing Captain Kachinov deliver sharp orders to officers, Amila knew this was no ordinary stop on the journey. A thick sheet of anticipation coated the air like a mantle of newly fallen snow. Officers escalated the tension, approaching each driver with frenzied orders: the captain and some officers would go to the square to buy provisions; soldiers were to remain with the wagons and enforce the same for all settlers. Amila heard them repeat the city's name several times–Moscow.

The captain and group of soldiers rode toward the expansive, noisy city center, taking along several wagons to bring back provisions. Waiting impatiently for the soldiers' return, Amila asked Pavel what he knew about Moscow. Gleaned from the few times he had passed through with the army, Pavel's response seemed a contradiction of pride and distress.

"They call the square beautiful, or sometimes red square, since the words are so similar in Russian," Pavel smiled. "It is the biggest square in the country and quite beautiful, full of excitement. It is said you can buy anything here if you have enough money."

Anchored near the high stone walls, they stared in awe at the merchant town. Competing sounds of horses, carriages, and transactions between market stall buyers and sellers echoed off the massive cobblestoned square. From her fellow travelers' looks, they were equally amazed.

"What is this on the other side?" Amila pointed toward the moat and imposing wall.

"It is the *kremlin*. In Russian, it means a fortress inside a city," Pavel explained.

Beyond the wall, Amila could see extensive grass areas and the top of many onion-shaped domes, perhaps cathedrals, and a bell tower. She stood high on the wagon and counted five stone palaces, similar in size to the newer buildings in St. Petersburg. However, no residents could be seen or sounds heard beyond the walls. The grounds and buildings seemed oddly neglected and run down, almost abandoned. In front of them, the *kremlin's* entry gate over the moat was lightly guarded. Amila was puzzled. "Does anyone live inside?"

"Not many, I think," Eyes downcast, Pavel spoke softly. "I know only that much blood has been spilled here by the people, the military, and even the rulers. Many years ago, Czar Peter decided this would no longer be the country's capital. He moved it to the new city of St. Petersburg, which is named for his patron saint."

Amila sensed his reluctance to say more and changed the subject. "Will we see other large cities on the way?"

"No. From here on, we will see only open land and a few small villages. The supplies must last us many weeks, until we reach Saratov."

Once reprovisioned, the officers immediately led the wagons south out of Moscow. Progress was slow. Each time a wagon stopped unexpectedly, Rein and Johann hurried to the source of the delay and assisted with repairs, assuming correctly it was another breakdown. Johann couldn't suppress his frustration. "I can fix almost any wagon, but repairing the same wagon over and over is maddening. Russian wagons are not made as well as German ones."

Rein agreed. While the poor condition of the roads was taking a toll on the sturdy army-issued wagons, they shouldn't be breaking down repeatedly. "But we're getting really good at fixing them, aren't we?" With the axle repaired, the wagons began to lumber forward again.

The monotony of long travel days made the two men look forward to evenings. Once stopped for the night, Rein and Johann ate quickly, then followed the soldiers to the area set up for the evening's drills. Each night, the soldiers gathered to practice military skills—sword fighting, loading and caring for black powder rifles and pistols, throwing knives at targets, and wrestling in hand-to-hand combat involving throws and takedowns. At first, the Russians were hesitant to let the colonists take part, but Rein and Johann were persistent in their desire to learn, and they finally agreed. The captain, who dropped by occasionally to make sure his regiment was diligently practicing, even seemed to approve. The strapping soldiers' muscles were honed to fighting, unlike Rein and Johann. The Russians thoroughly enjoyed leaving the two colonists bruised and bloodied, boasting good-naturedly of their prowess. But after a while, the contests became more evenly matched. Johann could best many of the soldiers in wrestling contests, and Rein often won at swordplay and knife throwing. Rein could see the Russians' attitudes toward them soften, a mutual respect growing amidst the physical combat. Georg, who wasn't interested in taking part but watched from the sidelines, began to call Rein and Johann his lieutenants for the new colony.

Some evenings or early mornings, the two joined soldiers hunting in the woods. Rein always brought his bow and often was more successful bringing home wild game than were the soldiers.

Late evenings, soldiers received a daily ration of vodka, which they invited their new friends to sample. It was more potent than any beer Rein had ever tasted. It loosened their tongues as well as his own, providing him and Johann with a safe opportunity to attempt Russian words, although some were not appropriate to repeat. The soldiers poked fun at the Germans' attempts to speak their language, but emboldened by the vodka, they vowed to keep trying. Rein noticed that arguments and fights rarely broke out due to this potent drink, as sometimes happened at home. For these Russians anyway, the liquor seemed to bring forth a peaceful state. The big, burly soldiers would sometimes even link arms and belt out Russian folk songs.

Days later, as Rein and Johann walked beside the wagon, they encountered a herd of fearsome-looking beasts calmly grazing near the forest's edge. They were similar to cattle but much larger and seemed unafraid. "What are they?" asked Johann. Rein shrugged. Both hung back in awe of the stately creatures.

One by one, the wagons and soldiers on horseback halted and respectfully watched from a distance. Each dark-colored animal had a thick, shaggy mass of hair on its humped back, neck, and forequarters, framing its giant head and curved horns. Far larger than any cattle, they didn't seem concerned about intruders.

Amila quietly asked Pavel the question on the settlers' minds. "Oh, they are called *zubr;* some call them bison. But don't worry, they won't attack us unless we provoke them. They are wild and just want to be left alone."

A team of horses began to whinny and paw the ground nervously. A few bison took notice, and a deep growling sound like the buzzing of bees began to emanate from the herd. They moved, almost as one, galloping a few steps quite swiftly considering their size, and drifted toward the cover of the forest before calmly stopping to graze. Again part of the landscape, the giant beasts seemed to have forgotten they had been disturbed.

Pavel continued to share information on the bison as Amila translated. "There's plenty for them to eat here and in the forest. We have watched them before. Along with the grass, they eat leaves, pine needles, twigs, bark, ferns, moss, and even mushrooms. It is said that, in the winter, they use their powerful heads to push through the snow to find food."

"Does anyone hunt them?" asked Amila.

"Yes, but only our rulers can say when. This is a royal hunting preserve, and they are protected because so few remain," explained Pavel. "For the hunts, thousands of peasants serve as beaters to drive the herd together so the nobles can shoot them. But they only shoot a few. They never kill them all."

Rein and Johann exchanged knowing glances. Amila closed her eyes tightly, unwilling to look in their direction.

Early one morning, Rein heard a stir among the herd of horses and rushed to see the cause of the disturbance.

He wasn't surprised to find Eva and Amila there, caring for a foal born unexpectedly to one of the Kalmyk mares.

Captain Kachinov intervened. "It won't be able to keep up. We'll have to shoot it."

Amila's grasp of the Russian language improved daily, and she quickly translated for Eva. They howled in opposition, positioning themselves between the colt and the soldier's gun. The captain shook his head and addressed Amila, amazed how quickly she was becoming fluent in the new language. He acquiesced. "All right. But you'll have to take care of it with no help from my soldiers."

Eva adopted the colt and kept it on a wagon with her much of the day, fashioning a halter from available rope. Every time the wagons stopped for repairs, she hopped down with the colt and let it drink milk from the willing mare. The young travelers delighted in the diversion. After a few days, the colt was running alongside its mother for part of the day, and the children would catch it and lift it back in the wagon when it began to lag behind.

As they progressed slowly along the route, Rein watched with interest as Christof used his mapping materials to chart their journey to Saratov. He liked the talkative young man who had been so forthcoming about his lack of interest in farming and agreed that perhaps Christof's skills lay elsewhere. He wasn't interested in the daily soldier drills, nor in hunting, as were many of the male settlers. Rein could hear the zeal in Christof's voice when talking about his work, the thrill of charting new lands. Rein felt the same about farming the land, which probably seemed odd to many.

"Christof, will you show me the maps you're making?" Rein inquired one evening by the campfire.

Christof enthusiastically rolled out the oversized sheets of highly detailed maps he was drawing by hand. "This terrain is easy to chart because it's fairly level, but the distances are so great between villages, I don't know if I can trust my calculations."

Christof told Rein he had asked if the army had accurate maps. "Captain Kachinov showed me the map he's following, and it contains little more than trails, with no distances at all. I pulled out a map from Germany, including one I made of the Hanover area. I'm pleased to say that he seemed quite impressed."

Christof had sought out Amila to help translate and explained that he was trained as a geographer. He asked if it would help the army to have maps like the ones from Germany. "The captain said that as an officer, he would highly value such maps. So, I'm charting our journey, calculating distances and details as best I can, to share with his fellow officers when we arrive in Saratov. Maybe there's a job for me here as a mapmaker after all."

One evening, Amila sought out Captain Kachinov to thank him for sparing the colt. She spoke slowly and cautiously, trying out new vocabulary she was adding every day. "It has meant so much to Eva and the children. The colt is almost like a pet. It has kept them busy during the long days." Amila had noticed the colonists and soldiers alike laughing at the children's antics with the pampered colt, scrambling to catch her, sitting along-side her in the wagon.

"Your efforts to learn our language are admirable, Lady Amila. Ah yes, the colt. It wouldn't have survived without them." A worried look formed on the captain's face. "It takes a great effort to survive here, for every living thing."

Amila smiled and thanked him for praising her language skills. Since Kachinov didn't speak German, he had not conversed with other colonists, who were lagging well behind Amila in learning the complex language. Changing the subject, she asked how far he thought they might be from Saratov.

"The delays have put us well behind schedule, I'm afraid. I've made this journey to Saratov many times, but never this late in the summer and never with so many wagons." He continued cautiously, lowering his voice. "May I ask, how much do you and the others know about the Volga steppe, the place you are going to settle?"

"We know very little. Only the amount of land we will receive, and that the empress is generously furnishing supplies and livestock to establish the colony. Have you been there, to the Volga steppe, as you call it? Anything you can tell us will be helpful."

The captain's brows drew together, and he frowned. "I can see that you are good, hard-working people. It is important that you know about the region. You have a right to know."

Amila listened. Interest turned to shock, and her left eyelid began to twitch uncomfortably. Shaking off the twinge, she tried to remember every word the captain uttered. When he had finished, she squeezed his arm with her shaking hands and ran to find Georg.

CHAPTER 10

November 1763

Amila rushed to the Müller's campfire, stammering, unable to organize her thoughts. Finally, Elisabeth interrupted. "Amila, what's wrong? You aren't making any sense."

"I have to tell you. You must listen. It's the Volga steppe; everyone must hear what the captain just told me," Amila pleaded. She saw Eva nearby and shouted for her to go find Georg, Rein, and Johann and ask them to come immediately. Amila sat huddled close to Elisabeth until they arrived, trying to recall everything she had heard.

"I went to see Captain Kachinov to thank him for saving the colt, to tell him it was a kind thing he did," she reported. "He began telling me about the Volga steppe, the prairie where we are being sent. He said we're good people, and he thought we should know what's there, what's waiting for us. Russia has tried to settle this region before. It is not vacant land. There's grave danger there!" She had their full attention.

"The captain's father was a officer in the Russian army. Thirty years ago he led a battalion whose job it was to defend the shores of the Volga River. On the east side of the river live wild tribes of Kirghiz nomads who roam the area and consider the land theirs. They're savage warriors and expert horsemen. His father's brigade and a second brigade sent there to defend the eastern shores of the Volga were all slaughtered by the Kirghiz!"

Amila took a breath and continued. "Large bands of thieves live on the river's west side, where the hills and forests provide hiding places. They rob and murder throughout the area. After the captain's father and the brigades of soldiers were killed, the Russian empress before Catherine opened up the Volga's west side to any Russian subjects who wished to settle there. More than a thousand Russian families came. They failed as farmers. Instead, they joined these bands of thieves. The captain told me Empress Catherine believes German and other European immigrants can succeed if they settle as a colony, a community, and have the strength of numbers to protect themselves. *We are to be this empress' experiment.* We're the first people in nearly 30 years that Russia has tried to bring here to settle this frontier. He warns it will be difficult—difficult for us to survive."

Heart pounding, Amila stopped at last and looked from one despondent face to the next. They needed time to absorb the shock. Georg broke the silence. "The Russian army. Will they be there to protect us?"

"Captain Kachinov told me his regiment will be based near Saratov." Amila saw some hope return to their faces. "He said Saratov may be far away from our colony. He's not sure where they are sending us, but he believes it is to land on the east side of the Volga, several days' ride from the army's base of operations, where the Kirghiz roam."

"That's the worst, but not all," disclosed Amila. She felt wretched bringing them such horrid news. "He asked about our winters in Germany. After I told him what they were like, he shook his head sadly. He said winters in Russia, even in the south along the Volga River, are brutally cold with deep snow and last much longer. The Volga freezes for at least three months every year. Spring finally arrives in late April, and winter comes early in the fall. He said we will soon find out how severe winter is here."

Georg called the vorstehers together to hear what Amila had disclosed. But they had little time to process the startling news. The foreboding of winter to come seemed to trigger a change in the weather. As the wagons pulled out of camp the next morning, it began to snow. The heavy, blinding snow stuck to the horses, drivers, and riders without remorse. Colonists quickly pulled winter scarves and kaftans sewn from the heavy fabric out of storage. Children were protected under the canvas covers of wagons, along with as many women who could squeeze in beside them. Rein and Johann joined men walking on foot beside the wagons, one hand clinging to the sideboard to assure they didn't get separated from the caravan.

Officers rode back and forth between the wagons, urging the drivers to push on. Amila heard them speak of a village. Within a few hours, they reached Petrovsk, the last village en route to Saratov, which was still miles away. With the storm showing no sign of abating and the temperature dropping, Captain Kachinov ordered wagons pulled into many tight circles, sheltering the colonists and ponies as well as possible. Men took shelter inside the circle while soldiers began to pull folded tents of thickly woven hemp from the army's wagons. With only a few rainy nights, the soldiers hadn't bothered putting up tents thus far; they simply slept in the open near campfires. Rein and Johann joined the soldiers to help assemble the tents, slowed by the blinding snowfall.

Amila heard the captain shout orders to officers, who began knocking on the doors of huts, speaking hastily to residents surprised to see soldiers in their village, much less at their doors. The officers rode from wagon to wagon, spreading word that peasants would open their homes to colonists and to follow quickly. Rein, Johann, Eva, the Müller family, and Amila approached one of the huts and entered, hastily shutting the door behind them.

The warmth of the cottage engulfed them as they shook the snow from their clothing. Across the room, their eyes met those of a large family. Spanning several generations, from the eldest tucked in close to the heat's source to small children huddled on the floor, the Russians stared curiously at the intruders.

The hut was smoky and dark, with torches instead of candles for light, a packed dirt floor, and no windows. A calf and lamb lay quietly at the opposite end of the large, one-room cabin, which looked to be the place the family cooked, ate, and slept. All were gathered around a massive fireplace.

Breaking the awkward silence, Amila attempted to speak to them in their native tongue. "Thank you for letting us come inside, especially the child. We were traveling by wagon to Saratov when the storm took us by surprise. We are grateful to you."

The guests were greeted with penetrating yet blank stares. Finally, a man stepped forward and addressed the men, ignoring Amila.

"I am Boris, head of this household. Why does she speak for you?" he asked, pointing to Amila, who looked uncomfortably at him but translated nonetheless.

"Please tell them that you are our spokesperson because we do not yet speak their language." Georg exposed a touch of guilt in his smile. "And thank them for sharing their home."

Once Amila translated the message, their hosts' mood lightened, replaced by curious stares. "We have many travelers who pass through our village, but never such a long line of wagons, and few who are not Russian," said Boris. "You are welcome here. Where are you going, and why this time of year? The soldiers should know better."

In the first real test of her still immature grasp of Russian, Amila explained they were from Germany and other countries traveling first to Saratov, then on to land near the Volga River, where they would build a village and farm the land. She told them nearly 200 colonists were traveling together in the wagons, with soldiers guiding the way. She explained they had been traveling for two months, and the soldiers hoped to arrive in Saratov by now. But delays, mainly due to wagon breakdowns, had prolonged the journey.

Then, for the first time, the matriarch of the family came forward and spoke directly to Amila. She introduced herself as Lena, Boris' wife. She asked if they would like food and drink. When Amila translated, they all nodded enthusiastically.

"We have rubles to pay for our stay here," Amila added hastily. She knew they must not impose on the family otherwise.

Lena nodded appreciably and moved toward the fireplace. They watched her and her daughters work efficiently. In no time, they returned with bowls of cabbage soup and *kasha*, buckwheat boiled in milk until it thickened to become porridge. The guests ate ravenously. Then the women brought wooden cups of *kvass* to drink. After tasting it, they agreed it was delicious, and Amila asked what it was. Lena shrugged and said it was simply their common drink, made daily of rye bread and beets.

"Do you realize we have been here several months, yet this is the first time we have been in the home of a Russian or been able to speak with families?" Rein sent an unexpected smile in Amila's direction, then smiled warmly at the family members. One of the daughters blushed deeply.

"Be careful not to be too friendly, Rein, or you will not only speak with Russians but leave with a wife," warned Johann. Rein cast an irritated glance for the needling. Johann thought it best to change the subject. "Amila, can you ask them about the hearth? It seems to keep the house so warm. I've never seen one like it, and I've helped build many cottages."

Boris motioned for them to come closer and feel the heat from what they called the oven or stove, not the fireplace. Also curious, Amila trailed to translate. Boris said it is the centerpiece of the home, made of clay and placed on a separate base so that the house won't lean to its side due to the stove's immense weight.

"I helped build this stove and cabin when I was a young man, learning from my father, God rest his soul." Boris motioned with his hands, explaining the stove is built in layers, with sand and pebbles to ensure the outer surface is safe to touch. He continued knowledgeably: the oven is designed to retain heat for long periods of time by channeling smoke and hot air through a complex web of passages, warming the bricks from which the oven is built. A brick flue in the attic slows cooling. He added that the oven is also used for cooking, not on top but inside.

"The stove is the place where *domovoi*, the Russian house-spirit, resides. He preserves peace and abundance in the family and so has to be fed wood ritually to be kept happy," explained Boris. "But it only needs to be fired once in the morning, and then it retains heat for the rest of the day. On the coldest days in winter, grandfather sleeps on top of the oven to keep warm. He is too weak to work but, as an elder, still governs the entire family, often making his point with a wooden stick," teased Boris.

Proudly concluding the explanation of the stove's inner workings, Boris said that he and his sons must go out into the storm to care for the livestock. As they moved toward the door toting the calf and lamb, the German men hastily donned their kaftans and followed the Russians outside.

Lena approached Amila, curious to know if this was one or several families.

"We are two families, traveling together, sometimes on the same wagon." Amila explained that Georg and Elisabeth were married and had a son. She added that Rein, Johann, Eva, and she were all single. Lena registered shock, turning to speak rapidly to her daughters, then back to Amila. "Young unmarried women are allowed away from their families before marriage?"

Amila explained that both her parents and Eva's were dead and that she had joined Elisabeth and her family for the journey.

Lena addressed Amila boldly. "You had better marry that tall, handsome one soon, or another will snap him up." It was Amila's turn to blush. She chose not to translate, instead inquiring about the warm outdoor clothing Elisabeth had been admiring. When the men left the cabin earlier, Elisabeth had turned to Amila and whispered that the kaftans were no match for winters in Russia. They needed whatever the Russian men were wearing.

Lena and her daughters proudly displayed the *dokhas* that covered one from head to heel for Russian winters. The women wore them as well, and one daughter brought hers to show. Made of animal hide, the *dokha* had long, broad sleeves and a turn-down collar that could be raised to cover one's head and was wrapped and belted with a sash. The collar was wound with a warm scarf or a shawl and tied at the throat.

"How is it you do not know basic things like stoves and *dokhas*? I can tell you are not stupid. But you must know these things if you wish to survive here," warned Lena.

Amila nodded and clasped Lena's hand. "There is much we have to learn."

When the men returned, covered with wet snow, they overflowed with ideas about building barns, storing food, and caring for livestock in winter. They continued to marvel at how odd it all seemed until their hosts settled in for the night. Benches and the table where they sat to eat doubled as beds. They fell into a deep sleep, blanketed by the warmth of the stove.

*R*ein was disappointed when Kachinov informed them only two days later it was time to push on. He knew it was critical to reach Saratov before the next storm, but they had much more to learn from the farm family. Rein and Johann had spent every minute trailing after Boris and his sons. After weeks of inactivity on the road, the physical work, even in the cold, was a welcomed change. While they recognized new ways to do things, Johann and Rein talked privately about how primitive Russian tools and farming techniques seemed compared with home. Rein was anxious to talk with the colonists lodged with others to see what they had learned. It was clear all had come to respect the power of winter in this new country. It snowed in Germany, but not this early and rarely this heavily. With this cold and snow in October, what would the rest of the winter bring?

The morning they left, Rein, Johann, and Georg grasped their hosts' hands, and Amila expressed sincere gratitude. Boris and Lena accepted payment for food and lodging, and Elisabeth was thrilled with her purchase of one of the daughters' *dokhas* as a pattern to follow. Lena hugged Amila hard, taking her chin in her hand and telling her to remember what she had told her.

After two days of uneventful travel in cold but dry weather, the officers circulated among the wagons with news: they would soon see Saratov over the crest of the hill or 'yellow mountain' that gave the city its name. Walking alongside the wagons, Rein and Johann quickened their steps to the hilltop. They stopped, awestruck.

"It isn't a river at all. It's a sea!" Johann's jaw dropped. "I can't see across it, can you?"

Rein shielded his eyes from the water's glare and squinted toward the horizon. The river dominated his field of vision in all directions. "How can a river be so wide? We swam rivers at home, Johann, but I wouldn't dare race you across this one."

As they stared at the Volga River, the wind whipping waves into whitecaps like the sea they had crossed to reach Russia, they heard similar reactions from colonists as each wagon crested the hill. On the near side of the river was the small city of Saratov, where huts and other crudely constructed buildings dotted the landscape. Rein had heard the soldiers call Saratov a frontier outpost, located here to protect the trade route along the Volga from nomadic raiders. Now he understood. It was the most unkempt, ramshackle city they had passed through on the entire journey. His forehead furrowed in thought. It was going to be an interesting winter.

Rein and Johann watched Captain Kachinov ride ahead into Saratov, most likely seeking where to direct the throng of wagons. The remaining officers halted the caravan on the hill overlooking Saratov. Blank looks on the colonists' faces and whispered conversations conveyed disappointment in the stark settlement they had traveled so long and far to reach. The military fort dominated the small city, said to have nearly 10,000 inhabitants. At the center was a two-story log house, which Rein supposed headquartered the army's operations and perhaps the new colonization program. A long line of buildings leaning with the wind bordered the headquarters, all located inside stockade walls. Outside the fort, an erratic patchwork of huts and larger cabins were pieced together with livestock pens and barns. A few properly constructed two-story houses were visible. All buildings were built of unpainted wood, and smoke billowed from chimneys. The imposing river dwarfed the city, completing the panorama.

When the captain returned, officers circled back, telling drivers to deliver the weary travelers to the barracks at the fort, where soldiers would also report. Rein helped Eva retrieve her small trunk, gathered his packs, and they entered one of the barracks buildings, glad to at least be out of the cold. The only light entering the barracks came from gaps between the unplastered walls of rough-cut timber. The wind whistled through the flimsily-built structure furnished with simple wood-frame cots atop a floor of packed earth. Rein glanced at Eva, unable to suppress comparisons with their previous housing—the large brick warehouse in Lübeck, then the dreary but solidly built barracks in Oranienbaum. Even our barns at home are built better than these, thought Rein. Disappointment stemmed from grave concern about spending a long Russian winter in these shabby buildings. He saw Eva shiver when she approached the airy wood-burning fireplace and wished instead for one of the efficient stoves that heated the Russian family's hut.

Once settled for the evening, Georg gathered the vorstehers to continue discussing Kachinov's revelations—the dangers awaiting them on the Volga steppe. Rein was comforted by Georg's approach—he asked the group's input to solve difficulties that lay before them. He urged them not to share the alarming news with other colonists but to keep them from worrying for now. After hours of talk, the weary men retreated to their cots with a plan.

The next morning, Captain Kachinov and his officers appeared to see how the colonists were faring and to tell them Ivan Grekov, the Chancellor of the government's Kontora, or Oversight of Foreigners, wished to greet them. Assembled outside the barracks on the cold, clear morning, Rein joined the mass of colonists murmuring among themselves, likely recalling Commissar Demidov's unwelcome directive a few months earlier. Rein remembered Grekov from his introduction by the commissar in Oranienbaum. Another arrogant aristocrat put in charge of my life, he brooded.

"I greet you today as Chancellor of the Kontora for Oversight of Foreigners. I am the senior officer for this program, and in this capacity, I command the military here as well," spouted Grekov in a perfect High German dialect. Standing on the elevated stockade house porch, he was impeccably dressed in the fashion of European nobility. He paused, arching his shoulders a little farther back, and scanned his audience before continuing. "Your arrival in Saratov brings you nearer your final destination as the first crown colonists for Empress Catherine's Volga settlement program. Unfortunately, we received word that the second group of colonists, those traveling on the Volga, have been detained about fifty miles north of here due to ice forming on the river."

The news created a stir, as many knew those traveling the other route. He brushed their concerns aside. "I assure you they are quite safe and will spend the winter quartered in villages nearby, traveling to Saratov as soon as the river is passable in the spring. Now I turn to more important matters. I suggest you spend your time this winter in productive ways, learning the Russian language and the culture of this great country. You will receive forage money and continue to be housed in the soldiers' barracks. As stated in your oath to become Russian citizens, you will be required to observe the laws of the empire at all times."

Abruptly leaving the assembly area, Grekov stopped momentarily to speak to leaders, exchanging brief greetings with Georg and others. Rein noticed Grekov pause when he saw Amila and turned to ask Captain Kachinov a question. The captain looked toward Amila and responded to Grekov, who nodded. Perhaps it was nothing, thought Rein.

CHAPTER 11

November 1763 - April 1764

*F*or the first time, Amila witnessed the industriousness of the German serfs when given the freedom to determine how best to use their time. Stranded for the duration of the winter, the colonists took the initiative to improve the deteriorating barracks, obtaining supplies and tools from the Kontora officials. Knowing many more colonists would arrive in the spring, the Russian bureaucrats were eager to let the colonists repair the inadequate structures, although they offered no assistance. The buildings were crowded and cold, especially at night. Still, an abundance of firewood was available, and teams of colonists made sure the barracks never ran short. Georg urged the settlers to spend their support allowances with care, reminding them funds had to last the winter.

Amila recalled Tundorf's description of their serfs at the horrid dinner with Duke Zweibrücken. It seemed long ago and a world away, but she remembered his words clearly: *My serfs and the children of my serfs are lazy beggars.* She knew it to be a lie and needed only to observe the colonists for proof. Amila spent less time worrying about Tundorf's ability to find her here. Given the remote location, she doubted any attempt on his part would be successful.

One morning Georg appeared, clearly flustered, and asked Amila to come with him. On the way to another barracks, Georg explained he was embroiled in a heated exchange with the minister, Adam Yauck. The Lutheran minister accompanying the Bremen colonists not only presided over church services but also served as the schoolmaster, holding classes for children in the barracks.

Amila listened, unsure why Georg had summoned her. It wasn't long until she understood Georg and the good father were arguing about whether or not the colonists should learn the Russian language.

Father Yauck held the position that the colonists and their offspring must resist all influence of the Russians. "We must hold fast to the Lutheran religion and our country's customs. I fear for our souls. These Russians keep to their old pagan rites and profess they also follow Christian beliefs. They even have a word for it, *dvoeverie*, double faith! They have spirits for everything—the house, the hearth, the harvest, even the bathhouse! And where are their churches and schools? Saratov doesn't even have a Christian Orthodox church."

He looked around, then spoke again in a hushed tone. "You know as well as I do that they are a backward, godless people. Our souls will be lost if we begin to assimilate. Intermarriage must be strictly prohibited. We must not fall into their sinful ways."

Georg pointed vigorously at Amila. "What if she had not been able to speak the language? Her language skills have been a godsend from the first moment of our ship's arrival, have they not? She listened to the empress' fateful admission, and her ability to speak with Captain

Kachinov alerted us to the impending danger of the Volga frontier. We won't be able to practice our faith if we're not alive."

A compromise was struck between the two: Paster Yauck agreed the colonists needed to learn the language and associate with Russians—as a necessity for survival. But the Lutheran religion, German language, and culture would be sustained and protected for future generations.

Georg concluded the discussion, and the matter was settled. "You tend to our souls. I'll try and keep our families fed and warm, so the congregation can grow and thrive." Soon after, Georg asked officers quartered nearby to use the winter months to teach the colonists Russian.

Amila noticed Rein, Johann, and other male colonists were continuing physical training with the soldiers. Captain Kachinov had taken Christof's offer for mapmaking seriously and had all but enlisted him in the army, requesting he first complete maps sketched of the route from St. Petersburg to Saratov.

It seemed to Amila everyone was busy except her. She passed hours with women in the barracks, tapping her fingers on the makeshift sewing table and feigning interest as Elisabeth and other women stitched warm *dokhas* from hides purchased from locals. Now a tolerable cook, she helped Elisabeth prepare stews in heavy pots hung on the fireplace. Feeling like a fish out of water, Amila wandered from group to group, not knowing what to do with her pent-up energy. Eva kept an ongoing vigil for illness in all the buildings. She treated the sick with herbs she had gathered and advised mothers about ailing children. Amila felt proud of the way Eva was making a place for herself as the colony's medicine woman. Yet her own activities were little more than meandering. She had no idea how to contribute and felt she clearly didn't belong. Perhaps when spring came and colonists left for their new home, she should go back to St. Petersburg to determine her next step. Surely a coach would be taking passengers north in the summer. Seeing Eva and Elisabeth chatting happily nearby tugged at her heart. She would miss them, but it couldn't be helped.

Amila quickly discerned that this city was different from any they had as yet passed through. Many nationalities of residents lived here with the Russians—among them Tartars, Mordovians, and Ruska Roma Gypsies. These people seemed nothing like the peasant family they had met in Petrovsk and certainly were not as welcoming. Amila enjoyed accompanying Elisabeth and Georg to market stalls where locals sold food and goods the colonists needed. The merchants were anxious to sell to the newcomers but otherwise kept their distance. As a trading and military outpost, the residents frequently saw people come and go. It wasn't a cohesive community, more like a permanent gathering of discordant camps of inhabitants, all viewing one another with suspicion. It wasn't long before the locals began to call the colonists *outlanders* and *nyemtzy*, a derogatory nickname bestowed on the Germans because they didn't speak the local language. It meant mute, speechless, and even stupid. Amila knew these names were unfair. It had taken her years to learn what little Russian she knew before she arrived and months of practice to improve her grasp of the language. The colonists had a kindlier nickname for Russians, saying they had moved to the land of the *kapustniki*, sauerkraut gobblers.

Rein followed Pavel through the darkness to the large wooden building, pleased to see a wide plume of smoke billowing from the chimney. He'd gotten to know Pavel on the journey to Saratov, both as a wagon driver and as a formidable opponent during sparring sessions with soldiers. Pavel spoke no German, and although Rein's Russian was improving, communication continued to be a challenge, usually resulting in Pavel leveling good-hearted jeers in Rein's direction. But Pavel knew how to ice fish—another skill Rein wanted to learn. Rein had cautiously followed him onto the frozen Volga ice earlier today, where a surprising number of locals were busy hacking holes with axes. Some already had piles of fish and were standing over their holes patiently holding poles with thick lines and baited hooks. This must be where many of the local fishermen were catching fish to sell, thought Rein. Pavel was patient. It had taken the whole day, but they had amassed a pile of perch, and several large zanders, which Pavel explained was a cross between a pike and perch. They took the catch back to Eva to flavor tonight's soup. Rein was able to explain that Pavel was invited to share the meal later in the evening. A smile covering his face, Pavel motioned for Rein to follow him outside the fort and down an unfamiliar street.

The low-slung building they now entered was furnished only with wobbly tables and stools. The long bar along one end of the room helped Rein conclude the building was a popular Saratov tavern. Hardly a table or space at the bar was vacant, but the two crowded onto stools at a table with other soldiers. Pavel ordered vodka for them both. After the first drink, Pavel's already good nature softened even more.

"There are many ways to die in Russia," joked Pavel, speaking slowly so Rein could understand. "Join the army and get beaten or starve to death, drink bad vodka, or walk under the path of a giant icicle as it falls from a rooftop. But the dumbest way to die is to fall through the ice while fishing."

Rein laughed and nodded that he understood. "Warning well taken. There's more to ice fishing than I thought." Looking across the room, he saw Christof and motioned for him to join them.

"My friend, you've been stolen away by the Russian army. You are becoming one of them," teased Rein. "It's good to see you. You remember Pavel from our journey?"

From the easy banter that ensued, Rein could tell Christof's grasp of Russian had greatly surpassed his own. As the vodka continued to flow, soldiers began to sing songs in unison. Pavel stopped talking and joined in. Some songs were sad, lamenting melodies and others were more raucous, bringing the rowdy soldiers to their feet with fists held high once the verses ended.

"What are you singing about, Pavel?" asked Christof.

"Ah, these are beautiful but sad songs all Russian peasants love," he sighed. "This one is the saga of Stenka Razin, a chieftain who arose from the people of southern Russia to be a liberator of the common people. More than a hundred years ago, Razin led a rebel army, proclaiming to his followers: 'I have come to fight the wealthy lords. As for the poor and plain folk, I shall treat you as brothers.'"

Pavel said the lyrics celebrate the thousands of peasants who joined Razin's army. "He was a pirate on sea
and land but fought for the people, for freedom, besting
the czar's troops and ships. He took control of the Volga,
robbing from ships and raiding the settlements along
the shores. It was told he was invincible!" Pavel wiped
his eyes. "The story has a sad ending. That's why the
empress takes no notice when we sing it."

He explained that Razin's army made an ambitious
but fool-hardy attack on Moscow, which failed. Razin
was taken prisoner, and his loyal followers were forced
to witness the torture and execution of their brave leader.
The remnants of his army retreated to the Volga steppe.
Villages sprang up along the river—filled with runaway
serfs, army deserters, fugitives from justice, escaped
prisoners, revolutionaries, debtors, vagabonds, and
adventurers."

Spirits lifting, he continued. "They have become a
rabble great in number and survive as frontier outlaws,
stealing anything they can. What remains of Razin's
army are *spitzbuben*, forest thieves who take refuge in
the wooded hills and ravines on the land where you are
going. The army is here to fight them…if we can find
them. The song ends with a warning: everyone knows
the Volga is too dangerous to settle, that only the lawless
can survive here. *To live on the Volga is to be a thief.*"

Rein met Christof's equally somber stare. Captain
Kachinov had told Amila about the thieves along the
Volga. This confirmed and even heightened the level of
danger. Perhaps the folklore was an exaggeration. He
must tell Georg what Pavel had said.

Looking around the dim, smoky room, Rein was
curious about the tavern's patrons who were not Russian

soldiers. "Christof, can you ask Pavel, who are these people? I've seen them walking the streets of Saratov and at the market stalls, but I have no knowledge of them."

"Ah, yes, we all come together here to drink vodka!" Pavel began to describe the bar's clientele. Rein understood bits but was relieved when Christof translated.

Pavel pointed with his chin toward one group, dressed in furs from head to toe. He called them Tartars and explained they come from the Far East, Turkish tribes who conquered these lands long ago. They are skilled craftsmen in wood, ceramics, leather, cloth, and even metal. They have long been known as traders and merchants, transporting goods back and forth from the east. Rein noticed their oval-shaped faces with dark, narrow eyes and thin beards.

Next, Pavel motioned to a group of Mordovian men. "They are peace-loving people who come from the Volga uplands, northwest of the river. They are skilled farmers, even able to grow tobacco in summer. We know them to be excellent breeders of horses, sheep, goats, cattle, pigs, and especially bees for making honey. Many of the horses the army buys come from their farms."

Rein observed that the Mordovian men were dressed like other Russian farmers he had seen. "If they're such skilled farmers, then why did the empress bring us here?"

Pavel laughed heartily. "You have no idea how much land is here. I've been to the south with the army. It goes on and on. You can travel for weeks before you reach the southern sea. There's plenty of land for everyone and not nearly enough farmers to feed all of Russia! So you see, the empress does need you."

"He's right," Christof agreed. "I've seen maps of the region to be settled south of here. It's a massive wilderness. You could place ten German provinces inside its borders! And then, the water of the Volga pours into a vast sea. The land surveyed and set aside for colonies is remote, except for a few small Russian settlements. And the government is giving its citizens land too. I've seen those plots and the orders. People in and around Saratov, whether landless peasants, retired soldiers, or even those who already own land, are being given many hectares as long as they work to make them productive."

Rein thought that explained why the Russians didn't seem to resent the colonists. He tried to imagine...enough land for everyone.

Pavel was most excited about the third group of people in the tavern. These he called Ruska Roma, or Gypsies. They were the source of lively music resonating in the tavern, where soldiers were gathered as men played instruments and Gypsy women sang and danced.

"The music and beautiful Gypsy women, this is also why everyone comes to this tavern, not just for vodka. Music must be in their blood." Pavel explained that Gypsies travel and live in wagons during summer, buying and training horses, singing, and dancing. In winter, they stay in local peasants' cottages and pay for lodging with money from selling or trading horses.

They left the table and moved closer to listen and watch. Beautiful indeed, with dark hair, green eyes, and delicate skin, the women wore bright, multi-colored dresses of flowing fabric. Looped rings dangled from their ears as they sang in deep, husky voices. The men played guitar-like instruments while the women spun and gyrated, swinging long scarves and singing mysterious lyrics to beautiful melodies.

It didn't matter that he couldn't understand the words. Rein had never heard or seen anything like it. The dancers began to move faster as the pace of the music increased. Rein must have been staring open-mouthed because one of the dancers noticed him and swayed closer and closer, within inches of his body.

Leaning back quickly, Rein accidentally bumped into a soldier, who pushed Rein forward with both hands, launching him into the arms of the dancer and sending both tumbling to the floor. Quite flustered, Rein quickly got to his feet and helped the dancer stand.

The soldier who had pushed him was laughing and pointing, shouting words Rein had heard enough during the wagon journey to know their meaning. Grabbing the soldier by the lapels of his uniform, Rein shouted, "Tell the lady you are sorry." The soldier cursed again and broke free, swinging a fist at Rein's head. He ducked and bear-hugged the soldier from the side, sending both careening into the bar. Music forgotten, the Gypsies scurried for cover. Fists swung freely throughout the tavern. Unfortunately, this time the vodka didn't make the soldiers want to hug each other and sing happy songs.

Rein and Pavel limped back to the barracks, Christof leading the way.

"Someone has to make sure you don't fall down in the snow and freeze to death," scolded Christof, half-serious. He had also partaken of the vodka but had sense enough to move far away when the fighting started. "I've never been a fighter and don't intend to start now. I'm impressed you two are still standing."

Eva was awake when they entered the dark building, weaving and occasionally bumping into bunks of sleeping colonists. The noise woke Amila, who came from the Müller's corner to investigate the stir. She gasped upon seeing the two bloodied men. "Oh no, what's happened?"

Eva sighed at Rein and got out clean rags, dipping them in a pail of water and reaching for soap. "It isn't the first time I've had to patch you up after a brawl."

Amila followed Eva's lead and picked up a cloth to minister to Pavel. She hesitated, not knowing where to begin cleaning his numerous wounds. "A brawl? What happened?"

Christof took delight in recounting the tavern scene, from the fascinating people to the Gypsy dancers, music, and ensuing fight. "Well, the most beautiful dancer came close to Rein, leaning in so near he had to move away. Well, he didn't really have to. But he did, and that's what started it all."

"It was for her honor," Rein smiled sheepishly and took the rag from his sister. He winced as he wiped the drying blood from his temple.

Pavel grinned, still tipsy. "Or perhaps, your honor, or both of you? You defended yourself and her honor quite well, my friend. And she was beautiful, wasn't she?"

Rein nodded slightly, gaze fixed on some distant image.

Amila wrung out a wetted rag and started wiping Pavel's wounds a bit too vigorously.

*O*ne gloomy winter day, Captain Kachinov arrived at the barracks with an invitation for Amila to dine with him and Chancellor Grekov that evening. She had grown to like the fatherly officer and welcomed his company, as well as any opportunity to practice speaking Russian. Although she was uncertain why she had been invited instead of the leaders, she agreed. Amila felt she should let Georg and Elisabeth know where she was going. After all, they were her family now.

"I'm not surprised they would ask you, Amila. I'm sure they would enjoy the company of a beautiful, intelligent young woman instead of a demanding negotiator like me," Georg smiled, then grew serious and hesitated before asking for a favor. "But I do have a request. Last night, the group leaders came together again to talk about the news you shared with us, about what we can do. We must find out where they plan to send us. We've requested a meeting with Chancellor Grekov, but he isn't receptive to meeting with us. If it's possible, could you ask where the first colony will be located?"

Amila pulled the one dress appropriate for the evening from her trunk and attempted to shake it free of wrinkles. Eva noticed and kindly asked if she could help. Amila nodded thankfully, knowing Eva's skill with a comb and brush could tame her frightful tangles. In the end, Eva secured one thick braid on top of Amila's head, letting stray tendrils frame her face.

Her hosts sent a small carriage, delivering Amila to one of the few prosperous-looking houses in Saratov. Chancellor Grekov and Captain Kachinov, quartered in the same home for the winter, greeted her at the entryway and escorted her through the cozy, nicely furnished parlor to the dining room. Amila stared at the thick rugs, formal table setting, and chandelier lit with candles. This used to be a part of her life, at least occasionally. She tilted her head sideways slightly and glanced around the room. Did she miss it? Feeling no immediate reaction, she put the thought aside, hoping she could at least recall her table manners.

Knowing the chancellor spoke both German and Russian, she asked him which he preferred.

"Ah! I'm surprised and pleased you have learned Russian in so little time," Grekov remarked. Amila responded, explaining how she had gained a fundamental understanding from her tutor and now took advantage of every opportunity to practice. They settled on Russian to include the captain.

Amila enjoyed the light conversation and unique food, especially something very rich in flavor called caviar, which they explained was eggs harvested from a large fish, the sturgeon, caught from the Volga River.

The captain recounted entertaining stories from the wagon journey, teasing Amila about saving the colt, now residing in the army stable with its mother. He told a light-hearted version of the bear incident, omitting Amila's fainting spell. He was complimentary of her dogged determination to improve her Russian and the respect she had garnered from the soldiers, notably one of the drivers.

Amila relaxed in the captain's company and couldn't help but recall the last formal event like it, back in Germany. "We had many bone-jarring hours in the wagon to practice. I learned a great deal from Pavel. It seems that serfs in Russia and Germany have much in common."

"I was quite surprised to find a noblewoman among the rabble of peasant emigrants," Chancellor Grekov declared. "Pleasantly surprised, I must emphasize. But what possessed you to join them?"

Used to this line of questioning by now, Amila gave a short response about the small estate where she had grown up, saying both her parents were dead. "The manor is now managed by my stepfather, so I welcomed this opportunity to travel." With the wine flowing freely, Amila knew she could be in danger of sharing too much and couldn't bear to utter the count's name. Surely her hosts knew that every colonist here had a compelling reason for emigrating. She left her explanation short, instead asking about him.

"I'm a Baltic German from the province of Estonia, a part of the Russian Empire. You sailed past our beautiful country on your voyage to St. Petersburg. I'm of Baltic nobility." The chancellor raised his chin. "My father is the baron of a large, rural estate. Alas, I am the youngest son, and the title passes to my eldest brother. So I took this civilian position to manage Empress Catherine's colonization effort."

He paused, pulling at his mustache repeatedly, and moved about nervously in his chair. He started to say more, then stopped. She sensed he was battling for control or might be truly unwell. Grekov cast a contemptuous glance around the room, a faraway look in his eyes. "I won't always be here in this place God has truly forsaken. Once the colonies are in place, I'm sure the empress will see the value I bring to her reign. I expect placement in her majesty's court in St. Petersburg before long."

Amila glanced at Kachinov, whose eyes conveyed something was amiss with the young chancellor. She tried to placate him. "This is a significant endeavor for the empress and an important position for you. I wonder if you know where the first colonists will be sent, to what parcel of land?"

"Of course. The empress and Commissar Demidov desire the first farming colonies to be located on the east side of the Volga, the *weisenseite*, or meadow side, several days' ride from here." Grekov leaned uncomfortably close to Amila. "But please, let us leave this talk for another time. Given your superior station in life, I wonder if you would be more comfortable quartered in a boarding house for the winter? It would be possible for us to pass the time together with more dinners such as this."

"Oddly enough, I am becoming used to the drafty barracks, even sleeping in wagons and on the ground. But I thank you." Amila retreated and turned to the captain. "I hope this doesn't mean I have soldiering in my future."

Kachinov laughed, and Grekov pretended to enjoy the joke, saving face given Amila's rebuff. Thinking it a good time for the evening to end, Amila inquired about the carriage. The captain excused himself, asking a servant near the entry to bring the carriage. As Amila left the house, Grekov insisted on walking her out. Once he had helped her inside, Grekov leaped in beside her and quickly slammed the door, ordering the driver to pull away. "I'll accompany you back to the barracks. This city is not safe. You shouldn't be out alone."

Amila moved as far from him as she could on the seat and craned her head out the opposite window. The captain was nowhere in sight. Noticing her lack of attentiveness, Grekov faced her, clearly perturbed. "In all honesty, I don't understand why you want to stay with the commoners in that crumbling building. It's no more than a barn. You must reconsider my offer."

"I thank you. But I have many friends among the colonists, including two women I'm very close to. They are like sisters to me, which I've never had. I'd miss them too much." She remained silent, wishing the horses would move faster.

Suddenly she felt Grekov's arms tightly encircle her shoulder and waist. He whispered in her ear. "Surely you know what I can offer you, what I want. A kiss goodnight and much more the next time we meet. I promise you will never regret it. You are quite beautiful. I have desired you from the moment I cast eyes on you."

Amila tried to push his arms away and succeeded momentarily, reaching for the carriage door. He grabbed her again, reaching inside her cape to touch the bodice of her dress. She struggled ferociously but was pushed up against the carriage door. "No! Leave me alone!" she screamed.

The carriage stopped abruptly and the door opened.

"Lady Amila, you've returned." Rein declared through clenched teeth, darkening the carriage doorway. Johann held the harness of one of the horses, accounting for the abrupt stop. "The barracks are nearby. We'll accompany you there."

Grekov silently slid across the seat away from the open door, nostrils flaring. Amila straightened her cape and quickly stepped out of the carriage without a glance back. "We'll see that Lady Amila gets home safely." Rein leveled a warning glance and slammed the door.

Grekov shouted an order to the driver and the carriage sped away.

"Thank you," Amila wept softly, hugging Johann and glancing over at Rein. "How did you know where to find me?"

"Eva told me where you were going, and we decided to watch for your return," Rein responded gently. She looked from one to the other, ashamed she had allowed herself to be in such a vulnerable position. Outrage quickly replaced the tears. "How dare him? I hate him. He's just like the count, just like the duke. I hate them. I hate them all!"

"*W*hat gives you the audacity to come here with these demands?" snarled Grekov to Georg, who stood at the front of the leadership group, finally granted a meeting with the Chancellor of the Kontora. Bureaucrats charged with implementing the colonization program were also present, the secretary furiously taking notes. A bookkeeper and other office workers were seated with Grekov at a table.

Rein quietly smoldered. He decided he could never master the role Georg played so well. He wanted to challenge Grekov to a bare-handed fistfight, or swords, his choice. Just so blood was spilled. Rein was among the handful of leaders accompanying Georg, who, as their spokesperson, had presented requests respectfully and explained their rationale for doing so. This wasn't the response they had sought.

Georg restated why they felt it critical that the first colony be located on the west side of the Volga, the hilly side. "These are not demands. Think of it as the success or failure of the colony. We can protect ourselves more effectively against bands of thieves who live on the *berg-seite*, the west side of the river, than the warlike nomads on the east side, where we would be in constant danger from raids. Farming would fail. Our request that soldiers accompany us to the first colony, due to the likelihood of bandits, will protect us further, and it is critical we have guns and ammunition as provisions."

The leaders waited respectively for the chancellor's response, hopeful he would understand that the success of the colony would reflect well on him as well. Rein knew many other questions were on the colonists' minds, such as how much land the colony would encompass and whether houses and buildings had already been built. But those questions were delayed until the most important issue was resolved, a safe location.

"Well, I decline your requests, all of them," Grekov snapped back with a wave of his hand. "You're here at the pleasure of the empress and will abide by the decisions she has empowered me to make. This meeting has come to an end."

Snow was falling heavily as leaders retreated silently to the barracks. To Rein, it felt like a familiar blanket of oppression, imposing brutal injustice over his life and the lives of those he cared for. Georg and the other members of the delegation ambled along, equally despondent. Once inside the barracks, they talked quietly among themselves.

Rein saw Amila approaching and turned in surprise. "I know we don't usually talk to one another, and that's the way you want it. But, I wish to thank you for watching out for me the other night. And to ask, the meeting with Grekov, did it go as badly as I fear?"

"When Eva told me where you had gone, I began to suspect the worst." A deep frown clouded Rein's features. "I don't trust that man. I've had a bad feeling about him since he was introduced to us months ago. And he has proven me right, has he not? Not only his behavior toward you but his treatment of us, of our rights. No, the meeting didn't go well. Grekov declined even to consider our concerns about the colony's location and a military escort."

Amila bristled. "Then I'm partly to blame, and the chancellor is taking it out on all of us. What right has he to endanger you good people?"

Hands on her hips and shoulders held high, her voice gained intensity and volume far beyond the confines of the two of them. "We're the first colonists, and we will make way for those who follow. We've come so far, too far to fail now. We can't let the unfair lord and serf system you are trying so hard to escape follow you here, to this new life! I know; I was part of the nobility who allowed you to be treated so. It must stop. We all know how much the empress wants us to settle this land. We have more power than we know. To be free and to survive in this hostile place, we must fight. We will find a way!"

When her tirade ended, Amila turned to see the leadership delegation had been listening. Like Rein, they had devoured her every word.

The next day, Georg called Amila aside and asked if he could talk with her alone. She winced, fearing she had offended the leaders with her outburst. She had slept poorly, remembering Tundorf's tongue-lashing for speaking her mind at the dinner table so long ago.

"Amila, I've never been so proud of you, speaking up like that. We were all a little surprised at the strength of your words but impressed nonetheless. We're fortunate to have you on our side."

Amila let out a long breath and felt her body relax.

"We needed that jolt to believe there is a path. Will you help us write a letter to Commissar Demidov in St. Petersburg? It must be a secret. We fear that if Chancellor Grekov finds out, we will suffer grave consequences." Georg and the other leaders believed the letter must convey concerns about the safety of the colonists, given the location being considered, and provide evidence, such as the information Captain Kachinov had shared.

"We believe that dispatches must somehow be sent back and forth to St. Petersburg during the winter months. There is hope if we can get a message to the commissar."

Amila thought for a moment. "Christof. He's working for the army, making maps. He's in and out of their offices all day and returns to the barracks at night. He'll know how to get a message to St. Petersburg."

CHAPTER 12

April - May 1764

"*W*e have a response from Commissar Demidov," Georg gasped, out of breath, when he found Amila working with Johann tending horses at the livestock stable on a clear April morning. After many false starts, spring at last showed signs of hanging on.

The past few months had been nearly unbearable. They had adjusted well enough to the short days, cold, and snow. It was uncertainty about the future that kept everyone on edge. Amila had worried whether the commissar had even received their letter. At least a response was proof that he had. Georg opened the letter for the first time and scanned it briefly before looking up at Amila.

"It says he received the letter stating our concerns, and the response has been sent to Chancellor Grekov in this same dispatch." Georg looked uncertain whether to be encouraged or discouraged. "There's nothing more except this: 'The empress is seeking a dependable settler population that will take root and flourish through her colonization program. Furthermore, the goal she envisions is for the lower Volga to be converted into a region of productivity and social stability, to serve as an exemplary influence in agriculture and industry for her native populations.' That's all."

Amila hurried back to the barracks with Georg for a hastily called meeting with the vorstehers. He shared the contents of the letter with guarded enthusiasm. "It sounds like Commissar Demidov is trying to placate both parties, with two letters arriving in Saratov in the same parcel. We just don't know the outcome. We must wait for the chancellor to tell us."

Amila was surprised when Georg asked her to go with the leaders to the meeting called by the chancellor the next day. She had successfully avoided Grekov the remainder of the winter and didn't think her presence would help their cause. She remained at the back of the room and kept quiet, her heart beating so loudly she was afraid others could hear.

"So, you contacted Commissar Demidov behind my back. He has, of course, sent me the response," Grekov uttered through clenched teeth. After a tense pause, he quickly and unemotionally read from the letter he had received. "Regarding the location of your colony, I have consulted with Empress Catherine, and she has made the decision. Land on both sides of the river has been set aside and surveyed for colonies. She agrees that the lower Volga is a primitive frontier and that the east side may be more dangerous. Taking this into consideration, the empress says you will be allowed to settle the west side of the Volga first. However, at a future time, the east side of the river will be settled, and the colonies there will become a wall which absorbs the blow of the nomadic tribes."

Grekov stood and paced back and forth, pulling nervously at his mustache while looking wildly at the colonists. "However, I have selected your colony's location on the west side of the Volga. We're sending you to the farthest reaches of the surveyed land to the south. And, if you ever conspire against me again, you'll be sorry." With this pronouncement, he walked briskly from the room.

Once the realization of the outcome sunk in, raucous cheers erupted. Amila cringed, looking toward the door where Grekov had exited, concerned he might still be near enough to hear. She was equally excited but had seen enough lunacy in the man to fear retaliation.

Georg found Amila and hugged her tightly. "It's over. This decision clears the way. We can go. Amila, you helped make this happen. You know that, don't you?"

She sniffled to fight back the tears stinging her eyes. "Thank you. We can... go."

On the walk back to the barracks to share the good news, Georg and the leaders gathered around Amila and stopped. "We have an offer to make you," he announced, wearing the expression of a proud father. "After much discussion among ourselves, we want to ask you to fill an important role in the new colony. No one would be a better secretary to help draft and write our laws, keep records, and make translations. And of course, you would take part in decision-making. We are unanimous in asking you this."

Amila looked from face to face to see if they could be sincere. "But, I'm a woman," she uttered weakly.

Laughter erupted from the group. "Yes, we are well aware you are a woman, Amila. You are also formidable and smart. You have much to contribute."

Her mouth curved into a smile. Incapable of words, she could only nod her head in response. As they cheered again and walked on, Amila fell behind, deep in thought. Her plans to leave—what would they think when she deserted them?

"It's a happy day, don't you think? And quite an honor." Rein had slowed to walk beside her.

She gave him a sidelong glance, surprised by any attention from him and especially anything resembling praise. "Do you mean that, or are you teasing me? It's wonderful, the location of the colony. I don't know what to think about the offer. I've struggled to find a useful role for myself here. I'm not good at so many things."

Rein took a moment, thoughtful and serious in his response. "Perhaps you are quite good at some things others are not." A second later, he flashed a playful grin. "Where else could we find a woman willing to walk boldly into a camp full of thieves? Now I am teasing you." He scurried forward to join the others before she had time to respond.

*I*f the colonists seemed industrious in winter, Amila now witnessed how the arrival of spring and a clear path to their new home generated vast energy reserves. The Volga had thawed and large, crudely-constructed wooden barges were arriving, weighted down in the water by supplies to equip the settlers' farms. The Kontora issued a loan of 150 rubles to each family to purchase supplies and equipment from the floating mercantile stores. Each family signed a document declaring the loans would be paid back after ten years.

As Amila walked through the tethered barges and stalls on Saratov's shore, she encountered families excitedly shopping for livestock and supplies. Coming from a country ravaged by war and desperate to feed themselves, colonists had scarcely expected to own this much property in their lifetimes. Each family was issued the unassembled parts of a wagon, a wooden plow, ropes, harnesses, hatchets, sickles, augers, drawknives, and chisels. These items remained on the barges, which were simply large rafts of uncut lumber lashed together. The barges would carry not only settlers but also supplies to the location of the first colony. Horses and cattle were to be herded south along the Volga shoreline, escorted by a detail of soldiers.

Amila stopped to watch the elders of a large family spanning several generations bargain confidently at one barge and then another. Settlers excitedly haggled for household items such as pots, pans, copper kettles, pottery bowls, eating utensils, fabric, sewing materials, and blankets. From local traders, they purchased livestock—Kalmyk ponies, cows or oxen, and smaller farm animals. Guns were not issued but were for sale. The vorstehers asked each family to purchase as many guns and as much ammunition as they could afford, reminding them they were settling on the side of the river where bands of thieves roamed.

As Amila wandered through the busy market with Georg, she overheard families speaking discouragingly about the prices. Georg shared his concerns. "Everyone expected the rubles to go much farther. We can negotiate with the locals for horses and livestock. But the government items seem double what they're worth. At these prices, there will be little left for food. I wonder if a large portion of the money is going into Kontora pockets."

Georg also expressed concern to Amila that some of the families were wasting funds they'd been given. Not used to having money, some were spending it on frivolous items as well as food and drink to celebrate their newfound wealth. "From our waste, the local shopkeepers and traders will likely become quite wealthy."

Amila saw Eva and Rein eyeing Kalmyk horses for sale from Gypsies and paused to watch. Eva was already the proud owner of the colt rescued last fall, which was faring well after wintering with its mother. Captain Kachinov presented the colt as a gift, saying she saved it, so it belonged to her. Amila was amazed how well the sturdy horses had handled the severe weather. During the winter, she had witnessed what Pavel had told her on the long wagon ride—the Kalmyk horse was most desired here because of its endurance and ability to thrive in extreme temperatures.

While the Kontora staff created its records of loans, Amila compiled records of each family, listing names, country of origin, and the trade or craft of the head of household. Her records listed 55 families and a total of 261 persons who would be traveling together to the first colony in June 1764. This included ten single men and two single women—only she and Eva. One family was from Finland and one from Sweden; the remainder from German provinces. Amila's records showed about one-third listed their primary trade as farmers. Others listed blacksmith, stableman, cobbler, saddler, gardener, wheelwright, butcher, weaver, tailor, baker, many merchants and builders, and the Lutheran minister and schoolmaster. Amila's most challenging task as secretary had been to review and interpret the "Laws for Colonists" that had arrived in March from Commissar Demidov's Guardianship Council for Foreigners office in St. Petersburg. She thought the German translation of the laws was poorly done and instead studied the Russian version. The tedious document was critical in that it detailed freedoms guaranteed to colonists: the right to practice their chosen religion, exemption from taxes and tributes for a specific number of years, as well as exemption from Russian military service. The laws also granted each colony's land and right of ownership and stated rules for self-governance. Amila had poured over the intimidating document, continually seeking clarifications from Kontora bureaucrats, who soon began to duck away when she approached. For the past few months, she carefully relayed what she was learning to Georg and the vorstehers.

Today's record-keeping up to date, Amila decided to walk back to the barracks to find Elisabeth and see if she could help with family provisioning. She was pleased to cross paths with Captain Kachinov. "This is an exciting time for you, isn't it?"

"Yes, it is," Amila alternated between feelings of elation and pangs of guilt, both sharpened by uncertainty. Go to the colony or go back to Germany? The imaginary cloud hovering over her pulsed with thunderous fears that the count would send his henchmen in search of her, or worse, come himself. She had talked briefly with Christof, now employed full time by the army, and he planned to stay and continue the mapmaking he enjoyed so much. Where should she go? "May I walk with you for a while? It's a beautiful spring day, at last."

"I can tell you're deeply troubled. What is it?" the perceptive man inquired.

It occurred to her she had someone to confide in to help sort through this dilemma. He had disclosed to her the realities of the place they were being sent. She had grown to trust the captain. "Do you mind hearing a long story? I would value your advice."

They continued to walk. Amila started at the beginning. It all gushed forth: Count Tundorf's plans to wed her to the old duke who was dying of a contagious disease; meeting the Russian recruiter as the last wish of Eva and Rein's mother; escaping the night before the wedding. Most importantly, she shared knowledge of the evidence in her possession that confirmed the count's treason and murder of his own serfs, one of which was Eva and Rein's father.

"They don't know, and I don't know whether to tell them. I didn't understand the documents until I had time to read them on the ship coming here. Tundorf must know I have this evidence, and I'm afraid of what he'll do. We laid a false trail when we escaped, but I believe he'll try to find me. I didn't realize it at the time, but now I know that the ship's log in Lübeck listed my name and destination. If he tries, he can find me."

Amila stopped abruptly and reached up to rub the nape of her neck with one hand. She shut her eyes. "Captain, he's an evil, insidious man. I know he's not above murdering whoever opposes him. The estate has been in my family for many generations. How can I let him have it? He abuses the serfs, overtaxing them to near starvation, and is destroying the woods and land. Most of all, he needs to face the consequences of murder and betraying our country. I must go back to Germany and challenge him. But how? And now, Georg and the leaders have given me an important role in the new colony. How can I desert them?"

Captain Kachinov took both of Amila's hands in his own. "No wonder you're troubled, my dear girl. What a heavy burden for one so young to carry, especially alone. As a soldier, as a man who takes honor to country very seriously, I consider this man's crimes unforgivable. I'm glad you were able to escape. And I agree you may truly be in danger. Now, let's think about what can be done."

Rein stood beside his mount with Johann and watched the spectacle unfolding on the river. It was unlike anything he had ever seen or would likely see again. "Do these Russians have any idea what they're doing? This can't possibly be safe. They'll never get there alive."

Johann muttered nervously. "It reminds me of the story of Noah. Except with the animals and people piling on a bunch of really rickety arks. Let's hope it doesn't take forty days and forty nights for them to reach the new colony."

"Can they all swim?" Rein could scarcely believe they were finally beginning the last leg of the journey. But transporting the settlers on barges? It was best he watched from a distance. He didn't want to dampen the excitement on the colonists' faces as they boarded. Yet he had grave concerns about the likelihood the rafts would stay afloat and the passengers safely aboard if they did.

A few soldiers and the river pilot—the helmsman who would steer the raft with their assistance—were already onboard each of the twenty large, wooden river rafts. Soon men, women, and children began to carefully step onto the barges, weaving until they could find space to sit in and around farm implements, food, and supplies. The transports also carried small livestock—young piglets, sheep, goats, and poultry—in small wooden corrals and crates positioned in the center. Children were charged with trying to quiet the animals. Chickens in crates cackled nervously, and the livestock's fearful bellows added to the chaos.

Rein, Johann, and several other colonists had been recruited to accompany the soldiers driving the horses and cattle along a trail near the coastline. It felt good to ride a horse after such a long and idle winter, and Rein was anxious to explore the countryside. They were to meet up with the barges at the location of the first colony, where the smaller Dobrinka River fed into the mighty Volga.

Rein sighed and looked to Johann for moral support. "They'll be all right, won't they?"

Johann grinned and offered his brand of comfort. "Oh, you mean Eva. Don't worry—you know she can swim like a fish. Or is there someone else you're worried about? Oh, yes, the children. We're all concerned about the safety of the children."

Rein rolled his eyes and fought back a grin. He mounted and turned his horse toward the path, Johann following and chanting behind him. "I'm sure they'll all get wet before the trip is over. But you and I both know there isn't a creature on that ark or in that river likely to drown Lady Amila."

They joined Captain Kachinov, soldiers, and a few fellow colonists on horseback where the herd was assembled. Rein craned his neck toward the partially visible river and still chaotic scene. He recalled the many steps

on this long journey and was filled with a rush of foreboding: The escape and long ride by horse to Lübeck;
the ship to St. Petersburg; and the months-long wagon
train to Saratov. Something had gone awry on each
leg—highwaymen, the ship captain's deception, and the
dangerous winter weather. He longed for an uneventful
trip this time.

Water lapped up against the raft's sides as they floated
down the expansive Volga. Scanning the horizon, Amila
observed a continuing succession of the river, prairie,
and sky. The long caravan of rafts floated peacefully past
small islands of various shapes and sizes, either barren
of vegetation or dotted with patches of steppe grasses.
Swallows skimmed low over the river's surface, oblivious of the powerful current.

It occurred to Amila that she needed to remember
how to swim. The barges were little more than logs
lashed together. She asked Eva and Elisabeth, "Can you
swim?"

Before answering, they peered over the edge, where
strong currents propelled the raft forward. They gazed
beyond at the powerful waves extending to the river's
far side, which they had been told stretched several miles
in some places. Eva spoke first, asserting that she had
been swimming in the Wörnitz River that wound around
the village since childhood. Elisabeth nodded, noting
Bremen also had a large river where they swam during
the warmer months.

Soldiers stretched out lazily as the barge pilot stood
confidently operating the long tiller, the lever that
controlled the submerged rudder steering the raft. Oc-

casionally, the pilot called for one or more soldiers to help steady the long paddle. Perhaps this was an ordinary mode of transportation for Russian soldiers, Amila thought. The colonists had been told the trip would take five to seven days, and the current seemed to be propelling them forward at a brisk pace. There was little wind, but the air coming off the water felt cool on her skin, and the barge's gentle rocking seemed tranquil enough.

"Don't worry. We won't need to swim," assured Amila. She wasn't entirely convinced but didn't want to worry Elisabeth, who was gazing nervously at her napping son. Eva eased her way toward the animal pens. Amila had long wanted to talk privately with Elisabeth, but they'd been busy preparing to leave. She took advantage of the opportunity.

"May I talk with you about something?" Amila peered over her shoulder to see Eva sitting with children caring for a small pen of goats.

Elisabeth nodded. "Of course, my dear."

"It's about, um, men. I simply don't understand them." Amila wiggled uncomfortably. "You and Georg, I've watched the way you treat one another. He's so patient and sweet to you and listens. He treats you with respect. I see the playful way you banter and tease one another. Even though your lives are difficult, with your son and Georg's responsibilities, you seem so close."

"We're very fortunate to have one another, to be so much in love," Elisabeth responded warmly. "It isn't always easy. At times I'm not sure I understand even him. Just like women, men are not all cut from the same cloth. Is there perhaps one man, in particular, you are wondering about?"

Amila's forehead creased. Her eyes darted from one side of the raft to the other. After a deep breath, she finally spoke. "It's Rein. It's clear he hates me. He has a right to. There are things that I…haven't told you. You see, it was my family's manor where his father died, and he was so close to his mother. So was I. She was the housekeeper at our manor, and she spent more time there, with me, than she could with Rein and Eva. He has spoken to me about that in anger. And many other things. I was there when their mother died, and he looked at me as though it was my fault."

Elisabeth nodded but remained silent. Amila's pent-up thoughts began to flow freely. "We escaped together, with Eva, and she's like a dear sister to me. The entire trip to Lübeck, Rein and I argued and were determined to part ways once we arrived there. But then, by coincidence, you and Georg invited us both to join your colony. We've tried to stay out of one another's way, but it isn't working. And then I hear stories about a Gypsy dancer, and I see the way women gawk at him. It's maddening. He annoys me. Elisabeth, I truly don't understand men, and especially that one."

A knowing smile crossed Elisabeth's lips. Having become acquainted with Amila in the past months, she chose her words very carefully. It would be best if her young friend worked this out herself. "He's a good man, don't you think? Cut from the right cloth? I've seen how he treats Eva and others, and he has a natural way of making friends, even with the Russian soldiers. He's smart, has strong values, and is a hard worker, helping with whatever needs to be done. Not to mention very attractive."

"Yes, I suppose that's all true." Amila shrugged.

"Well, have you considered that you see these qualities in him and like them? That perhaps you want to be closer to him? That you regret the harsh words and arguments? Maybe what you don't understand is that your feelings for him may have…changed." Elisabeth carefully introduced the idea.

Amila slid back from where they sat cross-legged. Recognition dawned. The words she spoke were barely perceptible. "That I care for him, love him? Is it possible?"

Amila's bothersome eyelid flickered again as she worked through an onslaught of ragged emotions followed, thankfully, by more rational thoughts. Can this be? She probed the overpowering feelings he awakened in her – love? This hardly felt like love. She always seemed to strike out at him, and he at her. Around him, but only him, she felt unable to control her emotions. She longed for him to treat her the kind and gentle way he treated others. But something always went awry. She felt sick inside when other women smiled at him longingly. Had she ever smiled at him that way? What if she did? Admittedly, she had lain awake wondering what it would be like to kiss him, to be held by him. *She desired him.* A flush crept up her body to her face.

Rational thoughts took hold. A noblewoman can't love or marry a serf. The count had Rein's father murdered, and if Rein knew, he would blame her as well. Could he ever forgive her? And if she did let herself love him, she might care so much that she would never be able to leave.

"Amila, are you all right?" asked Elisabeth, seeing her friend's distress.

"I think I've been hit by a force of nature. And I have no idea what to do about it."

*W*ith ships solidly booked for colonists, finding passage from Lübeck to St. Petersburg had been difficult, but Count Tundorf bribed enough authorities in the port city to board the first decent passenger ship leaving in the spring. In Lübeck, he was sickened to see waves of serfs and even middle-class tradesmen gathered at the docks deserting German provinces. He was furious when he arrived in St. Petersburg to find the same disgraceful scene but in even greater numbers. Thousands of colonists had arrived and were being welcomed with open arms in this shoddy, inferior country.

Riding in a carriage to the hotel, he leaned back and shut his eyes. He was determined to carry out the plan he and the German princes had agreed upon: do whatever was necessary to assure the first colonies failed. The exodus of serfs, the princes' rightful property, had to stop, and soon. He wasn't sure how, but he'd find a way. He snickered under his breath. Knowing right from wrong had never stopped him before.

Tundorf found it easier to track Amila's whereabouts than he had thought. He was disappointed to learn she was no longer in Oranienbaum, where other colonists were quartered. He'd told an office clerk at the Guardianship Council for Foreigners he was searching for his dear stepdaughter, who was missing. After rubles exchanged hands, he learned Amila Wallerstein had left by wagon with the Georg Müller family and was likely among the only group to reach Saratov before winter. From there, settlers would travel to their colony location in the spring. *This spring.* He had to travel there anyway. This would make it possible to kill two birds with one stone.

The count massaged his pulsing temples. If only he'd gotten rid of the documents showing he'd been paid, and paid well, twice—by the French and Prussian armies— for the wagonloads of supplies from his manor. But he'd kept the incriminating documents until well after the war ended, been hesitant to act. It made sense to retain the documents in case the French and its allies won the war. That transaction would have shown his loyalty to the French, keeping him in good stead with the new rulers, although it was treason against Prussia. But once the war was over and the French had lost, he decided to keep the records in case his financial situation didn't improve, and he might need to leave Germany permanently—for France. His knowledge of the inner workings of the Prussian army and proof of loyalty to the French would have procured a prominent position for him there.

Now, she possessed the damning documents that could lead to his execution. He began to sweat and felt a tightness across his chest. Fear. He'd seen it in the eyes of others, those who were about to die, but he'd never felt it himself. As a member of the German princes' *vehmic*, the secret punishment tribunal, he'd participated in executions. If neighboring princes learned of his treason and murder, he could be executed on the spot without a trial.

The blistering anger he felt toward Amila smoldered at a low boil in his blood. His life had gone according to plan until her subterfuge. Granted, he had to bend and break the rules often to stay ahead of the game, but he had been quite successful until now. And it would've worked this time if Amila had married the duke. How dare she humiliate him. He clenched the cane lying across his lap with such force it nearly snapped in half.

And Reinhardt Lundgren. He could hardly wait to get even with him. Nothing more than a low-born upstart, as his father Daniel had been. The count remembered with fury what that agitator had the gall to approach him and ask. Granted, Daniel did hold a contract established 15 years earlier with Amila's father, Count Philip. Hard to believe any proper nobleman would stoop to such an agreement. The blasted contract stated that Daniel's role as overseer and operator of the watermill on the estate's property must become more lucrative over the 15-year period, which it had. The problem was what Daniel was promised in exchange: Daniel would receive expanded rights for his family. The Lundgren family would continue to operate the mill but would also become free men with hereditary rights to the land they farmed and would no longer labor several days a week for the count.

Of course, he knew of the contract his predecessor had idiotically agreed to. And the mill was arguably the most profitable business on the estate. So he placated Daniel, assuring him he would look into it. In the meantime, the opportunity presented itself with the wagonloads of supplies bound for the Prussian army. He had taken great joy in burning the accursed contract once Daniel was dead. When Reinhardt came to remind him of the agreement, he suppressed the glee he felt informing the son the contract was void upon his father's death.

He'd lost 25 serfs in that transaction. On a lark, he'd appealed for the War Office to reimburse him for the loss of workers as war casualties. What a stroke of genius—they bit! He hadn't counted on that stream of revenue. But now, even those funds were gone, used to pay for his birthday hunt. Never mind, he'd soon rebuild the number of peasants under his rule. He had to. The serfs were his producers, labor force, soldier assets—respon- sible for all his income. And the mill, he'd find someone else to run it. How hard could it be?

For now, he needed transportation to Saratov as soon as possible. He closed his eyes again to wipe from his mind the image of hordes of German serfs boarding ships bound for Russia.

CHAPTER 13

June 1764

*A*mila began to stir as the sun rose over the water. Just like at sunset, sunrise projected a play of light with constantly changing streaks of gold, orange, blue, and lilac. Disquieting thoughts from yesterday's conversation with Elisabeth still clashed about in her mind, and she welcomed the many distractions around her. All the barges were tied in shallow water along the western, hilly shoreline last night when the light faded. The pilot, although young, seemed very sure of himself and firmly in charge. He had announced to passengers that beaching the heavily loaded rafts was unsafe until they reached their destination due to the difficulty of maneuvering in and out of the current.

But the shore may as well have been a mile away – passengers were ordered to remain on board at all times. Fortunately, though not happy about it, they were accustomed to using the privy buckets from the long ocean voyage. Amila was relieved to at least have plenty of water to drink and wash. She watched enviously as the soldiers swam ashore and untied heavy ropes from the thick stakes pounded into the ground the night before. The pilot eased the barge back into the current, followed by the convoy of rafts that had also hugged the shoreline the previous night.

With nothing to do but drift, she and Eva eagerly pointed out each new sight. Amila heard it called a wilderness. But she wondered, is a wilderness always this vast? The Volga was clearly its own brand of wild. Fish jumped from the water, so numerous the two young women finally turned their eyes instead to shore. They lost count of the number of streams and rivers they saw feeding into the Volga. The rafts floated nearest the hilly side, where the colony would be located. Here the land alternated between high bluffs with sandy shores and deep ravines with dark forests. Prairie winds caressed the lush, deep grass covering the land. On the east side, when the width of the Volga narrowed somewhat to observe the far shoreline, the same grass covered flat plains. Near them, deer timidly approached the water's edge to drink. When they saw timber wolves lope up and down the shoreline curiously eyeing the barges, passengers lowered their voices in respect for the fearsome predators. Missing from the landscape was any sign of human habitation. Hour after hour, day after day, they saw no villages or settlements anywhere.

"Look! Horses!" Amila stood and pointed. On the nearby bank, a small herd of horses approached the river, looking nervously toward the rafts. "If no one lives there, they must be wild!" She immediately began to devise ways to catch and tame them. She had sorely wanted to ride with the soldiers and colonists driving the horses and cattle, but Georg and Elisabeth had forbidden it, emphasizing it wasn't appropriate for a single woman to travel unchaperoned with a group of men.

Amila carefully stepped around the other passengers to seek out soldiers who might know something about the horses. They sat huddled in one area near the pilot steering the raft. "The horses don't resemble the Kalmyk ponies we bought in Saratov. Are they wild?"

By this time, the soldiers were used to her inquisitive nature and unfazed by the young woman's questions. They simply shook their heads. The barge pilot overheard her question and seemed eager to respond while never taking his eyes off the river or his hands off the tiller's handle. "I've seen some herds on this side, but it's rare. It's likely they crossed the ice in the winter to graze and find protection in the woods, then the ice thawed before they could return. Now the herd must remain on this side all summer. It's miles across—even though horses are strong swimmers, they won't try to swim that far."

Having found a soul willing to converse, Amila crouched down beside him and introduced herself. She learned his name was Luca Belova. She asked how he had come to know so much about the Volga and become a barge pilot.

"I've been on this river all my life. What I know I learned from my father and his father. This is the best job in all of Russia. We work for ourselves and ride the water all summer until the river freezes. Then we go where we like, spend the winter in a city or village, and start all over again the next year."

"I see you watching the water." She followed his gaze into the Volga's depths. "What do you see?"

He chuckled heartily. "People think we're crazy, we pilots, for just that reason. We must learn to read the river. The water tells quite a story." He explained that the water's color, its ripples, and swirls help him determine what lay ahead. By gazing into it, Luca could tell the water's depth, the strength of the current, and the locations of snags, rocks, and sandbars that could strand or sink a raft. He said the hardest part is it changes rapidly, depending on the weather and season.

Luca's voice imparted a reverence for the mighty river, reminding her of the way Rein talked about farming. "The Volga never stops changing: while there is the river, there is life all around. Eventually, all life comes to the shores of Mother Volga. I've seen herds of boar and the wondrous saiga antelope. Not even the army's hunters can shoot them – they run so fast they disappear into their own cloud of dust. And of course, wolves and bears, even the smaller ermine, sable, and fox, all come to the river."

Luca studied the wisps of clouds, then quickly returned his gaze to the river. "But the Volga's greatest gifts live in its depths. The river is brimming with fish. So many kinds I can't name them. I know where to go and what to look for – in the evening, I go ashore and catch them with a scoop net. I sell them to the army and to passengers. Of most value is the sturgeon, prized for its roe, or eggs. One of the giant fish can hold 40 or more pounds of eggs. That is a more difficult fish to catch." Luca looked toward the soldiers and then whispered. "I sell the eggs as *caviar* for a great deal of money."

Just listening to Luca speak about the river was exciting. But settlements were vacant from the landscape, and Amila wanted to know what he would say. "What about people? We haven't seen a village of any kind. Does anyone live along this part of the Volga?"

"No one you want to meet. Large bands of *spitzbuben* live on this side, stealing everything they can get their hands on," warned Luca. "Without the soldiers, it would be too dangerous for us to even stop near the banks, as we do each night. The thieves see these rafts and want everything we carry. They're probably watching us now."

Amila shivered, glad he spoke Russian so the other colonists couldn't understand.

Rein rode back and forth at the edge of the herd, gently urging horses and cattle across a river swollen by runoff. They balked and bellowed, then lurched into the water and swam safely across. Captain Kachinov said there would be many such water crossings in the five or six days he estimated it would take to reach the colony's land.

The captain had expressed his frustration for the colonists' late start. He recommended to Chancellor Grekov that they leave in April, knowing how much time the colonists needed to get settled and prepare for winter. It was now late June. Grekov had held up their departure, saying they had to wait until the scientific team completed its surveys of the entire area. Georg already had a survey map of their destination, so the delays made no sense to him or the colonists. When a message from Commissar Demidov in St. Petersburg arrived saying hundreds more colonists were on their way to Saratov, with many more to follow, Grekov at last agreed to let the first settlers depart.

Rein had formed a deep respect for the captain. Language was still a barrier, though his Russian was improving. Even when unable to understand what was being said, it was clear the soldiers held the fatherly officer in high regard. Just as on the trip from St. Petersburg to Saratov, Rein felt fortunate to have this man in charge.

The first day Rein and Johann had occasional views of the river from high bluffs, but the herd was now too far inland to see the massive river. That night the horses and cattle were weary from the day's walk and grazed peacefully before bedding down. Kachinov posted lookouts through the night.

The second day was warmer with more water to cross. They continued to follow the trail south along the Volga, making progress without mishap. Tired and dusty at the end of the long day, Rein was relieved he wasn't on lookout duty tonight. As they sat by the campfire, Kachinov walked through, talking to soldiers and the few colonists who, like Rein and Johann, had volunteered to move the herd.

"How will we know when we've reached our destination?" Rein asked, using his limited Russian and hoping the captain could understand.

Kachinov nodded and motioned for Rein and the other colonists to come near. He pulled out a map. "It will be obvious when we arrive. We will continue to follow the river and find it easily. It's a unique and memorable location. Look here," he tapped a position on the map showing high bluffs silhouetting an inlet on the Volga where a small river flowed from the hills. "We'll cross the Dobrinka River, and then we will find it. If their trip goes smoothly, I expect the barges to arrive first. And I have no reason to believe otherwise. The river pilots are a bit crazy but excel at what they do."

By the sixth day, children's complaints and cries drowned out the sound of gurgling water beating against the side of the raft. Long days trapped on barges were especially hard on the younger children. Movement was minimal, with no one allowed near the sides for fear they'd fall in. Amila stretched her arms high overhead and yawned. Her thoughts drifted to Rein and the soldiers. She wished for the hundredth time she could be on horseback driving the herd. For now, she longed for a walk along the shore or a quick swim.

As a diversion, children coddled the sheep, goats, and chickens, feeding handfuls of hay and grain and sloshing buckets of water handed to them by parents. Not unlike the children, animals showed signs of weariness, bawling and pushing against the confining slats of pens. Both adults and children fished with long wooden poles to fill time and add to the food supply. The fish they caught were salted heavily and dried in the sun or simply eaten raw. Colonists on each barge had packed food to be doled out carefully, not knowing how long the trip would take. From the locals in Saratov, they'd purchased dried fish, dried fruit, hard cheeses, and loaves of bread. It was still too early in the season for fresh vegetables.

Shouts carrying across the water from one of the barges brought colonists out of their doldrums. Throughout the trip, one barge had consistently lagged behind the others, meandering from side to side. The raft's movements now looked even more chaotic. Suddenly one corner bobbed under water, and cargo began to slide. Passengers pressed against one another, crawling away from the sinking edge. Panic-stricken parents moved erratically to grab their children.

"The barge is in trouble. Sit down and remain still." Luca commanded to his passengers. Amila translated quickly. After a series of shouts back and forth with other pilots, he began to steer the raft toward a sandy shore.

"What's happening?" Georg shouted to Luca, who spoke only Russian. Amila attempted to translate as Luca spoke.

"It's overloaded, or the weight is unbalanced. If the passengers panic, it may sink. We must get it to shore. Grab the ropes tied to our raft and swim to shore!" he yelled to the soldiers. "All others stay where you are."

Soldiers from each raft had evidently received similar orders and were heaving heavy ropes over the side as they neared the shore. They jumped in, swam, and then waded the rest of the way to shore, towing the ropes over their shoulders. All but the unsteady barge were now safely near shore.

Fearful cries carried across the water from the careening raft, now weaving dangerously and drifting even farther from shore. The pilot seemed unable to control the raft, even with assistance from soldiers. The unpredictable swaying caused several passengers to fall into the water. Others jumped, attempting to swim to shore. Those huddled on the raft looked on helplessly as the powerful current seized the swimmers and those who had fallen overboard downstream.

Soldiers on shore began to cast ropes toward the disabled raft but fell far short of reaching it. Those on board were doing the same, trying in vain to throw ropes to shore, with no success. Suddenly, a burly soldier on the sinking raft tied a rope around his waist and dived into the water, swimming hard across the current toward shore. Shouts of encouragement came from every direction, urging him on. Ropes thrown from shore finally reached him, and they pulled the swimmer, bobbing in and out of sight, to shore. Soldiers formed a line to heave the raft to the safety of the shallows. More ropes were thrown and tied on as they hauled the raft in closer. It was clear the soldiers needed help pulling all the rafts toward shore.

"If you're a strong swimmer, get to the shore and pull the ropes," ordered Luca. Men at once jumped into the river. It took Amila only a moment to respond, following Georg into the water. She dived and surfaced quickly, shocked by the cold water, and swam the short distance to shore. They grabbed ropes tied to their own raft and strained to hold on.

The troubled raft was pulled closer, but still in deep water. Its passengers had calmed and lay low against the soaked lumber, clutching one another to brace themselves. The pilot immediately shouted orders to help passengers swim from the battered raft. A child broke away from his parents to free the frightened goats and sheep, allowing them to jump into the water and swim to safety. Once ashore, the shivering men, women, and children could only watch as the raft careened once more, then sank in swirling waves, taking its cargo along.

Georg, Amila, and others ran down the grassy sloping riverbank, desperately searching for those missing, hoping they might somehow have reached the shore farther downstream. They found no one, only a vast expanse of dark green water rushing serenely past.

Amila heard Luca yelling for them to return, saying they must continue or all rafts might be lost. She and Georg rushed back to help the displaced passengers move toward other already crowded rafts, comforting them more than the brusque, Russian-speaking soldiers who pushed them along. As the last passengers were relocated aboard rafts, she and Georg swam back and grabbed outstretched hands to board. Luca and the other rafts' pilots eased the barges back into the current.

For the first time, the colonists had witnessed the deadly power of the Volga; it had claimed twelve lives. Amila and her companions were solemn. She was sure they would never look at the river the same way.

On the sixth day, Captain Kachinov passed calmly between the drovers and told them he was certain they were being followed. Rein listened intently, trying to make out every word. *Spitzbuben*, he heard him say, and the officers repeat again and again. He and Johann understood Russian the best among the colonists on the cattle drive, given the time spent sparring with soldiers on the months-long wagon train. Suddenly he recalled Pavel's song from the tavern and words of warning.

Forest thieves, explained the unflappable officer. He'd been on this overland route before to reach Kamyshin, a fortress on the southern border of the lands designated for new colonies. But he'd never encountered *spitzbuben*, though he knew there were many bands hiding in the forests. "As soldiers traveling from one fort to another, we never had any trouble. But we had more weapons and nothing they could easily steal. They will likely strike at night, scattering the herd and taking as many as they can."

Rein could hear the rapid exchange between the captain and his other officers, determining what should be done. He understood the part about gunfire and knew that would stampede the entire herd. Rein, Johann, and the other colonists spoke in hushed tones about what such a devastating loss would mean to the fledgling settlement.

"What if we surprise them before the herd can be scattered?" asked Johann. "We double back after dark and intercept the thieves before they can strike, take their weapons and horses?" Rein and Johann approached the Kachinov with the idea. He listened intently, consulted his officers, and fine-tuned the plan. They nodded in agreement and accepted Rein and Johann's offer to join the soldiers that night. "You must learn to fight them sometime. May as well begin now."

Under cover of darkness, Rein and Johann followed the soldier detail on horseback, retracing the herd's path earlier that day. After several miles, Captain Kachinov motioned to dismount and tie horses in a nearby stand of trees. If they had guessed wrong and the thieves were able to bypass them and scatter the herd, losses would be heavy. They were banking on the thieves taking the easiest route, following directly behind the herd. The captain had wisely circulated word to continue to act normally as if the thieves hadn't been seen. Rein hoped they were lazy and sloppy, like Tundorf's goons, Ebald and Axel. He shook his head, remembering the many times he'd evaded discovery as they patrolled for poachers, passing so close to Rein he could hear them breathing. Good experience for tonight's exercise, but he lacked his trusty bow.

The soldiers paused, hearing sounds directly ahead. Positioned at the front of the detail, the captain motioned to spread out and take cover on one side of the woods. Men on horseback, speaking quietly, were approaching, illuminated by moonlight on the trail. Rein counted about fifteen riders. The soldiers and colonists waited with rifles loaded and raised.

"You're surrounded by the army. I order you to dismount. Drop your weapons on the ground. Now!" ordered Kachinov.

The shocked thieves yelled among themselves and spurred their horses forward in an attempt to outrun the soldiers. Kachinov gave the order to shoot. Firing from the advantage of ground cover, the muskets found their targets as the thieves drew pistols and fired back into the dark woods. Shots from the black powder rifles knocked all but two riders from their horses. Several thieves were still alive but lay thrashing in pain, weapons already fired. Two riders had evaded capture, spurring their horses in the opposite direction into the thick, concealing woods. The soldier detail was on foot and unable to follow.

"Those two were probably the leaders. You two ride back to the herd and warn the others that two thieves escaped," Kachinov instructed Rein and Johann. "I don't think they'll attack the herd, but we need to be sure. We'll return soon."

As they followed the orders, galloping their horses back toward camp, Rein heard more shots fired from the direction of the encounter. He swallowed hard and glanced at Johann. So this was how the Russian army handled frontier justice. Wherever the thieves came from, thought Rein, let's hope it isn't near our land.

Amila desperately hoped Georg was right. After consulting the map and talking with Luca early that morning, he spread the news. The destination must be close. Parents urged children to summon final shreds of patience when Georg explained they must watch for high bluffs, then a large inlet where the river swung to the right. All eyes focused down-stream. A boy spotted it first and began to point and shout. "Dobrinka River! Dobrinka!" Cheers reverberated across the water when the highly anticipated landmarks came into view.

The pilots exchanged commands between barges and began to maneuver toward the inlet. Luca and soldiers forced the tiller that controlled the rudder hard right to turn the raft upstream against the current, steering toward the bank. As the current tried to push the raft downriver, the pressure he exerted on the tiller swept the raft closer to the inlet. Once inside the protected area and as close to shore as the rafts' momentum would take them, Luca and the other pilots shouted for soldiers to swim in with tow ropes.

Compared with the deceptively powerful current of the Volga, the Dobrinka River seemed mild. Once close enough to shore, soldiers helped passengers enter the waist-deep water. Forced to wait their turn, Amila and Eva looked at one another mischievously. Holding hands, they took the few steps to the edge of the raft and plunged into the welcoming water, shouting and splashing joyfully to shore.

"Pull the barges as far up the inlet as you can, all the way to the mouth of the river. Men, help pull. Women, please keep your children nearby," Georg shouted boldly. Watching, Amila smiled, certain the leadership skills he had honed over the past year would be pushed to new limits starting today. "The closer we can get to the mouth of the river, the shorter the distance to unload."

Summoning energy dormant for the past week, all united toward this common goal. Some with feet planted in the mud, others up to their waists in water, soldiers and colonists dragged the rafts farther into the inlet. Progress was slow, but the teams towed the creaking barges, still heavy with cargo, close to the seeping mouth of the tributary. Exhausted from the exertion, many collapsed on the bank.

Once the rafts were secured to shore, colonists swarmed up the embankment to the hilltop. Amila and Eva stood with the Müllers, gazing in all directions. Amila shielded her eyes from the sun to take in the dazzling panorama. Deep grass dominated the scenery in every direction, with flat land and a few rolling hills pushing out to the horizon. Where the little Dobrinka River met the mighty Volga, a deep ravine grew thick with trees. The bluffs they'd floated past were visible upriver, and the Volga consumed all the space beyond. But it was the tinted canvas of clear, blue sky meeting verdant plains as far as one could see that made Amila catch her breath.

She heard cheerful discourse mixed with the carefree voices of children. However, an undercurrent of disenchanted muttering swept through the crowd. Amila stood near Lars Heckmann, the shoemaker from Bremen, who from the beginning had opposed farming.

Lars looked out across the prairie. "I see only barren land, hear only the monotonous rustling of grass. Those gorges and ravines. What's out there? We have no shelter, as we were promised." His words reverberated among the non-farmers.

Head held high, the Russian officer leading the soldier detail addressed the colonists. "Everything you see is presented to you with the compliments of Empress Catherine." Amila translated, hopeful the shades of disillusionment evident on many faces would dim in time.

"The empress' gift. It must first be shaped by us with great toil. We have no assurance it will repay the labor and time spent," reflected Georg. "Did we think it would be paradise? Perhaps we've found a lost paradise, good friends!"

Riding near the back of the slow-moving herd, Rein could see the lead riders herding the animals around a mass of people moving amidst tall grass. He looked over at Johann, and they simultaneously breathed deep sighs of relief. Impatient to join their fellow colonists, they nevertheless remained with the herd until the weary animals stopped to graze. From what he could see, the livestock could eat and drink here until they were too full to stand.

Rein scanned the crowd. After an anxious, frenzied search, he found the tall, unbending, unmistakable silhouette of Amila. He looked toward the heavens and squeezed his eyes shut, finally admitting how worried he had been–about Eva and Amila. Relief washed over him, knowing they had all finally made it. But something else momentous rose up inside him. He acknowledged what it must be and wanted to cry out in joy. *He felt free for the first time in his life!* That headstrong woman who had plagued him every step of this journey did this for him, for Eva. We would never have come if not for her. Amila made our parents' dream come true.

Rein reveled in the feeling, but it threatened to over-whelm him. He shook himself to regain composure before approaching the others. He steadied his breathing and studied the terrain. Before him lay a virgin wilderness, like a green-gold ocean splashed with wildflowers. No plow had passed over these waves of wild growth. Rein could smell the prairie—heavy, luscious, and sweet. The panorama presented flat land clear of trees with gently rolling hills. Toward the mouth of the Dobrinka River, ravines were rich in oaks, pines, and firs.

When Rein saw the Dobrinka River feeding into the Volga, his heart beat faster. He hurried to Johann, pointing. "Our mill will be there someday! Like father's back home. And an orchard, many orchards, with all this water." The pair released their horses to graze and strode toward the colonists milling about.

Eva ran to Rein. He picked her up and swung her around in a playful embrace. She smiled and stepped back, turning her attention to Johann. "We're so happy to see you, to finally be here. It was the longest time on the rafts. Amila and I jumped in and swam to shore."

Rein nodded, unsurprised, as Amila approached, no longer dripping but still soaked through.

"We were so tired of that raft—we could wait no longer. It felt wonderful to get wet." Amila's face lit up when she saw his smile. The corners of her mouth turned up, and she held his gaze. "You've done it. You've brought the horses and cattle. We're safe."

"You seem surprised. It was a peaceful ride, wasn't it, Johann?" Rein winked and reluctantly looked away. "So, this is to be our new home." He could wait no longer. He left them and hurried down the bank to the barges, searching for something. Wading into the water, he pulled a shovel from supplies tied to one of the rafts. He returned to the top of the hill and started to dig. After a few tries, the thick grass gave way, and dirt piled up. Rein kept digging, his actions attracting a crowd. Some were puzzled by his actions, but farmers in the crowd knew what he was doing. Several feet down, he stopped digging, put down the shovel, and dropped to his knees on the mound, lifting handfuls of chestnut brown soil free of rocks and teeming with worms. Rein scanned the faces of curious onlookers gathered around and cleared a catch in his throat. "The soil is nearly perfect. It will grow all we need."

PART TWO

CHAPTER 14

June - July 1764

*G*athered in a circle on knee-deep grass, the leaders could finally implement the plan they'd been discussing during the long months awaiting transport. Rein begrudgingly took his place at the vorstehers' meeting, acknowledging its importance. So much to do, and already the end of June. He glanced at Amila, busy recording proceedings as a respected member of the decision-making group. A bit frazzled by her nearness, he attempted to focus on the discussion.

With the colony survey laid out for all to see, Georg pointed to agreed-upon areas best for temporary shelters and cooking fires, the community privy, and livestock. Colonists were busy unloading barges, harnessing teams of horses to help drag heavy items up the embankment. Children were roaming and playing while tending the smaller livestock, content to be back on land grazing the lush hillsides.

The survey showed the colony encompassed 27,683 acres, measured in Russian *dessyantine*. More than half was suitable for farming and the rest for grazing or woods. The map showed ten ravines, many groves of trees, a number of brooks, two small mountains, and the Dobrinka River. The survey listed the colony as "Dobrinka," influencing leaders to adopt the name until citizens decided differently. In the contract signed with the Kontora, the colony owned the land, the colonists were the "settler owners," and each family would permanently own its land with inheritance rights. To start, each family received more than 200 farmable acres, far more than a single family could manage in the first year.

Rein was amazed at the volume of land set aside for the new colonies. Before leaving Saratov, Georg had shared the map that encompassed land designated for all the colonies, confirming theirs was to be one community in a much bigger undertaking to settle this vast wilderness. Overall, land set aside for the empress' new colonies was about 50 miles wide and more than 75 miles long, including both sides of the river. The surveys assured the designated land avoided Russian settlements. The nearest town to Dobrinka was Kamyshin, a military fortress and small village located 27 miles south. They had traveled more than 50 miles south from Saratov without seeing a settlement of any kind.

To Rein, it was almost too much to comprehend. Our own land! He overheard complaints from many colonists about the isolation and bleak landscape. Wasteland, most disparaged. He could empathize with those who had never lived in the country or worked the land, having come to Russia expecting to live in towns and practice trades. Rein knew it was different for him, Eva, and Johann, who came from a country estate controlled by a lord, with no hope of ever owning land or even the cottage in which they lived. Dreams he'd never before allowed himself to contemplate took shape in his mind.

He could visualize what this place could become. He felt his heart might burst.

Envious that Johann had already been allowed to start work, Rein looked over his shoulder at the livestock area where his friend was busily assembling a wagon. When the leaders had asked Johann to manage the colony's horses and cattle, he smiled from ear to ear. The wagon would serve as Johann's makeshift shelter. He planned to build a barn and corrals and remain with the livestock day and night, unsure what kind of predators—four- or two-legged—might be about. Captain Kachinov's troops were setting up their camp near the herd's grazing areas and were to remain with the colonists through the summer.

While wintering in Saratov, Rein had pressed hard about the necessity to begin planting vegetables as soon as they arrived, and the other farmers agreed. Rein wasn't the only farmer who had brought a precious cache of seeds from the homeland. With the arrival of winter so early here, it would take every day of growth for cabbages, onions, turnips, parsnips, and carrots to mature before winter. They all knew growing and storing food for a long winter was critical to survival. He was itching to get started.

"We have no lumber to build cabins. When we asked the Kontora officials when we would receive lumber, they didn't answer. I don't believe they will provide lumber before winter." Georg's words brought Rein back to the harsh reality of a winter approaching before they were prepared. Leaders were discussing the most pressing immediate concern, shelter. They'd been told it didn't often rain along the river and that summer nights were cool. Since each family had the parts for a wagon and a canvas cover, these were to be utilized as summer shelters.

"What about using the rafts for lumber?" asked Amila during a pause. Members of the vorsteher glanced in her direction, still somewhat unused to having a woman among them express herself so freely. "Floating all that way, I had a great deal of time to talk with Luca, our pilot. He told me the barges can't be taken back upstream and reused. Grekov gave orders to float them to Kamyshin, where they'll be taken apart and sold as lumber. They're here. They promised us lumber." She shrugged and spread her hands wide, unsure what they would make of such a wild idea.

Hmm, thought Rein, impressed by Amila's clever suggestion, which generated a lively discussion, especially among the group's builders. He grinned inwardly, visualizing Grekov's reaction upon learning where his lumber had ended up. Relieved the meeting was breaking up at long last, Rein volunteered to hunt for fresh meat. After all, before the farmers could break ground, everyone needed to eat. He was still trying to grasp all this meant to them. We can hunt here! It's our land.

*F*ascinated by the openness and variety of the landscape before him, Rein was more interested in exploring his surroundings than hunting. Cries of quail and partridges led the chorus of bird songs. Hawks overhead fixed their eyes on moving grass.

He followed a game trail in and out of several wooded ravines, then climbed rolling hills until he reached a cliff overlooking the Volga. White cliffs extended far to his left and right, and a pebbly beach dotted the shore below before disappearing into the dark green depths. If he squinted, he could see the other side of the river where the cloudless sky hungrily swallowed the flat shoreline. The lush steppe grasses swayed beneath his feet, the earthy smell of the heavy green and gold spears lingering despite the gentle breeze. Rein moved his boot across the growth and recognized the beginnings of sage and feather grass.

From this vantage point of the settlement, he could see clusters of colonists scurrying about like a mound of disturbed ants. But he knew there was a method to the apparent madness. Georg was seeing to that, marshalling the workforce to take advantage of every daylight hour. Rein closed his eyes and bowed his head in thanks that he and Eva had linked their fate to this man and these good people. He looked back toward the river. Like the sea they had crossed, the Volga remained the biggest mystery of all.

He recalled the soldiers' campfire songs and stories about their beloved Volga. They called it a mythical river, the living spirit of a woman who flaunts her feminine curves as she meanders for thousands of miles. They sang her praises as a generous mistress, comrade, and companion who sleeps through the winter, awakening to become an unruly giant, her pulse beating once again. Rein recalled the warning: beware Mother Volga, source of life and death, hope and sacrifice.

Rein felt confident he could coax the land to feed them, and many knew how to hunt wild game. But the Volga was a powerful, unknown force that would test them. He believed the success of the colony, their very survival, would depend on discovering the river's secrets—quickly. He remembered the watermill at home, a tool whose power his father had learned to harness. The Volga had given them hope for a new life. Yet, it had already taken lives. Life and death. He retreated from the cliff contemplating whether the river would become their friend or their enemy.

When he returned to the colony, Rein was carrying large game birds the soldiers had called bustards, one in each hand. He quickly sought out Georg. "I need help before darkness falls. I've had luck hunting. You won't believe what's out there, what it means to feed us. Bring ropes, knives, and hatchets."

As darkness fell, Rein and a delegation returned tired but elated, dragging a large deer and several wild boar trussed on spits, ready for the fire. The delivery of fresh game attracted little attention. Instead, colonists were gathered listening to angry discourse near the rafts.

"You can't take them for lumber!" shouted Luca, speaking for the river pilots. Resting near the soldiers, they had entered the fray when they noticed colonists harnessing horses to one of the rafts and dragging it up the riverbank. The pilots rushed to stop the colonists. The settlers stood fast beside the beached raft, and the pilots were shouting at them from above the embankment. In between stood Amila, attempting to translate.

"We must have the lumber from the rafts to begin building winter shelters," asserted Georg, leaning forward to face Luca. "We don't know when or even if other lumber will arrive before winter. When it does, you can take it on to Kamyshin. We need this lumber. It's a matter of life or death for us!"

Amila took pains translating and tried to remain calm. Luca shook his head and talked rapidly to the other pilots. Just as it seemed fists would settle the argument, Captain Kachinov arrived and stood beside Amila, who explained the situation. While the pilots were not soldiers but employed by the Kontora, they considered the captain their superior. Men on both sides breathed hard, not willing to back away from a fight for the prized resources. Both sides stopped to listen to the wise captain, whom they were sure would take their side.

Through Amila, the captain asked Georg and the others questions. Whose idea was this? What were they going to build? Did they know how to build structures in the Russian way, without nails? After hearing the responses and shaking his head at Amila, he turned to the pilots.

"Where are you supposed to take the rafts, and do you know how they'll be used?"

Luca explained. "Our orders are to take the rafts to Kamyshin, where they will be pulled out of the river. You know this is the way it is done with all rafts. They must be taken from the river before it runs into the Caspian Sea, or they will be lost. The lumber is to be sold to villagers and money returned to Chancellor Grekov. We're to deliver funds to him in Saratov, and then we'll get our cut. It's the only way we get paid. Then we're to bring more colonists down the Volga on new rafts. We'll lose our jobs if we disobey."

The captain contemplated this for a moment before replying. "This is the first time lumber has been needed here in the wilderness. Perhaps it means looking at the sale of rafts in another way. How many rubles is the lumber worth? What if you didn't have to go all the way to Kamyshin to sell it and could return to Saratov sooner?"

Luca and the pilots looked at one another, understanding where this was leading. After a spirited discussion, they set a price and agreed to sell the rafts to the colonists.

Once Amila translated, Georg and the builders took their time discussing the terms and hesitantly agreed. They were unhappy about paying for lumber but planned to ask the Kontora to reimburse them. Then, cooperating again, especially when it meant leaving sooner to collect their wages and begin another rafting trip before winter, the pilots showed them a quicker, easier way to bring the rafts ashore and break them down.

Watching from the perimeter, Rein approached Georg. "You've solved another problem, Georg. And Captain Kachinov, he's a wise man, isn't he? I know you don't need another problem just now. But can I talk with you?"

Georg followed Rein to a quiet spot. "In the colony, we have farmers, builders, men who know many trades but no river expert to teach us about the Volga, its bounty, and its dangers. I believe we need someone among us who knows these things and can quickly teach us what we need to know to survive here. How to navigate it, how to build rafts and boats, how to fish. We don't even know what we need to know. But the pilots—they know. They've spent their lives learning about the river. Do you think we could convince one of them to stay with us until winter, pay them a fair wage, and teach us?"

George patted him on the shoulder. "I think the good captain isn't the only one who is wise. First, let's ask Amila for her help talking to Luca and the others. Then we'll ask the leaders. At this rate, the colony's treasury will be drained by winter. But you're right. We must learn the river's mysteries."

By sunrise, Rein and the other farmers had harnessed ponies to the crude plows furnished by the Kontora and broken ground on what would be the communal vegetable garden. If they planted now, they would have time to grow cabbages, onions, carrots, turnips, parsnips, and even cucumbers. Rein and the farmers had consolidated their seeds and decided how much space they needed to plow. Other larger plots would be plowed next for winter rye, the all-important grain that would take seed in the fall, go dormant under a blanket of winter snow, grow with the help of spring moisture, and be harvested around the time of Summer Solstice. Once they had their own grain, they could feed themselves year-round, so it was crucial they be ready to plant rye on the newly plowed ground as soon as late summer rains came. But, for now, the priority was vegetables.

Rein and others had visited farms near Saratov during the past winter and were shocked at the backward techniques and primitive tools they employed. Even in the fertile, black soil, which they called *chernozem*, Russian farmers were unable to produce yields as great as the poorest German soil. Rein was amazed the Russian farmers rarely fertilized or rotated crops to restore the soil, nor did they allow land to lie fallow some seasons. And no potatoes! When asked, the Russian farmers looked puzzled. They had never even heard of potatoes.

Rein had never seen such old-fashioned farm implements and wondered if even his father or grandfather had. The plow, or *sokha*, furnished by the Kontora was made of wood except for two iron plowshares. Rein found its design highly inefficient; it cut only a shallow furrow and was unable to turn over large clods or thoroughly break apart roots of grass and weeds. He was anxious to meet with their blacksmith to develop a heavier plow suitable for this soil type. Meanwhile, they must make use of what they had.

They had barely broken a hard sweat when Johann interrupted their work. "Georg has called the leaders together. A soldier just arrived from Saratov with news. Grekov has recalled Captain Kachinov and the soldiers. They've been ordered to leave at once."

When Rein and Johann arrived back at the settlement, they overheard the captain talking in a hushed tone to Amila and Georg, shaking his head. "Grekov again. I'm forced to follow his orders, as he is the head of the Kontora in Saratov. I will say this to you as a warning, but be careful what you repeat. He's a corrupt, unstable man. You heard the pilots say he was planning to fill his own pockets with the sale of the lumber and leave you without shelter for winter. We were to stay here with you until your colony had time to get established, to make sure you can protect yourselves. He has no concern for your safety. I believe he's bringing us back to Saratov out of spite, to get even with you for contacting Commissar Demidov without his knowledge. And perhaps for Amila's rebuff of his advances. You can't trust him."

Amila translated a short version of his message to Georg and the others, careful to follow the captain's wishes for discretion.

"It will leave us defenseless. What will we do?" asked one of the leaders.

Amila asked the captain for advice and translated, sentence by sentence, as he spoke. "Thieves will be watching. No one knows how many bands of robbers are out there. But the Kirghiz don't cross the river in the summer, only when the river is frozen. So you must take precautions immediately against the thieves. Build a tower and have an armed scout there at all times, especially at night. Tell the men to keep weapons loaded and ready. And when you leave the village, go in large groups, heavily armed. Perhaps we, or another detail of soldiers, will be patrolling the area and can help. But I'm sorry to say, you must take action quickly to protect yourselves."

Kachinov and his soldiers broke camp and prepared to leave. The river pilots were to return with them, except for Luca, who had agreed to stay in Dobrinka through the fall. Georg and the leaders asked the captain as many questions as they could. They learned where the nearest Russian settlements were located so they could buy and bring back food in winter. He told them they could also buy food and supplies at Kamyshin, the settlement located about a day's ride south along the river. It was a sizable village and military outpost with a battalion of 200 soldiers. Although he emphasized the Kamyshin fort was stationed there to protect the settlement and the empress' land to the south, not new colonies to the north, such as Dobrinka.

Woeful eyes followed the soldiers as they left the fledgling settlement. Once out of sight, the colonists turned to one another solemnly, knowing they were now truly on their own in the wilderness.

*C*elebration of arrival at their new home was cut short, replaced by the urgency to become vigilant. They followed the captain's recommendations to safeguard the settlement. Wagons, tents, and campfires were moved closer, tightening the circle around the encampment. Extra guards were posted with Johann and the livestock while an armed sentry stood watch day and night in the hastily built tower atop one of the hills.

Vigil determined work priorities. With more men needed for security, fewer were available for other tasks, the most pressing of which were tending the newly planted vegetable gardens, building what they were calling the common house, and preparing large plots where rye would be planted.

A disturbing realization hit Rein like a fist while plowing early one morning. He's not going to give us the seed to plant. Grekov and the Kontora he controlled so tightly were following a startling pattern when it came to support, almost as if he wanted them to fail or at the very least didn't care what became of them. Grekov had just recalled the soldiers. Why should they believe he would deliver the rye seed in time to plant? Before they left, Rein had been assured hundreds of sacks of seed were stored in a Saratov warehouse and would be transported to them once they arrived. It was already late. It wasn't coming. Knowing Grekov, he planned to sell the seed and pocket the money. Rein stopped plowing, patting the necks of the hard-working horses, and sought out Georg, who hardly needed yet another problem.

Riding as fast as their Kalmyk ponies would carry them, Rein, Amila, and Luca rode north toward Saratov

all day and by moonlight. Rein marveled at the endurance of the horses. He tired, but they never seemed to.
Neither did Amila. Born to ride, he guessed, like he was
born to farm. More comfortable on a raft than a horse,
Luca was holding up well enough.

Rein recalled what happened to precipitate the
rapidly organized trip to Saratov. Georg had been equally
distressed when Rein reported the seed was going to
arrive too late to plant, or more likely not at all. They had
to plant this fall for next summer's crop or go another
year without grain for the colony. As it was, they were
uncertain how they would survive the first winter. But a
second winter without grain for bread would be devastating.

Georg had expressed a related dilemma. Kontora
officials were scheduled to inspect the colony soon. If
Dobrinka had not achieved specific requirements, one
of which was having planted winter rye in the fall, the
Kontora would withhold forage money critical to feed
each family. That meant starvation, even before next
winter. Georg didn't hesitate to agree that a delegation
must be dispatched immediately to procure the rye seed
and that Rein should go. Rein had recently traveled the
overland route on the cattle drive, and Georg had seen
how skilled at fighting and weapons he had become if it
came to that.

They had discussed whether to bring the sacks of
grain back by wagon or by raft. Knowing wagons traveling alone would be an easy target for thieves, they
opted for the river. Luca agreed, assuring that one small
raft would carry it all and be much faster than the slug-
gish caravan of barges he'd led the last time. They could

trade the horses for a raft in Saratov, travel all night, and rarely bring the raft to shore.

However, Georg resisted when Amila argued she should go along. "I'm the only one who speaks Russian well enough to reason with them, to explain why we need the seed now. I'm as good or a better rider than anyone here. And I can translate between Rein and Luca."

Georg directed a fatherly look toward Amila. "It's your reputation I'm concerned about."

"Respectfully, Georg, we can no longer afford my virtue—there's too much at stake," she shot back. "Anyway, I traveled halfway across Germany with Rein. He's like a brother to me." An obstinate brother, she thought but didn't say so out loud.

Now, they were riding at breakneck speed across the same trails Rein had recently traveled at a painstakingly slow pace with the herd. On this trip, the trees and ground seemed to fly past. He had no idea how long it would take to reach Saratov. Perhaps only three days at this pace. Tonight, the clouds obscured the moonlight, and they stopped to let the horses graze and rest.

"I'll take first watch while you two sleep." Gun in hand, Rein propped himself straight-backed against a tree where he could watch the horses. Luca only waited until Amila translated and quickly found a place to lie down, as did she. Luca was already earning his wages for the colony. With the men busy farming and erecting buildings, he'd taught the women and older children how and where to fish and the best way to dry fish in the warm sun so they'd store well all winter.

Rein considered how different everything in this place was compared to Germany. Except, he thought cynically, the way aristocrats like Grekov treated serfs like him and the others. He expelled a heavy sigh. Why had he believed it would be any better here? He and Amila had talked about what they'd do once they arrived in Saratov. She wanted to reason with the chancellor and his staff, explain that the fields were ready, and they had simply come to hasten the delivery of the seed. They'd send Luca off with the horses to trade for a raft, which he believed would be easy to find this time of year. Rein hoped the plan would all fall into place easily.

After a few hours, Amila awakened and stretched. Straining to stay awake, Rein watched as she drank from the nearby creek, splashing water on her face and neck. She pulled dried fish and bread from a satchel and walked toward him, toting her gun.

"I'll take a turn so you can sleep." She handed some food to Rein.

"No, I can make it until morning. Get some more sleep."

"Don't you trust me? I can stay awake, and I know how to use this if anything happens," Amila held the gun in front of her. Once the soldiers left, Georg ensured all the colonists, even the older children, learned how to load and fire the single-shot muskets and smaller pistols purchased in Saratov. Amila also kept a knife sheathed in her boot—added to her arsenal soon after the attack by highwaymen.

"Why are you always looking for a fight?" Rein immediately regretted his words, realizing he was tired and no match for her energy.

Half-awake, Amila paused before blurting back. "If I don't fight, who will fight for me? Not my father. Not my mother. Everyone's gone who was on my side. And certainly not Count Tundorf! He's been my enemy since I can remember."

He sat blinking at her, too exhausted to argue. They had ridden all night, not knowing whether to be more concerned about thieves or wild animals. But neither had threatened them. They were traveling as safely as they could, with no campfires. He wanted to trust her.

"I'm sorry I doubted you, Amila. Yes, I believe you do know how to protect us. I do need sleep." He yawned and got to his feet. "The horses seem content to graze on this side of the creek. You know horses better than I. If anything, or anyone, is approaching, they'll hear it first." Rein carried his satchel to a level spot nearby, propped his gun in the crook of his arm, and lay down. As he closed his eyes, a thought occurred to him. For the first time, he had insight into the ferocity that drove her.

When they rode into Saratov on the third day, the three riders barely recognized it. The small city they'd left only a month before was teeming with people and livestock, all of which coated the few main streets with pulsating, nervous energy. Masses of what must be newly arrived colonists aggressively bartered with vendors for horses, livestock, and farm items. Urgency radiated from the small city as families snatched up goods by the wagon-load.

Rein, Amila, and Luca dismounted and led their horses through the noisy throng. Amila and Rein exchanged glances with the same wide-eyed realization. These settlers, most of whom were fellow countrymen and women, were preparing to leave for colony locations very soon, late in the brief Russian summer. They'd have even less time to prepare for winter than the Dobrinka colonists.

Hearing a nearby family speaking German, they stopped. "Where are you from? When did you arrive?" Amila pressed. The husband looked puzzled and responded that they were from Neroth, Germany, and had spent the winter in Oranienbaum. They'd only recently arrived by barge and were told by Kontora officials to prepare to leave for their colony location within days.

"Who is your colony's leader, and where can we find him?" asked Rein. Soon after, they sought out and met with Fritz Meier, the leader of settlers departing soon for a location on the Galka River. A glance at the Meier's colony survey showed the Galka River was north of Dobrinka, perhaps only ten miles away. After several hours of intense dialogue, Meier had run out of questions, and the Galka leader had been briefed on insights they could provide, along with many warnings. Rein encouraged Meier and others to visit Dobrinka as soon as they could. Meier shook their hands and thanked them profusely, then left hastily to share what he'd learned with other leaders.

With concern for the newly arrived colonists still weighing heavily, Amila and Rein walked side by side toward the Kontora office. They'd sent Luca to trade the horses for a small raft.

"Those are good ponies. I wish we didn't have to give them up," lamented Amila, almost to herself. She glanced up at Rein, guilty for the selfish comment. After all, the loss of a few horses was trivial compared to the challenges others were facing. "I know. It must be done. The new owners will be lucky to have them. With all the activity on the river, do you think Luca can find anything left unclaimed to float us back?"

Rein smiled. "He'll have a better chance than we would. I wouldn't know what would float and what wouldn't."

Amila stopped as they reached the Kontora office. "I don't want to run into Grekov. He hates me. I have no fondness for him either."

Rein remembered the carriage incident. "I don't think he hates you, Amila. It's me he probably dislikes the most. Anyway, he's unlikely to show his face in the office where real work takes place. Our request for seed is insignificant compared with the movement of this many new colonists."

Amila pulled out the seed order Georg had printed and signed so carefully. She swallowed hard. "You stay outside as we discussed. I'll present the seed order. All we need is their countersign and seal, and we take it to the warehouse to collect the sacks of grain." Rein nodded and leaned against the building outside the door.

Once inside, Amila pushed her way into one of several lines to see a Kontora official, all of whom appeared to be simultaneously overwhelmed and annoyed.

"And this is where we process colonist requests and store all the records," she heard Chancellor Grekov say proudly, spreading his arms wide to show clerks lined up behind the counter, interacting with the colonists.

"Very impressive, chancellor. Only a man of great intelligence and superior breeding could direct such a massive program," replied a richly dressed man following Grekov.

That voice. Amila turned away in horror and clasped her hand over her mouth to stifle any sound that might escape, a strangling dryness constricting her throat. Count Tundorf, here in Saratov. She looked toward the door and suppressed a desire to run. Rein was just outside the door. If they went out that way, they'd surely see him. Heart beating wildly, Amila left her place in line and walked slowly toward the exit, keeping her head tilted down and away from the pair.

Once outside, she grabbed Rein's sleeve and pulled him around the corner, covering his mouth with her hand when he abruptly asked what she was doing. Pale and breathless, she found a weak voice at last. "Count Tundorf. He's here, inside with Grekov." She crumbled to the ground, unconscious.

Amila opened her eyes to familiar voices. So, she'd fainted again. Just like the time she thought Eva was being attacked by a bear. She sat bolt upright on the small cot and recalled the moments before she collapsed. On her feet in a moment, she looked wildly around the room.

Rein quickly reassured her before she tried to dart out the door. "It's all right, Amila. You're safe."

"I've got to stop doing that." She rolled her eyes toward Rein apologetically and, for the first time, noticed Christof. "Do you think he saw us?"

"No. We did get a lot of attention from strangers, though, with me carrying your limp body through the streets looking for Christoph's lodgings." Rein thought how different it felt to carry her in his arms this time, recalling her fainting spell after encountering the bear. "I just kept telling people this often happens because you have such a delicate constitution and that you'll be fine once I get you out of the heat."

Amila blushed and held back the nasty retort forming on her lips. He had taken care of her, after all. But did he always have to tease? She turned her attention elsewhere. "It's so good to see you, Christof. When we left, you were traveling and making your maps for the army. I didn't get to tell you a proper goodbye."

He smiled warmly and approached her, taking her hands in his. "Rein was telling me all about Dobrinka and showing me the location on the map. I'll come to chart the area and visit you soon. But how are you feeling? And who is this man who can reduce the mighty Amila to a swooning maiden?"

"Oh, Christof. If only it were a laughing matter. It's my stepfather, Count Tundorf. He's an evil, horrible man, capable of anything. He harms everyone and everything he comes in contact with. Unfortunately, Rein knows all too well what he is capable of doing. It's the count I'm... running from."

"Ah, I wondered what brought you here, Amila," said Christof, still holding her hands warmly. "I've told you my secret, why I'm here. But this is much more serious, my dear. I sense that danger has followed you across the continent."

Amila turned to Rein. "I can't believe he's here. What are we going to do?"

Uncomfortable at having intruded on the emotional reunion between the two, Rein had withdrawn to the far edge of the room. He joined the conversation hesitantly, feeling troubled. Consequently, his tone was biting and his voice overly loud. "Why do you think he's come all this way? It must be an attempt to try and take you back. But he has no more power over me. He's not lord of anything here in Russia. He has no serfs to squash like bugs, no lands to ruin, and no ability to tax the food from our table and clothes off our backs. I welcome meeting him face to face."

"Rein, he's dangerous. He wants more than to take me back." Amila tried to calm him. "There's more…that you don't know."

Rein moved closer and scowled. "What do you mean? What haven't you told me?"

Amila backed away, avoiding his gaze. She looked out the window and saw twilight approaching. "It's getting dark. We need to figure out how to get the seed and find Luca. I'll tell you…after we've left, on the way back to Dobrinka."

"What can I do to help?" offered Christof. "Do you want me to come with you to the warehouse?"

Rein brooded over the offer for a moment, looking back and forth between them. "No. We don't know how we're going to proceed now, and you might get in trouble. You must live here and get along with Grekov. But watch them for us, if you can. In many ways, Grekov is like Tundorf. At every turn, he's taking advantage of his position to cheat us and pocket the money. Grekov's actions threaten our very survival. Be careful. He's also dangerous."

Amila went to the desk and found paper and a quill. She wrote a brief message and folded it. "I'm sorry for such a brief visit. Promise you'll come to Dobrinka?" She handed Christof the note. "Please give this message to Captain Kachinov as soon as you see him."

CHAPTER 15

August 1764

They found Luca at the river's dock, humming with activity even at dusk. He shouted a hearty welcome when Rein and Amila approached. "Hello! Look! A raft, and food, too! I got a good price for the ponies. Where are the sacks of grain?"

Rein quickly shushed Luca after hearing references to grain. He didn't need to speak Russian to detect their friendly pilot had found time to visit a tavern. They stepped onto the raft to subdue Luca, hoping to discourage attention. On the walk from Christof's lodgings, they'd had time to talk about how best to procure the grain without authorized papers. The plan was to use an approach familiar to Kontora officials: bribery. Amila had pulled rubles out of one of the hidden pockets in her dress, willing to apply the funds to a good cause.

Rein hoped bribing the guards would work. Otherwise, they would have to break into the warehouse and take the grain. He was willing to do that. It wasn't really stealing because it was the colony's grain. But last winter, they'd seen colonists jailed for lesser offenses.

After convincing Luca to stay with the raft and quietly await their return, they covered the short distance to the warehouse.

"Good evening, gentlemen." Amila smiled warmly at the two guards as she addressed them in Russian. Rein trailed behind. Amila pulled out the seed order signed by Georg and handed it over. "We are here to collect thirty bags of rye wheat seed for our colony, Dobrinka. We're ready to plant and have arranged to transport it ourselves by raft."

The guard held the order under the lone torch illuminating the warehouse door. "Why are you picking it up in the dark? This order is missing the Kontora authorization to receive the supplies." The two guards peered at the paper together. They might not be able to read but knew to look for the Kontora seal. "Something is not right here. You have to come back tomorrow." The guard handed the order back.

"Oh, can't we convince you to let us take the seed tonight?" Amila hesitated but finally accepted the paper. "We must leave tonight to take other supplies back to our colony. I've brought this laborer to carry the sacks. It will save the Kontora the trouble of delivering it to us, more than a week's travel down the river and back. Your superiors will be pleased with your initiative. Please take another look at the order?"

This time she handed them ten rubles along with the order. "You know, Oleg, it would save the Kontora all that time if we fill this order tonight. And a bottle of vodka would certainly sweeten the transaction if you could be so kind?"

Under light of the moon, they followed Luca's instructions to help launch the heavily laden raft from the riverbank. Luca was now sober and fully awake, having slept through the loading of the seed. The sacks of grain were safely elevated and covered by canvas in case of turbulent waves or rain.

Rein collapsed on the raft once safely on their way. Amila noted that Rein was earning this crop from start to finish. He'd plowed the fields, bribed the guards to get the grain, then carried and loaded the heavy sacks from the warehouse to the dock by himself. He'd soon plant and watch over the crop for the next nine or ten months before it would mature for harvest.

"Your 'laborer' is tired." Rein splashed water on his face and reached for the food Luca had bought for the return journey. Amila felt drained after the day's events and wanted nothing more than to sleep. This was no time to begin the horrible revelation she'd promised to tell. Rested and now sober, Luca contently hummed as they floated peacefully down the Volga. Amila crawled under the canvas to sleep.

Rein was waiting for Amila to awaken. Staring in her direction, he watched as she appeared from under the canvas. Light of day brought no more excuses. She hastily drank water and ate bread and cheese to summon energy as Rein watched impatiently.

Amila sat down near him. His intense gaze made her fidget about. She looked over at him, unsure how to begin, but knew she must. "I've kept this secret from you and Eva, not knowing how to tell you." She stumbled over her words, "But you need to know. You're in as much danger as I am. I didn't understand it until we were on the ship crossing the sea. It was only then I had time to study and understand the documents, what they meant."

"Amila, what are you talking about? What documents? You aren't making any sense."

"Can't you see this is hard? Don't yell at me. I'm trying," she pleaded. From his position at the raft's tiller, Luca looked at the two with concern. Amila assured him it was all right, not to worry.

"I'm going to start from the beginning." Amila took deep breaths, spoke slowly, and forced herself to maintain eye contact. "The day Maria, your mother, died, she asked to see me. Eva brought me to your cottage. She told Eva to go outside and watch for you and spoke with me alone before you arrived. Maria gave me a packet of documents she had taken from Count Tundorf's study."

Amila saw the sadness on Rein's face recalling that day. He was respecting her wish for patience but shook his head, still confused.

"Your mother knew what a horrid man Tundorf is. Since his marriage to my mother, Maria had helplessly witnessed his vile acts. Your mother took the packet from the count's study because she knew it was important. Through a crack in the study door, she saw how carefully he had hidden it, apart from all his possessions. That's why she did it—she believed it was proof of some secret, evidence to protect us from him."

Amila swallowed and started again. "I smuggled the pouch out of the castle with the few belongings I brought when we left. I didn't have time to study its contents closely until we were on the ship. The documents are complicated. It took time to determine their meaning. But finally, I began to understand…the horrible truth."

Rein nodded slowly, looking out at the river. "I saw you on the ship trying to find enough light to read. Yes, I was watching you. And then, I saw how you reacted afterward—angry and then afraid."

Remembering how she felt when finally interpreting the documents' meaning, she shuddered. "All the documents are very official, bearing the count's seal and signatures as undersecretary of the Prussian war office. Two documents are the same, except one is written in English and the other in French. They both list an inventory of supplies for the army and large payments made to the count. The order was for 25 wagonloads of food and other supplies from Nassenwald Manor to be delivered to the Prussian army's field locations a few months before the end of the war. When I looked closely and compared the two documents, I saw that one was an invoice to the Prussian war office. The other, the French document, was an invoice to the French army, the enemy! The count was paid twice for the wagonloads of supplies."

Blood drained from Rein's face, and his eyes bore into hers. Her voice quivered, but she had to finish, although the shattered look showed that he knew. "Rein, it was the wagonloads of supplies your father delivered when they were ambushed and killed by the French. Tundorf…he arranged the ambush and killing of our people! He is guilty of murder and treason!"

Rein stood and clenched his fists. A mournful cry shook his body, touching Amila's heart. Her tears began to flow.

"No, no!" Rein took two steps and dived into the water, surfaced, and began to swim, wildly at first, then toward shore. Luca, already disturbed by the intensity of his passengers' conversation, called out. "What's going on? What's wrong?"

"Can we put into shore here?" Tears blurred her vision, and she wiped them angrily away. "He needs time. He'll come back, I hope." Released from the horrible secret, Amila felt no relief—only guilt and blame for the crimes and for the telling, inflicting a wound that might never heal.

Luca brought the raft close to shore and secured it, assuring Amila that the smaller size and weight of the rafts made it easy to control compared with the huge colonist barges. Wading in the last few feet, she welcomed the numbing of the cool water. She climbed to the hilltop and wandered along the cliff searching for Rein. Finally, she sat down in the tall grass and hugged her knees, leaning forward to rest her head.

Amila heard footsteps and a harsh voice overcome with pain. "Why didn't you tell me? You had no right to keep this from me."

She looked up at the large shadow he cast. "You've been angry with me since the day your mother died. We've hardly spoken, and when I do speak to you, it seems to offend you. How could I tell you such a horrible thing? And I was afraid of what you might do. Go back to Germany, kill Tundorf and hang for it. Your mother was afraid of what you would do to the count if you knew…". Her voice trailed off.

"Knew what? I thought she didn't know Tundorf was responsible for Father's murder?"

"She knew something else. Will you come walk with me?" Amila stood and wiped her eyes. Walking beside him, she was able to avoid looking at him when she told him the count had raped Eva and continued to pursue her after that.

"Once your mother told me, I had Eva stay with me in my room when she had to be in the castle late at night. The count would watch and attempt to catch her alone. More than once, he followed her to my chamber. We slammed and locked the door in his face." Amila held her chin high. "Rein, Eva didn't want you to know." She gently extended her hand to touch his arm.

He recoiled, moving out of reach. "We all have good reason to hate him." Nostrils flaring, his voice conveyed a desire to kill.

Eyes downcast, Amila drooped in despair. She feared this reaction. The bitterness and resentment were unmistakable. Again, she felt completely alone.

Emotions worn razor thin, they climbed down to the raft and found Luca sitting near the raft's tow rope on the shore. He looked from one to the other, wondering what terrible words had passed between them. They silently boarded the raft and pushed off the bank. Swept up by the Volga's strong current, they began to drift away down the river.

Once underway, Amila sat opposite Rein and spoke gently. "When I saw the count yesterday, I was terrified. I've been afraid since I learned what the documents mean. He must know I have them. That's why he's here—to get them back or kill me trying."

Not sure if he was listening, she felt compelled to share the rest. "The note I left for Captain Kachinov yesterday informed him Count Tundorf is there, in Saratov. Last

winter, I told the captain what Tundorf had done, that I
had evidence. He's such a good man, and I needed to tell
someone. He was as shocked by the crime as we are. So,
I asked if he could think of a way to use the evidence to
convict the count. I don't know how, but I'm determined
to ruin him. I'm going back to make sure Tundorf pays
for his sins and claim Nassenwald as my property."

"He'll pay for his sins. I can assure you he's not going
to get away with this." Rein's voice oozed hatred. "Yes,
Amila, he's going to come looking for you. I'll be ready
when he comes, or I'll find him. And kill him."

"What good are you to Eva if you're in jail or hang for
murder? Can you get that through your thick, lame brain
bent on revenge? I wish I hadn't told you!"

Rein opened his mouth to respond, then abruptly
stopped. He turned and moved as far from her as the raft
would allow and sat facing the water. Amila covered her
face with her hands. We're right back where we've always
been, she thought. Only this time, it's much worse.

*L*uca knew the river. Without him, they would have
passed Dobrinka in the dead of night, thought Rein.
Knowing they were close, Luca had taken the raft to
shore when darkness blended with cloudy skies forced
them to stop the second night of the trip. The next morning, it took only a few hours to reach the settlement. The
rest of the trip to Dobrinka was swathed in silence, a
stark contrast to the first day.

When they unloaded the grain sacks, Rein saw the
disappointed looks on the faces of many colonists. The
farmers understood the significance of the seed. But the
rest would rather the sacks were filled with flour, corn,

and beans. Georg had sent wagons to Kamyshin to buy food with the forage money they'd been given, but the group had not yet returned. Game was still plentiful and fish abundant. Their diets lacked variety, but at least they had food. Rein knew they were still eating better than at home during war and drought years. But winter was coming, and with it, fear of hunger.

Rein saw Eva in the crowd, and she ran to hug him. He attempted a smile.

"What's wrong?" Eva looked suspiciously from him to Amila, who gave her a quick hug and left, saying she was exhausted from the trip and needed to find Elisabeth.

"Nothing, Eva. I'm just anxious to get back to the fields," Rein kept his eyes cast down to avoid Georg, always quick to notice something amiss with one of his flock. He headed straight to the fields, his sanctuary. Farmers were already beginning to scatter the rye seed into the freshly plowed soil. He sought out the more demanding physical work, joining the men and women working in the rolling hills of tall, native grasses being cut for hay. It would take many days to cut, dry, bundle, and store the heavy grass to feed livestock during the harsh winter.

All he wanted was to work from dawn until dark and let exhaustion claim him. The intense labor diminished but didn't block the pain. Now that he knew the truth, Rein experienced his father's death all over again. It all made sense now. How closely the count had scrutinized the loading of the wagons and his push to have the drivers ready to leave on time. All the while, he was coordinating the ambush with the French. Tundorf planned it to the last detail, even calling in Rein and the other farmers afterward, not to express sympathy but to inform them that, unfortunately, their families would not be paid their share for the food, grain, and hay in the wagons since the Prussian war office would not pay for undelivered supplies. Then the traitor had asked Rein to stay as others left and delivered the final debilitating blow—given Daniel's death, the contract between the Lundgrens and the former count that would free his family was revoked.

How convincing the lies had been! The devil had paid himself twice, stolen from the struggling farmers, and still demanded more in taxes. The ambush, the death of his father and all their friends, was for nothing more than money to fill a nobleman's pockets. Amila was right. This new knowledge had filled a well of anger and desire for revenge he'd never experienced. And sweet, innocent Eva. The thought brought bile to his mouth. He spat.

As the day wore on, Rein admitted to himself begrudgingly that the torment was more than knowing how his father really died. Though he had tried so long and so hard, he could no longer deny his feelings for Amila had changed dramatically.

Hearing her say she planned to go home to bring Tundorf to justice, to reclaim her lands made him want to call out—no, don't go! Until that moment, he hadn't realized how much he wanted to be with her, now and always. He had ignored twinges seeing Amila with Christof on the long journey, attributing it to curious interest. He had wondered what it would feel like if she was attentive to him instead. But in Saratov, he was nearly overcome by jealousy seeing them greet one another so warmly. Of course, it was Christof she cared about. He wiped the salty sweat from his brow before it or tears stung his eyes. How could a serf marry a noblewoman? And even if he could—Amila's family was responsible for what had happened to his father. Was she blameless in the crime? It was as if his heart told him one thing and his head another. He stared helplessly at the settlement beyond the field, wondering where she was now. Let her go. If she wants to go back to Germany and that life, you have to let her go.

As he continued to swing the scythe, Rein felt the physical release he craved. He began to encourage and praise his fellow workers—mostly non-farmers who had plunged themselves into labor they were not yet well adapted to do. Nevertheless, they were proving a willingness to bend their backs to the sokha. He'd been amazed at how quickly they'd learned to harness the horses and plow the fields, scatter seed from a half-sack slung on their shoulder, and sweep the scythe. Nor were they too proud to carry water and spread dung. One day they would become fine farmers. He must seek fulfillment in the work they were doing together.

Amila perked up when Elisabeth came to her rescue by suggesting she find a task other than helping the women prepare for winter. She was not skilled at cooking, sewing, or the multitude of duties in which the women were immersed. Eva had found her purpose, seeking and drying wild herbs for medicinal uses. Amila could think of only one place to help: the stable.

She found Johann engrossed in the construction of winter livestock shelters. Several colonists, including children, were already assisting. "Welcome back. Word has spread about your domination of the Kontora."

"I can always count on you to exaggerate and poke fun, can't I?" Amila's feelings were still painfully tender. She could tell he was genuinely glad to see her. "I've been kicked out of women's activities due to lack of skill and, to be honest, lack of interest. I wonder if you could put me to work?"

He stroked his chin and cleared his throat before responding. "Well, all right. You're hired, even though your skills are, shall we say, untested."

Johann explained to her what they were building. "Since we don't have lumber, we're bringing small, downed trees from the ravines, standing them upright, and placing them tightly together to construct walls. Next, we'll wattle the remaining trees, brush, and vines. Then comes the fun part—smearing the walls with a mixture of clay, earth, and grass for weatherproofing. I think the children will like that part the best. The roof will be added last. I think we can use the smaller tree limbs and brush, then cover it all with dirt at the end. We're keeping the roof low to conserve as much animal heat as possible."

"Johann, you're a genius," declared Amila. "I'm not surprised you'd come up with this. I know the Kalmyk ponies are used to being outdoors all winter. I was astonished by how well they adapted to the snow and cold in Saratov. But the other livestock needs protection to survive. This shelter will save them."

Johann's cheeks turned rosy. "Well, it will have to do until we get lumber to build suitable barns."

Amila took her position beside the workers, forcing branches and brush between trees already leaning against the structure. It calmed her wavering emotions. One minute she felt angry at Rein for his reaction, that violence should follow violence, accomplishing nothing. The next moment her heart ached for the anguish she had caused him. It was a relief, finally, to tell him the horrible truth, but did she need to lash out at him so ferociously when she could see the depth of his pain? But still, why did he walk away and shut her out? He's disgusted and wants nothing to do with me, she thought. He must blame me as well as Tundorf for his father's death. The sooner she could go back home, the better. But a dilemma tugged at her heart as she watched the children scurrying about, bringing armfuls of branches to the adults who were so precisely placing the odd-shaped materials into gaping holes to create crude stable walls. Was it these good people, this way of life, or just Rein she was so hesitant to leave behind?

Hours passed, her mind muddled with conflict. As twilight approached, she turned to see Johann explaining their progress to Rein.

"It isn't pretty, but it'll work for one winter. What do you think of my new apprentice? She came and asked me to put her to work. Elisabeth and the others suggested she look for other tasks. She's a little slow and stubborn but willing to learn. Claims she knows something about horses."

Amila continued to work without turning around. Johann was confused—sure the teasing would evoke a spirited retort.

"I came to see where you want to store the hay bundles." Rein's voice was flat. Johann looked from one to the other, puzzled. Neither of them had reacted to his jabs. Maybe the trip didn't go as well as everyone thought. "You can stack the bundles here, near the stable."

Rein nodded, turned, and walked back toward the fields.

As the sun began to set, Johann walked beside Amila to the settlement. "I'm not blind, Amila. Something's not right. What happened on the trip?"

She bit her lip. "Oh, it's obvious, is it? You deserve to know. Count Tundorf is in Saratov. We avoided him successfully, but nevertheless, he's here in Russia for a reason. Don't worry. You and your cousin's family are safe. As Rein says, he has no power over any of you here. But I'm afraid he's come to take me back or punish me for what I've done. That's all I can tell you right now."

Johann stopped in his tracks as Amila continued to trudge slowly back to the Müller's camp.

CHAPTER 16

September - October 1764

*E*very direction Amila turned, the settlement was ablaze with activity. Cooler weather spurred winter preparations, consuming all the energy the colonists could squeeze from each day. Yet, until today, an unspoken shroud hovered as winter approached.

"We won't have enough lumber to build cabins. The builders recommend we use all the lumber from rafts to build one large common house. We must live in underground shelters this winter to survive." Georg and the vorstehers had delivered the grim news in a gathering of the colonists several weeks before. "By now, it's clear no lumber is going to arrive in time to build cabins of any sort. Nor can we cut and fell enough lumber from the small stands of trees in time."

When he tried to continue, Georg's voice was drowned out by cries of shock and outrage. Colonists turned to one another in disbelief. No one had heard of such a thing. "We're already being pushed beyond our limits," complained a settler with a large family.

Georg shouted above their crowd. "Please listen! We know it can be done, and it will keep you and your families alive. We've visited Galka and have seen how they're digging their winter dwellings. Friends—we have no other choice. We're more fortunate than our neighboring colony—at least we'll have a common house. They'll have only dugouts all winter."

Leaders from Dobrinka and Galka had visited an outlying Russian settlement and seen the underground cave dwellings still used by the poorest Russian peasants. The vorstehers had visited Galka, the second of the founding colonies, the week before and seen their progress. Located 11 miles north of Dobrinka, Galka was the nearest of the other four mother colonies populated thus far. In Galka and the other three, settlers had arrived by wagon in August and September, with little time to build and no time to plant vegetables or rye. Messengers from Saratov reported that hundreds of new colonists had arrived and would winter there, as the Dobrinka colonists had last winter. They were told by Kontora officials that all the lumber available was being used to construct barracks for these new colonists.

Dobrinka colonists continued to grumble about the dugouts but eventually gave in. They began to dig underground caves, or zemlyanky, as Russians called them.

On her way to help Johann with the livestock shelters, Amila observed the excavations. Two or more families joined in digging pits into the earth or the sides of small hills. Once large enough for families, the dugout was topped by a squatty hut and entry door poking itself up over the ground's surface. Like the animal shelters, walls of huts were constructed with limbs, brush, and twigs and then plastered over with a mixture of mud and dry grass. The tiny gabled roof was covered with limbs, boughs, brush, and dirt. A small vent was cut into the roof to allow smoke to escape from the small cooking and heating lamps that would burn on the dugout floor.

Georg had explained to colonists that families would have to sleep in these dugouts each night throughout the long winters. During the coldest, snowiest weather, many people—especially the children—could shelter inside the common house. This building was to provide the colony's communal kitchen, where massive hearths at each end would provide heat and cooking fires. The large room would serve many purposes—church, school, infirmary, and meeting room. The remaining wood scraps from the rafts were to be used to build a few small outbuildings for food storage and crude benches and tables for the single room in the common house. When Georg had adjourned the meeting, colonists continued to grumble but seemed ready to act on the plan.

Amila's path took her near the sizeable common house now nearing completion. Builders had used the simplest construction techniques, dovetailing ends of logs together in the absence of nails. The clefts between logs were chinked on the inside with moss and a mixture of clay and grass on the outside, similar to Johann's live-stock shelters and the dugouts. Today, workers were covering the gabled roof with bark and grass.

Luca caught her attention. "I've been looking for you. I've decided to go to Kamyshin for winter. It's already time for me to leave. But I need to talk with Rein once more. Can you help me speak with him?"

Amila dreaded the task after having avoided Rein successfully since the raft journey but accompanied Luca as requested. They found him with Johann digging their zemlyanky into a hillside with a south-facing exposure.

"Luca asked me to translate. He's ready to leave for winter."

They paused and leaned on their shovels as Amila began to translate. "He advises you to keep the small raft in the water until the first ice begins to form. He says if you tether it to shore with ropes and float it into deeper water, you can use it as a platform to catch much larger fish. Then, when heavier ice begins to form, pull the raft high onto the shore."

Luca was looking back and forth between Amila and Rein, noticing the stark lack of eye contact. He tugged on her sleeve, reminding Amila to tell him about the sleigh. "He says you will need a sleigh during winter. Travel on the Volga in winter is easy with a sleigh. You can travel much faster than in the summer on land or water. If you pick two good horses for a team and take him to Kamyshin, he'll help you buy a sleigh and teach you how to use it. Then you can put it in the back of a wagon and haul it back here with the team of horses."

Finished conveying the message, Amila dispassionately turned and walked down the path to the stable. Luca followed. He caught and held her by the shoulders, forcing her to face him. "Whatever is giving the two of you so much pain must end. Can you not forgive him, and he you, for whatever has happened?"

She wiped at the tears clouding her vision. "Rein will never forgive me for who I am and the pain I have caused him. I'm afraid too much has happened."

Count Tundorf knew he'd found a kindred spirit in Chancellor Grekov. Even though the self-aggrandizing drivel about his current position and future value to the empress seemed endless, the count immediately recognized how their aspirations could complement one another. It was worth the time spent grooming him these past weeks. The tedious dinners together were paying off. Grekov was seeking out his company nearly every day now, glowing in another high-born noble's constant attention and praise. In fact, the attention he craved seemed obsessive. Soon, he won't even know whose idea it was to sabotage the colonies. Tundorf nodded and smiled, leaning forward to feign interest in Grekov's latest gibberish.

"Throughout my education, I excelled in all subjects, but perhaps most in the arena of financial concerns. My well-versed knowledge makes me the best candidate to oversee the profitable areas of colonization, such as the purchase and sale of grain, livestock, lumber, and farm implements. In fact, I've already begun to manage these transactions with great personal success."

Tundorf's eyes widened. This insight into the colonization program's funds could be useful in time.

Grekov continued. "My officials have just returned from inspecting the five crown colonies. I'll soon send a progress report to Commissar Demidov in St. Petersburg, who, of course, reports directly to the empress. I'm afraid I'll have to report that the colonists are behind in every endeavor, a failure of their own making due to laziness and wasteful spending. I fear they have squandered every ruble they've been given in drunkenness and luxury without restraint. Fortunately, the commissar will likely judge these colonists as worthless subjects through no fault of my own. When my officials present their reports, perhaps you would like to attend?"

The count forced a smile. "It would be my honor, chancellor. What a wonderful opportunity for me to learn to better govern my estates. And I'd welcome news of how my stepdaughter and the colonists of Dobrinka are faring."

"Indeed! I'd like to hear again about Lady Amila, the future Countess of Wallerstein." Grekov breathed the words like an endearment.

He never seemed to tire of hearing the same story, thought Tundorf, willing to recite it yet again. "Yes, she's such a lovely young woman and will inherit vast acreage, forests, property, and Nassenwald Manor. You see, in our province of Germany, inheritance passes to the oldest child, male or female. As an only child, my dear Amila is the sole heir. She was betrothed to a duke of very high standing. However, he became deathly ill, and the engagement was broken. Amila was quite disappointed and set off on this adventure to deal with the loss. While it is not befitting a lady to travel alone, she has had the constant companionship of her servant Eva as chaperone. I'm sure the hardships of pioneer life will soon dampen her desire to see the world. I plan to take her home and again advise her regarding a wise matrimonial choice. Of course, the new Lord of Wallerstein must be of noble birth."

Grekov beamed. "In my brief encounters with Lady Amila, I've been impressed by her charm and beauty. With your assistance, I believe she can be persuaded to favor my attention. Perhaps when she returns here with you, we can become better acquainted?"

"That's a wonderful idea, chancellor! I will see to it." Tundorf suppressed a chuckle. It took long enough. But finally, he's taken the bait.

Count Tundorf noted the pretentious way Grekov formally seated himself on a platform at the front of the room to preside over the officials' report on the five crown colonies. Thinking it ludicrous but willing to go along with the chancellor's efforts to impress his visitor, Tundorf sat respectfully near the back of the room. The count received confirmation of Grekov's primary objective when he asked that the report be delivered in German, which many Kontora officials were also able to speak.

The two Kontora officials who had traveled south under soldier escort described the first three of the five crown colonies they had visited, pointing to them on a map. The two colonies nearest Saratov were Sosnovka and Talovka, located only a few miles from one another, and colonists had arrived in mid-August. Sosnovka had 96 families and 404 individuals; Talovka had 76 families and 298 individuals. About 10 miles farther south was Sebastyanovka, where colonists arrived in September. Sebastyinovka had 63 families and 229 individuals. The officials reported little progress had been made at all three locations, where settlers struggled to prepare for winter.

One official did most of the talking. "Due to their late arrival, they were unable to plant crops. Leaders complained that no lumber had been provided for housing. They are engaged in digging underground dwellings, as is the Russian peasant custom. They inquired about the delivery of food during winter and were informed, as you instructed, that they must contract with nearby Russian settlements for food, using forage money as payment. I feel I must report that the leaders of all three colonies expressed grave concerns about their ability to provide for themselves through the winter, although they are the closest to Saratov."

"Is that all?" Grekov strummed his fingers on the table. "Now the other two, farther south."

"The colonists at Galka total 195 within 64 families. They arrived in August, were also unable to plant crops, and are struggling to prepare for winter. They too, are without lumber and are digging underground dwellings, fishing, and drying wild game for winter food. However, the mood among Galka colonists seems to be more positive, perhaps because they are in close contact with the Dobrinka community, located 11 miles farther south."

"I'm afraid the contracts with colony leaders state we must withhold forage money from all colonies that have failed to till the soil and plant crops," Grekov replied, detached.

The two officials looked at one another in bewilderment. Finally, one spoke up. "In all fairness, commissar, settlers of the four colonies did not arrive early enough to plant vegetables nor did they receive the rye seed. Losing their forage money will make it difficult, perhaps impossible, to purchase the food they need to survive the winter."

"It's not your place to question my decisions," the chancellor spewed back. "I alone have been empowered by the empress to see that contractual requirements are met. They must face consequences for their actions. Now, your report on the fifth colony."

"Dobrinka is the colony farthest south. It has 55 families and 249 individuals, mostly from German states. When compared with the other four, Dobrinka is the most advanced." The official paused to seek encouragement from the other clerk, who nodded his support. "They arrived in late June, giving them more time to prepare for winter. They, too, are creating dugouts for winter. However, they have built a large common house that will be used during the day for cooking, school, church, and an infirmary. They have several outbuildings and root cellars to store the food they have grown and gathered. Their community vegetable garden is extensive, and their harvest is nearly complete. They seem to be quite enterprising at fishing the Volga, with large stores of fish dried for storage. They are hunting wild game, drying the meat, and curing every pelt for various uses. They have even built livestock shelters and harvested summer grasses for winter forage. Because of a greater command of the Russian language, the colony has made contact with Russian settlements near and far to buy food, which they plan to transport by sleigh. Perhaps their most impressive achievement was the successful planting of winter rye on large plots, which benefitted from fall rains and will be ready for harvest next summer."

The official swallowed and cautiously continued. "The industry of the colony's members and its leaders is to be commended. We conclude our report by saying that perhaps this colony will serve as a successful model for others in future years."

The official realized he'd shown too much enthusiasm when he saw Grekov's pinched expression. Both clerks lowered their eyes.

The chancellor spoke through clenched teeth. "I'm curious to know, where did they get lumber to build the 'common house,' as you call it?"

"They disassembled the barges used to float settlers and supplies down the river. I believe there were about 20 large rafts," stated the official meekly.

"And who gave them permission to do that? All rafts were to be taken on to Kamyshin and sold as lumber."

The official remained calm. "We understand that the Dobrinka colonists paid the river pilots for the rafts, who then returned to Saratov ahead of schedule, turned in funds to the Kontora treasury, and collected their wages."

"And where did they get the seed to plant the rye?" Grekov fidgeted in his chair and pulled at his mustache.

"We were told a man and woman from the colony came to Saratov and picked up the seed themselves from our warehouse," offered the official.

Grekov's shrill voice resonated across the room. "How did you allow this to happen? Once again, these rebels dare to take matters into their own hands, and somehow you failed to stop them. They have deceived me and stolen Kontora property for the last time."

The count watched from the back of the room as Grekov fought a losing battle of control. He had not seen this side of the Kontora director. Tundorf maintained a serious demeanor, nodding supportively at appropriate moments. He tried to contain his excitement. Oddly, the rush was akin to the thrill of the hunt, closing in on the kill.

*W*ith pastures near Dobrinka depleted, Amila had begun taking the colony's horses and cattle to more distant areas to graze. Autumn rains had brought late growth to the steppe grasses, producing green sprigs throughout the clumps of tall, golden stalks. The animals were content to wander the prairie and ravines in search of this highly nutritious late-summer forage.

Usually, Amila would be as content as the horses to spend a clear, sunny day on horseback. However, knowing Count Tundorf was in Saratov plagued her, leaving her on edge, wondering when he would come after her. She was furious he had such power over her. She'd be safe once winter set in because travel would be nearly impossible. The fact that she felt weak and help-less enraged her the most. She had told Johann only that Tundorf was in Saratov and that she didn't know why. If Rein wanted him to know more, he could tell him. She'd already lost Rein because of the horrible secret. She feared Johann's reaction would be the same. Anyway, it was she who was in danger.

Amila was comfortable riding all day, watching over the herd, but noticed Johann was not. Abiding by the rule never to leave the settlement alone or unarmed, Johann and two older boys accompanied her and the herd. She noticed Johann couldn't stay mounted for long. He was more at ease leading his horse. But he was forced to remount when the herd descended a trail into a deep ravine. Johann and Amila looked at one another with surprise when they heard loud whinnies and snorts from what sounded like other horses ahead.

Amila's excitement grew. "There can't be other horses here, can there? Not ours anyway." They eased their mounts farther into the small canyon for a closer look. The ravine opened up into a well-protected valley. "Look, wild horses!"

Across the valley, Amila saw a small herd of horses acting skittish but not running away. Like the Kalmyk ponies, these horses were medium-sized, but her knowl-edge of high-quality equine traits judged them superior in many ways. They had more muscle, smaller heads, beautifully curved necks, and chestnut-colored coats with a deep golden sheen. Amila had not thought of her precious Gabe in some time but did now. The way these horses moved, especially the stallion, reminded her of Gabe's agility and vitality.

"They're breathtaking! They don't act completely wild. Do you think we could tame them? They'd be incredible to ride, and their bloodline would improve our riding stock."

"Slow down, Amila! We already have more horses than we can manage. And too many to feed this winter, so don't get any ideas."

"But look how healthy they are. Those horses must know how to take care of themselves in winter. It must have something to do with this protected valley." Amila stretched her neck to take in the expansive, fertile basin.

"Before we lose some of our herd to that stallion, we'd better start back."

"Oh, all right. But I intend to remember this place so we can find it again." Amila was relaxed with Johann, having slipped into friendship as equals, oblivious of former roles.

After gathering the herd and ascending from the ravine, they stopped once again to let them graze. Johann rode up beside Amila. "I've been wanting to talk with you about something, well, someone."

"Shall I guess? Is it Eva?"

"How did you know?" Johann stammered. "Well, I guess it's sort of obvious. I'm not very good at hiding my feelings for her, am I? What I wanted to ask is, do you think I have a chance with her? You know her better than anyone, probably better than Rein does."

At the mention of Rein, Amila frowned. She didn't see him often but knew he had left with Luca for Kamyshin to bring back a sleigh. She was able to avoid him most of the time. "Johann, I'm not very good at matters of the heart. Have you talked with her?"

"We spend time walking in the evenings and talk about everything but...this. I know how young Eva is, but she seems wise. And the way she takes care of the children and anyone who is sick, she's just amazing. And so pretty. She even laughs at my jokes."

"Oh, Johann, it sounds wonderful for both of you. Just take your time. There's no hurry. You know that I love her like a little sister, so you'd better take good care of her."

"I plan to do just that." Johann grinned from ear to ear as they turned the herd toward home. Moments later, jerking horses to a stop, they stared at one another in alarm. Hoping to be wrong about what they had just heard, then they heard it again. Gunfire, many shots fired, coming from the direction of Dobrinka.

Amila defiantly disagreed when Johann told her and the two boys to stay with the herd and keep out of sight until someone came back for them. "I'm coming along. They can handle the herd."

By the time they neared the settlement, the gunfire had stopped. Amila and Johann dismounted out of view and crawled forward to peer carefully over the hill. Heart racing, Amila covered her mouth to keep from crying out. Ten or more brawny strangers aimed muskets at a mass of colonists huddled together. Ear-piercing screams and sobs emanated from the group, whose eyes were riveted on three attackers, each of whom held a woman or a child tightly, pistols to their heads. Several settlers lay still on the ground, blood-soaked clothing visible even from a distance.

"I have to help them." Johann scrambled backward toward his horse.

Amila rolled toward him, grabbed his shoulders, and held firm. "Johann, they'll kill you, and they'll kill the women and children they're holding. You can't charge in like that. More people will die!"

"Then what can I do? Eva is there! I can't stand by and watch." He struggled free of her arms, but it forced him to pause.

They again crawled forward, helplessly watching as the horrible raid unfolded in a surge of coordinated actions. While attackers held the women and children at gunpoint—assuring the throng of colonists would not storm them—thieves ransacked the settlement. Scraggly looking robbers poured in and out of storage build-ings with armfuls of carefully stored food, filling crude carts, each hitched to a single horse. In the distance, they heard shots coming from the stable and could see thieves heaping carcasses of pigs, sheep, and goats into carts. The robbers invaded each family's camp, seizing guns, knives, and ammunition but also rummaging through wagons, stripping them of blankets, winter clothing, pots, and pans, and rushing with armfuls to the carts. As soon as a cart was filled, a thief would jump in and whip the horse to a gallop, disappearing over the hill.

A lone man sat on a horse with arms folded across the saddle horn, unfazed by the screams and chaos. He watched dispassionately as two thugs held Georg while a third hit him repeatedly in the stomach and face.

They stopped briefly while the man on the horse spoke brusquely to Georg. With no reply from Georg, they inflicted more blows.

"That's the leader," whispered Johann. "I'm going to get as close as I can and take a shot at him. I have to get within range. When you hear my shot, wait a few seconds and then fire your pistol over their heads so no colonists are hit. They'll see the smoke from your gun—that will give me time to reload. Then get on your horse and ride away as fast as you can."

Amila nodded and held her position low on the hill. She felt light-headed and dreaded what might be happening. She gulped deep breaths over and over, determined not to faint this time.

Johann edged back to retrieve his black powder rifle from the leather sheath on the horse's saddle and checked to ensure it was primed and loaded. Then, with the cocking mechanism detached, he crawled on his belly and elbows, inching forward. After several nerve-racking minutes, he had crisscrossed over hills, downward and closer to the settlement. At last, he stopped, as close to the leader as he dared move. He carefully aimed and leveled the single-shot rifle then squeezed the trigger, releasing a spray of sparks forward from the muzzle and another sideways. A second later, the man on horseback reeled and arched backward, clutching his shoulder, nearly falling from the saddle. Blood oozed from the leader's shoulder as his horse thrashed wildly.

Amila waited a few seconds before firing her pistol in the leader's direction but over his head. The leader struggled to regain control of the horse. Less than a minute later, Johann had reloaded and fired another shot, this time barely missing the leader.

Soon, the wounded rider regained his balance. Seeing smoke rise from two locations, he barked orders as he rode across the settlement out of range of Johann's rifle. Word spread rapidly among the thieves, who mounted horses and jumped in the last few carts to move out.

The attackers holding guns on the three colonists held their positions. The leader yelled something to the colonists, and the three thieves holding the women and child dragged them to their horses, using them as shields. They mounted with hostages in tow. A woman screamed and ran to the thief holding the child. He kicked out with his boot, knocking her off her feet. The leader and riders with captives spurred their horses to a gallop and disappeared over the hill following the carts.

"I'm going to follow them." Johann had quickly backtracked to Amila and their horses. He seemed unsurprised Amila had disobeyed his order to ride to safety. "Go in when it's clear, and then take men with you to bring back the boys and the herd. First, make sure Eva is all right."

"I will. Be careful, Johann." Amila knew the boys and the herd weren't in the path of the retreating thieves. But the marauders might send others to steal the herd.

Amila galloped over the hill into Dobrinka, past women and children wailing over the bodies of the dead. Men and women stumbled into one another, searching for loved ones, weeping and clutching them tightly upon finding them wounded, but alive.

She found Eva safe and already caring for the wounded. Eva stopped briefly, then rapidly looked beyond her, searching, eyes wide with fear.

"Johann is all right. He's the one who shot the leader. He's gone to follow and rescue the captives. Please, help

Georg." Amila ran to Georg, who was conscious, face covered with blood and weak from the beating. Elisabeth was sitting on the ground cradling him in her arms, wiping away the blood with the skirt of her dress. Amila crouched beside them, looking from one to another, and grasped Elisabeth tightly on one shoulder.

"He's going to be all right, Elisabeth!" He has to be, thought Amila. She spoke to Georg. "Johann shot the leader. He's gone to follow them and bring back the captives. We have only one more horse here, mine. I'll send someone on that horse to help Johann. The herd is several miles back, and the two boys are watching them. I'll gather some men to walk back to the herd with me. We'll make sure they get back safe."

Georg nodded approval. She charged off in search of men to help, and soon one was armed with a gun the thieves had not found, galloping on her mount over the hill to follow Johann. Several men located more guns and ammunition overlooked by the thieves and started over the hill toward the herd. Amila grabbed bridles and followed, running through the battle-scarred village after them. She struck her leg with the bridles, vowing she was through fainting—forever.

$\mathcal{R}$ein returned from Kamyshin two days later to a community he barely recognized. Gone was the energy and enthusiasm, replaced instead by a mass of battered, discouraged, grieving souls. With winter fast approaching, the food supply was depleted and most of the small livestock taken. Grave concerns about survival weighed heavily, but fears went unspoken. The first task was to bury and mourn the dead. Nine Dobrinka men and one boy had lost their lives, beginning with the young watch-tower guard whose throat had been slashed before he could sound an alarm.

Soon after his return, Rein went to the stable to find Johann. Listening to his account of the savage attack, Rein felt searing pangs of guilt for being absent.

"If you'd been here, you'd be dead. I'm sure of it," Johann assured Rein. "I'd have been killed, too, if not for Amila. No weakness from her. And this time, she didn't faint. She threw her arms around me and held me back when I nearly rode into the village alone. She doesn't mind worth a damn, but she thinks pretty clearly in a crisis, for a woman."

"Yes, Amila rarely flinches. I'm relieved she's all right." His creased forehead and wavering voice threatened to divulge conflicting feelings. "She seems indifferent, but I've learned that's not always true. What happened after the robbers fled?"

Johann told Rein he'd followed the thieves who took the two women and child hostage, finding them on the trail unharmed. "The robbers left them a few miles outside the village. After we returned them to Dobrinka, I doubled back and followed the thieves' trail. It leads to what must be their lair." Johann described an easily defended stronghold on a hill surrounded by woods. It was a few hours' ride from the settlement.

Johann was relieved to report the boys and the herd they tended were safe. As soon as he could, Georg had sent a rider to warn the colonists at Galka. "They have little food to steal but have livestock and weapons. The messenger reported back that Galka had not been attacked, and they were taking precautions."

"The thieves must have been spying on the colony for months to plan the attack so thoroughly." Rein clenched his fists by his side. "They waited until the harvest was in and food was stored, until all the work was done. They knew exactly where to find the food and stables, even most of our weapons. They must've known the horses and cattle were taken out for grazing each day, so we wouldn't be able to follow them on horseback." He shook his head in disgust.

Johann responded angrily. "They even knew Georg was our leader and would have access to the colony's treasury. They beat him badly, but he didn't tell them where the money is hidden."

Rein knew it was his brave friend's shot that had stopped the attack and likely saved Georg's life. "Do you think they're still watching us?"

"Aye. I'd bet my weight in strong, dark ale they are. Are you thinking what I'm thinking?"

Rein nodded. "Let's set a trap."

Hours later, they'd exhausted a variety of scenarios and hoped the one they were about to present wasn't so outlandish the leaders would reject it.

Amid the cloud of devastation hanging over Dobrinka, leaders were meeting to discuss how to survive given the loss of food, livestock, most of the weapons, and basic necessities. Then, Rein and Johann burst into the meeting.

"We haven't come this far to let a lazy band of thieves best us! We're not giving up," Johann announced with a gleam in his eye, backed up by his childhood co-conspirator. "Rein and I used to dream up ways to beat tougher outlaws than these. We have a plan."

CHAPTER 17

October 1764

Still yawning and pulling their frayed jackets tight against the cool morning breeze, three boys casually herded the cattle and horses away from Dobrinka to graze an area several miles north. Johann smirked. "They're looking quite vulnerable, wouldn't you say? And we thought we were going to be simple farmers."

Rein grinned collaboratively but continued to busy himself with a pitchfork in the livestock pens. If only he could be as light-hearted as Johann about today. Instead, he'd worry for the both of them. Relieved the day was finally here, he still battled doubts that all the pieces would fall in place. Their very lives, and the survival of the colony, depended on it.

Around the settlement, Rein saw colonists going about daily activities to maintain the appearance of normalcy. It wasn't really an act—there was always more than enough work to do. He liked the nuances of the plan the leaders had suggested. The entire colony was taking part, which made it more believable but also increased the risks significantly.

Drawing on Captain Kachinov's lesson from the cattle drive, they had discreetly confirmed they were being watched. Don't look over your shoulder, the wise captain had told them. Don't let them know you know they're watching. Soon enough, they saw the men spying on them relax and show themselves. Rein and Johann carried on as if nothing were amiss.

Late last night, once the spitzbuben spies had left for the day—and the night before they believed the herd would be attacked—twenty armed colonists had advanced covertly to the valley where the herd was now being driven. There, they hid themselves. But, with so many weapons stolen in the raid, the delegation had barely enough guns and ammunition to arm themselves.

Once the herd was out of sight of Dobrinka, Rein and Amila saddled and mounted horses. Johann checked that the canvas cover was secure on the wagon, tethered a third horse, then climbed into the driver's seat. The team strained to pull the wagon's heavy load.

Amila and Rein rode briskly toward the thieves' lair. Having followed the robbers after the attack, Johann knew the exact location. They stopped short of the hide-out's heavily wooded entrance. They lay waiting behind a hill at a vantage point, allowing them to observe who was entering and leaving. Johann should arrive with the wagon soon.

"What if they've already left? What if they don't fall for it?" Amila whispered impatiently. Rein cast a tender look in her direction. Her eyes were fixed on the hideout entrance, and it gave him a moment to gaze undetected. He could hear her uneven breathing and was close enough to see her eyelids flutter nervously. Being alone together, this close, intensified his feelings and added strain to an already tense day.

"Look!" she grabbed and squeezed his arm briefly and tucked her head lower. A group of armed riders suddenly poured out of the woods and galloped their horses in the herd's direction. They stared intently to count the number of riders.

"Go Amila, now! Ride hard," Rein reached but missed the chance to return her touch. "Tell them the thieves number fewer than fifteen armed men and to use their ammunition carefully. And if you don't get there first..."

"I know, stay out of sight. I'll get there first," she assured, rushing to her horse.

And please be careful, he wanted to shout. Instead, he watched her disappear in a cloud of dust. She was the colony's best rider, mounted on Johann's fastest horse, but she had to take an indirect route to avoid the thieves. And she must arrive first to deliver the message to the herdsmen in the valley. He felt helpless seeing her ride away. Yet there had been no talking her out of it.

Boots thrust deep in the stirrups, Amila pressed her knees tightly against the horse's sides and leaned forward. One hand wound in the horse's mane and the other tightly gripping the reins, Amila's knuckles turned white as she braced herself against her steed. Her hips moved with the horse's rhythm, reading its body language. They flew across the landscape like a team.

Amila knew the strength of this Kalmyk pony by now. He was sure-footed and could nimbly jump over rocks, pass through narrow gaps, and traverse barriers smoothly. But most of all, this horse loved to run. She had never seen him tire of it, even compared with the other Kalmyks, all of which possessed great endurance.

Amila knew she was the colony's fastest rider. She was light but had a strong upper body and could keep her seat at a gallop for long periods. Oh, she'd been thrown enough times to respect the power beneath her but had argued long and hard to be chosen to ride and warn the men hiding with the herd. She didn't intend to let them down.

Eyes straining through errant wisps of hair blowing across her face, Amila immersed herself in the sound of pounding hooves. The hills and ground rushed past. Space didn't matter; her mind was fixed on the goal—get there first. Landmarks committed to memory while taking the herd to graze flew by. She was close.

Cresting a hill, Amila saw the valley entrance and jerked the reins hard to turn the pony. The horse slowed enough for her to scan the horizon where the thieves should be approaching. Seeing dust, Amila slackened the reins, leaned forward, and urged the horse into the valley.

Johann waved a white cloth as he and Rein calmly approached the entrance to the thieves' stronghold. Rein held his hands above his head, remembering the Russian phrases Amila had made him rehearse over and over. "Don't shoot! We're from the Dobrinka colony. We want to meet with your leader. Please tell him we want to buy back the food, just some of it. Please, we beg you."

The man guarding the entrance looked shocked that anyone would approach the hideout and even more baffled when he heard their intention. He kept a rifle aimed at them, then shouted the stranger's message to another guard stationed deeper in the woods. Rein could faintly hear more guards relay it again until the sound faded.

"Take their weapons and bring them in," echoed the response.

Once they had searched and found no weapons, a guard motioned for them to follow. A second guard fell in step behind. Rein pointed to the horses, and the guard laughed and shook his head, a third guard leading them away. They followed the guards up a secluded path just wide enough for a two-wheeled cart to pass. The maze of trails split, again and again, assuring that strangers entering alone would quickly be swallowed by the woods and at the thieves' mercy. Rein wondered why they hadn't blindfolded them. His jaw tightened. They didn't plan to let them leave alive.

The guards led Rein and Johann deep into the forest, past a mass of rickety shacks littered with piles of rubble. Women and children, hair in tangles and dressed in dingy rags, huddled around small fires or sat atop felled tree trunks. Residents eyed the strangers suspiciously as they passed. The stench of unwashed bodies, decay, and excrement hung heavy in the stagnant woods. Finally, a stream appeared, flowing through the ramshackle village toward them as they walked continually uphill. Following the guard, they saw the source of the water, a spring pouring from the hillside. Beyond the spring were stepping stones leading upward to what appeared to be ruins of a castle. Several of the least damaged walls had been fortified to create living quarters.

Two armed guards stood outside the protected lair where the procession halted. Rein glanced quickly at Johann, both committing to memory the number of armed men they'd seen so far.

A man emerged from a damaged portion of the stone wall that served as a door. His arm tied up in a sling, he faced them squarely with shoulders arched back and head held high.

"I am Viktor Rodshenko, the chieftain you are seeking. You are either fools or very brave men. How did you find your way here?" The man had a commanding voice, deep-set eyes, a bushy mustache, and a ratty beard. But it was his large nose that dominated his facial features, casting a shadow on his pock-marked face.

"We're from the settlement near the Dobrinka River and found our way here by the tracks your carts left." Rein said in the difficult language he had practiced. "We're neither fools nor brave men. We're simply trying to feed our families, to survive our first winter here. We want the food back, and we'll pay you well for it. There's enough to share to keep us all alive through the winter."

"You will pay us for the food we stole?" Rodshenko repeated in a husky, mocking voice. Guards nearby joined in his laughter. "Bring them."

The guards pushed Rein and Johann up the remaining steps into the crude dwelling. Light penetrated the door and the cracked walls, enough to see roughly hewn chairs and a table.

Rodshenko sat down first and motioned for them to follow. "Russians have a saying: 'If fate suddenly sends you a windfall, take as much as you can.' That is what we did. Tell me again what you want. And why I shouldn't just kill you?"

Rein explained the rehearsed offer. "We're strangers in this land, but we're making our homes here. We have many families to feed and are desperate to get our food back. We don't know what else to do except to come to you and plead. If you kill us, you will receive no payment. But, if you agree, we will pay you well for even half the food."

From his position beside Rein, Johann fidgeted and gave Rein a sidelong puzzled look. He spoke urgently but slowly to Rein in clumsy, broken Russian. "Rein, why are you saying half the food? You know the empress gave us more gold than we need. It's more than enough to buy it all. My cousin and his family, I can't let them starve. Isn't this why we brought the gold in the wagon?"

"Quiet! The leaders sent me here to do the talking." Rein gritted his teeth and raised his arm, ready to back-hand Johann, who shrunk back in silence.

"I'm sorry for his outburst. He's a fool and doesn't speak for us. I do. We will pay you 500 rubles, in gold, for half the food, weapons, and supplies."

The chieftain's eyes narrowed to slits. "If you have the rubles, why would you not just go to settlements and buy food for the winter?"

"We thought about that. But we don't know where the settlements are that have food to buy or how much to pay. And once we're snowed in, we have no way to bring supplies back. As I said, we are strangers here."

Rodshenko considered that. "And how and when would you pay?"

Rein spoke confidently. "Have your men bring the food out in carts and leave it outside the woods. We'll take some of the food back in a wagon, starting with one load, and then return to get the rest. We will pay you some of the rubles today and the rest when we return. Then we'll leave you in peace and never return."

"You negotiate a hard bargain." Rodshenko paused to think before going on. "I agree to the terms, but only if we receive at least half in rubles today. We must now buy food for our village."

"You'll be paid half today. I want your word that you'll honor our agreement." Rein extended his hand.

"Of course." Rodshenko grasped the outstretched hand.

*A*fter hastily informing the Dobrinka men hiding in the valley about the enemies' numbers and imminent approach, Amila rode to the protected area where the boys had gathered the herd. She gave them each a pat on the back and reassured them as best she could. Their orders were to stay hidden and keep the herd calm. From their hiding place, Amila and the boys could see where the thieves would enter in search of the herd. The sturdy cattle and horses were to be used to stampede toward the thieves, but only as a last resort if ammunition ran out. Amila glanced across the valley, briefly wondering where the wild horses had gone.

A few minutes later, riders following the herd's trail appeared and began down the entrance to the valley.

The sound of coordinated gunfire rattled the canyon walls as colonists hiding in the brush fired and reloaded quickly, determined to make every shot count. One by one, the surprised thieves dropped to the ground. Others kicked their mounts forward to seek cover but found only an open valley before them. Amila counted seven men on the ground. Two more fell from horses as they failed to outrun rifle shots. That left fewer than six men to turn and take a stand against the colonists, by now running out of ammunition.

Knowing they were out of range but cut off from the trail behind them, the few thieves still alive stopped briefly to talk, then spurred their horses toward the far end of the valley. Amila knew the valley well by now. By the time they found the path out of the canyon, it would take hours for them to reach their stronghold.

Cheers resounded off the canyon walls as the smell of black powder rose from the air.

*O*ccasionally daring a glance in Johann's direction to summon composure, Rein followed the chieftain down the path. Ahead, Rodshenko led them through the myriad of trails. Seven armed guards surrounded him and Johann as they neared the exit to the thieves' stronghold.

With no weapons and no horse, the chieftain acted confident that no threat existed. Once the procession left the woods, Rodshenko stopped. He pulled a pistol from his belt. "Now, show us where you've hidden the gold."

"No! We have a bargain. You can't do this. You gave me your word." shouted Rein.

"It was spitzbuben's word. As you said, you're strangers here. Sadly, this won't save your colony. After winter, those of you still alive should go back where you came from. This is our land, and you have no right to be here," Rodshenko exuded calmly. He pointed his gun toward Johann and cocked the hammer. "Show us where the gold is hidden, or your foolish friend dies."

Eyes downcast, Rein pointed, and he and Johann despondently led them to a nearby ravine where the wagon rested covered with canvas.

"We won't soon forget today," said Johann as he hesitantly pulled back the canvas. The wagon was empty, except for loaded pistols within easy reach of the two captives. In one motion, each grabbed a gun. Johann skirted the wagon to hold a gun on a bewildered Rodshenko, whose weapon was holstered in his belt. Holding the pistol to Rodshenko's head, Johann threw the chieftain's pistol to the ground and dragged him toward the woods. Simultaneously, Rein fired at the guard nearest him, then dived under the wagon where another loaded pistol was stowed. Within moments, colonists hiding in the wooded ravine near the wagon moved into position to fire on the armed thugs, who lacked cover from the surprise attack. The colonists continued firing until all lay dead or writhing on the ground.

"Not you! We need you, Rodshenko." Johann revealed he knew more Russian than he had let on, while keeping the pistol to the leader's temple. "I told you we wouldn't soon forget today."

Rein jumped on top of the wagon and swung a brightly colored cloth tied to a stick above his head, signaling colonists hiding over the hill with wagons and horses to come and begin collecting their possessions.

"We'll keep you alive to give orders." Rein stared coldly at Rodshenko. "If you cooperate, we'll leave you with something more precious than the gold you were bent on stealing—your life. And if you're hoping the thieves who went after the herd are going to ride in and rescue you, forget it. They got the same treatment."

Rodshenko stared at the horizon. Then, finally, he turned and led them slowly back into the hideout, telling the few remaining guards to drop their weapons and let them pass.

Within the space of a few hours, forty colonists filled the robber's own carts full of dried fish and game, winter vegetables, and all the weapons and ammunition they could find. They loaded livestock carcasses found hanging and even located many of the stolen household possessions.

Rein witnessed the sunken faces of women and children as the carts passed. His heart ached for them. It wasn't the life they'd wanted, and they likely had nowhere else to go. And most or all of the men would not be returning. Their panicked stares and woeful cries seemed sickeningly familiar, akin to the aftermath of the thieves' recent attack on Dobrinka.

Once the carts exited the narrow path, colonists transferred the items to larger wagons and abandoned the carts, heading home.

After much debate, while planning the counterattack, they had decided they must free Rodshenko, whose cooperation was necessary to retrieve their possessions. Rein knew Captain Kachinov's solution would be to shoot the chieftain once his usefulness had ended. Georg held firm they must bring him back to Dobrinka under arrest. Dobrinka had no jail in which to hold him for any period of time, much less the entire winter. The colonists took all the weapons, including those belonging to the thieves. Not willing to shoot an unarmed man, even a thief, they released him.

"The army in Saratov will soon know the location of your stronghold and what you have done," warned Rein. "Stay away from Dobrinka and the other colonies. We are as strong as you and will become stronger."

"I'll see you both dead the next time we meet," threatened Rodshenko.

"If we don't kill you first." Johann replied. "I'm the one who put that bullet in your shoulder in the first place. I'll be happy to finish the job."

CHAPTER 18

November 1764 - February 1765

$\mathcal{T}$he tantalizing smells of simmering meat and strains of familiar music lifted the spirits of Dobrinka residents, a diversion from losses suffered in the attack. Rein thought it might be too soon. As he studied the hope-filled faces gathering for the harvest festival, he realized Georg was right, as usual. The colonists needed to celebrate together what they had worked so hard to accomplish and do it before the harsh winter set in. Snow already covered the ground, but the sun shone brightly. It would take more than snow to put a damper on this highly anticipated day.

Most of the food, weapons, and personal possessions had been recovered in the daring counterattack on the thieves' hideout. No colonists were injured, and those wounded in the thieves' earlier attack were improving under Eva's care. Lives lost at the hands of the barbarous spitzbuben would not be forgotten, but the indomitable new citizens of Dobrinka resumed their lives, ever more wary of the dangers surrounding them. As often as he could, Rein checked on the widows and children of those who'd given their lives. Perhaps next year he'd be able to do more, even give of himself.

Planning the harvest festival, or Kerb as it was known in German states, proved to have as much healing power as the event itself. Everyone took part in some way. Not quite like the annual festivals of the homeland, it nevertheless had the makings of a tradition. As Georg emphatically declared to the vorstehers, the harvest festival must take place. It was more like a sermon than any of his previous speeches. "Our citizens must make time to celebrate together our ability to survive in this new home and give thanks for what we have. This event will strengthen our bonds as a community, help create lasting memories, as well as give us the strength to deal with past and future challenges."

Finally, the Kerb festival day was underway. Children ran back and forth, urging their parents to hurry, while lighthearted banter echoed off the tall pine trees near the common house where the crowd was gathering. Sights and scents were already living up to the anticipation.

It was to be their first feast. Using the new communal kitchen, skilled cooks had kneaded together finely chopped meat and scraps from freshly butchered pigs and beef to make sausage. The mixture was seasoned with salt and herbs then stuffed into casings of pig intestines. Now the sausages simmered in cast iron pots, diffusing a mouth-watering scent to hungry onlookers. Pounds of dried and fresh mushrooms harvested from the woods were frying in animal fat. The children had worked hard to find and sun dry enough wild pears, blackberries, and strawberries, which were baked into kuchen sweet bread. Eva concocted a tasty drink from wild licorice root and dried spices. Rein heard Johann repeatedly apologize for the absence of ale but promised to brew it next year after the first grain harvest.

Just enough packed snow covered the ground so that children could try out sleds fashioned from split firewood lashed together with rope, large pieces of bark, or anything they could find large and flat enough to slide.

Rein proudly displayed the colony's first sleigh. Men gathered around to prod and test its strength, scrutinize weaknesses in the Russian design, and discuss ways to build an improved version. Make it more durable and faster with metal runners, they agreed. The primitive, all-wooden sleigh had two rows of seats lashed to wide skis. Poles rose from the skis on both sides where two horses' harnesses were attached. The Volga was beginning to freeze, but the ice was not yet thick enough for travel. Nevertheless, children lined up as Rein offered rides on snow-covered trails around the village.

Harvest festivals of Germany featured market stalls with farm and household items for sale. With no new goods available, colonists brought their own possessions to sell or trade with neighbors. Warm winter clothing was much in demand. Enterprising women had made felt boots from sheep's wool and long coats and hats of leather. Elisabeth and others sold dokhas, the long, leather coats with neck scarves and sashes worn by the Russians. The colony's cobbler and his sons sold all the leather boots they'd been able to finish and took orders for more.

Once the feast was consumed, a musician played folk music on his violin while the boldest, both young and old, danced the landler, a fast-paced folk dance well known to Germans. Caught up in the revelry and wearing their least-worn dresses, Amila and Eva joined the dancers. Boys and men whooped, stomped, and clapped while girls and women twirled daintily, lifting their skirts to show off their legs and ankles. Dancers kept rhythm by stomping their feet and slapping their thighs and the soles of their shoes. Laughter sometimes overpowered the music, as dancers lacking practice missed steps and bumped one another playfully.

The colonists sang along when the musician played a well-known tune, "Down in the Cool Meadow, a Mill Wheel Turns." Arm-in-arm, families swayed to the music. Tears stained their cheeks as they remembered the homeland and those left behind.

Amila saw Rein and Johann standing nearby and waved. Neither of the men had joined in the dancing but lingered at the edge of the crowd watching. Still stepping in time with the music, she and Eva twirled and glided off the dance area toward the two onlookers.

"You are both much to blame for this celebration," Amila chided, eyes twinkling in the bright sunshine. "How do you always come up with new ways to get in and out of trouble? What a clever ruse! I mean, I want to thank you both for your bravery. Your clever plan saved us from starving, not to mention taking weapons out of the thieves' hands and putting them back in ours. I wish I could've seen the chieftain's face when you drove away with our wagons overflowing."

"Thank you, Amila. It's a sight I won't soon forget." Rein stammered slightly. He hoped it sounded like a reference to the chieftain. During the dancing, he had tried not to stare. Yet it was impossible not to notice how beautiful she looked in her bright blue dress, green eyes vibrant, her movement almost hypnotic. More enticing than the Gypsy girl, he thought for the hundredth time.

He turned proudly to his sister. "I see you haven't forgotten how to dance the landler. Both of you, I mean."

Johann burst in, noticing the awkwardness. "Amila, you may have forgotten some dance steps, but at least you were trying. More than I can say for myself. Not everyone can dance as well as Eva. But I do want to thank you for something as well—it's long overdue. You kept me alive during the attack, taking hold of me like you did, making sure I didn't storm in foolishly to face the thieves. I never knew you had such a powerful grip. I was afraid of what you might do next if I didn't listen."

"I'm sure I could've found a rock to throw at you. Just listen to me from now on." Amila laughed and pointed a finger in warning.

"Yes, Lady Amila, whatever you say, milady," teased Johann, overdoing a respectful bow.

She giggled. "My first request is that you never call me that. Do you want to ruin my reputation here? I'm just a stable hand."

"If only you were," Rein murmured, then turned and walked away.

This time, she wouldn't let him get away with it. Amila followed and caught up, taking a mighty swipe at one broad shoulder to turn him around. "You have a bad habit of doing that, you know. Saying something to me, then walking away, sulking. Are you afraid of me? Tell me what you whispered before you walked away."

He took a deep breath and met her intense gaze. "I'm not afraid to talk to you, Amila. Sometimes, I'm just afraid of what I might say. I said, 'I wish you were a stable hand.'"

Johann and Eva remained several steps back, watching wide-eyed.

Amila stepped closer and looked up at him, hands on her hips. "And why is that, I wonder? So, you wouldn't have me to blame for what happened to your father? Or maybe I'll swoon over you like every other woman who crosses your path? Admit it. You just can't stand who I am. Admit it!"

Rein tilted his head slightly. "Is that what you think? That I blame you?"

"Of course, you do. You've made that very clear." Glancing back at Eva and Johann, Amila lowered her voice so only he could hear. "I can't help who I am any more than you can. I can fight my nature every day of my life, but I can't change the class in which I was born. I'll go away and make things right. I told you that. As soon as spring comes, you'll be rid of me. Eva needs you here. They all do. No one needs me. Not a soul." This time, Amila walked away.

*W*inter melancholy was taking its toll. Each morning, Rein was among the throng of ghost-like creatures emerging from rabbit holes. He shielded his eyes to adjust to the light after the long period of darkness. Colonists gazed at one another and the sky, hopeful the weather was growing warmer and days longer. Still, winter wore on and on, each day desperately cold, new snow adding to the deeply packed ice, illuminated only by a sun lying low on the horizon. With only eight or nine hours of daylight, colonists took advantage of every minute.

Each morning, parents trudged through the crunchy snowpack taking children to school at the common house. Even toddlers were welcome, too young to take part but able to draw strength from the giant hearths and the energy of the other children. The building bulged with more than 50 children. Rein watched as Amila and other women joined the schoolmaster to help manage the energetic mob.

The corner designated as Eva's infirmary swelled with patients. Along with other women who shared her knowledge of herbs, she had collected wild plants, buds, flowers, seeds, and roots all summer and fall to address as many illnesses as possible. Most in-demand were cornflower and stinging nettle for coughs and fever; white chamomile for a variety of stomach complaints; birch buds for healing wounds; horsetail shoots for frost-bite and burns; and mint for a wide variety of disorders. Unfortunately, despite Eva's skill and tender care, some patients were lost. Already three young children and two women had died from maladies so severe she couldn't save them, no matter what she and the others tried. With each loss, Eva mourned and wondered what more she could have done. Father Yauck attempted to console her. "You have tried your best, Eva. Nature grows no herb that can conquer death."

In addition to serving as schoolmaster, the Lutheran minister held church and prayer sessions in the evenings and every Sunday. So critical was he to the community's spiritual well-being, it was agreed he should reside in the common house full-time. Families with small children, the sick, and those simply needing a brief respite from their dark, dank burrows took turns sleeping in the common house. They hadn't the strength to feel guilty about the special treatment. They'd willingly return to their underground dwellings after a night or two, some-what revitalized, making space for others in greater need.

Leaving dugouts on days consumed by blizzards was impossible. Trapped below ground, Rein recalled the only sound was the wind wailing, and the only light came from small cooking fires and tiny lamps burning fish oil or animal fat. When blizzards ended, often after several days, snow blocked doorways. The lethargic colonists dug themselves and their neighbors out, emerging into a wonderland of pristine snow sculpted into massive drifts.

On days the weather was bearable, settlers spent precious daylight hours gathering enormous amounts of firewood necessary for the common house and tiny dugout fires, caring for livestock, hunting, and ice fishing. Women were able to sit in wagons above the frozen ground, protected from the wind by the canvas covers, spending time sewing, weaving, or simply talking. On those days, the sky shone bright blue, reflecting a blinding sheen from the thick ice covering the Volga.

Rein often visited Johann at the stables. The toughness of the Kalmyk horses was again apparent. They were allowed to wander, finding grass poking through the snow and pawing the ground until they reached more nutritious sprigs at the base. Rein didn't ask, but he knew Johann gave special treatment to the teams trained to pull the sleigh. Johann stayed in the animal shelter each night, having created an elevated sleeping area that took advantage of the warmth generated by the livestock. At night, he and his helpers built fires around pens to keep wolves from attacking. Unfortunately, as the winter wore on, the wolves acted more brazen. Johann kept rifles loaded and within reach.

By January, it was evident the dark, cold days and nights in dugouts were presenting mental and emotional hardships on the usually buoyant inhabitants of Dobrinka. The forced idleness spent crammed into dark dugouts left them brooding, bickering, and depressed. They had experienced the Russian winter the previous year but were lodged in Saratov in large barracks and had adequate food. The disheartened settlers began to talk seriously about going home, recalling the shorter, milder winters. Anything would be better than this, they complained. Others, like Rein, kept quiet, knowing he no longer called Germany home.

Rein felt fortunate he had thick, warm clothing and outerwear to safely go outdoors even on the coldest days, like today. The cold penetrated his bones despite his dokha and leather boots with felt liners Eva had toiled so hard to sew. On his way to the common house to meet with the colony's other men, he used a thick branch to knock the dagger-like icicles from trees and the roof. "Pavel warned us about the icicles," he mumbled to no one in particular.

With no indoor space large enough to hold all residents, women and children remained in dugouts during the meeting. Georg had called the men together in hopes of lifting spirits as well as addressing valid concerns. "Take heart! Already the days are getting longer. It's late February, and we have more daylight every day. Spring is not far off. This winter will be the worst for us. By next year, every family will have a cabin. Think what that will mean—a village of as many as fifty cabins. We'll have large barns, perhaps a mercantile, and space for craftsmen to create and sell their wares."

"That's all well and fine for next winter if we really do get the lumber promised to us. But my children are hungry," yelled a father of four.

"We have cattle, sheep, some pigs. We should butcher them," added another.

It was true. Food stores were running dangerously low with so many to feed, regardless of food stores recovered from the thieves and the ongoing ice fishing. Hunting wild game was difficult in the deep snow. Rein was making frequent runs by sleigh to Kamyshin and Russian villages, trading hides or paying with money from the colony's funds, filling the sleigh with as much food as it would carry. It was barely enough.

"We've talked about that among the leaders. We agreed we can't butcher more livestock. There is no meat without a bone—we need breeding stock to build herds for next year. We must continue to think about the future. Consider our poor neighbors in Galka. Think what they must be going through, with so little food stored and no common house," Georg reminded them.

Rein stepped forward. "I'll make more trips to Kamyshin. Let's see what's needed the most."

This seemed to appease the colonists, along with a plan to do more ice fishing. Soon, the meeting ended.

As Rein filed out with others, Georg caught him gently by the sleeve. "I'm worried about you, with so many trips alone in the sleigh. I judge a man by the way he bears his burdens. You are determined to bear yours without assistance. I see you taking unnecessary risks. It's getting worse with the wolves, isn't it? Although you've never told me, I've heard the stories, and I know it's dangerous. Rein, what are you trying to prove? At least take someone with you."

Rein's faraway look told Georg he wasn't getting through. "No, it takes too much space in the sleigh. I need it for extra supplies." He looked away, focusing on the wall. It wasn't the first time Georg had cornered him to try and talk sense into him this winter. Rein didn't know what to say or how to say it. He hurt so much. The only escape was the freedom he felt racing along the ice as fast as the horses would carry him. There, he was free from thought, free of her. Rein squeezed his eyes shut. "I'll go to Kamyshin again tomorrow."

Rein lost all sense of time and place in the sleigh's movement. The team pulled in a smooth cadence, gaining traction from newly fallen snow covering the Volga. It was a rare warm day with a clear, blue sky. With conditions like this and the sleigh empty, it would take only a few hours to travel to Kamyshin. Unless the weather changes and the wind whips the snow into a frenzy, he thought.

Rein had brought trade items such as tanned leather hides and furs, which were always in great demand, and rubles from the colony treasury. Two muskets were loaded and within reach at his side and a whip in his hand. He never used it on the horses, didn't need to. It was reserved for the wolves. Perhaps today, he'd be fortunate. But he'd begun to expect the challenge, even welcome it. He admired the Russian timber wolves. Could any creature be freer? He could recognize some family traits among their small packs: the reddish tones of their heavy, coarse fur, their size. The way they hunted together showed great cunning. But what he admired the most was their incredible tenacity, their will to survive.

They were clearly starving this late in the winter, and would do what they must.

Pleased to reach the military outpost of Kamyshin without mishap, Rein stopped at the trading post. He'd been there so frequently this winter that the proprietor knew his intent. In all, he purchased or traded for 300 pounds of flour, sugar, cured meat, and cheese, securing the packages in the sleigh. After watering and feeding the horses, he left right away, hoping to arrive home before the wind began to blow. He felt the horses adjust to the sleigh's extra weight and pull harder. By coming alone, as Georg had objected to, he was able to transport twice as much food.

Halfway through the return trip, the horses picked up speed. Rein knew the team's burst meant wolves must be approaching. Instinct thrust the horses forward to outrun the advancing threat. The scene had played out so many times during previous trips it was almost an expectation. Yet this was life or death, more than a game. As the hungry pack gained on the sleigh, Rein grabbed one of the loaded rifles and his whip. The lead wolf approached the horse on the right, and it kicked violently, sending the wolf rolling in the snow. Others took its place, closing in to snap at a horse's leg, trying to avoid the sharp hooves. Time and time again, Rein lashed out with the whip and found the backs of the wolves, leaving them whimpering. But they continued to attack.

He dropped the reins and pivoted in the seat, choosing his target. The sleigh lurched, and the shot missed, allowing the wolves to close in. Rein grabbed the second rifle and took more time to aim. He squeezed the trigger, and immediately, a wolf fell, struggling to regain its footing on the ice. The starving wolves surrounded the wounded pack member and viciously attacked him. Rein grieved for their loss and his role in it. They'd do anything to survive. He turned away and quickly reloaded both guns. The horses needed no urging. They raced toward Dobrinka.

Even though it was only late February, the day felt spring-like, glorious. Why not, she thought. It had been months since she'd been on horseback or away from the village. After helping teach the children that morning, Amila dressed warmly, stowed a pistol in her belt, and checked the knife in her boot. As busy as Johann was at the stable, she was able to catch and saddle her favorite—the fast Kalmyk she had ridden the day of the counterattack. Only a boy working with the livestock saw her leave. She put a finger to her lips, stowed the pistol in the leather holster attached to the saddle, and slipped away. She'd be back before anyone even noticed she was gone.

Months trapped in the dugouts and the uncertainty of her future had left her queasy and confused. However, her spirits lifted immediately once the pony began to move, the real or perceived pain in her stomach beginning to subside. She realized suddenly why she so badly needed to ride—it was like running free.

Giving the horse its head to choose the path, it avoided deep, crusty snow and drifts that refused to melt. Amila kept the horse moving toward a destination she'd been thinking about all winter—the secluded valley. She knew the route well. It was the valley where they often took the herds to graze, the place they had lured and fought the thieves. That was one of the few days she hadn't seen the small herd of wild horses. She wondered if they were there now, hoping they had survived the brutal winter.

On the trail alone, she was better able to think. Amila yearned to be the kind of woman her mother had been and would've wanted her to be. She had grown to love these inspiring people—the bonds they showed for their families and friends alike, their willingness to work so long and hard for so little in return, and the hardships they endured for their freedom. This winter, they risked their very survival to preserve that freedom. Tundorf was a coward by comparison.

An involuntary shiver racked her body. She must be vigilant. If he were capable of murder and treason, he'd do anything to save himself. He had chased her across the sea and two countries. With spring approaching, she must beware. As soon as travel was possible, she must go back to Germany, present the evidence and turn him in. Once the count was jailed for his crimes, Rein would no longer have this dangerous obsession to kill him. And maybe Rein would forgive her for what had happened to his father. She longed for his forgiveness. Vivid recollections of their continually intense interactions left her rattled and disturbed. She recalled the hurt and confusion reflected on his face when she'd told him she planned to leave in the spring. Did they always have to lash out at one another? There must be some way to treat one another that didn't end in bitter words. She contemplated her role in each interaction. Hadn't her mother always admonished her stubbornness, saying it wasn't a trait to be admired in a young lady? Amila's smug response was to deny being stubborn. Instead, she called it determination, even tenacity. Perhaps both she and her mother were right —the good with the bad. Amila vowed to try and separate the two, especially when Rein was involved. She breathed the warm air deeply and felt the sun penetrate her body. The vow gave her the clarity and hope she had been seeking.

In no time, the horse had found its way to the valley entrance. Amila let the sure-footed mount wind its way down the path, intermittently packed with rocks and ice. She noticed the path was surprisingly well-traveled, probably by the herd of horses. This meant they were alive. Her heart beat faster.

Her horse shied when surprised by a lone rider. Hardly more than a boy, astride a horse that looked much like the ones in the valley, he approached her on the winding trail. Then, whether out of fear or surprise, he suddenly charged toward her, emitting a shrill sound like a battle cry. Amila's first reaction was to turn and gallop away. She was attempting to turn but had just enough time to shift sideways, blocking the path. The rider was upon her in a moment. Unable to stop his horse, the two collided, causing the boy to fall from his horse onto the icy trail.

She was tempted to flee. But he was just a young boy and lay still on the ground. She quickly dismounted and knelt beside the oddly dressed child, alarmed to see a trickle of blood beneath his head. The sound of laughter made her turn with a jolt, where she saw a group of men dressed like the boy. They must have watched the encounter. She was certain the men were not Russians. Their long black hair, lack of beards, and clothing assured that. They were short and squarely built with large heads, round faces, and darkish yellow complexions. Dressed in heavy, flowing robes from the neck down to large black boots, they carried knives tucked into leather sashes at the waist. She saw no guns, but several carried bows and arrows.

Turning her horse on the narrow path and remounting quickly, she spurred her pony up the trail. Suddenly one of the stout, black-eyed men appeared out of the brush, blocking her path. He effortlessly grabbed her moving horse's halter, jerking her to a stop. He spoke gruffly in a series of unharmonious phrases, unlike any language she'd ever heard.

One man knelt beside the boy and shook him. Amila realized he must have hit his head on a rock when he fell. The boy didn't move.

"Is he alright? We have to help him." Amila dismounted and approached the boy. The man holding her horse's reins grabbed her around the waist, looking toward a man still on horseback as if for orders. The leader uttered several phrases and nodded toward the boy.

Amila's captor pulled a leather strap from his belt. She struggled ferociously and screamed when she realized he intended it for her. "No! Let me go!" He deftly grabbed her arms and bound them with the strap, then roughly lifted her back up on her horse, tying the strap and her hands to the saddle horn. Then while holding her reins, a single agile movement lifted him back astride his horse.

In unison, the riders remounted and began to ride away, leaving the boy behind. Until now, Amila had not noticed that the riders led horses tethered by long leather straps. That must be why they're here, she thought. They came to get the horses that live in the valley. Amila looked back at the boy on the ground and forward at the strangers leading her away and shuddered uncontrollably. *What have I done?* She fought back a dizzying panic, willing herself to remain conscious.

The horsemen followed the trail that led up and out of the valley's far side, clearly familiar with the route. Then the band of riders started down a steep, icy embankment toward the Volga. Her horse balked but kept its footing as they reached the bottom and started across the frozen river.

CHAPTER 19

February 1765

*I*t was late afternoon when Rein drove the sleigh through Dobrinka to the livestock area. The horse attacked by the wolves had minor wounds on one leg needing immediate care. Luckily, he knew Eva and Johann had treated more severe wounds, and the horse would recover.

When he saw Johann anxiously pacing, pausing only to talk to himself, Rein knew something was desperately wrong. "She's gone. Amila rode out alone. One of the boys saw her leave on horseback at mid-day. She told him not to tell. But he got worried when she didn't come back. I've been waiting for you."

Rein felt the air drain from his lungs. "Why would she do that? She knows it's dangerous." As soon as he uttered the words, he knew the answer. Hadn't he been doing the same, taking unnecessary risks, welcoming the challenge of the wolves as if nothing mattered? "Do you have any idea where she would ride?"

"I'm afraid it's the canyon where we see the wild horses. We can follow her trail and get there before dark if we hurry. Johann ran toward two horses he'd already saddled.

Johann led the way down the winding trail entering the valley. Both noted fresh tracks. Near the trail's end, they saw the child lying on the ground. Johann dismounted, crouching beside the oddly dressed boy. "He's alive. Unconscious, but breathing."

Rein inched ahead, forcing himself to peer around the next bend. Mind numb, he fought off the terror of finding her lying dead. Finally, he reached the open valley with no trace of Amila or her horse. He jumped from his horse and knelt on the ground, tears of relief and remorse pouring from his eyes. Why had he risked her love out of a need to blame, to avenge a wrong not of her doing? He pleaded for another chance if he could only find her alive.

He studied the tracks that showed many horses had passed this way. Rein followed the tracks on horseback up the slope and out of the valley, stopping where hoof prints descended the steep embankment onto the river ice. Racing back to Johann, he jumped off his horse, trying to breathe evenly. "There's no sign of her or her horse."

Johann had used his bare hand to apply pressure to the boy's slowly seeping head wound. Rein took the sash from his coat and wrapped it around the child's head to bind the wound. "I followed the tracks to the ridge. Many horses passed that way, down onto the river. I have to believe someone has taken her, that she's being held captive. Johann, I must find her!"

Johann touched his friend's arm gently and nodded. "I know."

Rein mounted, and Johann picked up the boy, carefully placing him in Rein's arms. Sensing urgency, the horses moved briskly up the trail as shadows claimed the valley floor. When they reached Dobrinka, Rein rushed into the common house with the boy while Johann ran to find Eva.

Terror subsided slightly when Amila saw the destination, an encampment of many circular huts dotting the horizon near herds of horses, sheep, and goats. Men, women, and children outside the dwellings greeted the riders warmly.

A woman approached, walking nervously through the returning horsemen, searching for someone. Amila dropped her head, certain it must be the child's mother. The woman stopped beside the boy's horse and scurried panic-stricken from one man to another. No one seemed willing to speak to her. Finally, she approached the leader. Amila heard the leader's response, words she couldn't understand but knew their meaning. The woman wailed mournfully. The leader addressed her again, and the woman turned to glare at Amila. Casting a long, angry look, the woman disappeared into a tent, reappearing with a whip. She spoke sharply to an old man who had followed her from the hut, then hurried toward Amila, who had been allowed to dismount, hands still bound. The mother lashed out viciously with the whip, forcing Amila to drop to the ground and cover her head and face with her hands, crying out each time the whip cut through her clothing to bare skin. After a few moments, the dreaded sound and the blows stopped. Amila lifted her head slightly, still whimpering. The old man was holding the whip still in the mother's hands. He gently took the whip and placed his arms around her. They wept together softly.

Darkness was consuming the settlement when the old man released the woman and stepped back. She continued to cry and retreated to the tent. Still cringing on the ground, Amila shrunk away when the old man approached. Instead of using the whip he now carried, he extended his other hand to Amila to help her stand. He motioned for her to follow him into the tent.

Warmth penetrated her freezing body, making every welt and gash sting painfully. Amila saw the woman bent over the fire, still weeping. The old man pointed to an animal fur near the wall, and Amila limped over and huddled on the floor, wincing silently. The worst wounds were those that landed on her scalp, back, and arms. Her coat and clothing had blocked many blows from penetrating her skin, but welts had raised everywhere the whip landed.

Amila knew it might be a mistake but had to try. She slowly rose and walked to the mother and knelt at her feet. Amila uttered words she hoped would be understood. "I am so sorry. I am so very sorry," she repeated respectfully in Russian, looking up into the woman's face. "I didn't mean to hurt him. I know it's my fault. I didn't mean to hurt your son."

Suddenly Amila saw the mother straighten and stiffly bow her head to a man who had entered the tent in time to hear Amila's words. She turned slightly to see who had commanded such respect.

"She can't understand you, but I can," he said in Russian with a heavy accent. He had the same long black hair, facial features, and build as the horsemen but was dressed formally in a long robe of bright colored wool. It was an air of superiority, both confident and frightening, that set him apart. "I am Batyr Khan, leader of this tribe. I will tell them what you said." Amila listened as he translated her words to the odd, guttural language. She stood and kept her head bowed, as did the mother and old man. When he stopped talking, the mother and elderly man she assumed was the boy's grandfather nodded, acknowledging her message but refusing to look at her.

"Thank you." Amila dared not say more to the leader.

He came closer and studied her, then sat down by the fire, motioning for all three to sit as well. Amila knelt and cowered. Batyr Kahn addressed her in Russian. "I came to tell them I grieve for them. The horsemen who went out today saw what happened and told me. The boy was perhaps too young to accompany the riders and too eager in his actions. But his mother and grandfather were anxious for him to learn our ways and be accepted, so they sent him along. His father died a few years ago." He abruptly changed subjects. "Who are you? Are you spitzbuben?"

Captured and beaten, Amila chose her words carefully. She was well aware of the special name given to forest thieves living along the Volga. "Not spitzbuben. My name is Amila Wallerstein. I came here from Germany with colonists who are settling on the west side of the Volga. We have a settlement on the Dobrinka River. It is our first winter here."

"How many of you? And why are you here?" He probed, forehead creased.

"I suppose we're here because the Empress of Russia invited us to come, to settle the lands near the Volga. We have 55 families, about 200 men, women, and children. We plan to farm the land, to grow crops and fruit trees."

The Khan's face was taut. "Do you have yurts like ours? Will you herd sheep on the steppe, on this side of the Volga?"

"No. Our colony's land is on the river's west side, and we have no rights to the land on the east. We have horses and cattle, a few sheep and goats. But most important to us is farming the land." When it seemed he had no more questions, she asked timidly. "May I ask who your people are? And what is your tongue, the language you speak?"

"We are Kirghiz, descended from Batu Khan, the grandson of Genghis Khan." He asserted proudly. "We speak the Mongolian language of our forefathers. I learned your language from selling horses to Russians across the river."

"What will you do with me?" Amila braced for the answer.

"You are responsible for the child's death," came his indifferent response. "According to our law, you are the property of his family to do with as they please. You will work for them and live with them for now. I told them not to hurt you anymore, that you are more valuable if you are strong. I expect them to sell you in the slave markets when we travel to the Uzbek city of Khiva in summer. We don't want Russian or any other blood mixing with our own."

Mouth open, lungs drained of air, Amila sat rigid, unable to move. She would never see Rein again.

She'd been gone more than a day. Rein paced beside the pallet where the boy sat. He was conscious and able to eat and drink. Eva believed he was now well enough to travel in the sleigh. A storm had passed, and the weather was cold but clear once again. Rein had loaded the sleigh and now waited impatiently for Georg.

Rein had pressed himself to remember everything he could about the people he believed to be Amila's captors. Captain Kachinov and Pavel recited stories about the nomadic tribes called Kirghiz. They roamed the vast steppe on the east side of the Volga grazing herds of sheep and horses, occasionally selling horses and trading with the Russians. Kirghiz made large encampments and remained in one location for the winter. Rein recalled the captain's tragic story about his father's regiment: the Kirghiz were fierce warriors and expert horsemen who had slaughtered battalions of Russian soldiers— including the captain's father—thirty years ago.

Rein spoke rapidly when Georg and Johann finally appeared. "Eva says the child can travel. I'll go upriver toward the valley where the tracks lead out onto the ice. I'll find their encampment and return the boy. Take gifts, some tools, and furs. Pavel told me they trade with Russians."

George nodded. "This time, you must take someone with you. What if you can't find them? What if the wolves attack again?"

"I'll find her. And I've dealt with the wolves many times. Georg, I can't put anyone else at risk. You know as well as I—they'll either let us go or kill me, whether it's one or ten men. I must go alone."

By first light, the team was hitched to the sleigh, and the boy reclined under a pile of furs and hides. The day promised to be bright and clear with twinges of spring. Rein hugged Eva then held her face in his hands. Johann stood nearby. "I have to find her. You must have suspected – I love her so much." Laying his feelings bare at last left him unburdened, free.

Eva smiled and nodded. Her eyes held back tears. "I know how you feel about Amila. So does Johann and everyone who knows you. You were just the last to admit it. But what if you don't...".

"You must believe I'll find her, and we'll be back. If something happens, then you know I tried, that I wanted to go. And I think you have someone here who'll take care of you." Rein nodded to Johann.

"She does. But come back with that stubborn stable hand of mine. She owes me a horse." The two friends shook hands and ended with a clumsy hug.

Rein took his seat in the sleigh and flicked the reins hard. The horses responded; the scraping of the rails— usually so soothing—blocked out all other sounds. Within an hour, he found the location where the horses' hooves had left the riverbank and urged the team across the ice. In the bright sun, Rein was able to follow faint tracks on the ice. It was the first time he, or anyone from Dobrinka, had traveled miles across the Volga to the opposite side.

Amila didn't understand what she was being asked to do. She felt numb and wanted only to huddle on the hut floor. The mother, whose name she had learned was Juma, was shouting orders, tugging at Amila's clothes, and pointing to a wooden basin behind a partition. After Juma stood in the basin and pretended to pour water over her own head, Amila understood she was supposed to bathe.

She stepped behind the blanket and began to undress, wincing as she pulled layers of fabric off her skin. Amila stood in the basin assessing her wounds. Luckily, few had bled, leaving only angry, red welts. Juma handed her a soft chunk of what she assumed was soap, a small wool cloth, and set a bucket of heated water in front of her. Amila gently poured water over her head and shoulders, unable to remember when she'd last been able to wash properly. Mindlessly, she began to wash away layers of dirt and grime, cringing as the soap bubbled over the swollen welts.

When she was finished, Juma handed her a large wool cloth. Amila wrapped it around her and searched for her clothes. Peering from behind the blanket, she saw her clothing smoldering in the fire pit located in the middle of the yurt. She panicked. Although the tent was surprisingly warm, those were the only clothes she had. Amila finally got the attention of Juma, who was enthusiastically stirring the clothing into the flames. Her captor brought a large stack of brightly colored clothing, including undergarments and winter outerwear, and dropped the pile in front of Amila, glancing momentarily and without remorse at the injuries she had inflicted. From Juma's urgent tone and clapping hands, Amila understood she was to hurry and dress.

By late morning, the snow-packed trail led Rein to the outskirts of the Kirghiz encampment. At a distance, he could see unusual round huts and herds of horses and sheep gathered near a protective windbreak. Rein closed his eyes for a moment and took a deep breath. She must be here. She must. Please, let her be alive. He could bear anything, as long as she was alive, and he could finally look into her eyes and tell her how he felt. Slowly, he urged the horses forward into the village.

The arrival of a sleigh alarmed Kirghiz working outdoors. By the time he was amid the tents, he was surrounded by men with lances aimed aggressively. Rein halted the horses and ever so slowly raised his hands above his head. He'd been over it in his mind. He must show them the boy was alive and well as soon as he could. He carefully reached back to uncover the child, slowly shifting so they could see his every movement. As the boy began speaking rapidly, the Kirghiz relaxed the hold on their weapons. A man hurried to a tent and shouted inside.

A woman emerged and ran to the boy. "Usen, Usen." She wrapped him in a tight embrace, tears of joy wetting both their faces. The old man watched the reunion with relief, turning to Rein to express kind words. A young man carried the boy into a tent, and the woman and elderly man followed.

Rein stood by the sleigh while men began rummaging through items inside, no longer concerned he was a threat. He looked around the encampment nervously, speaking Amila's name and asking in Russian if they knew where he might find her. He'd heard the child speak his unusual native language and wasn't surprised when no one understood. Am I too late? His eyes darted around the encampment.

A formally dressed Kirghiz man emerged from the largest tent and motioned to Rein, who eagerly followed him into the dwelling where men were gathered and talked noisily. His eyes adjusted to the uneven light of the fire, and he scanned the room, searching frantically.

Amila's back was against the tent wall, knife in hand. She thrust it forward and sideways to fight off the advances of several men, who seemed to be enjoying her clumsy attempts at self-defense. Finally, one tired of it and swatted the knife from her hand. They moved closer, groping and pawing at her hair, face, and body while laughing and speaking loudly. She had nowhere further to retreat.

"Amila!" Rein shouted with blustering force across the room.

She heard his voice over the bedlam. "Rein!" She reached out her arms.

He crossed the distance in giant strides, flinging the smaller men aside, punching one with his fist, until the path was clear. He stopped in front of Amila, turning to shield her, and stared rabidly into the surprised faces peering back. Veins throbbed in his neck. His chest heaved, sending an unmistakable message to would-be challengers. Seeing only stunned expressions, he turned to Amila.

As if no one else existed, he lifted her off the ground into his arms, pressing his cheek against hers, and held her tightly, swaying gently back and forth. The responsive woman returning his embrace assured him it wasn't a dream. "You came for me!" she murmured softly. At last, he set her down and tenderly cradled her face in his hands, smiling through tears of joy. "Are you truly surprised? Amila, I can't live without you. I waited too long to tell you and almost lost you. Can you forgive me?"

"Is this your woman?" issued a commanding voice from the center of the room. Forced to acknowledge others observing their reunion, Rein turned to the powerful Kirghiz man speaking Russian. Amila leaned in close to Rein. "This is Batyr Khan, the chieftain of these Kirghiz people."

"Yes, she is my woman," Rein responded boldly, a protective arm extended. Amila gazed up at him adoringly. He continued, knowing his Russian was not easily understood. "I have returned the injured boy, who is now well. And I brought gifts."

The Khan's gaze scanned the room until his eyes found and rested upon the leader of the horseman who had returned the previous day. In his Mongolian tongue, he yelled orders to the men in the yurt. The native men sheathed weapons and moved away from Rein and Amila. The chief spoke to women nearby, who scrambled away. He calmly squatted by the fire pit in the middle of the yurt and motioned for Rein and Amila to join him, diffusing tension inside the smoky hut. Rein held Amila's hand tightly, and they moved forward. They sat quietly until the women returned and placed food they called *balamyk*, bread fried in animal fat, mutton and goat meats, and a strong, fermented drink they called *kumis* before them.

The Khan motioned for them to eat and drink. "You wish to trade for the woman?"

Rein calmed his nerves by taking a bite. He attempted his best Russian. "Yes. I wish to take her home."

"What was she doing there, out riding all alone?" the Khan asked.

Rein looked at Amila to allow her to answer, keeping a protective arm around her. "I went there to see if the beautiful horses had survived the winter and just to ride." She stumbled on the words and lowered her eyes.

Batyr Khan huffed. "Is this how your women behave? Go riding in winter by themselves? If we had not found her, she would have been killed and eaten by wolves."

"She is, how do you say it, strong head?" responded Rein, sending a quick forgive-me glance toward Amila, who looked annoyed but knew better than to disagree.

"Ah, head-strong, stubborn." The Khan nodded, chuckling, and explained to the others in his language. "You must punish her, and she won't do something that stupid again."

"I hope she won't want to do that again." Rein squeezed her hand and gazed at her tenderly.

"The horses you saw are ours," the Khan said firmly. "We allow them to wander in the winter, and at times small herds cross the frozen river and remain there for a year. We always come back for them."

Then the Kahn, in his deep, resonating voice, conveyed a message unlikely to be forgotten. "Your woman told me why your people are here. We are nomads, Mongol tribes, and very proud people. The Kirgiz have pastured our flocks here for five hundred years. Our burial mounds are proof we own all land east of the Volga. The west side of the river is the Russian side."

He took a drink of the kumis and urged them to do the same. "The name Kirghiz means 'unconquerable.' It is said our warriors make other Turks tremble. When I was a young man, the Russian army came and tried to take our land. We killed their soldiers—all of them. We will do it again if they challenge us."

Rein and Amila listened solemnly, waiting until he had finished. Then, Rein asked if he could bring gifts from the sleigh. The leader nodded. When he returned, his arms were filled with small tools, a bearskin, and household goods. Colonists from Dobrinka had generously given up precious possessions when they heard he was going to try and bring Amila back.

"You will be allowed to go. You saved the boy's life, and I give you hers in return. Take back this message— tell your people never to come to this side of the river."

Rein and Amila rose, and she bowed to him. "May I have my knife back? I am not good with it, as you can see, but keep it in my boot, always." The Khan nodded to the man who had taken it.

Rein thanked the Khan for caring for Amila. He laughed and shook his head, "Hah! You arrived just in time. I had given her to my men to do with as they wished. In summer, she would have been sold as a slave in the east." He followed them out the yurt opening, shouting a series of orders to his men.

Anxious to depart before the leader changed his mind, Rein helped Amila into the seat beside him and covered her with furs. As they were leaving, Juma ran toward the sleigh with something in her hands. She hugged Amila and spoke to Rein, her face conveying heartfelt gratitude. She handed Amila a small wooden box with a hand-carved lid before turning and quickly retreating to the yurt.

As they drove the sleigh slowly through the camp, they heard a man screaming in agony. They watched with horror as Batyr Khan stood nearby as a warrior slowly drove a fiery lance repeatedly into the limbs of a man tied to a post. Finally, a knife to the man's heart silenced his cries. Amila recognized the dying man—it was the warrior who had led the horsemen, the one who had left the boy lying in the snow to die.

*W*ith darkness approaching, Rein knew they must press hard for Dobrinka. But as soon as they reached the river, he pulled the sleigh to a stop and held Amila in his arms. "I love you so!" he breathed. Amila pulled him under the furs. Both still shaken, they held one another, letting pent-up emotions flow in sweet whispers.

Before starting across the river, Rein prepared Amila for the worst. Clouds were gathering overhead, but the sleigh would be visible as they crossed the ice. "Wolves will see us from miles away. I need for you to hold the guns. If they attack, take the reins and keep the horses moving while I shoot. Amila, I know you can do this." She nervously took the loaded rifles and held his whip, knowing well the pain it could inflict.

As the sleigh glided across the frozen river, the horses sensed the wolves' approach. Ears pricked forward and muzzles snorting, the two sturdy native ponies sped up to outrun the starving pack. The wolves attacked the horse on the left, the lead wolf jumping again and again to bite its neck while others snapped at its back legs. The horse's frenzied kicks found their target, forcing the yelping wolves back.

Recoiling toward Rein on the sleigh's narrow wooden seat, Amila shivered, less from the cold than from the savagery. Minutes before, Rein had calmly prepared her for the likelihood of an attack, the ferocity of which she had heard about but never seen. Now the ice was black with snarling wolves closing in, mouths open, teeth bared, and coats bristling while paws fought for traction on the snow-covered ice. If the wolves brought down one horse, the second would fall, the sleigh capsize. She gulped the frigid air burning her lungs, trying to swallow her fear. Amila glanced at Rein. He had repeatedly experienced these attacks alone, transporting provisions for the colony. It was reckless, putting himself in peril this way. She winced, knowing it was her actions propelling them into danger today.

Rein's steady voice asking for a musket calmed her slightly. She handed him one of the heavy, single-shot rifles. Resting it across his lap, he quickly wrapped the leather harness straps around Amila's trembling hands, shouting above the din to steer the sleigh forward through the lightly falling snow. With the wolves too near the horses to shoot, Rein clenched a whip with his free hand and lashed out, landing stinging blows on the wolves' backs and heads. They fell back, giving the horses time to gain a slight distance from the pack. At last, Rein could fire. Immediately, a red patch spread across the snow.

The sinewy wolf stumbled and fell, struggling in vain to regain its footing. The other wolves halted the chase, turned on their wounded brother, and ravenously tore him to pieces. Knowing the wolves would not be sated for long, Rein picked up the second musket, fired, and another wolf dropped on the ice.

Amila and Rein watched the gruesome scene for a tenuous moment, feeling kinship with the wolves' powerful instinct to survive the brutal Russian winter. Then Rein reloaded both rifles. Amila turned the sleigh across the Volga River and urged the horses forward. It was still more than a mile across the massive river to the safety of the west shoreline.

One danger averted, heavy snow began to fall in place of the feathery flakes. High winds swirled the stinging crystals, limiting vision beyond the sleigh. Soon, Amila and Rein wore the white of the storm, the wet, spring snow clinging to their coats and faces, to the horses and sleigh. Rein had driven the sleigh in heavy snowfall, but never in a blizzard with such hypnotic power. He tenderly wiped the snow from Amila's face and pulled her closer, lifting a fur hide over her head. Gritting his teeth against the bitter air, he wrapped the scarf of his dokha tighter around his head and face. His Russian friend's words hounded him: *beware Mother Volga, source of life and death, hope and sacrifice.* Rein gave the Kalmyk ponies their heads, trusting in their instinct to survive. The horses heaved the sleigh through drifts in a direction Rein hoped was Dobrinka.

Amila shouted above the wind's deafening howl, pleading with Rein to take cover. He relented and she pulled the hide over their heads, sheltering them from the storm's wrath. Whatever happened now, they would face it together. Surely they hadn't come this far, only now truly finding one another, to die like this.

Long minutes, perhaps an hour, passed with agonizingly slow, steady movement of the team. Unable to see more than a few inches, Rein peered out from under the hide occasionally, still blinded by blowing snow. Suddenly, he heard a different kind of scraping. The sleigh's runners were no longer on ice. The horses seemed to gain stronger footing and began pulling hard along the shoreline. Dobrinka must be near. The team turned and pulled hard up a slight incline, then kept moving forward. Even though the wind continued to roar, the snow stopped swirling around them. The horses pulled the sleigh farther, deep into a recess free from the wind and snow.

"Amila, are you alright?" Rein asked, shivering and numb, barely able to form words. The horses had found a protected ravine, and near the end, they had pulled the sleigh into the opening of a cave.

Amila lifted her head from under the hides, put her warm hands on his face, brushed the snow and ice away, and pulled him close. "You're freezing. You must get warm."

Together, they shook snow from their clothing and the pile of hides. "I have to see to the horses, especially the one that was attacked." He carefully stepped off the sleigh, eyes beginning to adjust to the dim light that penetrated the cave. Snow drifts were quickly sealing the entrance behind them. Beyond the entrance, walls disappeared into the darkness. They had come through a small opening, and the cavern appeared to be narrow and deep. He stepped forward to the horses as they began shaking snow and ice loose from their coats. They brushed the snow off the horses with hides now free of snow.

"You saved our lives." Rein gently wiped snow from the horses' faces and manes. Exhaustion and relief flooded his body, but he had to keep moving and think.

"We aren't safe yet." Rein took both rifles from the sleigh and handed one to Amila. "If we found this cave, others may have. This could be a winter lair for predators. The horses haven't sensed anything, so maybe there's nothing to cause worry. We have to find out."

Both shivering from the cold and the ordeal, they walked slowly together, guns ready. The light was becoming so dim it was difficult to see farther back into the cave. Amila stumbled on something and almost fell. She reached down to touch it. "Rein, pieces of wood. It's all over the cave floor." In tandem, they began dragging pieces into a pile near the sleigh at the cave's entrance.

"The wood must drift into the cave when spring runoff makes the river rise. If that's the case, the flooding might keep animals out of the cave." Rein went to the sleigh and retrieved the flint rock he kept with him. "We need something for kindling."

Amila thought only a second. "Wait just a moment. This clothing they made me wear has many…layers." She pulled the knife from her boot and turned away shyly to cut and then tear pieces of fabric from her white underdress. She handed them to Rein.

He placed the fabric in a pile and expertly scraped the steel of his knife against the flint until a spark ignited the pile of cloth. Then, carefully adding chards of wood followed by larger pieces, a fire soon ignited and lit the cave's walls.

With the fire blazing, they made sure the smoke could escape through the opening of the cave. Rein picked up a piece of wood burning on one end. "We have to see what's back there." He carried the gun, and Amila held the makeshift torch as they walked farther back, the floor rising slightly in elevation. Just when it seemed they had reached the end, the torch illuminated another opening. They climbed to reach a smaller entrance. With his musket held ready, Rein threw a piece of driftwood into the room. No sounds came from the dark cavity. Their torch was becoming dim.

"We're losing our light. We have to go back."

"No, wait." Amila used her knife and cut more long strips of cloth from her underdress and wound them on the torch, blowing to reignite it. They approached the raised opening and entered cautiously. The torch illuminated a smaller room at the end of the cave. As Amila moved the torch from side to side, they looked at one another in amazement. "What is all this?"

"I don't know, but it's been here a long time." Curiosity overcoming fear, they peered at the dust-covered items strewn about the small room and sitting along ledges in the cave walls. They saw crosses, daggers, porcelain and pewter dishes and cups, and kettles of copper and cast iron. Inside the kettles lay small glass containers still sealed and filled with what might be spices, dyes, and oil, discolored by age. Larger bottles lay empty and scattered along the cave floor.

Rein sighed. "That must've been the wine and vodka."

As soon as the torch began to flicker, Amila cut more strips from her underdress and added them to the branch. She giggled timidly. "Soon, I'll have nothing left of this layer."

Rein approached a lone trunk of warped wood that lay open and half-filled with an assortment of trinkets—jewelry, pins, pendants, and small, porcelain boxes with lids. "It looks as though they took the valuable items and left these behind. Let's take a pot back to melt snow, and I'll tell you what I think this might be."

CHAPTER 20

February 1765

So this is what serenity feels like, thought Amila, watching Rein move methodically around the cave. Outside, the storm raged on. Inside it felt calm, even soothing. Delight at being together filled the air. It took nearly losing him to find this, and she didn't intend to give it up—ever again. She kept the fire burning while Rein returned to the hidden room, retrieved a small bowl and oil from one of the corked bottles, then ignited the makeshift lamp. He brought back a second copper pot and melted snow for the horses. After unharnessing and examining them, he asked Amila for more strips of cloth to clean and dress the injured horse's wounds. Drinking thirstily, the horses lay down near the back of the cave, wary of the fire. Rein retrieved the bread and dried meat loaded early that morning—which seemed a lifetime ago. They had nibbled nervously at the unusual food provided by the Kirghiz women but were now ravenous. After warming the food by the fire, they ate and drank melted snow boiled in the pot and poured into pewter mugs.

"What do you think it is we found back there?" Amila asked between bites. It occurred to her they'd seldom been alone together, excluding times they were embroiled in arguments. Yet they had successfully traveled across countries and a sea together for nearly two years, albeit in the company of Eva and a throng of colonists.

Rein relaxed beside her. "It may be pirate treasure. I remember Pavel and other soldiers telling stories and singing songs about a river pirate named Stenka Razin, who raided ships and forts along the Volga a hundred years ago. He was beloved by the peasants for attacking Russian nobility but was finally captured and executed. It was rumored he had a castle hidden in the hills and caves along the Volga where he stashed stolen goods. The ruins where the thieves' chieftain lives may be what's left of Razin's castle, and this, the last of his treasure."

Hunger and thirst sated, they huddled close to the fire. Already sharing a bearskin for warmth, she looked directly into Rein's eyes and took his hands in hers. "What I did, riding away when I knew better... I almost got us both killed. The Khan was right about me. It was thoughtless and put us in danger. I'm sorry."

Rein started to speak, but she lifted a finger to his lips. "No, let me speak for a moment, please. I promise I won't walk away if you won't." She gathered her thoughts, guarded about the admissions she had long wanted to share with someone. "I pretend to be so strong as if I don't need anyone and can make it on my own. I must because—I've had to. Ever since my father died when I was so young and my horrible stepfather took over, he made it difficult for me to trust anyone, especially a man."

She paused and shifted to face him, eyes reflecting the firelight. "In you, I've found someone I can trust. I see the way you treat Eva, who is as precious to me as she is to you. I've seen how you treat others with respect and kindness while also playing the big brute who can best the Russian soldiers. The way you care for the land is... reverent. Your devotion goes all the way to your soul. And you've changed, Rein. I've seen that too. This new life, this new home, it agrees with you. I've seen you become confident and proud, determined. Where others see obstacles, you see opportunities."

She closed her eyes and took a deep breath. "All I could think when I was taken captive was that I would never see you again. That I had missed my chance to be with you because I was stubborn and unable to ask your forgiveness." She paused to summon the courage to go on. "What I'm trying to tell you is, I've never known anyone like you— that such a man walks this earth. When my mother told me I must marry, I hoped to find a man whom I could love forever. I have."

So near she could feel his warm breath, she could wait no longer. Actions guided her. Amila closed the remaining distance until their lips met. She had never kissed a man and had wondered how it would feel. A powerful sensation entered from the outside and reached deep inside. He pulled her onto his lap for a long, penetrating kiss that left them both gasping. They stopped and took great gulps of air, pressing their foreheads together and laughing out loud at the magical feeling they had just shared.

"Can I talk now? I'm not sure I can, but I must try." He cradled her in his arms and stroked her hair. "I have to admit some things to you, Amila. At every turn, I've tried not to love you. At home, each time we rode to Donauwörth to see the recruiter. Escaping the castle and riding to Lübeck...besting the thieves in the forest. Seeing you on the ship and every single day on the wagon journey to Saratov."

Brushing back her hair with his hand, he continued. "And I've been jealous, Amila. I've been jealous of you and Christof. I brooded every time I saw you together. I was sure you loved him over me." Amila tried to interrupt, shaking her head vigorously from side to side to reassure him.

"I hated using you to flirt with the sailor so he would open the door to the hold. It was all I could do to keep from strangling the man. Even when you acted like a spoiled, selfish child, I think I still loved you. But I kept trying not to feel anything, to push you away."

He stopped to trace the contours of her face with his fingertips, then kissed her softly. "The way you do things makes me smile without smiling. Your ability to solve problems and help others, seeing the way you care for Eva, Johann, the children, it touches my heart. When I heard you make that speech to the leaders about not giving up, I wanted to take you in my arms and never let you go! When you were captured, I was willing to die to get you back. I will no longer push you away or deny that I love you."

She cried out, hearing his words. But she had to know. "So, can you forgive me for what happened to your father and the others? For my role in it?"

He grimaced. "There's nothing to forgive. It was not your doing. I tried to blame you for every noble's treatment of us. You're not like them and never have been." He pressed his lips against her hair. "You feel and smell like heaven must!"

Amila giggled, still timid, being so close. "They made me bathe. And while I was washing, Juma burned my clothes and stirred the fire with great enthusiasm. That's why I'm wearing Kirghiz clothing and the vanishing underdress."

"You look beautiful. Even though I tried to deny that I loved you, I've never denied your beauty." He couldn't help but tease. "When you fainted—twice—and I carried your limp body, you looked so beautiful and…peaceful. Do you think you'll be doing that again? I enjoyed the calm."

"Hmm. I'm sorry to disappoint you, but I shall never faint again." She stood up boldly, an idea igniting her to action. "I'll help you wash. Can I?"

Rein stood and held his arms out to his sides. "Do as you wish with me."

She clapped her hands gleefully. "First, we'll need to melt a great deal of snow and get it hot. Then, after I wash you, I'll wash your clothes. But don't worry, I won't burn them." From the sleigh, she retrieved the small wooden box Juma had given her. She had peeked inside, finding it held lumps of the sweet-smelling soap given to Amila to wash. Both pots were filled with snow and heated on the fire. Two more were brought from the upper cave, one more for water and one to stand in. Rein began to strip off the clothing he'd worn for months. When the Volga froze and the colonists were forced to live in dugouts, washing had become a rarity.

"We haven't a blanket to hang for privacy, so you'll just have to, um, turn around." Rein obediently turned away. Off came another length of Amila's underdress to use as a washing cloth. She watched intently as layers of clothing were shed. Even though the cave was warm, he shivered and removed the last of his clothing, facing away.

Amila stared, unable to move. What she thought would be great fun was now a very real man standing naked in front of her. She had long ago conceded that Rein was handsome. It was on the face of every woman who looked his way, which continually annoyed her. But now, here he was for only her to admire. Who was the naked Greek god in the drawing her governess had shown to her? Ah, yes, Adonis. The memory of the statue and this real-life vision made her face burn scarlet. Amila was tall for a woman. But Rein was a head taller. His shoulders were broad, and his back and arms rippled with muscles from a lifetime of hard, physical labor. His waist tapered, then thick muscles outlined his buttocks and legs, all the way to the floor. Gone was the summer bronze on his arms and legs. And most of this lily-white skin had never seen the sun. She swallowed hard.

"Oh. You're cold. I'm sorry. I was just....you'll have to bend down so I can reach your hair." He obediently crouched down, still turned away. Amila began pouring hot water from a pewter mug over his head, wetting his now loose shoulder-length hair. She poured water down his shoulders and body to warm him and began lathering the soap into his hair with her fingers. "This soap was in the little wooden box from Juma. The same soap she had me use to bathe. I wonder if she was trying to tell us something about our poor washing habits."

Choking a bit on the soapy water, he teased back. "I wish I had been there to help."

Amila poured more water to rinse his hair and told him to stand up. She started on his shoulders, lathering soap into the cloth, then on to his back, buttocks, and legs. More mugs of hot water washed the suds away, leaving the cauldron in which he stood rapidly filling with warm, soapy water to soak his feet and legs.

"I'm finished with this side. Ready for you to turn around."

Rein paused. "Are you sure? I can wash the rest...if you're not sure."

"I'm...sure." She took a step back.

Rein slowly turned around to face her. Their eyes caught and held. Then she slowly looked down the length of his body. She covered her mouth with the back of her hand, eyes wide, color draining from her face.

He swished his feet around in the cauldron. Suddenly they both began to giggle. "Here, I can finish." He grabbed the cloth. Amila yanked it back. "No. I started this, and I'm going to finish." Some of the tension eased, she began to work more quickly, washing and rinsing each area. She hurried to scrub his legs, then rinsed and stepped away.

Rein stepped out of the pot and moved nearer the fire, shivering. Amila grabbed the thickest fur and wrapped it around him. She combined the remaining clean water into the pot at the edge of the fire, and in went his trousers, shirt, and stockings with a soap shard. She stirred with a stick.

Rein watched her busy herself by the pot.

"I have to finish and hang up your clothes, or they'll never dry." She smiled at him briefly, then averted her eyes.

Having spent so much time with Amila—in all sorts of predicaments—Rein had come to realize her eyes always gave her away. One eyelid twitched when she was afraid or when something momentous was about to happen. A raised eyebrow meant either she was thinking deeply, or her temper was about to flare. Most telling was the luster of her deep, green eyes themselves—sometimes a sparkle, sometimes a gleam—her eyes seemed to be a window to her soul. Averting her eyes now might mean she was alarmed by what she had seen. This would test the newfound intimacy between them. "Amila, did your mother tell you anything…about men and women?"

"No!" She rushed to say, relieved he had broken the silence. "I was young when she died and, no, she didn't tell me anything. Neither did I have a sister nor an aunt, no one to explain. I'm very… naïve about such things. I could have asked Elisabeth but didn't have cause. I know about animals, horses, of course."

"I'm naïve too, but I know a little more than you." Rein was equally uneasy. At least neither of them walked away. This was progress. "We don't have to worry about it. But we need to make the cave more secure before we can sleep."

$\mathcal{R}$ein pulled on his boots and wrapped the hide around his shoulders. "Help me push the sleigh farther toward the opening of the cave. If the horses found the cave, other animals might, even in this storm." They unloaded the sleigh and turned it on its side, blocking the entry where the blizzard continued to rage.

The leather hide slipped off Rein's back while they were working. Amila snickered at the way he looked—wet hair sticking to his shoulders, wandering around the cave wearing only his boots. Once the sleigh was in place, he brought the two guns and extra ammunition near the bearskin where they would sleep.

"I'll be right back. I want to make one more trip to the upper cave." He repositioned the fur around his shoulders and took along the oil lamp.

As Amila added wood to the fire, she experienced the most unusual sensation—even in the brief time Rein was gone, she missed him.

He returned with a hopeful smile. "Can I ask you one more thing before we sleep?" She nodded.

A trace of doubt creased his forehead. He knelt on the fur beside her and opened the palm of his hand to reveal a ladies' ring retrieved from trinkets in the pirate trunk. "Amila, I love you, and I want to spend the rest of my life with you. I know we come from different classes, that I'm just a poor farmer, and you are of noble birth. But I'm free now, and I'm ambitious. I believe we've been through much to overcome our differences. Will you, will you marry me?"

Tears of joy streamed down Amila's cheeks. Her memory flashed back to childhood, the lonely years without her father, and then the loss of her mother... the count's cruel treatment and designs on her life. Yet, she had finally come to realize this was the man she'd longed to meet someday—he was right here all along. "Yes, yes!" She put her arms around him and smothered his face with kisses. "You mean we can be a family? You and me, and Eva as my sister, and maybe someday Johann, too? And children of our own?"

"Yes, all that, I hope." Rein grinned and looked at her tenderly. He fitted the ring on her finger. "I think the pirates missed this one. I'll buy you a ring someday, but this will do for now. We have my mother's wedding ring, but Eva should have it."

The unusual gold ring fit her finger. Holding her hand closer to the tiny lamp's amber glow, she saw the tarnished golden color gleam slightly. She could see several bands twisted together with clasped hands adorning the top. "It's beautiful. Yes, Eva must have your mother's ring. I have my mother's, and it means a great deal to me. But this ring will always mean the most."

Amila snuggled up close to Rein. They sat on the leather hide, and he pulled the bearskin around them. Their lips met again. This kiss tasted different to her. The passion was still there but wrapped in tenderness, conveying less urgency. The resulting breathlessness was the same, however. Amila gently pulled free of his embrace. She stood decisively and began to slowly undress in front of him. Nervous fingers worked the unfamiliar clasps on her outer dress of wool, and it dropped to the floor. A second brightly colored dress of softer fabric fell to her ankles. The shortened underdress revealed long, shapely legs as pale as his. Never letting her eyes leave his, confident in their growing intimacy, Amila loosened the laces on the bodice, pulled it down her shoulders, and wiggled free.

Rein's mouth hung open, and words failed the first time he tried to speak. He tried again. "Amila, I never dreamed a woman could be so beautiful."

She smiled, confident of her decision and enjoying the effect she was having on him. She lay down beside him.

"Do you mean…are you sure?" His heart pounded in his chest.

"Rein, we could have died today. We've spent years arguing and misunderstanding one another. I almost lost you. Life is unrelenting in this new land. We could die tomorrow. If that happened, my greatest regret would be not…knowing you in this way."

He held her gently, seeing her wounds for the first time. "Amila, the red marks and cuts on your neck, arms, and shoulders. What happened?"

Amila shared what Juma had done when she thought her son was dead. "I had forgotten about them. They don't hurt badly anymore."

Rein pulled her close. "It would be both torture and treasure to wait to be with you," he said.

She relished the newfound boldness between them, feeling she could talk to him about anything without fear. Such a gift! Shyness gone, their eyes locked in a visual embrace. Together, they pulled the hide over their heads.

Much later, Rein added more wood to the fire and quickly returned to lay beside her, cradling her in the crook of his arm. He read the mischievous gleam in her eyes. Eventually, they slept.

$\mathcal{F}$ire burning low, one of the horses nuzzled Rein from a sound sleep. Light shone through the cave opening. Silence had replaced the roar of wind-whipped snow.

"The blizzard may be over." Rein held Amila in a tender embrace, reluctant to move. "We can't stay here, although I can think of nowhere else I'd rather be. We must get back to the village, or I'm afraid we'll starve." His words ushered in an uneasy silence. They both knew what that meant—returning to their dugouts to wait out the rest of the winter. No longer being alone together, like this.

"It's already late February. Spring can't be too far away, can it?"

"Once the Volga ice begins to melt, spring is near, Luca told me. It'll be all right, Amila. Although, I'll have to go back to watching you from a distance."

"Watching me?" She stretched and reached for clothing.

Rein put on his clean, now dry, clothing and added wood to the fire, prompting the horse to go back to its side of the cave. "I'm always watching you, though I try not to let you see. Since we began this journey, you've rarely been out of my sight—like it or not. I've seen the joy and sadness. I saw fear in your eyes, times you were afraid, and how bravely you tried to hide it. I knew you were attempting to solve some problem, but I didn't know what it was."

Her lower lip trembled. "If it was fear you saw, then you know the cause."

"Please, don't hide anything from me again. One day we'll be free of his shadow, somehow."

Using firewood to push the snow away from the cave opening and free the sleigh, they squinted into a wilderness of white. Rein studied the landmarks. Aware that wolves may already be prowling, he rapidly hitched the horses to the sleigh.

Amila went back to the cave and returned dragging a pot full of jewelry, trinkets, pewter cups, and bowls. Together, they lifted it into the sleigh. "It'll give the women something new, perhaps repay them for the possessions they gave up to trade for my freedom. Eva can use the bottles for her herbal concoctions." Her eyes reluctantly scanned the cave and the fire's dying embers.

"Can we come back again before the ice melts and it floods?"

They exchanged a knowing look that resulted in a quick embrace. Rein held her at arm's length and longingly gazed as if to memorize every feature. "Oh, the power you have over me, dear lady. I will gladly bring you back here every chance we get. But now, we must go."

She sighed. "Do you know where we are?"

Rein pointed north and nodded. "With the storm passed, I can tell by the cliffs. I've been to Kamyshin so many times, and I know the landscape well. The horses almost found their way home. Dobrinka is only a mile or so north."

Amila cuddled close to Rein on the short sleigh ride to Dobrinka. Word spread rapidly of their arrival, and Eva and Johann came running. Johann's bear hug nearly crushed Amila. He grinned widely and glanced back and forth between the two. "Two of my favorite people, together. You aren't shouting at one another. Do I detect a truce?"

In response, Rein put his arms around Amila, pulled her close, and gazed into her eyes. "More than a truce. I can't promise to agree with her all the time, but I do promise I'll be by her side, no matter what."

Eva cried out with joy and relief. "We couldn't help but think the worst." Then she noticed Amila's exotic clothing and the pot filled with unusual items. "What happened? Where have you been?"

Amila wrapped her arms around Rein's waist and held tight. "It's a long story." She gazed serenely at him. She knew which parts of the story she would share.

CHAPTER 21

April – August 1765

*T*he boy dropped his fishing pole and ran into the village. "Look what's coming down the river. It's a giant raft!"

Plowing in a distant field, Rein heard the commotion. He gave the horses a rest and joined the throng on the riverbank gaping at the spectacle before them. His eyes darted around until he found Amila. It was a day they'd been waiting for, praying for, thought Rein. And perhaps the first time the Kontora had followed through on a promise, even though a year overdue.

Amila joined Rein on the steep bank, peering out at the unruly mass of lumber. He slipped his arm around her waist. "We'll miss the dugouts, won't we?"

"Oh, no! I refuse to spend one more night underground. I'll go live with you in our cave if I have to." She grinned and kissed him on the cheek. "Look, isn't that Luca?"

Luca was piloting the knotted mass of logs, shouting to those onshore to bring ropes and hurry. That much Russian everyone could understand. The long, thick logs were lashed together haphazardly, snarled lengthways and overlapping with no apparent order. But they were floating, and they were here. Several men rode on the pilot's raft with Luca. It appeared that Kontora officials had fulfilled another promise—to send laborers to help build cabins, having assured the colonists "every Russian who can lift a hatchet is a carpenter."

A month earlier, when the weather finally warmed enough to allow the colonists to move above ground into covered wagons, the builders had presented a plan for the construction of the village. They'd received word from Saratov that lumber would arrive soon. Just in case it did happen, they planned to be ready. If the Kontora had failed to deliver, Rein wondered how the disappointment might affect the families. This was the emotional lift they all needed. To Rein personally, it meant he and Amila would be able to marry and have the privacy they longed for in a cabin of their own.

Ever confident the logs would arrive, the builders had placed rocks on the plot of land to show the location and dimensions of the cabins. They presented the proposed design to an attentive, hopeful audience one spring evening. The twenty-by-twenty-foot cabins would be built side-by-side, five in a line, with shared walls to conserve lumber. Builders pointed and walked the area, eagerly explaining how cabins would be arranged in a square for better defense against intruders. In summer, the courtyards would serve as vegetable gardens, more easily protected against foraging animals, wild and domestic. Each cabin would have sparse furniture at first: a simple table and chairs made from scrap lumber.

An all-important decision was the type of fireplace for heat and cooking. Here, builders disagreed on the approach. Some wanted to build German-style hearths. Recalling their stay with peasant farmers in Petrovst, others suggested the Russian-style ovens that warm the entire house and provide cooking areas. In the end, they settled on the more efficient Russian ovens layered with clay, pebbles, and sand.

No longer doubting the delivery of the long-awaited lumber, the builders and as many colonists who could crowd the shoreline welcomed Luca and the carpenters with every rope and muscle they could muster.

$\mathcal{A}$mila and Rein sat side-by-side on a grassy hillside overlooking Dobrinka and the Volga, now free of ice and flowing smoothly. They anxiously anticipated time together every evening when work concluded, the only time they were alone. More than a month had passed since their tryst and safe return.

"Rein, I've been thinking," began Amila from their hillside rendezvous.

"Uh-oh. I've noticed that when you're thinking, trouble is often brewing." Rein still enjoyed every opportunity to rib her.

She rolled her eyes. "This is very important, and I can't figure out how to solve the problem. It's about books. The children need books written in German so they can learn properly. I've been thinking of my role here and what I can do. And I enjoy teaching children as much as I enjoy horses."

She paused and took his hand in hers, knowing she was coming to the difficult part. "I had many books growing up. They're still in my little study at the castle, I'm sure. If only I could think of a way to bring them here. I suppose it might have to wait until we go back and charge Tundorf with his crimes. We have to go, Rein. You know we do."

Most pressing was their renewed fear that Tundorf would find his way to Dobrinka and endanger Amila, now that routes from Saratov were open. Rein made Amila promise to remain in the safety of the village, and if she went riding, to do so only in a group that included armed men. They shared details of the danger she faced with Georg and the vorstehers, so they, too, would be vigilant. Still, both he and Amila were constantly on edge. They had no idea what Tundorf might do to regain the incriminating evidence she held, certain that he was most assuredly going to try. They had discussed at length how and to whom they could present the evidence so that he would be arrested and Amila safe. No solution in Russia seemed plausible.

Rein's jaw tightened. He detested the power his former lord held over them. He woke in a cold sweat many nights, wondering if the evil man was near. The mention of returning to Nassenwald ended in vigorous disagreement every time they discussed it. He wanted the count to pay for his crimes. But he couldn't seem to make her understand how difficult it would be for them to leave Dobrinka for the year or more it would take to travel there and back together or how dangerous such a trip would be if she went alone.

Rein faced her. "Amila, I admire that you are undaunted by challenges. But we have discussed this. Do you recall what Commissar Demidov told us, all of us? We can't return to Germany. At this time, it doesn't seem possible. And even if we could go, how would we pay for such a trip?"

"I thought you might ask that, so I brought something to show you." Amila pulled a medium-sized cloth bag from a pocket of her dress, carefully spreading out the contents on her skirt. She proudly turned to show him. "I smuggled them out of the castle the night we left and carried them in the hidden pockets of my travel dresses. Once winter came, I buried the bag in the Müller's dugout."

Rein's eyes bulged at the diamond, ruby, and sapphire studded jewelry set in gold and silver. His quick response sounded harsh. "Where did you get those?"

"They were my mother's. I thought you would be pleased." Amila's smile faded. "Her wedding ring from my father is the only piece that means anything to me. I can't remember seeing her wear any of the others. Don't you see? We can sell them or use them to bribe the Kontora, or whoever need be, to make the trip."

Since that night in the cave, they had made a vow—no more walking away. This was the closest Rein had come to breaking that vow. He gathered his thoughts before speaking. "I've been trying to forget the conflicting lives we led, Amila. And yet you proudly show off these possessions? That jewelry, it makes me remember the hunger and suffering we grew up with, the oppression we faced every day to pay for your wealth."

Eyes welling with tears, Amila stuffed the jewelry back into the pouch. "I understand. But you're wrong. That's what they used to symbolize. Not anymore. When I see them, I see justice— Tundorf in jail. It's his turn to suffer for what he's done. And I see other things we desperately need here, more than just books. The children need clothing and shoes. We need better tools, like iron, for the plows you want to make. The parts we need for the watermill you keep dreaming about. Fruit trees for the orchards. When I look at this jewelry, that's what I see."

Rein hung his head and shut his eyes. Then he put his hands over hers and gave the pouch and her hands a gentle squeeze. "I'm sorry. I didn't even give you time to explain before I judged you. You're right, of course. Putting the count behind bars is the only way to assure your safety and bring him to justice. I can't believe I'm agreeing, but I don't see another alternative. We'll go back together after the summer crops are planted. We can bring back a wagon full of books."

Amila threw her arms around him with such force that he fell back onto the grass, willingly lying beneath her. She kissed him hungrily until they both fought for breath. "I'm so happy that you finally agree. But that kiss had nothing to do with getting my way. It's because I love you. And I have something wonderful to show you."

From her finger, Amila removed the special ring Rein had found in the pirate cave and placed on her finger that night. Once she had polished it, they had both been amazed to see that it was gold, even the clasped hands atop the ring. She brought it near her eyes to focus. Very carefully, she loosened a tiny hinge. Then, laying the ring in her palm, she extended it to Rein. "Look!"

Opening the hinge enabled the thick band to swivel apart into three separate thin bands. The hands unclasped, revealing a heart on the third band. "Isn't it amazing?"

Rein touched the tiny rings with his finger as if they might break. Then, as deftly as before, Amila realigned the three bands back together to form one ring and again laid it in her palm for him to inspect. "We'll sell my mother's wedding ring as well. But this one—never."

Rein leaned closer. He gently took the ring and eased it back on her finger. "Yes, this is for us. Three bands—for then, for now, forever."

$\mathcal{A}$t last, it was over. It had been the longest winter and spring Count Tundorf had ever experienced, stuck in a ramshackle town lacking decent food or accommodation and only the boorish Chancellor Grekov for company. Finally, summer had arrived, and at last, he was on his way to unleash pent-up fury.

A month earlier, he and the chancellor had met with a band of thieves in their stronghold. Not just any thieves, but the very ones who had attacked Dobrinka so savagely last fall. Once Müller's report of the attack had reached Saratov, including the colonists' clever ruse to retrieve their stolen goods, the missing link fell into place. The colonists' expectation that Grekov would send the army to arrest the leader had included the location of the thieves' lair. How remarkable—and convenient— that they'd left the leader alive.

It was amazing how easily it had all come together. All winter, the chancellor's outrage toward Dobrinka festered. The more vodka he drank, the more crazed his outbursts. How dare they acquire the seeds and lumber behind his back, depriving him of selling them to add to his personal treasury. Grekov railed that a dangerous precedent could be set with other colonies attempting to bypass his authority. He bragged that within another year, he'd amass a fortune large enough to begin a comfortable life elsewhere.

Cautiously, Tundorf had presented ideas to Grekov. Their goals were the same, he assured him. The count wanted the colonies to fail in order to staunch the flow of German emigrants into Russia, as the German princes had sent him to do. And, of course, he longed to bring home his poor, misguided stepdaughter. The chancellor wanted to teach the rebellious Dobrinka colonists a lesson so that others wouldn't dare follow their lead. Why not combine forces, he had suggested to Grekov one long winter evening. He offered Amila's hand in marriage, and the partnership was forged.

In a little more than a day, he and Grekov would arrive at the rendezvous location to join forces with Viktor Rodshenko, chieftain of the most powerful band of robbers on the Volga. Hungry for revenge after his embarrassing defeat last fall, Rodshenko was easy to bring on board. Persuading him to attack and destroy Dobrinka, burn the buildings, ruin the crops, and drive away livestock—at any and all cost of lives—was a simple task.

Rodshenko had supplied the count with details of the settlement's layout and information necessary to plan the attack. In return, they had assured the robber baron that the Russian army brigade patrolling the Volga region would be far north that day and that they could plunder the entire village before it burned. But it must burn. The count was firm about that. Finally, they'd sweetened the pot, offering the chieftain a large sum of money to be paid in full once the act was carried out. All Tundorf asked in return was the loan of two of Rodshenko's toughest men and the opportunity to locate one of the female colonists as the attack began. Tundorf assured Rodshenko they would then make a hasty departure, wanting to be far away when the ensuing messiness occurred. At that point, Dobrinka would belong to the thieves to deal with as they wished.

The chieftain's desire for revenge and possibility of ongoing attacks on all the colonies thrilled the count. Although his forces were sorely depleted from the counterattack last fall, Rodshenko assured Tundorf he could recruit neighboring bands of thieves to join him, swelling his forces to ensure victory. He would require the other robber bands' unconditional loyalty for the battle, and they would share equally in the plunder. Dobrinka would be the first colony to fall, but far from the last. Rodshenko assured them that soon all colonies would suffer the same fate. The spitzbuben would once again rule the steppe west of the Volga.

CHAPTER 22

August 1765

"*S*pitzbuben! Spitzbuben!" The young guard yelled from the watchtower and fired his rifle in the air. Then, in a flash, he climbed down the rope ladder, jumping the last eight feet to the ground.

Stinging bile rose in Rein's throat. It isn't possible! The middle of a summer day? Why attack now? From his position in the field, he was among the farthest from the protection of the wagons and common house. Rein looked toward the hills where the boy had likely seen raiders approaching. He saw nothing—yet. Everyone should have time to reach the settlement safely.

Rein joined men and women running toward the wagons from fields, gardens, livestock paddocks, and the half-built cabins. Previously arranged in a neat semi-circle barrier around the common house, the wagons were now scattered among the winter dugouts and cabins under construction. Behind the jumble of structures was the common house, which backed up to the steep bank leading down to the river.

"Women and children to the common house! Lock the doors once everyone is inside," Georg ordered, and fellow settlers took up the chant. Colonists snaked through the area, grabbing rifles, pistols, powder horns, sabers—anything resembling a weapon—from wagons and dugouts. Rein knew they should already be safely inside the common house, Amila with the school children, and Eva in the infirmary. But he didn't have time to make sure.

At once, a throng of raiders crested the hill and spread into a broad line. Some rode horses, some drove wagons or carts, and others stood alongside. All carried weapons—guns, swords, or spears. Rein scanned the horizon and estimated the enemy at more than one hundred men. Their menacing formation and fearful yells caught Rein off guard. This was no stealthy raid to steal food and possessions. This was a bone-chilling frontal assault—bent on murder and destruction.

Georg darted back and forth behind the line of wagons rapidly dragged together and tipped onto their sides for protection. "We must fight for our lives, men. Think of your families! We have more than fifty guns and the advantage of cover." The Dobrinka men and older boys crouched behind the wagons with muskets leveled at the marauders. "Wait until they come within range, then shoot and reload in waves."

Rein took stock of his weapons. Both rifles were loaded and powder horn within reach, his saber securely fastened at his waist. Surely it wouldn't come to that. His bow and a quiver of arrows lay at his side.

Johann knelt behind a nearby wagon and called over to Rein. "I saw Eva and Amila. They're safe inside with the others. Here we go! We haven't come this far to let a few stinking thieves stop us!"

"I'm glad you're on our side, my fearless friend!" Rein's heart beat wildly, every muscle tense.

With a thunderous surge, the attackers came barreling down the hill into musket range. Gunfire erupted from the settlers; sparks and smoke rose into the air. Thieves fell from horses, and carts capsized. More riders and men on foot appeared and poured over the hill. Rein's eyes widened at the onslaught. No single band of thieves could be this large! It was clear the colonists were greatly outnumbered. Every shot must find its mark.

Count Tundorf had been over the plan repeatedly with Grekov and the two ruffians from Rodshenko's band who accompanied them. Now, if they were just smart enough to remember what to do for the handsome reward they were promised. The count, Grekov, and the two thugs had split off from the small army of bandits and arrived through a ravine to the north of Dobrinka, crossing the small river and tying horses in a wooded area. Grekov nodded nervously when ordered to stay with the horses until they returned.

Hearing gunfire, at last, Tundorf and the two thieves quickly crossed the short distance to the riverbank and approached the back of the common house near the cliff's edge. He was certain the women and children would be gathered inside. The building contained a few large windows, all tightly shuttered against intruders.

The count and his henchmen eased forward to a back window, disappointed to see they were locked from the inside. He peered through a crack in the shutter. The axe in one of the thug's hands might not be needed. He inserted his saber between the two shutters, gently lifted the wooden bar off its slats on the inside, then eased a shutter open. Inside, the dimly lit building was crowded—women and children huddled together facing large doors in the direction of the battle, not expecting an attack from a back window. Tundorf pushed both shutters open and gestured for the thieves to enter first.

Once inside, the darkness of the room and gunfire outside aided the attackers within. Each ruffian grabbed a child, aiming a pistol at their head. The mothers' screams made the intruders' presence quickly known, and women reached for their children and pressed against one another to move further away. The count aimed his two pistols at the frightened settlers.

The crowd parted, and several women came forward with muskets, stocks anchored against shoulders, leveled at the intruders. Amila and Eva were among them.

"Drop your guns, or we'll shoot the children." Tundorf's order was frighteningly calm. "You don't know how long I've waited for this moment, Amila. And you, too, Eva. You're still my property, you know. They'll shoot the children unless you drop your guns, now."

Hearing his voice made Amila's knees weaken. She cocked the trigger on the rifle and stole a quick glance at Eva, whose face was flushed but was holding steady. "I've waited just as long to confront you as a murderer and a traitor. And now it's clear you're a coward as well, threatening children. Release them!"

Furious with the delay, Tundorf ignored the accusations. "All I want is for you to come with me, Amila. We'll leave the same way we came in, and no one will be hurt. A fair trade, don't you think? Everyone will be safe. Put down your gun and come with me."

Still, Amila didn't move. He aimed his pistol at one of the children, a small girl. "You know I care nothing for them. I will shoot her."

"No!" Amila swallowed hard, eyes spanning the room. "I'll go. Eva, everyone, put down your guns and move back." She bent slowly to put her rifle on the floor and walked toward him. Eva and the other women hesitantly laid down their guns.

"We'll come and find you, and then we'll kill you," spewed Eva. "You have no power over us here, you wretched, sickening man!"

A shot from one of the count's pistols shook the room, and Eva fell backward to the floor, a bright red stain appearing down the front of her dress. "Eva!" Amila screamed and ran to her side.

"Bring her, now!" They released the children, pushing them back into the crowd. An assailant grabbed Amila's arm, dragging her toward the window as she struggled fiercely to free herself. Tundorf crossed the short distance and punched her in the stomach. She buckled onto the floor. He pulled out a sash and tied it across her mouth, then grabbed the colonists' rifles and threw them out the window. The assailant lifted Amila's limp body over his shoulder and climbed out the window. In a few moments, they had vanished.

Rodshenko must be responsible for an attack of this magnitude, thought Rein. With no success, he tried to catch a glimpse of where the leader might be hiding. The thieves kept charging in numbers much greater than the attack last fall. With the advantage of cover, the colonists initially produced heavy losses on the attackers, their dead and wounded bodies flattening the tall grass. But the thieves were now closing in. Fearlessly driving their wagons and carts near the settlement, they spun to a stop and tipped them over for cover, cruelly shooting their own horses for shields.

Twice Rein and Johann retreated with the settlers, abandoning wagons that now provided cover to the enemy from which to fire. The defending colonists now found cover behind half-built cabin walls, the last line of defense protecting the common house.

Abandoning his musket because it took too long to reload, Rein fired arrows rapidly at attackers leading the charge. Each hit its mark, causing the raider to fall and writhe in pain, unable to advance. Johann, kneeling nearby, continued to fire his black power rifle, deftly reloading in twenty to thirty seconds. Between the two of them, they were keeping many attackers at bay but were attracting unwanted attention. Rein saw a group of raiders motioning as though they planned to rush the two.

Rein shouted over the sound of the muskets. "Johann, I'm running out of arrows!"

Johann closed the distance between them. "I'll load, you shoot." With three muskets and powder horns before him, Johann could quickly put loaded rifles in his friend's hands. Rein waited until he had a clear shot at the men trying to rush them, picking them off as they started to charge.

Out of the corner of his eye, Rein saw smoke and flames rising near a small group of attackers. Rodshenko squatted behind a wagon, fanning an oil fire. The heinous purpose was soon apparent: Rodshenko and his men began showering flaming arrows onto the roof and sides of the common house. Smoke billowed on the grass and bark-covered roof. Flames erupted and spread rapidly.

All the colonists' guns now rained on the source of the flaming arrows, briefly slowing the barrage but giving the ruthless assailants time to close in from the sides as flames engulfed the common house roof.

"Cease fire! Cease fire!" Georg was sickened hearing his own words. "We must surrender. Get the women and children out of the building!"

Rein lowered his gun. He knew in his heart that it must be done. He and Johann exchanged a knowing glance, recalling Rodshenko's threat should their paths cross again.

In the distance, a loud rumble filled the void left by the silenced guns. The sound escalated, accompanied by a cloud of dust rising from the hill beyond the village. All heads—colonists and thieves alike—stared at the source vibrating the ground beneath them.

Suddenly, a brigade of mounted Russian soldiers crested the ridge, spread in a single line, and halted. At once, soldiers attached bayonets, the fearful snap of long spikes locking on muskets billowing to the battleground below. "Charge and fire at will. Take no prisoners!" Saber raised to the sky, Captain Kachinov sent the powerful surge of soldiers to engage the enemy.

The colonists clenched their fists above their heads, tilted their heads back, and roared in support of the advancing army. Out of ammunition and arrows, Rein and Johann froze and watched the gory scene unfold.

The brigade bore down on the thieves, swerving in from one side to cut off the robbers from the colonists and smoldering building. Soldiers fired their rifles at close range. With their single shot spent, they closed in with bayonets, ruthlessly ripping into flesh and bone. Defenseless against the size and intensity of the charging

horde, thieves ran frantically, scrambling in all directions—bolting toward the ravine, the river, any haven for
escape—except for Rodshenko. He calmly stood and shot
flaming arrows at the oncoming soldiers. The captain
reached him first, cutting him down with his saber.

Now free to move, colonists rushed to fling open the
doors of the common house. Women and children burst
through, coughing from smoke and searching for their
families. Rein and Johann joined men running inside to
help women and children exit the building.

"Rein, here!" Johann's agonizing plea summoned
Rein to the back of the smoke-filled room. Elisabeth sat
on the ground, cradling Eva in her arms, hands pressing
the wound across her ribs to staunch the flow of blood.
Johann picked up Eva and carried her out to safety,
followed closely by Rein and Elisabeth.

"Please, help her," pleaded Johann. Elisabeth began
to tear strips from her dress to cover the wound across
Eva's ribcage. Rein took his sister's hand. It was warm,
and she was conscious. Suddenly, pain ripped through
Rein's chest. He stood and spun around, disoriented.
"Amila. Where is she? Where is she?"

"A man came and took her." Elisabeth struggled to
form the words. "He and two men held guns on the children. He said he'd let them go if she went with them. We
all put down our guns. Then he shot Eva. They dragged
Amila away."

"Tundorf." Strength waning, Eva's eyes implored
Rein. "Save her."

With the largest thief carrying Amila over his shoulder,
they rushed down the path into the ravine where Grekov

waited with the horses. The chancellor grimaced to see a cloth tightly binding Amila's mouth.

The count barked orders. "Get her on that horse, no matter what you have to do to her." Amila kicked viciously and twisted to escape. Finally, the two ruffians were able to load her onto a horse. One mounted behind her, holding her so tight she could barely breathe.

Riding north up the ravine, the sound of gunfire became more distant. Soon the only sound was the horses' labored breathing and hooves pounding the trail. As they disappeared into a heavily wooded area, Tundorf told them to stop. This is as good a place as any, he thought.

"Get her down and hold her." They dismounted and held Amila's arms.

Tundorf roughly pulled the sash down around her neck. She spit in his face. "You will die for what you've done."

He slapped her with the back of his hand. Blood flowed from the side of her mouth, dribbling down her chin. "Not another word until I ask you to speak, or I'll hit you again. Now, where is it?"

Amila winced as she spat words at him. "Take me back, and I'll get it for you."

Tundorf sneered. "There's nothing to go back to. By now, the serfs are all dead, and the village is burning, including my documents. But I want to know where they are. I'll send someone back to make sure they burned."

Amila arched her shoulders and lifted her chin. "You may as well kill me now. I'll never tell you anything. You had our own farmers murdered. You shot Eva in cold blood. You filthy coward."

He hit her again, this time with his fist across her chin. Amila's head snapped back, then drooped onto her shoulder.

Grekov had shrunk back from the scene, rocking back and forth, wincing and wringing his hands. Finally, he stepped timidly forward. "Amila, don't you see, we've rescued you. Your stepfather only wants what's best for you." He turned to face the count. "Look here—you, you got what you wanted. I insist you stop hurting her."

In a single motion, Tundorf pulled his saber from its sheath and stabbed Grekov through the chest. He pulled the saber free and watched the astonished man crumble to the ground.

"You idiot. Did you really think I'd allow a simpering fool like you to marry her and have her estate?" Tundorf asked calmly as the man writhed, wallowing in a widening pool of blood. "It was never you. I will marry her as soon as we get back to Saratov. You see, it happens all the time. A young lady loses her mother and comes to rely on her stepfather. The new heir will be my son."

The count rolled Grekov over onto his back and saw that he was still breathing. "You've served your purpose. I have you to blame and no one to say otherwise. I'll tell the authorities in Saratov that I came to bring Amila home and found you here attacking Dobrinka in league with the thieves. Everyone knows you're mad. I've stopped the madman!" He drove his sword into Grekov's heart.

Even the hardened thieves stood motionless. "Get her back on the horse. Let's go." All is going according to plan. By now, the destruction of Dobrinka must be well underway, he thought as they rode away.

*W*hat will he do to her? Rein forced himself to think clearly. He raced to the corner of the still smoldering common house and removed the stones, digging with his hands until he found the leather packet. Quickly he untied the leather strap and pulled out the documents. So, Tundorf hadn't learned its location.

Taking the packet, he grabbed a pistol and rifle, powder horn, bow, and found a few arrows. He checked to secure his saber. Racing through the battle scene, he was overcome by the devastation. Women and children wailed over the dead. Colonists darted between the fallen, trying desperately to help those still alive. Others relayed buckets of water from the river to douse the fire on the common house roof. A wife reunited with her wounded husband sat holding him in the middle of the chaos. Captain Kachinov and the soldiers had disappeared to deal with the last of the forest thieves.

Rein rushed to where Johann and Elisabeth were caring for Eva. "I'll see him dead for this and all his crimes."

"End it, and bring my sister back," whispered Eva, with all the force she could muster.

"Be careful, Rein," Elisabeth warned. "The two men—they held guns to the heads of children. If they'll do that…"

Rein touched Eva's cheek and looked back and forth between Johann and Elisabeth, pleading without words for them to save her. Johann held Eva's hand, his distressed look conveying to Rein he must stay with Eva.

Running through the chaos, Rein caught one of the thieves' horses and mounted it. He found tracks behind the common house and followed them into the ravine where the horses had been tied. Knowing the terrain well, Rein spurred his mount to a gallop and followed the tracks out of the ravine along the trail. He looked up to judge the time of day and knew the summer sun would provide light for many hours. Around a bend in the trail, he encountered the body of Grekov, mouth and eyes wide open, sprawled in a pool of blood. Why was Grekov a part of this, and why would they kill him? Rein urged his horse forward.

At the top of a bluff, Rein saw the riders at a distance. They were following a trail near the river, approaching a wooded area he knew well. Tundorf led and Amila rode in front of one of the thugs, followed by the third attacker, holding the reins of a fourth horse. They didn't appear to be in a hurry, having left the village before the soldiers arrived and thus were unaware of the outcome. Rein would have the advantage of surprise. Soon they descended into the woods and disappeared. Familiar with the ravine they were entering and the riverbank trail ahead, Rein kicked his horse and galloped to open ground.

Rein dismounted, left his horse, and scrambled to the woods' edge on the steep hill overlooking the Volga. The riders soon emerged. Quieting his rapid breath, he waited until the trio of riders had nearly passed, confirming what he'd seen from a distance: Count Tundorf led, followed by Amila held tightly by her captor, and the second outlaw trailed behind, leading a fourth horse. Rein couldn't risk an arrow hitting Amila. He aimed his bow at the trailing rider.

The arrow hissed past. A moment later, Rein had a second drawn and aimed at Tundorf. As the trailing outlaw gasped and fell from the saddle, his mount reared, and the two remaining riders spun their mounts. Rein's second arrow missed wide.

"Rein!" cried Amila. She fought fiercely to free her arms, but her captor's grip was too strong. She threw her head backward and felt the crunch of his nose. His grip went slack momentarily, allowing Amila to dive toward the ground. Hands still bound in front, the hard ground knocked the air from her lungs.

Tundorf drew a pistol and charged toward Rein.

Rein dropped the bow and swung his musket from his back to his shoulder, aiming at the count. In a blink, the space between them narrowed. The crack of two shots rang out, and Tundorf's charging horse let out a terrified bray and reared, unseating its rider.

Rein dove sideways to avoid the approaching horse's hooves. Unsure if he had hit the target, Rein attempted to stand and steady himself. Feeling sharp pain, he touched his shoulder. Blood was seeping from where the shot had grazed him. Tundorf limped towards Amila and the remaining thug.

As Amila regained her breath and tried to stand, a rough hand grabbed her hair and jerked her upright. "I'll teach you." Nose bleeding, the thug held her arms to her sides with one arm. She heard the rasp of a long knife being unsheathed, followed by the cold touch of steel against her throat.

The count stood next to Amila and her captor. Seeing Rein stooped in pain, Tundorf drew his saber. "You? I remember you. Your father was Daniel." Shocked they'd been followed, he shook his head in disbelief and turned to the thug. "Don't let her go! Remember the reward you've earned!" He looked at the lifeless body of the other brigand. "Looks like your pay has just doubled."

With difficulty, Rein rose to his feet and gathered his strength. Taking a deep breath, he drew his sword with his right hand, pointing it at the count. "Yes, Daniel was my father, one of the honorable men you had murdered." He took a step forward. "I'll see you dead for what you've done."

Eyes focused on Tundorf, Rein calmly addressed Amila's captor. "You...drop your knife and set her free. This isn't your fight. Rodshenko is dead, and your friends are running for their lives. The Russian army will be here soon. Save yourself while you can!"

Rein's words unsettled the thief. He looked back and forth nervously between Rein and Tundorf, who could see the outlaw balk. "He's lying. Don't believe him. It's a trick!"

"Is it?" asked Rein, "Then why am I here? Rodshenko was among the first to die. He accepted his fate, cut in half by the captain's sword. Soldiers are on their way."

"I'm not dying tonight," said the outlaw and pushed Amila towards Tundorf, who slung his free arm tightly around her neck.

"Come back, you coward. I'll triple your pay," yelled the count.

"No reward is worth this." He ran to the nearest horse, mounted, and galloped down the path leading away from the river.

"Amila, are you alright?" Rein shouted. Hands prying at Tundorf's stranglehold, she nodded.

"How charming. The peasant boy in love with the lady of the manor," the count mocked.

"He's worth a thousand of you, and he's my husband!" Fighting for breath, Amila's pent up emotions gushed. "You've lost—the property, the farmers and villagers, they'll never be yours. You'll never control us again."

Tundorf put his saber to her throat. "I'll kill you."

"Let her go, and I'll give you the evidence you're seeking." Rein pulled the worn leather packet from his belt. "Let her go, and it's yours."

Tundorf sneered. "I'll take it from your corpse."

Amila fixed her gaze on Rein, her eyes flashing a clear message. *It ends now.*

Tundorf dropped his saber. Reaching behind his back, he drew a second loaded pistol from his belt and aimed it at Rein. Arms still bound at the wrist, Amila lifted her knee and pulled the dagger from her boot, gripping it tightly. She jabbed the dagger backward, deeply penetrating Tundorf's thigh. He cringed and fired the pistol into the air. The hilt of her knife protruding from his leg, Tundorf recoiled in pain. Amila dropped to her knees, free of him.

Rein charged, closing the gap in three steps, and swung his saber. Time stood still. Rein could sense the presence of his father toiling beside him in the field and see his mother and Eva warming their hands by the hearth. He felt the air split by his saber as it closed on the evil man's throat. Tundorf jerked, futilely grasping at the wound and staggering backward. He managed one last gurgling shriek before tumbling down the steep embankment behind him. His lifeless body splashed into the river.

Rein knelt beside Amila and took her in his arms, helping her stand beside him. They faced the river, watching as Tundorf's body drifted into the current and disappeared.

Amila turned to Rein. "We're finally free."

CHAPTER 23

October 1765

*W*ith much to celebrate yet many wounds to heal, the citizens of Dobrinka planned the second Kerb with great care. Now late October, a three-day celebration was in full motion.

So much had happened in the past two months. Twenty-seven of the colony's men and older boys were lost in the brutal attack by the spitzbuben. Young and strong, Eva recovered from her gunshot wound under the tender care of Johann and Elisabeth. Captain Kachinov and his detachment of soldiers assured the thieves who had banded together to destroy Dobrinka would never again attack the colonists with such a united force. After capturing and executing those who took part, they followed the last few stragglers back to Rodshenko's stronghold and destroyed it, burning the ramshackle dwellings to the ground. The women and children living in the fortress were allowed to pack meager belongings and relocate to Russian settlements. The captain warned colonists to be vigilant—small bands of thieves would likely continue to menace settlers along the Volga.

Following the death of Chancellor Grekov, revelations of his widespread corruption came to light. Members of the Kontora staff came forward with proof the chancellor had been diverting funds intended for the colonies to his personal accounts. Likewise, the despicable actions of Count Tundorf were now clear. In his Saratov quarters, Captain Kachinov found correspondence proving the count was in league with German princes to carry out misdeeds assuring the early colonies failed. The objective—to halt the empress' massive recruitment program enticing German serfs to the Volga frontier. Amila and Rein added to the posthumous charges against Tundorf. In a communique to King Frederick, they included the documents proving Tundorf was guilty of murder and treason against the Prussian Empire.

Dobrinka now resembled a village more than a settlement. With cabins newly built in neat squares along the Volga banks, the colonists would no longer be forced to live underground. Families had well-built cabins complete with efficient Russian stoves to endure the harsh winters. Georg and the vorsteher council frequently consulted with the other four crown colonies as all struggled to survive the turbulent first years. Rein eagerly shared his knowledge of farming with the fledgling colonies, and together, they made plans for the first watermills along tributaries feeding the Volga.

Dobrinka's first crop of winter rye was harvested in August, every kernel of grain saved for food or replanting—excluding the portion Johann needed to brew beer for Kerb. Using the new, more efficient iron plows forged by the blacksmith, Rein and the Dobrinka farmers plowed and planted larger plots in winter wheat and rye, with seed delivered on time from the newly appointed chancellor of the Kontora.

Taking advantage of water diverted from the Dobrinka River, huge plots of summer vegetables were grown, and the industrious settlers—even those who had not planned to become farmers—enthusiastically harvested the bounty. The cabbage crop so prized by Germans provided not only sauerkraut for the Kerb feast but also the ingredients for a new dish introduced by Russian neighbors. The savory bierocks were of seasoned meat simmered with cabbage and onion, baked in yeast dough until golden brown.

"Friends and citizens of Dobrinka and our honored guests, Captain Kachinov and Christof Bengler, we welcome you to the Volga German celebration of the Kerb!" Georg Müller spread his arms wide in the opening address. "We have much to be thankful for, yet many losses to grieve. We'll never be able to repay what you've done for us, our dear captain and Herr Bengler. We honor you today for saving many lives and the colony."

Citizens cheered in deafening roars and clapped their hands to honor the heroes. As food was served, Amila and Rein walked arm in arm to greet the captain and Christof. The captain had arrived the previous day, and Amila and Rein had proudly given him a tour of the village, including the cabin they would move into today.

This was Rein and Amila's first opportunity in many months to see Christof, who had just arrived from field-work mapping the Volga wilderness. It was well after the attack that citizens of Dobrinka learned of Christof's critical role in the rescue. As the talkative young man approached, he audibly drew in his breath upon seeing Amila. "You look stunning and so happy, my dear friend! I understand congratulations are in order. We are to be guests at the grand occasion of your marriage later today.

I must admit, I'm jealous of the man who has captured your heart."

Amila threw her arms around Christof and kissed his cheek. She did feel beautiful today, wearing the lacy white wedding gown Elisabeth had sewn. Eva had tamed her unruly hair, arranging it in curls cascading down her back, adorned by a band of wildflowers accentuated her flashing green eyes.

She stepped back, and Rein warmly clasped Christof's hand, comfortable this time with Amila's embrace of the young man. A torrent of emotion flooded Rein as he gazed at his bride. "This ravishing woman has captured my heart and soul. I have finally earned her love."

Amila's eyes locked on Rein's, and she tightened her grip on his arm. "I remember well, Christof, the wise counsel you gave a young woman so hesitant to believe in love. You told me 'love is a force of nature—you can't do a thing to stop it.' I finally understand."

The group laughed light-heartedly, all keenly aware of the challenges Amila and Rein had overcome to reach this momentous day. Rein turned to the captain and Christof. "Without both of you, none of us would be here today. But there is something I don't understand. How did you know about Tundorf's plot and when the forest thieves would attack?"

"The credit goes to Christof." The captain explained. "After your visit to Saratov and warning about the count, he kept a watchful eye on him and Grekov."

"It was a long winter, and I was quartered nearby," Christof explained. "Neither of them knew me, so they didn't notice when I checked on their activities. I suspected they were up to something. When they left together early in the spring, I learned they had gone to meet with Rodshenko and told the captain."

Kachinov nodded. "Amila had informed me about Count Tundorf. I knew he was capable of horrible acts. Grekov ordered me to stay away from the southern colonies that week and instead go north. It was an easy decision to disobey his orders. I only wish we had arrived sooner."

Christof knew the Captain was too humble to say more. "You will be pleased to hear the rest of the news. Saving the empress' first crown colony and exposing the corruption of the chancellor has not gone unnoticed. Our queen has shown her gratitude by promoting the good captain to major."

Amila hugged Major Kachinov, and the group added hearty congratulations. "Thank you all. Empress Catherine is now more aware of the dangers you face. She has granted additional troops to safeguard the colonies." Uncomfortable being the center of attention, he quickly changed the subject. "Amila, now that you and Rein are to be married, what will you do about your estate in Germany? Do you plan to return?"

Amila squeezed Rein's hand and leaned close before explaining. "We made the decision together. I have a distant cousin in Germany whom I met once. He's a kind and gentle man. I've written to him, and he will move to Nassenwald and serve as caretaker of the Wallerstein estate. He promises to restore the land and treat serfs fairly if they choose to remain there. Many serfs may wish to emigrate here or elsewhere, and my cousin understands they must be allowed to do so. And justice has been served by King Frederick: because of crimes against Prussia, Tundorf's small estate has been seized, and the king has generously forgiven the large debts the count incurred against Nassenwald."

"If Amila and I are blessed with a child, she or he will be heir someday," Rein was quick to add. "We'll tell her when she's old enough. She can choose her path, just as we have."

Amila couldn't contain her enthusiasm. "Would you like to know the best part? The new caretaker will ship us all the books from the castle. Unless Rein yearns to see more of the world, I have no desire to leave. This is the life I want to live and the man I want to share it with."

Later that day, Major Kachinov walked Amila Wallerstein down a path of wildflowers to wed Reinhardt Lundgren in a ceremony conducted by Dobrinka's Lutheran minister. As he once again placed the triple gold band adorned by clasped hands on Amila's finger, Rein recited the words "For then, for now, forever." The community witnessed the joyous event with the Volga River as a dramatic backdrop. Eva had a moment to hug her new sister before Johann gently lifted tiny Eva and kissed her. He whispered something in her ear that made her smile and blush.

"Let the dancing begin!" called the violinist, joined by several musicians new to this year's Kerb. Amila extended her hand, and Rein led her forward.

TEN YEARS LATER

Summer 1775

*C*ommissar Yuri Demidov pointed toward a high bluff on the western shoreline. "And there, Empress Catherine, is Dobrinka, the first of your crown colonies to settle the wild frontier. I understand they now call themselves Volga Germans."

"I recall those first arrivals. I believe I welcomed them personally." The empress peered out from under the canopy of her imperial barge, shielding her eyes from glare reflecting off the water. Atop the embankment, she saw a neatly organized community of wooden houses and one large building near the edge of the bluff. "Volga Germans. Interesting," she whispered.

Demidov gave the barge pilot instructions to slow as they approached. Whistles sounded, and the squadron of several hundred oarsmen simultaneously lifted heavy, painted blades from the water. A mass of curious onlookers had gathered on the high bluffs to see the armada of richly adorned barges painted gold and scarlet and flying flags of the royal crest. A majestic flotilla of vessels accompanied the imperial barge, all propelled by oarsmen.

Forewarned the empress might sail past the colonies, the residents of Dobrinka waved their hats, and children jumped up and down. The sound of thunderous cheers carried across the water, reaching their beloved queen's ears. She smiled and waved in response.

Demidov sighed as he looked at the settlers crowding the shoreline. He had never been this far south and had anxiously anticipated a look at the fledgling community that had led the way and finally begun to thrive. It had been ten years since the empress had appointed him Commissar of the Guardianship Council for Foreigners to oversee her massive colonization program. Demidov silently reviewed the program's successes and failures. Over the first four tumultuous years, nearly 30,000 predominantly German emigrants had answered the empress' manifesto decree to come to Russia. Losses had been heavy on the 2,000-mile journey—only about 23,000 reached the colonies alive. Then, the steady flow of emigrants had stopped abruptly when Empress Catherine halted the massive colonization program.

On the days-long trip down the Volga, Empress Catherine and Demidov saw some of the 104 colonies now dotting both sides of the river. Demidov shook his head, recalling the colonists' misfortunes. Once they arrived, these pioneers had suffered even more losses—after ten years, his administrators estimated the population to be only 21,000. Yet still, the tenacious Germans persevered—determined to build communities and coax the soil to feed their families.

"As I have reported, losses among the emigrants have been quite heavy," Demidov admitted, pressing his lips together in a frown. "The most deaths continue to be from Mongol raids, forest thieves, as well as Russian peasant rebellions. However, it is the colonies on the east bank that suffered the greatest loss of life and property from the attacks of the Kirghiz."

Sadness clouded the empress' features. "Ah, yes. You've told me about the raids. I knew these colonists would eventually sacrifice many lives. They have suffered dearly to provide a buffer between the eastern hordes and my Russian citizens."

"Ah, dear queen, you have done much for these people and for the good of your empire. The conditions against which they struggle are harsh and yet beyond our control and theirs as well," Demidov responded skillfully. He often justified to his queen the dangers from which the Volga Germans suffered–sickness, wild animals, rebel raids, savage tribes, and robber bands— as challenges all pioneers must face and against which no government can furnish protection. He summed it up: "The colonists' survival has depended upon seeing their enemies everywhere and in everything. The mass of virtues nature has given them serves them well."

Unfortunately, "everywhere" included his own Kontora bureau, though he would never admit it. He was certain she knew. Very little happened in her kingdom that Empress Catherine didn't learn about. If it hadn't been for his own organization's corruption and poor management, more colonists might have survived, Demidov admitted to himself. One could say they had succeeded despite the Kontora bureaucrats.

"Of your many achievements, this may be your greatest, my dear empress." Demidov spread his arms wide, motioning toward Dobrinka and beyond. "I believe your Volga Germans will someday feed most of Russia. Like Mother Volga, they have become one of your empire's greatest resources."

EPILOGUE

AMARILLO, TEXAS, UNITED STATES

Winter 2013

"*K*arena, why are you so excited? It's just a little ring." Lisl followed her daughter into the civic center hosting the Antiques Roadshow. "Yes, it's gold. And we know it's old. What matters is that it's still in the family and that you want to keep the tradition alive."

Escaping the chilly Texas Panhandle wind at last, Karena lovingly took her Mom's hand in the crook of her arm and urged her forward. "Aren't you curious, just a little bit? When will we ever have a chance like this?"

A few months earlier, Lisl had seen the news article announcing the Antiques Roadshow's stop in Amarillo on its annual tour of mid-sized cities. Among the many appraisers attending this year's event, one was of great interest: a Russian historian and gemologist specializing in antique jewelry. Once she'd mentioned it to Karena, there'd been no question as to whether they would attend, although Amarillo was more than a hundred miles from the farm where Lisl and her husband raised wheat and cattle.

Arriving early, they progressed quickly through the line to meet with Nina Turgenev, the appraiser they were seeking. Lisl removed the triple gold band and gently placed it in Ms. Turgenev's hand. Her eyelid twitched ever so slightly, alerting her that something notable was about to happen.

For several minutes, Ms. Turgenev closely examined the ring using a ten-power magnification loupe. She spent most of the time scrutinizing the clasped hands that adorned the top of the band. Finally, she lifted her eyes and smiled. "What can you tell me about the history of this ring?"

"It's called 'the family trinket' for some reason and has been in our family for many generations," said Lisl proudly. "Our ancestors were from Germany, emigrants who helped settle the Russian frontier along the Volga River in the 1760s. We assume it's from that time period or later. It's been passed down as a wedding band. You can see it's well worn,'" Lisl paused, knowing little else about the heirloom.

"Ah, yes. I'm quite familiar with Volga Germans. When people of German descent come to me with family jewelry, they're often descendants of emigrants who settled the Volga. Your Volga German farmers made quite a positive impact, feeding most of Russia for well over 100 years. That is, until much of their land was taken away during Russian uprisings in the late 1800s and early 1900s. Then in the 1940s, Stalin forcibly resettled those who had not already left. Well, enough of that," she concluded almost apologetically, certain they knew their own ancestors' history.

"No, please. We never tire of hearing it," Karena interjected. "We have a great deal of information from our family's records and from the Volga German historical society. But there's always more to learn."

Seeing the line of people waiting behind the two women, the gemologist returned to the work at hand. "Have you had the ring appraised?"

"Yes. A jeweler told us it's pure, 24-carat gold," said Karena. "But we're more interested in its history, its origin. We believe the ring has quite a story to tell."

The gemologist pointed to the ring with tweezers. "May I open the fulcrum?" she asked politely. Lisl smiled at the expert's knowledge and nodded.

Ms. Turgenev used the precision tool to remove the tiny pin that acted as a fulcrum or pivot, enabling the single band to swivel apart into three thin bands. The clasped hands separated to reveal a heart on the third band. After examining each band, she aligned the three bands back together to form one ring, replaced the pin, and set it down on the cloth-covered table between them.

"Well, here is what I can tell you. It's a 'fede gimmel' ring, named for the Italian phrase 'hands in faith or trust.' The hallmark of this type of ring is the motif of two right hands, one female and the other male, clasped together and holding a heart. It was quite popular across Europe, including Russia, in the 16th and 17th centuries."

"We always assumed the hands symbolized the union of two people," Lisl said.

Ms. Turgenev continued. "On this tour, your Volga Germans have brought in some fascinating pieces. However, none are quite as old or unique as this one. Because of its age, this ring is very rare. It's not from the 1700s, more likely the early 1600s, and is exquisitely handcrafted. The high quality means it was probably commissioned and designed for nobility. It's much more than a 'family trinket.'" she added.

Lisl and Karena exchanged a sidelong glance, wide-eyed.

"If you're interested in selling the piece, I'd be pleased to represent you," added Ms. Turgenev.

"Oh no. We'll never sell it," Lisl responded immediately, and Karena nodded in agreement. "To the family, the three bands symbolize the past, the present, and the future. Now, Karena is engaged and has decided to make it her wedding ring."

Ms. Turgenev stifled a frown, fairly certain that would be their response. "So, the tradition will continue. Let me know if you change your minds."

"We are curious. Can you estimate its worth?" asked Lisl.

"As a ring, it's worth only the value of the gold, which is significant. As an antique, much more. If I were you, I'd insure it for upwards of $200,000."

"To us, it's priceless. We thank you so much." Lisl slipped the ring back on her finger and shook the expert's hand. Mother and daughter linked arms and left together.

Author's Note

Growing up in Follett, Texas, a small farm community of predominantly Volga Germans, I learned to appreciate my heritage as a German from Russia. When I was in college, my grandparents, Martha (Ehrlich) and Jona Laubhan, presented me with a book called "Ehrlich: a Family History, 1763-1970," which reinforced interest in my ancestry. Reading historical fiction over the next 40 years, it seemed an important story was missing: I had a nagging desire to tell the exciting, tumultuous story of the first Volga German pioneers, focusing on their unflinching resolve to make a better life for themselves and future generations.

While conducting research and writing this book, I developed a deep respect for these resilient pioneers. Through family histories, I learned about the earliest years in Russia, including encounters with the wolves on the frozen Volga River. It was that story and others that kept guiding me toward this project. In this book, I have tried to address the question: how did the earliest colonists survive? Nearly 30,000 people emigrated over a four-year period, before Russia halted the colonization program. Many perished on the 2,000-mile journey from German states to the Volga frontier, and thousands died settling the region. Those who arrived early clearly laid a path for others to follow and, within ten years, the pioneers had successfully established 104 colonies on both sides of the Volga. The Volga Germans tamed a wilderness never before cultivated, converting knee-high grass into productive farmland. The farms they established eventually fed much of Russia.

The significance of the Volga Germans' achievements must be celebrated, not diminished or forgotten given the horrific treatment by Russia in the late 1800s through the 1940s. During that time, Russia imprisoned, deported, and relocated the ethnic German people. As a result of those devastating events, the Volga Germans emigrated again, this time to the United States and other countries. Once again, they brought with them their farming expertise, work ethic, strong values, and sense of community, forever benefitting their new homelands.

The Empress' Gift is based on fictionalized renderings of actual events and written recollections, retaining as much historical authenticity as possible. The book's timeline has been compressed somewhat to allow for a continuous narrative. While the book's characters are fictitious, many were inspired by historic individuals, including relatives who arrived several years after the first pioneers. The story was developed from many original family documents and other vital sources. Of utmost importance were the vast resources of the American Historical Society of Germans from Russia (AHSGR: www.ahsgr.org).

I am pleased to share credit with many contributors. I wish every author could have such a fantastic support team! Family and friends have provided ongoing motivation, support, and valuable insights for the past seven plus years. Special thanks go to my husband, Randy Rye, sons Jim Stafford and Elliot Stafford, sister Janette Laubhan, and friends Gail Johnson, Teresa Ivie Robison, Sandy Lang, Sydney Burton, Renee Cottrell, Marsha Evans, Diane Trenfield Wilson, and Terry Powell. Without my son Jim's interest in family history and ongoing encouragement, I would not have completed this book. The project has appropriately been a multi-generational family effort.

Authors and creative writing professors Alyson Hagy and Ann McCutchan generously lent expertise in strategic direction and writing style. Finally, my sincere gratitude goes to Sherri Hutton and the excellent staff at Rowe Publishing (www.rowepub.com), who painstakingly led me through the entire process. As a first-time author, I appreciate their patient, professional guidance and support.

— Ellen Laubhan